The Ultimate Sacrifice

She moved the stethoscope for a few heartbeats, then again. Her other hand rested on his bicep, gentle and reassuring. Michael shut his eyes and tried to hold still.

"You okay?"

Her voice was very close. He opened his eyes and looked at her. "No."

"You stopped breathing."

"Oh. Sorry." He swallowed and took a deep breath.

"If I'm making you uncomfortable—"

"Never." He looked at her. "Never, Hannah."

She studied him, her eyes full of uncertainty. "I thought you—I thought—" She broke off and looked away. He watched her throat jerk as she swallowed. "I thought I was going to have to give your brothers some very bad news."

The words—the wavering emotion in her voice—hit him hard. He'd spent so many years worrying about everyone else that it was a shock to hear someone express worry over *him*.

Have you read all the Elemental books?

Elemental (novella)
Storm
Fearless (novella)
Spark
Breathless (novella)
Spirit
Secret

SACRIFICE *The Elemental Series*

BRIGID KEMMERER

Teen

KENSINGTON PUBLISHING CORP.
www.kensingtonbooks.com

ACKNOWLEDGMENTS

This book almost did me in. You're holding this book in your hands because my husband, my agent, and my editor are the most patient, encouraging, supportive, and motivating people on earth. Holy cow, I am not exaggerating when I say this book wouldn't have gotten written without their support.

Michael, my husband, is my best friend, and he makes a great sounding board. He also gets me going when I need it. Thanks to the newest addition to our family, he's just as sleep deprived as I am, but you'd never know it. Honey, thank you for everything.

Mandy Hubbard, my agent, is beyond compare. When I thought I'd hit rock bottom, she threw me a rope. One day I'm going to meet her in person and tackle her with hugs. Thank you, Mandy, for everything.

Alicia Condon, my fearless editor, is the most patient person alive. I am fully convinced she's unflappable. I'm so lucky to have her in my corner. Thank you, Alicia. When I say I can't thank you enough, I mean it.

As always, tremendous thanks to my critique partners Bobbie Goettler and Alison Kemper Beard. You guys have been there since the beginning. I'm so lucky to have you as my friends. I can't imagine being on this journey without you.

This book involves a lot of firefighting and paramedic information, as well as encounters with law enforcement, so it required a lot more research than I was ready for. Extra special thanks and hugs to Kimberly Hart-Smith and Ed Kiser of the Riviera Beach Volunteer Fire Department, as well as Jim Kalinosky of the Baltimore County Police Department. When people offer to help me with research, I don't think they're ever ready for the amount of information I'm going to need, so I owe you all a tremendous thanks for answering all my questions. I took all of their knowledge and twisted it to fit my needs. Any errors are mine alone.

Many people read chapters (or the whole manuscript!) at the drop of a hat, and the book is better for their insights: Joy Hensley George, Jim Hilderbrandt, Nicole Mooney, Nicole Kalinosky, Sarah Fine, Rachel Shaw, Nicole Choiniere-Kroeker. Thank you all, so much.

Extra-special thanks to the Kemmerer boys, Jonathan, Nick, Sam, and Baby Zach, for being the best kids a mom could have. When I first started writing about the Merrick brothers, I never knew I'd end up with four boys of my own. I love you all. So much.

Finally, thanks to you, my readers, for going on this journey with me. When Becca saved Chris in that parking lot, I never knew how much the Merrick brothers would have to say. I'm so glad I've had the chance to tell their stories, and that you've been there to enjoy them. I can't tell you how much I appreciate your emails, your tweets, your Facebook messages, and your letters. Thank you.

CONTENTS

Sacrifice
1

Fearless
275

SACRIFICE

CHAPTER 1

Michael Merrick stepped off the porch, put his bare feet in the grass, and waited for a bullet.

He'd done this every night for a week.

The air held still, waiting with him, cloaking the yard in darkness. Breath eased from his lips, fogging in the early November chill. He wished he'd thought to grab a fleece pullover, but he'd barely paused to yank a T-shirt over his head.

Someone was out here. He knew it.

He'd known it for the last six nights.

Dried grass wove between his toes, but the earth carried no warning. Just the awareness that someone moved through the trees.

The first night he'd sensed something, terror had clung to his back, sending him bolting from room to room, slapping light switches and creating so much racket it was a miracle he hadn't woken the neighbors too. His brothers and Hunter had gathered on the porch, their breath shaking in the night air. They'd been ready to fight. They'd been ready for war against the Guides who hunted them.

It never came.

But every night since, Michael had felt . . . *something*.

Or maybe not. Maybe this was 3 AM stress and paranoia setting up shop in his brain. His fear from the first night had morphed and taken new shape, turning into something more akin to fury.

He didn't know who was out here, but he wanted to kill them for threatening his family.

"A rookie sniper could take you out without a scope."

Michael jumped and swore and spun, pulling strength from the ground without thought. He choked on his breath. A sniper wouldn't even need a bullet; a heart attack would do the job.

Hunter Garrity stood on the deck, his feet also bare, though he'd had the good sense to grab a sweatshirt. Moonlight glinted off the piercings in his brow. Casper, his German shepherd, was alert by his side.

"Sorry," Hunter said softly. "Thought you heard me."

"What are you doing out here?" Michael snapped, keeping his voice as quiet as possible. "Go back to bed."

Hunter ignored that and joined him by the steps, putting his own feet in the grass. The dog stopped by his side and whined. "Someone's in the woods."

Of course Hunter would sense it, too. He was a Fifth, which gave him a connection to all the elements. He would have been a Guide, too, if he'd followed in his father's footsteps. Fate hadn't worked out that way.

Hunter glanced over when Michael didn't answer. "You should wake Nick. He could divert a bullet."

Michael studied the line of trees. He didn't want to wake everyone again. His brothers already spent each day riding a blade of tension; he didn't need to fill their nights with panic.

He hated this. It reminded him too much of the nights he'd spent awake after his parents died, trying to figure out how to keep his brothers safe. Then, he'd been worried about money and the other Elementals in town, the ones who'd sworn to leave his family alone. Now he was worried someone would shoot them all before he could get out a warning.

"Go inside, Hunter."

Hunter turned his attention back to the trees, probably giving each individual leaf a militaristic assessment. "It's only one guy. Maybe two. We could circle around—"

"At ease, soldier. I told you to go inside."

Hunter shut his mouth, but he didn't move. He was worried, though—worried and furious, the way Michael was.

He'd never admit it, of course. But Michael could feel his unease through the ground. Hunter hung close like a child who wouldn't venture too far from a parent in an unfamiliar situation. *I can face this as long as I'm not alone.*

Hunter hadn't been like that at first. He'd been reckless and impulsive and unsure where he fit in this world. When Hunter's grandfather had thrown him out of the house, Michael had just offered the kid a place to crash. He hadn't realized he'd be inheriting another brother to take care of, a sixteen-year-old who could handle himself like a Special Forces soldier but trusted people about as much as a beaten dog.

Hunter trusted him now, though. He'd never say as much, but the proof was in the way he stood here, following Michael's lead.

Michael's senses pricked. Whoever was in the woods had moved closer. He—*they?*—was being stealthy, picking through the underbrush.

"Could it be Calla?" said Hunter, voice softer than thought.

"I doubt it." Calla Dean was the only person in town who wanted this war against the Guides. For years, Michael had assumed he and his brothers were the only full Elementals in town. They'd lived in fear that the Guides would discover their existence and send someone to kill them. They'd taken great care to hide their abilities and live in secrecy.

Then Calla Dean had come along.

Like Hunter, she was sixteen years old and a junior in high school. Unlike Hunter, she was a Fire Elemental with a psychotic streak. She didn't want to hide. She wanted the Guides to come—and she'd done everything she could to get their attention. Innocent people had already died because of Calla's obsession with this war.

She wouldn't be sneaking through the trees. She'd be lighting them all on fire.

Maybe he *should* wake Nick. His brother would be able to read the air and tell them what he sensed.

No. His brothers were safer inside the house, asleep and oblivious.

Maybe if he kept telling himself that, he'd eventually believe it.

"What do you feel?" he asked Hunter.

Silence for a moment. "Not danger. They're just . . . there." Hunter glanced over again. "Is Hannah here?"

"Why would Hannah be here?"

Hunter gave him a look. "To spend the night?"

"No, she did not *spend the night.*"

Hunter shrugged and looked at the woods again. "Gabriel thought you were sneaking her in since we hadn't seen her around lately."

Typical Gabriel. "For god's sake. She's been busy. Would you just go back in the house?"

Hunter stayed right where he was. "Whatever. She's *your* girlfriend."

Yeah, and Michael had been avoiding her since the first night he'd sensed someone in the woods. Hannah was smart and fierce and had the uncanny ability to look right through him.

He wasn't ready to share his secrets. Not yet. Not ever, if spilling the beans meant putting Hannah and her son in harm's way.

She wasn't stupid. She knew something was up.

She wasn't happy either, considering she hadn't responded to either of his texts earlier this evening.

A branch snapped, and Michael froze. Casper growled.

A shadow slid between the trees. Hunter shifted forward, his stance getting lower. He put a hand on Casper's collar.

"Take it easy," Michael said, his voice as low as he could make it. "Just wait."

Hunter didn't say anything, but metal clicked.

Michael looked down. A gun had appeared in Hunter's hands.

Michael caught his wrist, keeping the weapon pointed at the ground. "What the hell do you think 'take it easy' means?"

The shadow in the trees stopped short.

"If it's a Guide, they'll be armed," Hunter hissed. "Don't be stupid."

They stared at each other for a long moment. Michael wasn't sure he *wanted* Hunter to put the gun away. He could feel his heart in his throat. Hunter's breath was shaking, just a bit.

The woods hung still now, no sense of motion at all.

Then that shadow bolted. Casper barked and ran.

Hunter jerked his arm free and took off after them both.

Michael swore and followed.

This immediately felt wrong. He didn't want to leave his brothers vulnerable—and that's what sleep felt like now. Vulnerability.

Why the hell hadn't he woken them up?

"Stop!" he yelled, hoping his brothers would somehow hear him. "Hunter, damn it, stop!"

Then he shut his mouth. He shouldn't yell—not unless he wanted to wake the whole street. This war made everyone in the neighborhood a liability. A risk. A threat. The last thing he needed was some middle-aged dad stumbling into the line of fire in his boxer shorts.

Besides which, he was terrified Hunter was going to pull that trigger and shoot some moron hiding a few joints in his pocket.

But Hunter hadn't fired, and Michael could see him slipping between the trees about twenty feet ahead. He hardly needed the visual: at this distance the earth could feed their path to him. They'd never lose him on foot. The underbrush helped, too. Rocks and branches shifted out of the way of his bare feet, letting him gain ground.

The earth couldn't offer the nuances of emotion, but it knew enough to recognize a panicked run. Whoever they were chasing was terrified of getting caught.

Not a Guide, then.

Hunter's breath echoed over the crunch of his feet through underbrush. Their quarry was quick—he'd gained ground—but this kind of desperate running would burn him out fast.

"Hunter! I said stop." Michael was fast. He could almost grab the back of Hunter's sweatshirt now, but he didn't. "He didn't attack us. We're chasing *him*."

That made Hunter draw up short, sliding to a stop in the dirt, breathing hard. "Casper! *Hier!*" The dog barked again, somewhere in the distance, but he returned to his master's side.

Hunter pushed hair off his face and swore. The gun was still in his hand, pointed at the ground. "You don't *know* this isn't Calla."

True, he didn't know this wasn't Calla. She was violent and unpredictable and refused to discuss anything that had to do with avoiding a war. Michael hadn't heard from her since last week, since he'd told her his priority was to protect his family— not to start a war with the Guides.

Regardless, he wasn't a big fan of shooting blindly into the woods. "What if this has nothing to do with us, and you shoot some unarmed kid?"

Hunter slid the gun into his waistband at the small of his back. He was scowling. "I'm not reckless."

Branches snapped in the distance. Michael felt every step as the runner drew farther away.

"See?" he said, catching his breath. "A Guide would know we could follow him."

Then they heard a splash, and Michael lost any sense of their target.

Hunter took off again. "Why would some unarmed kid jump into the creek in November?" he called.

Michael ran after him. "Maybe he fell."

But he'd felt the instant the runner's feet left the earth. Running to the water had been deliberate. Whoever this was had known Michael could follow him on land.

Maybe he didn't know Hunter would be able to follow him in the water.

Stoney Creek wasn't really a creek at all. It stretched half a mile across, the towns on either side connected by a drawbridge. Farther south, there was a stretch of beach, but here, at the edge of their neighborhood, the woods ended at a sheer drop into water. By the time they reached the bank, Hunter had lost his sweatshirt. He didn't even pause: he leapt into the quickly moving current, jeans and all. Michael dove in beside him.

The sudden cold caught him in a vise grip. For an instant, he couldn't think. He couldn't *breathe*.

But then his body kicked into action, sending his heart pounding with adrenaline. Forget Nick. Michael should have woken *Chris*. His youngest brother wouldn't need to chase this guy. Chris could probably convince the current to drag him back to shore.

Too late now. Icy water attacked with the sting of a thousand needles, protesting his presence. He fought to make his arms drive through the water, but the current churned thick with power, fighting his every stroke. Michael kicked and the water dragged him under. Those pinpricks of cold turned to full-size nails hammered into his skin.

Power.

Maybe jumping into the creek wasn't about avoiding anyone's abilities at all. Maybe this guy was a frigging Water Elemental.

Brackish water fought its way into Michael's mouth. He tried to force it out, but the current was a living thing, prying open his lips, burning into his nostrils. His lungs begged for air and water surged down his throat. Instinct forced him to inhale, allowing more water to knife its way into his chest. He tried to cough but inhaled more liquid.

The water dragged at his body, pulling him deeper. The pressure on his chest increased. Bitterness clawed at the back of his tongue, more water trying to force its way into his lungs. His legs couldn't kick. He'd been so worried about a bullet, and now he was drowning.

No, not drowning. Sleeping. He didn't need to fight anymore. He could sleep, right here.

Sleep.

He'd never warned his brothers. They'd be asleep in their beds, easy victims.

His body touched the bottom, and the sand whispered to him, scraping his skin, offering power. Michael couldn't make sense of it. He was too tired.

Something caught hold of his arm. Should he fight?

That struck him as funny, in a very distant way. He couldn't even *move*.

Or was this Hunter? Was this a rescue? Maybe they'd be dragged to shore and *then* shot.

Maybe he imagined the grip on his arm. Maybe the current had him, and he'd float to the bay. Maybe he'd finally see the ocean.

He seemed to float forever.

His face broke the surface, but his lungs didn't try to inhale. November air slapped his cheeks, but he didn't care. A moment later, his back hit the sand. Then his head did.

Suddenly everything hurt. His lungs *burned* with cold. He wanted to fight but nothing would work. He couldn't see stars or sky or *anything*.

Maybe he wasn't really out of the water. Maybe this was true death.

Fear ripped through him, offering some clarity. He could feel everything. The cold bit down to his bones. His muscles could only offer aching pain. He was definitely on shore—the sand beneath his body pulsed with power. Michael's fingers moved against his will, digging into the sand, feeling each grain drive under his fingernails.

Something heavy hit his chest. And again, this time using force to lift his shoulders and slam him back into the earth.

Then a third time. Michael jerked and coughed, and water poured out of his mouth. He choked and tried to breathe. More water. More coughing. His eyes still wouldn't focus.

And then they did.

Chris crouched over him, barely recognizable in the darkness with water dripping through his hair and off his cheeks. His eyes were furious instead of worried. He punched Michael in the chest again, but this time it had nothing to do with revival. "You idiot, I could have killed you."

"Chris—what—" Michael couldn't get his voice to work. "Where—Hunter?"

"Right here," his voice called from a short distance away, just as rough and broken as Michael's. Fabric shifted through sand as he tried to stand. He must have found his footing, because bare feet slapped against the beach. Michael struggled to sit up.

Chris got out of his way, moving to sit closer to the water. He swiped sandy hands against his jeans and turned his glare on Hunter. "I guess you survived."

"Yeah," Hunter rasped. He dropped to his knees beside Chris, and Michael thought he was going to collapse there in the sand.

But he didn't. Hunter raised his hand and put the barrel of his gun in Chris's face. "I survived. So you'd better start talking."

CHAPTER 2

Michael couldn't wrap his head around this. His youngest brother had been in the woods? Had been running? They'd been standing behind the porch sensing *Chris?*

What do you feel?

Not danger.

It hadn't been Chris every night. Michael was sure of it.

Mostly sure.

No, he couldn't be sure at all. It hadn't been Chris the first night, but Michael didn't go around checking beds every night. His brothers were sixteen and seventeen years old. They knew better than to sneak out of the house, especially now.

Yet he was staring down at his little brother while someone else held him at gunpoint.

"Hunter," Michael said slowly. "Put the gun away."

"Not until he gives us a good answer." Hunter cocked the gun.

Chris threw himself at Hunter, driving the other boy to the ground, slamming his wrist into the wet sand. Something heavy skittered along the beach until Michael lost track of the gun in the darkness. Hunter swore and tried to swing a fist, but the trip underwater must have taken something out of him, too. Chris was on top and had leverage—not to mention power. Water crawled up the sand to flow around them, then retreated.

Casper barked and whined, prancing in the surf, waiting for a command.

Chris braced an arm against Hunter's neck and leaned in. His voice was low and lethal. "Don't you ever put a gun in my face again."

"Hey," said Michael. The water flowing around his knees was ice cold. "Stop. Chris, let him go."

Hunter's voice was strained and breathy. "Aw. Poor Chris. Scared?"

"Fuck you."

"Fuck *you*." Hunter struggled to get an arm free. "You're the one turning on your family."

Chris lifted Hunter to slam him back against the beach. "The only person who ever turned on my family is *you*—"

Casper barked and surged forward.

"Hey." Michael grabbed the dog's collar. He needed to defuse this. Soon, before Chris lost control of his power and the water posed a threat again. The earth was feeding him strength now, so he put a hand against brother's shoulder and kept his voice low. "*Hey*. Come on. Chill out. Let him up."

Chris hesitated, his breathing rough and rapid over the slow roll of the waves. Michael waited. The twins, Nick and Gabriel, had always had each other, but when Chris was younger, he'd looked up to Michael. Some of that closeness had faded since their parents had died, leaving Michael riding that fine line between brother and parent, but Chris would listen to him.

Usually.

Hunter's eyes shone darkly in the starlight. He didn't move, but Michael could feel his tension through the sand.

After an eternal moment, Chris's arm shifted. He eased the weight against Hunter's neck. Michael let out a breath.

Then Hunter jerked free, swung a fist, and punched Chris right in the throat.

Chris collapsed in the water—but it was his element, and it fed him strength immediately. Hunter tackled him, but Chris was ready. He let Hunter's momentum carry them into deeper water.

And then they were fighting in earnest.

Michael sighed. Casper whined.

When they got going, sometimes Michael just wanted to say *fuck it* and walk away. He was tempted to do that now. His joints ached and his lungs burned. He hadn't slept in days.

Wind blew in from the water to make the trees rustle, bringing the scent of saltwater from the bay. He gave the dog's collar a tug. "Come on, Casper."

Michael went for the weapon first—because he didn't want to take the chance of Hunter getting his hands on it. He asked the sand for the location and found the gun a short distance down the beach.

When he looked back, Chris had Hunter pinned in the surf. The waves had turned more aggressive, crashing into them both. It wasn't quite deep enough to hold Hunter's face underwater, but close.

"Come on," said Michael. "Both of you." His voice hadn't lost the rough edge, and he didn't bother hiding his irritation. "Using abilities out in the open is reckless." The Guides didn't need much evidence to justify killing a full Elemental.

Chris was breathing hard. "I let him up once already."

Michael smacked him on the side of the head. "Well, let him up again! Jesus, it's three o'clock in the morning and we're half a mile from home! Knock it off and start walking or you can both spend the night stuck in the sand."

Chris didn't move. His jaw was set.

Hunter snorted and shook water off his face. "Whatever."

Michael dropped to a knee in the sand and leaned down close. "Try me."

Hunter glared back, but Michael didn't look away. He had a limit. They'd found it.

Chris broke first. He let Hunter go with a shove and a curse, turning his back on them both to head for the house.

Michael straightened and put out a hand to pull Hunter to his feet.

After a moment, Hunter took it. When he was on his feet, he pushed wet hair out of his eyes and turned to follow Chris. Somewhere in the distance, a siren kicked up, and Michael hoped a well-meaning neighbor hadn't called the cops about all the crashing around in the woods.

He caught Hunter's arm. "What's up with you two?"

The response was clipped. "Ask Chris. He's the one running around in the woods when we're all waiting for a war to start."

"I'm asking you."

Hunter jerked free. "What, he gets a free pass for being shady, and you're going to come down on *me?*"

Michael didn't have an answer for that.

Hunter scoffed and stormed into the woods, his dog by his side. Another siren joined the first. Then a third. They sounded closer.

"Christ," Michael muttered. This was all he needed. He had no idea how he'd explain what they'd been doing out in the water. Another gust of wind pulled at his damp clothes, making him shiver.

Then he caught the glow of something red, far ahead between the trees.

A lot of red. Michael stopped short.

Chris reappeared, crashing through the underbrush. His eyes were wide and panicked. "Mike," he gasped. "Fire. There's a fire—the houses—"

Michael stopped listening.

And started running.

Hannah rocked with the motion of the fire truck and rubbed her forehead, trying to scrape off a layer of sweat or soot or whatever was caked under the edge of the helmet.

Three calls back to back, and she was ready to return to the firehouse so she could lose the gear, take a shower, and go home. Her twelve-hour shift had ended at midnight, yet here she was, still riding the truck at 3 AM.

But they'd gotten yet *another* call while packing up from the

MVC on Solley Road, and Chief Kidder had fired up the sirens without asking her opinion.

A week ago, an accidental all-night shift would've meant she could look forward to an early-morning cup of coffee with her boyfriend, Michael Merrick.

Then again, a week ago Michael hadn't been giving her the cold shoulder. Lately, he was always too busy to do so much as talk on the phone.

Fine. Whatever. Like she had time in her life to deal with re- lationship drama. This was why she didn't date. She had one male in her life who really mattered, and he was five years old and called her Mommy.

The sirens screamed overhead, and she wished they could ride without them for once. Her head was killing her.

Kidder tapped at the dashboard computer in the front com- partment, then turned around to talk over his shoulder through the window. "Dispatch has called for three additional alarms on this one. Apparently we've got more than one house on fire."

Great.

Normally the thought of a massive job helped her focus. She could turn off her emotions and put the task at the forefront of her mind.

Tonight she was just tired.

Irish spoke from across the compartment, his voice a low rasp that didn't get a lot of use. "How many houses?"

Kidder checked his computer. "Five. Single-family. Sounds like a whole cul-de-sac."

Irish gave a low whistle, but didn't say anything else.

But she agreed with his assessment. Hannah glanced across at him, found him studying her, and quickly looked away. He smiled, a flash of white in his dusky face. "Looking tired, Blondie."

Hannah rolled her eyes, then realized it made her look like a petulant sixteen-year-old. She pulled her helmet firmly down on her head and studied the window really hard.

She still couldn't decide if she liked him. His name wasn't really Irish, of course, any more than hers was *Blondie*. He'd joined the station a month ago, showing up three days later than expected because of some paperwork mix-up. His real name—Ronan O'Connor—had been on his locker, and she and the rest of the company had expected a red-haired, freckled kid with an Irish accent, fresh out of fire school.

They hadn't expected a twenty-six-year-old seasoned firefighter.

They also hadn't expected a black guy. Not unheard of, but it made him the only one in the firehouse. Jerry Crondall, one of the older guys who killed off his brain cells with cigarettes and liquor, had taken one look at Ronan O'Connor and said, "Hey, kid, are you what they call Black Irish?"

The new guy had sighed and started unloading his gear. "No, man, I'm just Irish."

And that had stuck.

He was still looking at her. Hannah glanced over. "What's your problem?"

Her words were harsher than he deserved, especially since his brown eyes weren't mocking, just assessing. But she'd learned pretty quick that she needed to take the offensive or risk becoming the station doormat. It didn't matter that she could run lines or carry O2 tanks or break down a door like the rest of them. Without a penis, she had half the guys in this company thinking she was inferior. Being a *sweet little thang* would just reinforce it.

She already had to deal with the nickname Blondie.

"Seriously," Irish said, his voice low. "You look tired."

Like he knew her at all. "We're all tired."

He leaned sideways to call over her shoulder. "Chief. I think Blondie—"

Hannah kicked him right in the shin. "Don't you *dare*," she hissed.

If he said she couldn't handle another call, she would pull the Halligan bar off the side of the truck and introduce it to his skull.

Irish smiled and held her eyes. "I think Blondie and I should be on search and rescue."

Chief didn't even look over his shoulder. "You got it."

Hannah didn't say anything. Search and rescue could be

easy—if people had gotten the hell out of their houses—or it could be horrible. Like if she had to drag some obese guy down a flight of stairs.

She didn't know whether to hug Irish for confirming she had another call in her, or to smack him for being such a cocky shit in the first place. He was telling the *chief* what their assignment should be? What next, running the department?

Just when she was about to zing him with a comeback, she realized they'd turned onto Magothy Beach Road. She could see flames through the trees up ahead, toward the water.

Five houses. Single family. Sounds like the whole cul-de-sac.

Her heart stuttered to a stop.

Then it kicked into action again.

She caught sight of the street sign. Chautauga Court.

"Shit," she whispered.

Michael.

CHAPTER 3

M ichael stopped at the tree line and stared. Chris and Hunter were breathing hard beside him.

Five houses sat around the court. All blazed with fire—except the Merrick house, where no flames were visible, but smoke seemed to seep through the roof. At the others, smoke poured through roofs and flames shot high against the sky. Discordant smoke detectors screeched from each. The sirens coming up from Magothy Beach Road were louder.

Compared to the others, the Merrick house sat like an afterthought in the midst of this inferno. No motion, complete darkness.

Michael couldn't remember if he'd turned on a light.

He couldn't move. He couldn't think. Smoke burned his already abused lungs, but he couldn't cough. The heat was blistering, even from this distance.

His brain was frozen on his thought from fifteen minutes ago, when he'd been standing right here with Hunter.

His brothers were safer inside the house, asleep and oblivious.

But the Merrick house wasn't actively burning. Good? Or very bad?

Michael swept his eyes along the tree line behind the houses, looking for any sign of his brothers.

"Gabriel!" he yelled, sending power into the ground, seeking . . . anything. "Nick!"

Nothing.

He tried again, louder, spinning in a circle, as if his brothers would come sprinting out of the woods with a crazy story about what had happened.

Nothing.

Michael only spotted two people: the Hensons. They stood in the backyard next door, silhouetted by the flames. The woman clutched at her husband—whether in panic or from injury, Michael couldn't tell. They were an older couple with a yellow lab and too many grandkids to keep track of. Mrs. Henson had dropped off dinners almost every night for a month after Michael's parents had died. Michael mowed their lawn every week through the summer and plowed their driveway in the winter.

Flames poured through their upstairs windows. Their siding was buckling from the heat. Mrs. Henson was clutching at her husband in the backyard and screaming for Charlie.

Their dog. Trapped.

"Our house is smoking," said Hunter. His voice was shaking. "I can't sense anyone inside."

Michael looked at him. That statement could mean two things.

"Where are they?" said Chris. At some point he'd grabbed Michael's arm. His breath was shaking, his eyes a little too wide. The earlier indignant fury was gone from his expression, and now he just looked young. And frightened.

In a flash, Michael remembered Chris five years ago, flames reflected in his eyes exactly like this. Then, Michael had dragged his youngest brother out of a burning house much like this one. Chris had been choking, gasping for air.

Then, he'd been punching Michael, crying, yelling, his voice breaking. "Go get them! Get them!"

Their parents.

Red and white lights strobed between the houses, under-scored by the sound of hydraulic brakes and sirens cutting out. The sound should have been reassuring, but it wasn't.

Michael didn't want to believe Calla was behind this—but five houses. Five points on a pentagram—a symbol typically used to call the Guides. She wanted a war. This couldn't be a coincidence.

Or it might not be Calla at all. It might be an attack.

He immediately regretted yelling for his brothers. "Hide in the woods," Michael said. "Now."

"No!" said Chris. "Michael—we have to get—we have to get them—"

"I'm going to. I'm telling you to hide."

"But—"

"Goddamn it, Chris!" His own voice broke. "I'm not losing all of you! Go!"

Chris's face went whiter, if that was possible.

So did Hunter's, but he took hold of Chris's arm and started dragging. "Come on. We can hide."

Chris jerked free—but he followed.

For a moment, Michael wanted to call them back. He wanted to form a human chain and drag them all into the house behind him.

But he didn't know what he'd find inside.

He realized he was standing in the open, lit up by roaring flames.

A rookie sniper could take you out without a scope.

Everything suddenly sounded like a premonition. Michael sprinted onto the porch and grabbed hold of the door handle without thinking, throwing the French door wide and rushing into the kitchen.

Smoke hit him in the face, and Michael jerked back, coughing. The smoke detectors were screaming, three times as loud now that the door was open. He dropped to his knees and spent a minute relearning how to breathe. The air in here was hot and dry and tasted like ash. Pulling his damp shirt up over his mouth and nose helped, but not a lot.

He crawled forward. Darkness cloaked him immediately. He lost track of the door in less than five seconds. Every inhale tasted of smoke, along with something acrid and sour as he got farther into the kitchen. He put his hand down on something

unfamiliar that crumbled under his fingers and wished the flashlight weren't in the garage.

Michael stopped. The garage. Full of landscaping equipment—including fertilizer and chemicals.

Was the house still on fire? Was he crawling through a ticking
bomb?

He inhaled to yell for his brothers again, but his lungs didn't
want to inflate all the way. Michael coughed and pushed forward, trying to rush now.

His shoulder hit the cooking island *hard*, and Michael swore—
but at least it helped orient him. The doorway to the front hall
should be straight ahead.

Gabriel could survive in an inferno, but Michael knew smoke
made it hard for him to breathe. Nick could handle a loss of
oxygen—but he couldn't take a fire's heat for long.

Please be together, he thought.

Then he amended that.

And alive. Please be together and alive.

Michael wished he had Hunter's gun, so he could shoot these
screeching smoke detectors. With their persistent beeping, he
couldn't hear anything in the house. No movement, no voices.

Everything seemed very still in the darkness.

His hands found the slate flooring of the foyer. Every forward
movement brought another handful of grit, both a blessing and
a curse. He hadn't found his brothers collapsed in here, and that
could be a good thing or a bad thing.

Maybe he should have used his cell phone to try to call them.

He choked on the thought, unsure whether he was laughing
or crying. He put his forehead on his hands and inhaled again.
When had he gotten so *tired?*

Glass shattered somewhere up ahead.

Michael jumped and felt as if he were waking up. Somehow,
he'd ended up on the floor. He fought to get to his hands and his
knees, but his limbs felt too heavy. His shirt had come off his
face.

More glass shattering. Then a loud crack.

Someone was in the house.

Michael got his hands beneath his shoulders, and he managed to push back, toward the kitchen. He needed to hide.

Left hand. Right hand. This was more difficult than he remembered.

The house was so dark.

He needed to find his brothers. He needed to warn them.

He hit the cooking island with his hip, and it almost stole his balance. His head slammed into something, and flickering starbursts filled his vision.

He couldn't tell which way was up. He couldn't find his hands.

More starbursts. This felt like drowning again.

A hand grabbed his shoulder, and Michael flung himself back. Was this a Guide? Had they come after him? The smoky house, the lack of fire—all of a sudden this felt like a trap. Michael couldn't see anything in the darkness, but his attacker wouldn't be able to either. If they couldn't see him, they couldn't shoot him.

Every motion still felt slow, as if it took too long for messages to make it from his brain to his limbs. He barely had an opportunity to move before someone else grabbed him. Or was it the same person? He had no idea.

Something metal clicked, and Michael tried to swing a fist.

But then he inhaled, and his entire world clouded over.

Hannah heard Irish swear, and she swung her flashlight, trying to find him. The beam of light barely penetrated more than a few feet, and lit up nothing more than smoke in the hallway. But still, she didn't need to feel along walls to navigate through the thick darkness.

She knew this house.

She knew this staircase. This wall. This archway. This kitchen, where Michael would make her coffee and ask her quietly about her day.

She'd known the door they had to break through to get in here. The windows she'd had to smash to release trapped heat and smoke.

She and Irish weren't going to find anyone conscious in here. They'd be lucky to find someone alive.

Her breath shook for a moment, loud behind her mask.

Stop it. If she lost herself in thoughts, she'd never be able to get through this job.

Thoughts like how Michael and his brothers hadn't been sitting out front, waiting anxiously for the fire trucks.

Thoughts of Michael's hand pushing the hair back from her face. Or how he could be gruff and rough around the edges with everyone else, but his voice would go soft and gentle, just for her.

Thoughts of his brothers, who'd invited her and James into their mix without judgment.

"Michael," she whispered, the name echoing back to her through the mask. "Michael, please don't be in here."

"Blondie!" yelled Irish, his voice muffled behind his own mask. "I've got a body. Grab his feet."

Her heart stopped.

Then her brain caught up, letting her training kick in. A patient needing assessment, just like any other rescue.

A body didn't have to be Michael. It didn't have to be one of his brothers.

Yeah, like there's some random guy lying in the middle of the kitchen.

But she was moving now, and that's all that mattered. She couldn't see for crap, but she caught hold of ankles and lifted when Irish said he was ready.

Ankles. Good. Ankles could mean anyone. They'd get this guy outside and assess his condition.

She wasn't fooling herself.

The body hung limp and heavy between them. Hannah's flashlight bounced and arced along the smoke as they made their way through the foyer, never quite lighting on the patient's face.

Then they were through the broken front door, into the frigid night air, into the bright lights from the fire trucks and ambulances.

Michael.

No surprise. No shock. She'd *known,* from the minute she'd picked up his ankles.

She choked on another breath and was glad she still wore the mask, feeding oxygen into her face. She was lucky to recognize him, his face and clothing were so filthy and caked with soot. His head lolled back, his face slack, with dark smudges around his nostrils. Smoke inhalation, for sure—how long had he been in there?

They got him on the ground. Irish was speaking into his radio, calling for an RSI—a paramedic trained to insert a breathing tube.

Holy shit—that meant Michael wasn't breathing at all. Hannah yanked her helmet and gloves off and flung them into the grass. She pressed her fingers against his carotid artery, searching for a pulse.

"Call for more on rescue," she said in a rush. "Four other people live in that house." She shifted her fingers, searching. "Come on, Michael," she whispered, putting her face down close to his, feeling for breath. "Come *on.*"

Nothing.

She was distantly aware of Irish beginning chest compressions. Of firefighters rushing up the steps behind her, preparing to search the house.

When Irish called out the count, her training kicked in, and she bent to press her mouth to Michael's. She should be using a bag and a mask, but she didn't care. He didn't have the two minutes it would take for her to run to the truck.

His lips were ice cold. She tasted soot on his skin.

He wasn't moving.

"Damn it!" she yelled between breaths. "Where the hell is the RSI?"

Oscar Martinez, a guy she'd gone through fire school with, spoke from beside her. He was a full paramedic, but he couldn't intubate. He was trying to thread an IV needle into the back of Michael's hand. "Next house over. Some teenagers got the whole family out the back, but they're in bad shape. We're waiting on another ambo from station fourteen."

Michael couldn't wait that long. How long had he gone without a pulse? How long had he been in that house?

He'd sent her two text messages today. She hadn't bothered to read either of them because she'd been too pissed at the way he'd been blowing her off.

Two text messages. Two frigging text messages. How hard would it have been to read them?

Hannah choked on her breath again. "Come on," she whispered. She pressed her hand to his cheek. "Come on, Michael. Wake up."

No response. She blew another breath into his mouth, but his chest barely rose.

"Your brothers need you," she said.

Irish glanced up. She met his eyes and saw the resignation there.

This might be a lost cause.

Her own eyes blurred.

And then she heard the rumble, as the ground started to shake.

CHAPTER 4

At first, Hannah didn't understand what was happening. The sound wasn't loud; more like a slow roll of thunder. The vibration of the ground under her knees felt more like a large vehicle starting up than anything else.

But then it grew stronger, until she had to put a hand on the ground to keep her balance. Someone somewhere was shouting. It took her a moment to make out the word.

Earthquake.

Irish didn't stop the chest compressions, but she could see he was struggling to maintain his balance too.

A loud crackling echoed from her left, and she snapped her head up.

"The sidewalk!" said Oscar. He'd dropped to a knee, and now had a hand on the ground.

He was right—the sidewalk was splitting, slow cracks crawling along the pavement.

Firefighters were shouting, both live and from the radio on her shoulder. The team that had rushed into the house a minute ago came flying through the door, stumbling on the steps.

She'd thought nothing could overpower the cacophony of the trucks and radios and discordant fire alarms, but the new sounds brought on by this earthquake were deafening. Metal shrieked from everywhere, and Hannah could swear she saw the porch supports at the front of the house start to buckle. From the street, more shouts, more splitting pavement. Metal on metal as fire trucks began to slide and collide with each other.

"What the hell is going on?" said Oscar. He must have lost the needle; Michael's hand was bleeding.

Wind ripped between the houses, sudden and cold, pulling smoke and debris from across the court. More shouts from the hose teams as water blew back, away from the flames, showering the rescue team with ice-cold droplets. Fire was in the air now, bits of flaming ash flying wildly.

One of the porch supports groaned, then cracked fully. The roof over the porch sagged.

"We need to move," said Irish.

But they couldn't. The ground bucked again, and Hannah watched the grass split and separate. The gap spread in a line from Michael's body all the way to the road. She swore and shifted to the other side of his body, beside Irish.

It gave her a better view of the destruction around her. At the house next door, wood cracked and split. The house swayed for an eternal moment, as if buffeted by the wind.

And then it collapsed.

Flames and smoke billowed from the destruction, and the hose team fought to stay on their feet, aiming water at the structure, trying to keep the fire from spreading. Water sprayed wildly in the wind.

Then the ground rumbled again, and the sidewalk around the hydrant fractured. Water shot from the ground in a massive fountain. The fire hoses lost pressure and died.

Another rumble. The grass cracked and split again, stretching off into the darkness. The front yard seemed to be shifting in pieces, rolling like the sea. The house behind them creaked and threatened to collapse like the first. The fire trucks on the road bounced and shifted. People were yelling now, fear in their voices. Her radio was going crazy as people called orders and updates. She couldn't make sense of any of it.

Another house across the court collapsed. Firefighters ran to escape the flying debris.

More wind blasted her cheeks, bringing smoke and ash.

And then, out of nowhere, one of Michael's brothers skidded to his knees beside her.

One of the twins. She had no idea which. His clothes were filthy too, his skin darkened with soot.

She put a hand on his arm to push him back. "Gabriel—"

"Nick," he corrected her. He grabbed Irish's arm. "Stop."

Irish didn't stop—though his efforts lacked the fervor of his initial attempts to save Michael's life. Hannah could read it in his expression. It had been at least three minutes.

The ground rumbled and shifted again. Irish swore and fought to keep his balance. "Kid, you need to get out of here before that house falls."

"It's his brother," Hannah said. Her voice broke. "Nick— Nick, I need—"

"Stop. Both of you stop." Nick's voice was rushed and panicked. He grabbed Irish's arm again and almost shoved. "I said *stop*."

Irish stopped. Time seemed to hold still, the earth shifting below them, the wind slamming into them.

"Just stop," Nick said again, his voice more steady. Wind whipped at their clothes and made Hannah shiver. The house behind them gave another loud creak. "Wait."

She stopped. Held her breath.

For an instant, she thought maybe Nick knew something they didn't, that all Michael needed was his brother's presence and he'd sit up and ask what was going on.

Michael didn't move.

Stupid, she told herself. She knew the limits of the human body as well as anyone else. Her eyes wanted to fill, but she could hold it together for his little brother.

Nick put a hand on his brother's neck. "Michael," he said softly, his words somehow carrying over the wind. "Mike. Wake up."

Irish looked at her over Nick's head. He shook his head.

"Nick," she said, putting a hand over his. "Nick, the smoke— it works fast. His lungs may be too badly damaged—"

Nick sucked in a deep breath and pressed his mouth over his brother's before she could even finish that thought.

Michael's chest rose from the pressure and fell when Nick drew back.

And then rose again.

"He's breathing!" Hannah grabbed his wrist and felt for a pulse. Irish reached for his neck.

Michael's eyes opened. He squeezed them shut and blinked a few times. His arm jerked out of her hand.

"Take it easy, man," said Irish. "We're just—"

Michael shoved him away and fought to get off the ground. Irish and Oscar tried to hold him there.

"Let me go. Let me go." His voice was like crushed stone, rough and painful to her ears. He sounded disoriented and afraid. "Someone was in the house. My brothers—" His voice broke. "I need to get my brothers. I need to get them before they're found."

"Hey. Mike." Nick put a hand on his shoulder and got in his brother's face. "We're okay. Look at me. We're okay."

Michael went still. The rumbling earth slowed and went still. "Nick. Hannah."

"Yeah. It's okay. We're okay."

"Gabriel?"

"Everyone is okay."

For the longest instant, Michael just stared at them, the wind blowing fiercely between them. His eyes shifted past his brother, to the destruction of the houses on the court, to the fire hydrant spraying water high into the air. Fires still burned everywhere, and emergency lights flickered off everything.

He glanced at his own house, barely standing.

Then his face crumpled and he threw his arms around his little brother's neck. "Not okay, Nick. It's not okay."

Nick let him hold on. "You'll make it okay, Michael. Just breathe."

And just then, thunder cracked overhead. The sky opened up, and rain poured down, putting out every last lick of flame.

* * *

Michael sat on a stretcher inside one of the ambulances, but he had no intention of letting them take him to the hospital. Thanks to the downpour, his clothes were soaking wet again and he was freezing. Someone had offered him a wool blanket, but he'd refused.

His brothers had taken them, though. They were sitting in the back of another ambulance, waiting.

He needed to get them and leave.

He had no idea where to go.

The rain had stopped the blazing fires around the court, but it still rattled against the roof of the ambulance. Michael could see cracked pavement from here, lines of fractured asphalt weaving between the rescue vehicles left on the court. Rain wouldn't do much to repair this kind of damage. He'd caught a glimpse of one collapsed home and didn't have the guts to look at the others.

His whole life, this was what his parents had been worried about. This was what the *Guides* were worried about.

He'd never caused this much destruction. He'd never lost control to this extent.

Then again, he'd never been so close to death, either. Looking at the damage, he didn't want to consider how bad it must have been for his powers to take over without his knowledge.

He didn't want to see the destruction. He might not have started the fires, but his earthquake had completed the disaster. He didn't want to see them bagging bodies and towing disabled trucks. He didn't want to hear crying from the few survivors, and he sure as hell didn't want to see who'd survived—because it would make him think of those who hadn't.

Maybe someone could close the back door of the ambulance.

Hannah sat on the little bench in front of him, trying to shine a light in his eyes.

He brushed her hand away. "Hannah. I'm fine."

"You don't sound fine."

He couldn't meet her eyes. "Yeah, what do I sound like?"

"Like you have gravel instead of lungs. Look at me."

He didn't want to look at her. He wanted to snap and tell her to get the hell away from him before he hurt her, too.

But then her hand caught his chin, and just like every other time she touched him, he couldn't move. He'd gone so long without a gentle touch that even now, after six weeks, some small part of him still couldn't believe that she *wanted* to touch him.

Her tiny flashlight clicked back on. "Let me check your eyes."

Her voice was gentle, encouraging, but it carried a note of command. A mother's voice.

He looked at her. Blue eyes, their brightness dimmed a bit from exhaustion. Blond hair cut just above her shoulders, gone flat and tucked behind her ears. She'd lost her coat somewhere along the line and sat there in a T-shirt, worn red suspenders, and reflective pants. Soot smudges were everywhere. He wanted to pull her into his lap and not let go, to reassure himself that there was something in his life that couldn't disappear between one heartbeat and the next.

Then the light was in his eyes and he couldn't see anything.

"You really need a trip to the hospital," she said quietly.

"My eyes are fine." He *did* sound like he had gravel for lungs. He cleared his throat. It hurt. He wasn't sure whether to blame that on the near-drowning or the smoke inhalation. Probably both.

"I'm not worried about your eyes." She lowered the flashlight and clicked it off. "You need a chest X-ray."

No, he didn't. He might not be all the way healed, but Nick's power over air had done its work. What he needed was to get out of here.

What he *wanted* was to hold Hannah's hand against his face and not let go. What he *wanted* was to tell her everything.

And yet, he didn't.

"I'm not going to the hospital." He wanted to fidget, but there was nothing to fidget *with*. He dug his fingers into the edge of the stretcher mattress.

"I don't know how you're sitting up talking to me. Are you aware we were calling for someone to put a tube down your throat so you could *breathe*?"

Michael didn't look at her. The panic of the moment he'd woken was still too fresh. He wondered if he would've been able to stop the earthquake if he'd woken up strapped to a gurney with plastic tubing shoved into his lungs.

Hannah finally sat back, letting her hands fall to her lap. "They'll make you sign something, if you refuse treatment."

Was that supposed to be intimidating? "Fine. I'll sign whatever so I can get out of here."

She frowned, and Michael kept his eyes on the rack beside her head, regretting the sharpness of his tone. His fingers were lined with soot and dirt. It felt as if his swim in the creek had happened hours ago. Days, even.

She didn't move. He didn't either.

Silence fell between them, punctuated by shouted orders from outside along with bursts of static-laced information from her radio. He didn't know the codes or the lingo, but then he heard, "*I've got three possible DOAs in house two. Request assistance. Over.*"

Michael rubbed his hands over his face. He didn't know which one was house two, but he knew all his neighbors. Would it be the Stapleys, the young couple who'd only lived here a year, the ones with a new baby? Or maybe the Mellisarios. They had three kids. Sarah, John, and little Andrew. Michael remembered them coming to the house for Halloween—

His chest tightened, and he worried he was going to lose it again, like he had in the front yard. He tried twice to make his voice work. "Can you—are you allowed to turn that off?"

She turned a dial on the radio. It didn't go silent, but almost. "Your house is the only one that wasn't actively burning. How did you stop it?"

He swallowed. He'd never be able to sit here and lie to her for long, but at least this answer was easy. "I don't know."

"Do you remember what happened?"

He remembered going through the back door. He remembered crawling through smoke and darkness. He remembered breaking glass and splintering wood.

He shook his head.

"We found you in the kitchen," said Hannah. "Do you remember getting there?"

"Someone broke in while I was looking." Michael looked at her. "I think they did something . . ." He tried to force his brain to work, but his moments in the house were unclear, his thoughts as fragile and fleeting as wisps of smoke. "Did you find anyone else in there?"

"No." She paused. "You might have heard me and Irish. We broke in to search the house. We smashed out the windows to let smoke out, then came through the door."

Could that have been it? Could he have mistaken their rescue for an attack?

Michael drew back and rubbed at his face again. Sweat and dirt made his eyes sting.

Hannah spoke again, her voice quiet. "If you won't go to the hospital, would you at least let me call a paramedic to listen to your lungs? I don't want—"

"Hannah. No." He started to shift off the stretcher.

She caught his arm. "Me, then. God, at the very least, let me get a pulse-ox to make sure you're actually getting some oxygen."

He sighed and eased back onto the thin mattress. He wondered if she realized how easily she could get him to follow orders, just by letting him feel her skin against his.

Hannah flipped on a machine behind her, then snapped a plastic clip onto his right index finger. She pulled a stethoscope out of a tiny cabinet, then shifted to sit beside him on the stretcher.

It put her thigh against his, and even though he wore soaked jeans and she wore bunker pants, he imagined he could feel her warmth.

"Just breathe normally." She plugged the earpieces into her ears.

He nodded. It took everything he had not to lean into her.

Then her hand slid under the back of his shirt, and she might as well have hit him with a live wire.

"Sorry." She winced and pulled the stethoscope away. "Cold hands?"

As if that were the problem. He shook his head quickly. "No. It's fine."

She put the metal and plastic back against his skin, her fingers warm where she touched him. Michael breathed and wished his worries could condense to the space inside this ambulance, just for a moment.

She moved the stethoscope for a few heartbeats, then again. Her other hand rested on his bicep, gentle and reassuring. Michael shut his eyes and tried to hold still.

"You okay?"

Her voice was very close. He opened his eyes and looked at her. "No."

"You stopped breathing."

"Oh. Sorry." He swallowed and took a deep breath.

"If I'm making you uncomfortable—"

"Never." He looked at her. "Never, Hannah."

She studied him, her eyes full of uncertainty. "I thought you—I thought—" She broke off and looked away. He watched her throat jerk as she swallowed. "I thought I was going to have to give your brothers some very bad news."

The words—the wavering emotion in her voice—hit him hard. He'd spent so many years worrying about everyone else that it was a shock to hear someone express worry over *him*.

He realigned everything she'd said to him since the moment he'd woken up, and everything he'd said to her.

Fine. I'll sign whatever so I can get out of here.

He put his hands over the place where her fingers rested on his arm. He wanted to do more than that, to collapse on her shoulder, to curl up and clutch her against him, but if he fell apart now, he'd never get it together.

He ducked his head and kept his voice low. "How do my lungs sound, Doctor?"

After a breath, she rested her forehead against the side of his face. She smelled like soot and ash and sweat, but under that was something warm and sweet, like sugar cookies. When she blinked, her lashes fluttered against his cheek. "I'm not a doctor."

"Paramedic."

"Not yet. You know I still have another year of—"

He couldn't take it. Michael wrapped his arms around her and crushed her against his chest. His breathing was shaky, and he didn't trust his voice, but he held her, and she let him.

No, she held him *back*.

"It's okay," she whispered. "It'll be okay."

"It's not," he said, his voice thick. "Not even a little bit."

Despite everything his family had gone through, they'd always had a *home*. He'd made sure of it. The shelves were never overflowing with food, and there'd been a year when he'd turned off cable and made the guys share one cell phone, but they'd had a roof over their heads and beds to sleep in. Always somewhere to come back to.

And now they had . . . what? The truck? The car?

Considering the earthquake, he wasn't sure they even had that much.

Then one of the demolished homes on the cul-de-sac caught his eye. They had a lot more than some of these families.

All this destruction. How much had been his fault? If these homes hadn't collapsed, would the radio be reporting rescues instead of dead bodies?

His breath shook again. He wanted to ask how many people had been killed, and whether Hannah knew names yet.

At the same time, he was afraid to ask.

"When you two are done, I have a few questions."

At the sound of the dry voice, Hannah pulled back quickly, and Michael let her go. He recognized the man standing behind the ambulance, and he wondered if it was a good thing or a bad thing that the county fire marshal had shown up.

"Dad!" Hannah said, for all the world sounding like a teenager caught with a boy in her room. "What are you doing here?"

"Working." He paused, then raised an eyebrow. "Aren't you?"

Michael knew he wasn't imagining the disapproval in the man's tone. Hannah and her father had a tense relationship. If Hannah's mother weren't in the picture, they probably wouldn't speak at all. Jack Faulkner was never rude to Michael—but he wasn't exactly patting him on the back and inviting him over to watch the game, either. The fire marshal had arrested Gabriel and charged him with arson six weeks ago. Once the real arsonist was behind bars, Jack had been civil to Michael. Not quite friendly, but not cold.

Suspicious? Michael had no idea. Hannah said her father treated everyone like a potential criminal—including her.

But to his surprise, when Jack turned steely grey eyes his way, there was compassion there. "How are you doing, Mike? You okay?"

The question, the casual concern, threw him off. Michael's own parents had always been warm, their home always open to others—to their detriment—and Hannah's father was the opposite of that. They'd sat across a table for dinner on Hannah's birthday and talked business and sports. Easy topics, nothing personal.

That night felt like a year ago.

But maybe this was the real Jack Faulkner. Maybe a crisis brought out the *dad* in him, breaking down the awkward barriers.

Michael nodded and had to clear his throat. "I'm all right."

"What about your brothers? Are they holding up?"

Michael nodded. He rubbed a hand over the back of his neck. Sweat and grit. Sand, soot, whatever. He'd kill for a shower. A hot one. "More or less."

"You have somewhere to go?"

For an instant, the question didn't make sense. Why would he *go* anywhere?

Then reality knocked on his skull. The fire marshal was asking if he had a place to *stay*.

It hadn't even occurred to him yet, but now that he had to

consider it, Michael had no idea where to take his brothers. Insurance would come into play at some point, but it wasn't like he could call up his agent and money would appear in the checking account tomorrow. They could ride on credit cards for a while, but feeding and housing five people on Visa's dime would only last so long.

But what was he supposed to say? He knew from experience that he couldn't admit uncertainty in front of anyone official. He held back any emotion and wished his voice didn't sound as if he were speaking through ground stone. "I have to make a few calls. I'll work it out."

Hannah slipped her hand under his and laced their fingers together. The motion felt comforting—but somehow defiant, too.

Michael couldn't tell if Marshal Faulkner noticed. Rain was collecting on the shoulders of the man's jacket. "It might just be smoke damage. There are a few local companies who can help with that. You'll have to get an engineer out to check the foundation after that earthquake."

Or Michael could just walk a loop around the house and feel it out for himself.

As if the insurance company would take his word for it.

Marshal Faulkner turned and looked past the ambulance, his eyes on something in the distance. "A lot of damage here. You guys are lucky."

Lucky. Yeah, right. Michael hadn't felt lucky since . . . ever.

The fire marshal stepped closer. "How did you put the fires out so quickly?"

Michael opened his mouth to respond, but Hannah squeezed his hand, *hard.* "Don't answer that."

Michael blinked. She'd asked him pretty much the same thing. "I—I . . . what?"

Her tone was even. "He's not being nice. He's trying to *interrogate* you."

The fire marshal barely spared her a glance. His attitude didn't change; it was still official, reassuring. "Hannah, why don't you let me speak with Michael privately?"

"Why, so you can try to trap him with questions?"

"No, so I can spare him a trip in a squad car and his brothers a night with DFS."

Michael straightened. DFS was the Department of Family Services.

"What does that mean?" He suddenly wanted out of this ambulance, as if social workers had secreted his brothers away already. Tension held him rigid, and the only thing keeping him sitting here was the knowledge that acting like a panicked freak would do more harm than good.

"It means if I take you in for questioning, I'm responsible for making sure your brothers are taken care of."

"We just dragged him out of his house, unconscious," Hannah said. "Why don't you find someone else to question?"

"There is no one else right now, Hannah."

The words hung there in space for a moment, and Michael flinched, realizing what that meant.

The fire marshal continued, "I had one of your brothers under arrest a month ago. Should I have kept him that way?"

"My brother didn't do this."

"Then help me prove it. Answer my questions. Take a walk through your house with me."

Michael hesitated. The night had been too long, the events too quick to string together. He needed an hour to sit down and think.

Marshal Faulkner took a step closer. "A rookie cop could put two and two together on this one, Mike. Your brother was a prime arson suspect a month ago—and while he ended up with a rock-solid alibi during interrogation, *you* didn't. Your house is the only one still standing. They're talking about bringing in bomb dogs to see if that *earthquake* was really a natural occurrence. I'm not trying to rough you up here, but I need something that doesn't look so damning or I'm going to have to drag you in on principle."

Michael looked away. Didn't an officer need a warrant to search the house? Should he be calling a lawyer? Could he even get one at three in the morning?

When his parents died, they sure hadn't left a manual.

Chapter Three: When You're Suspected of Criminal Wrong-doing.

Wind sliced into the ambulance, biting through his damp clothes. He shivered.

A terrible, dark part of his brain wanted to start shouting. *Yes. I'm guilty. I should have stopped this. Instead, I made it worse.*

He swallowed, and his throat was so tight that it hurt.

The fire marshal hadn't looked away. "If you want me to get a warrant, fine, I'll get one. But if you're not doing anything wrong, then what's the big deal?"

Michael rubbed at his temples. Maybe if they went in the house, he could choke down half a bottle of aspirin. Or a whole bottle of whiskey. "Fine. Whatever. Let's get this over with."

CHAPTER 5

Michael wanted to check on his brothers first. He remembered the months after their parents had died, how he'd spend all day worrying that they wouldn't get off the bus after school. Back then, he hadn't been sure which to fear more: the Guides who had wanted to kill them for their abilities—or the social workers who had wanted to split them up into the foster care system.

Right now didn't feel too different.

His brothers and Hunter were huddled at the back of another ambulance, just a short distance away. Only Chris had abandoned the wool blanket, and he was sitting on the bumper, rain threading through his hair to paint reflective lines on his cheeks. Hunter's dog was curled up beneath the tailgate, behind Chris's legs. He looked up and beat his tail against the ground when Michael came over.

His brothers watched him approach, but didn't move. Michael looked at each of them in turn, as if he could reassure himself just by seeing them alive and well and *together*. Their faces were drawn and cautious, their skin caked with dirt and soot.

None of them said anything. They didn't have to. He could read the uncertainty behind their guarded expressions like a billboard sign.

What's going to happen?
Where are we going to go?
Are we in danger?

They always thought he had answers. He almost never did, but he was pretty good at faking it. "Is anyone hurt?" he said.

"No," said Chris.

"They're lucky," Marshal Faulkner said from behind him. "I understand two of you kids pulled a family of five out of . . ." He consulted a notepad, then pointed at a burned pile of rubble. ". . . that house."

"Me and Nick," said Gabriel. "They were right by the door. I guess that makes *them* the lucky ones."

His words were sharp edged, a reaction to authority, and it was almost enough to make Michael snap at him. But he heard the fear beneath Gabriel's snark, and he understood the reason behind it.

It gave Michael the answer to one question: his brothers hadn't been trapped in the house at all. He'd crawled through smoke for nothing. He'd lost consciousness and started an earthquake for . . . nothing.

He swallowed his own self-doubt before they could see it. "Anyone who's still sitting up and talking is lucky. Can you guys wait here for fifteen minutes while I check the house?"

"Where else are we going to go?" said Nick.

His words weren't snarky at all. It was a genuine question.

"I'm working on it," said Michael. "Sit tight." And then he started walking.

Hannah and Marshal Faulkner were right on his heels, but he needed to get some distance from that ambulance before his brothers figured out that he didn't have a clue about what to do or where to go. He didn't even know the right answers to keep himself out of a police station.

When he hit the grass in front of his house, however, he stopped. The sidewalk was destroyed, but from what he could tell, the damage didn't reach far below the surface. All the front windows had been smashed out, and the boards of the porch looked warped. The front door was hanging open, half off its hinges.

Splintered wood surrounded the area around the lock and the knob.

"Wow. You really did break in," he said to Hannah.

"Yeah." She paused. "It's procedure. The windows—we have to let oxygen in—"

She sounded guilty, and Michael shook his head. "I'm not *blaming* you, Hannah."

"People blame the fire department all the time," said Marshal Faulkner. "Broken windows are the least of their worries."

His tone sounded conspiratorial, but Hannah's earlier warning had Michael on edge. Was this a ploy, to get him to talk? Or just his girlfriend's dad cutting him some slack?

Michael kept his mouth shut and climbed the steps.

A rapid cracking sound echoed from inside the house. Michael stopped short at the doorway.

Marshal Faulkner clicked on a flashlight and didn't seem concerned.

"Is someone already in here?" said Michael. Some part of him rebelled against it. This was his *house*. No one had a right to be in here.

Then again, the shattered windows and broken door wouldn't do much to keep out vandals. He'd need to board the place up. He started making a mental list.

"Someone is checking the walls," said Hannah. "Making sure there's no fire left."

Gabriel would know for sure, but Michael couldn't think of a reasonable way to ask for him to join them. When they stepped through the door, he automatically reached for the switch, then told himself to stop being an idiot.

"We killed the electric for the street," offered Marshal Faulkner. "Gas and water, too." He swept his flashlight across the foyer floor.

Michael almost wished he hadn't. All the wide beam showed was a cone of smoke and dark dust swirling in the air. The light found the stairway bannister: all black. The carpeted steps, too.

"Jesus," Michael whispered. He was glad his brothers weren't here.

The flashlight beam moved higher. "We can't go upstairs," said the fire marshal. "I don't like the look of those steps."

Michael thought about what that meant. He had his phone in his pocket—if it had even survived the swim in the creek. The case was water resistant—an investment he'd made after losing a phone in a koi pond once. He checked now and found it working. Did his brothers have theirs? What about clothes? Schoolbooks?

Identification? Car keys? His own wallet was plastered inside his back pocket, but his ID and credit cards seemed intact. He had no idea what his brothers might have on them, if anything.

Marshal Faulkner hadn't waited for a response. He'd moved into the dining room. Michael watched the flashlight beam play along the floor, the walls, then the table.

Everything had a fine layer of soot.

The marshal stopped at the far side of the room, until Michael couldn't see him through the haze, just the bouncing beam of his flashlight. "How long did the fire burn?"

Michael shook his head. "I don't know."

"When we broke in, we didn't see anything actively burning," Hannah said. "The place was hot and full of smoke."

The fire marshal's flashlight stopped in the doorway to the kitchen. "Do you remember stopping the fire?"

"No." Michael suspected Gabriel had, but it wasn't like he could say that. His brother certainly wouldn't have used a fire extinguisher. But Michael had no other explanation. If he admitted not being here when the fire started, would that look better or worse? He didn't know.

Then his eyes followed the light beam as it stopped on the door at the opposite side of the kitchen, leading to the garage—where he kept all his landscaping equipment and supplies.

If this house had gone up in flames, he wouldn't have just lost their home, he would have lost the business, too.

"No fire in here," the marshal said. "Just smoke damage."

"How can you tell?"

"No burn pattern," said Hannah. "Look at the floor and the walls."

He couldn't see anything but dark grey ash everywhere.

The light centered on him. "You all right?"

Maybe the residual smoke was getting to him. He cleared his throat. His eyes burned and he rubbed at them. "Yeah," he ground out. "Fine."

Hannah found his hand in the darkness. She squeezed once.

He didn't squeeze back—but he didn't let go either. He followed the arcing light back into the foyer.

Here, he could see what they meant about the burn pattern. The carpeting was black, but *too* black. The stairwell had been on fire. He could smell the difference, too, now that he was paying attention. Something stronger and more acrid than the smoke alone.

The flashlight hit the living room carpeting and illuminated the edge of the sofa.

Or what was left of the sofa. Michael only recognized it from its position in the room. No more green upholstery. Nothing left but the arm of a charred shell.

The fire marshal stepped back into the archway separating the foyer from the living room, shining his light along the carpeting, then along the ceiling.

The drywall had burned away, and Michael was looking at charred beams and exposed insulation. Then the light skittered down the opposite side of the room, where a few bookcases and cabinets had been built into the wall.

Michael remembered being eight years old, resentful of his three toddler brothers who never shut up. He remembered sulkily "helping" his father install those wall units, probably just an excuse to keep him out of his mother's hair.

Why are we building this, Dad?

Because your mother wants bookcases.

Then why isn't she building them?

Because I want to give them to her.

He couldn't remember how much he'd actually helped, but he remembered holding a hammer, his father's hand secure over his as he showed him how to hit a nail. He remembered being proud of the finished product, of his mother's reaction.

Now there was nothing left. Just a burned shell of where the bookcases used to be.

Hannah edged closer to him. "If this is too much—"

"It's fine. I'm fine."

It wasn't. He wasn't.

Hannah didn't move away. Her voice was very soft. "You're shaking."

He was. He made sure his voice wasn't. "It's nothing. It's cold."

A new voice spoke from down the hallway. "Want me to grab a blanket off one of the ambos?"

Michael turned, glad for the distraction, for the reason to look away from those goddamn bookcases. *I'm sorry, Mom.*

Like he was a kid again, and he'd broken her favorite dish or something.

No, worse. Like he'd burned down her house.

You did burn down her house.

"No, thanks," he said. "I'm good."

The new firefighter clicked on his own flashlight, creating another beam in the hallway, his feet crunching on grit as he came over to join them. When he got close, Michael recognized him as the firefighter who'd been with Hannah. The guy was tall, taller than Michael, and built like a linebacker. He had a bar in one hand, one end resting against his shoulder. A camera-like device hung around his neck.

His flashlight beam lifted almost to Michael's face, so he could see everyone clearly, but no one was blinded. His expression was some mixture of surprised and intrigued. "I still can't believe you're upright and talking."

Michael wasn't sure what the right response to that was. "Give me an hour."

"I checked the walls on this level. Thermal imaging doesn't show anything. I think you're clear."

Again, no appropriate response came to mind. This man had dragged him out of a house unconscious. He'd helped perform CPR. He'd watched Michael lose his shit.

Actually, if he'd walked in here a minute later, he would have seen Michael lose it for a second time.

"Thanks," Michael finally said.

"No problem."

"This is Irish," said Hannah. "Irish, this is Michael."

Michael knew he should be following social niceties, but his brain wasn't providing the automatic responses. Maybe it was the dark, maybe it was the residual haze of smoke in the living room, maybe it was the fact that his life had literally turned into a pile of crap around him. But he could only stand there, silent, staring at Irish like he had two brain cells left.

"Could you shine that light over here?" said the fire marshal.

His words broke through the awkward tension. Irish pointed the flashlight toward the other beam.

"Look." Marshal Faulkner gestured with his flashlight along the floor. "Can you see the pattern of the burn?"

Michael just saw a whole lot of burned carpeting. "It's all burned."

"Look. Follow the light. See how it's darker along this line?"

The light traced a path through the thin smoke, following a stretch of charred carpeting.

Then Michael saw it, a clear line of darkness through the rest of the blackened material. "It's darker. Why?"

"Burned hotter," said Irish, as if it were obvious.

Hannah glanced up. "Accelerant does that."

"Like gasoline?" Calla had used accelerant to start the fires a few months back. She'd been drawing pentagrams in the houses she destroyed, in an attempt to call the Guides. Was this a pentagram? It was too dark to tell, and he couldn't ask without sounding more involved than he was.

Guides marked houses with pentagrams, too, but he'd never heard of it being done by fire. Then again, anything was possible. Neither she nor the Guides would have needed accelerant to start a fire—unless they wanted to send a message. Like now.

Everything here pointed in both directions, leaving Michael feeling like he sat squarely in the line of fire.

Hannah's father shrugged. "Could be gasoline. Or kerosene. Lighter fluid. Anything, really. Pretty clear pour pattern. No one tried to hide anything here." The light flicked back to Michael. "Deliberate. No question. Not that I had any doubt, with four other houses going to ash right this second."

"Who would do this?" said Irish.

His tone was the same as the fire marshal's: not quite an interrogation, but almost. Michael waited for Marshal Faulkner to say something cop-like, maybe, *I'll ask the questions here*, but he didn't say anything. Maybe he was waiting for the answer, too.

At least Michael didn't have to lie. "I have no idea. Is that Ryan Stacey kid still behind bars?"

"Who's Ryan Stacey?" said Irish.

"Local kid," said Hannah. "He was setting houses on fire a few months ago."

Ryan had been helping Calla. They didn't know that, but Michael did.

Not that he could volunteer that information.

"Ryan Stacey didn't do this," said Marshal Faulkner. "Not from prison. New question."

Michael coughed. He felt like the room was spinning. "Shoot."

"Looking at this room, your house should be rolling like the rest of the street. I'm going to ask you again. How'd you stop the fire?"

Michael had no answer for that. He ran his hands across his face. "I don't know. I don't—it must have burned itself out."

"That's not how fire works, and I'm pretty sure you know that as well as I do."

He did know that. He also knew he didn't have any answers to give. His thoughts were still trying to make sense of the fires—and who had started them.

There was someone in the woods.

Was it *just* Chris? Or someone else? Was it a coincidence this happened when he'd been chasing his brother?

Had he been lured away?

He didn't know. He couldn't even answer his own questions, much less the fire marshal's.

Michael rubbed at his eyes and wanted to sit down. "Are you going to arrest me because the fire *stopped*?"

Marshal Faulkner held his eyes across the haze. "Not yet."

"He's not going to arrest you at all," said Hannah. Her voice was firm.

"Hannah—"

Irish cleared his throat. "I'm going to go help run lines."

"Take her with you," said Marshal Faulkner.

Hannah inhaled to object, and her father said, "Don't think I won't order you out of here."

"It's okay," Michael said. "He's doing his job."

"Come on, Blondie," said Irish. He gave Hannah a pat on the shoulder and gestured toward the front. "We're shorthanded anyway."

Blondie. Michael tucked that away in his head to think about later. Along with the casual way Irish had touched her.

But she gave Michael a last, lingering squeeze of her hand. "Find me before you leave, okay?"

"Okay."

And then she was gone, following Irish through the door.

Leaving him there with the fire marshal.

Michael wondered if he could make a run for it, or if the guy would take that as guilt and just shoot him.

But then Marshal Faulkner said, "I'm going to let you take your brothers out of here."

His voice was almost kind, and for an instant, Michael wished he was seventeen again, that the marshal *could* call DFS and find someone else to make all this go away. He nodded. "Okay."

"Not far. You understand me?"

"Yeah," said Michael, making no effort to hide the exhaustion in his voice.

Marshal Faulkner pulled a card from his coat and held it out. "I want you to call me later, after you've gotten some sleep. After you talk to the insurance company and get yourself settled."

Michael reached for the card. He nodded.

The man didn't let go of it. "I expect to hear from you within twenty-four hours. Clear on that, too?"

"Yes. Clear." He took the card.

"Good." The marshal clapped him on the shoulder. "Come on. Let's go see if you have a working vehicle."

CHAPTER 6

The truck was undamaged, so Michael had a working vehicle. Three, really, if you counted Hunter's Jeep and their SUV, but they wouldn't all fit in the jeep, and the keys to the SUV were upstairs, in a backpack or on top of a dresser. Unreachable, at least for now.

His brothers and Hunter said nothing when he showed up at the ambulance again, the fire marshal at his side. They silently piled into the truck while Michael turned on the heat. His brothers climbed into the back, while Hunter sat up front, Casper curled up between him and Michael.

He wondered how long he could sit here with the car in park before they'd realize he had no idea where to go.

He wondered how long this shocked silence would last.

Did they blame him? Not like it mattered. Michael blamed himself. His fingers felt like icicles, and he flexed them in front of the vent, willing the car to warm up more quickly.

They were waiting for him to say something. To *do* something. Their expectations sat like a weight against his skin.

He shifted into gear and glanced at the clock on the dash. Four o'clock in the morning. He could check into a hotel at 4 AM, right?

Nick cleared his throat from the back seat. "I texted Adam. He says we can go to his place."

Adam was Nick's boyfriend. He was nineteen and he had his own place—but that didn't mean they'd all fit. Michael glanced at Nick in the rearview mirror and tried to ignore how driving over the fractured driveway pavement felt like driving over downed trees. "You have your phone? Who else has one?"

They all did.

Michael had no idea why it was important, but his worries eased just a notch knowing he could reach them if he had to.

And where would they be going?

He wove between the remaining fire trucks sitting in the cul-de-sac. He hadn't seen Hannah since she'd walked out of his house, and he hadn't been able to look for her. Her father had actually walked him and his brothers to the door of the truck.

"Tell Adam thanks, but we'll go to a hotel."

"And then what?" said Nick. "Sleep in these clothes? Live on fast food?"

"You think the five of us are going to fit in a one-bedroom apartment for long?"

"You think the Holiday Inn is going to let us check in looking like this? With a *dog*? At least at Adam's we can wash our clothes and get something to eat."

"Nick—" Michael sighed. Those were all good points, and he was too tired to argue. "Fine. Whatever." He reached out and spun the dial to turn the heat higher. He couldn't stop shivering.

The roads were deserted at this hour. Rain speckled the windshield, and he clicked on the wipers as he turned onto Ritchie Highway. Beside him, Hunter had his fingers buried in Casper's fur. His forehead was against the window.

At the first stoplight, Michael glanced in the rearview mirror and took stock of his brothers again. Nick looked weary, his eyes half open. Gabriel looked pissed, his jaw set, his eyes glaring straight ahead. Chris was looking out at the darkness, the streetlights reflecting off the bare spots on his cheeks where the rain had washed the soot away.

"Thanks for stopping the fires," Michael said. "The rainstorm was smart thinking."

Chris didn't look away from the window. "It wasn't just me."

"I know. I'm thanking you all."

Gabriel's eyes locked on his. "Maybe you could thank us by telling us what the fuck is going on."

Michael kept his foot on the brake. "What?"

"What do you mean, *what*? We looked for you, asshole. You weren't in that house when the fire started. You weren't in the woods. You weren't *anywhere*." His voice gained volume. "We found Hunter and Chris, but you weren't—we couldn't—"

"Easy," said Nick. "Take it easy."

"*Fuck easy*, Nick! Until that earthquake started, we didn't even know if he was—"

"Wait." Michael slammed the gearshift back into park and turned in his seat. Gabriel looked primed for a fight, like he was ready for his oldest brother to take a swing at him. He looked like he'd welcome the opportunity.

But Michael looked at Chris. "You didn't tell them?"

"Tell us what?" said Nick.

"We couldn't tell them," said Hunter. His voice was tired. "By the time they found *us*, we were surrounded by paramedics, and then the earthquakes started—it was all too fast."

"Tell us *what*?" Gabriel demanded.

"I thought someone was in the woods," said Michael. "It woke me up."

"Me too," said Hunter.

"What did you guys think?" said Michael. "That I snuck out?"

"We didn't know what to think," said Nick. "The fire started fast."

"I almost couldn't stop it," said Gabriel. "I had to keep it to the front of the house. I was worried about it getting into the garage."

So Gabriel *had* stopped it. "You probably saved the business."

"I was more worried about all that shit blowing up. Whoever did this had a plan." Another pause. "And power. A lot of power."

"Do you think it was Calla?" said Michael. "I haven't heard from her in a week. She's been pissed that I won't help her start a war."

"This would be a good way to start one with us," said Gabriel, his tone dark. "But I have no idea. I didn't see anyone."

"Who was in the woods?" said Nick.

No one said anything for a long moment, but the confusion and fury in the car redirected toward Chris.

He didn't look away from the window. "Sometimes I go for a walk, okay?" he snapped. "It's not like anyone is sleeping lately."

"But you *ran*," said Hunter.

Now Chris whipped his head around. "I didn't know it was you! You would have run, too!" Then his gaze darkened. "Or maybe you would have shot someone. Who knows?"

"You're lucky I'm not shooting you right now."

"You're lucky I didn't *drown* you—"

"Hey!" said Michael. He knew most of this was misdirected fear and uncertainty. That didn't mean he wanted to listen to it. "Knock it—"

A horn blared from behind them, and they all jumped. Another car had stopped behind them, and Michael realized they'd been sitting here for a while, just blocking the intersection.

He turned around in his seat and put the car back into gear. He ran a hand through his short hair, feeling dirt and burned particles dislodge. Once they made the turn onto Ritchie Highway, he glanced in the rearview mirror again. Aggression hung so thick in the air that he wanted to open the windows to clear the cab.

"Have you been sneaking out every night?" he said.

Chris didn't say anything.

"Chris!"

"He's scared," said Hunter.

"Fuck you," said Chris. "If you want to sit around waiting for an attack, fine. I can't do it anymore."

They came to a traffic light, and Michael rotated in his seat to face his youngest brother. "Are you out of your mind? What the hell were you thinking, Chris? We could have—those fires—"

Chris wouldn't look at him. "You think I don't know?"

Gabriel hit him on the back of the head. "And you thought that was a good idea?"

"I stayed near the water. And who the hell are you to talk about *good ideas*?"

"You know what, Chris? You can—"

"All right, stop!" The light changed and Michael turned back to face the road. He knew better than to let them ramp Chris up. Nick was always reasonable. Gabriel would fight, but he was direct about it—and once he was done, he was done.

Chris would stew in his own thoughts for hours. In retrospect, Michael wondered if he should have been watching for this, for Chris to isolate himself.

He was too tired for all this analysis. And his brothers were too keyed up. He needed a distraction.

He looked at the brightly lit storefronts along the highway. McDonald's had a huge OPEN 24 HOURS sign out front.

"Text Adam," he said. "Tell him we're bringing breakfast. What do you guys want?"

Hannah stood under the stream of hot water in the firehouse locker room and put her forehead against the shower wall.

Even odds said she could fall asleep right here. Or put her fist through the wall.

Or cry.

She saw a lot of terrible things in her line of work. Last night had been among the worst—and she hadn't even been part of the recovery crew, pulling dead bodies out of collapsed homes. She hadn't heard a total body count yet, and she wasn't going out of her way to look for one.

She'd seen a half-melted Elmo car on one of the driveways of a collapsed home—the same toy James had at home—and she'd almost lost it.

Sometimes her brain would form a story around something

like that. She'd imagine the little boy who played with that toy, and then imagine his home engulfed in flames. She'd imagine him inhaling the smoke, choking, maybe trying to scream for his mother—

Stop. She *would* be crying against the wall of this shower if she didn't knock it off. It wouldn't do for the fire marshal's daughter to be a blubbering mess, even in the privacy of the shower. If she started letting herself get worked up here, she'd never keep the few shreds of respect she'd managed to earn.

Think of something else.

So she thought of Michael. She thought of him in the back of the ambulance, the way he'd clutched at her.

She'd never seen him like that.

He hadn't come to find her after her father was done with him, though. She'd finished dragging the fire hoses back onto the trucks with Irish, and then Chief had ordered them to pack up and head home. She'd sent Michael a text to tell him she was leaving, but then she'd noticed that his truck was gone.

And then he didn't respond to her text.

Before tonight, she hadn't been sure where things stood between them. Dragging him out of a fire and watching him in the midst of a tragedy hadn't changed that. He'd grown distant enough that she'd started to think his feelings toward her had cooled—but tonight he'd gripped her hand while they were walking through his ruined home, showing no indication of letting go.

Maybe he would have been like that with anyone who offered him a shoulder to cry on, but she didn't think so.

She remembered a few weeks ago, when Michael had been concerned that Nick, one of the twins, was hiding something. He was failing tests at school and getting in fights with his brothers. Michael had confided in Hannah, and they'd tried to figure it out. Based on her own experience, she'd been certain that Nick had gotten his girlfriend knocked up.

She couldn't have been more wrong: Nick wasn't interested in girls at *all*. His girlfriend had just been a cover.

The night Michael found out the truth, he'd sat on the back porch with Hannah and told her what happened.

"Are you okay with it?" she'd asked.

"Of course," he'd said, not even needing to think about it. "If I'm not okay with it, he's never going to be."

And he was like that with everything. Strong. Stoic. A rock for anyone who needed one.

If she examined their relationship too closely, it looked a little strange. She'd given up hope that she'd ever be able to date someone, what with her pseudo-cop father and her five-year-old son. Guys her age—twenty-two—never wanted a ready-made family, and they didn't understand why she couldn't go clubbing 'til two in the morning or spend the night at their place. They didn't understand that work and school and motherhood barely left her with five spare minutes in a row.

But then she'd run into Michael Merrick. Only a year older than she was, with his own ready-made family. He worked as many hours as she did, and he hardly had time to scrape together for a girlfriend either. In a way, their relationship felt very high school. The closest they'd come to "spending the night together" was one morning when she'd gotten off work at 3 AM, and "early cup of coffee at his place" had turned into making out. She'd showered in his bathroom and borrowed one of his T-shirts—leading his brothers to get the wrong idea—but they'd never gone farther than that.

Back in high school, they'd never run in the same circles. He'd played baseball and worked for his parents, while she'd rebelled against her father's strict parenting. Michael had been a year older, too, and she'd dropped out halfway through her junior year. It wasn't like they would have bumped into each other at the prom. Still, she remembered eighteen-year-old Michael so clearly. He'd walked through the hallways like he owned the place, every pore on his body radiating *don't mess with me*.

He carried himself like that now. When they'd first gone out—for a cup of coffee, nothing more—she'd been a bit wary, worried that when he learned about her profession, he'd act like he needed to "out-man" her. But there really wasn't anything *macho* about him. No bravado, no chest-puffing, no sign of a domineering asshole.

He'd been a gentleman. He'd bought her coffee and pulled out her chair—little niceties she wasn't used to, because she sure didn't expect that around the firehouse. But every time he talked to her, his voice had been rough and quiet, as if every word were a secret just for her. It had made her shiver in a good way.

Tonight, he'd looked broken. She'd been afraid to touch him, as if one brush of skin would send him shattering into a million pieces. But then she *had*, and he'd clung to her as if he'd been afraid to let go. Some people might see it as weakness, but she didn't. She knew how it felt to have life yank the rug out from under you. She knew what it meant to need someone to hold you, to share the weight of the world for a minute. For a *second*. She would have held him all night.

And then her father had shown up to act like Detective Dickhead.

As usual.

A locker door slammed over on the guys' side of the dorm. Hannah ignored it, insulated on the women's side. She wasn't the only woman in the department, but there were few enough that sometimes it felt like it.

She should probably get going. She pushed the damp hair back from her face and slapped the faucet to kill the water.

She could hear male voices more clearly now, but with the dorm area door closed, she couldn't make out more than muffled tones, then laughter with an edge. Giving someone shit, from the sound of it.

Men. She sighed and reached for her towel.

Her phone was on the counter, and the screen lit with a message. Hannah pushed the button, hoping for a return text from Michael.

Her mother.

I have lunch packed for James. Need me to take him to school?

Hannah smiled. While her father treated her as if she'd never live up to his expectations, her mother made up for that lack of warmth tenfold. Hannah looked at the time and texted back.

I should be home in time.

A new message almost immediately.

I don't want you to have to rush. You work so hard.

Maybe it was the timing of the message, or the emotion of the preceding twelve hours, but Hannah could swear she felt tears rushing to her eyes again.

Maybe her mom could sense it, because another message appeared almost immediately.

Don't worry about rushing. If I don't see you in the next 20, I'll take him. I'll put a note in his lunchbox from mommy.

Hannah smiled. Her mom always thought of details like that. She'd probably draw a picture and sign it from "mommy," full of Xs and Os.

Hannah made a mental note to empty the dishwasher or vacuum the living room or something, just to let the woman know her efforts weren't ignored. She put the phone on the counter and used the towel to scrub vigorously at her body. If she rushed, she could make it home in time to see James.

The phone lit again, and Hannah grabbed it from the counter. It wasn't like her mother to keep a text conversation going. The woman needed emoticons explained, for god's sake.

But it wasn't her mother. It was Michael Merrick.

Sorry I couldn't look for you. Are you OK?

Hannah stared at the message for a while. Too long—she realized she was still standing here naked and freezing.

Yeah. You?

He didn't respond for the longest time, and finally she had to get dressed or deal with hypothermia. She put the phone back on the counter and reached for her clothes.

Another locker slammed from the other side of the wall, then more male laughter. Hannah pulled on a long-sleeved tee and wished her hair were long enough for a ponytail. She didn't have time to dry it—not if she wanted to get home in time to be a responsible mommy.

She slung her bag over her shoulder and flung the door open.

It left her staring straight into the men's locker room. The door was propped open, steam in the air.

Irish was standing at a sink, wearing jeans and nothing else, shaving his face with slow, even strokes.

Hannah was standing there with her mouth hanging open. She quickly shut it and looked away before he could notice.

They'd been next to each other all night—at one point performing joint CPR on a woman they'd found in the basement of the fourth house—so it shouldn't have felt so intimate.

But it did.

A faucet turned on, and she heard something tap against the sink. "You crashing here, Blondie?"

"Going home." She had to clear her throat. Were her cheeks on fire? It felt like her cheeks were on fire. Had that been a tattoo on his shoulder?

Don't look. *Do not look.*

God, she'd just been thinking of Michael falling apart in the ambulance, and now she was gawking at another firefighter. Someone she had to *work* with.

"You need something?"

Now she was standing here like a stalker. She forced herself to look at him. He was just *shaving,* for goodness sake. It wasn't like she was watching him in the shower.

If her brain would stop supplying images, it would totally be okay.

"Aren't you going home?" she said.

"A bed's a bed," he said. "I'm back on at noon." He looked over. "How's your boyfriend?"

Her boyfriend. Michael Merrick. Right.

"I don't know. I texted him, but he hasn't responded yet."

"I didn't know he had a history with arson in this town."

"He doesn't. Not really."

"I walked through that house, Blondie. That fire wouldn't have stopped unless someone put it out."

A low whistle sounded from behind him. "Look at Blondie getting an eyeful. Your daddy know you're into the dark boys?"

Hannah jerked back, sure her cheeks were flaming—though now she couldn't decide if she was more furious or embarrassed.

Irish didn't stop shaving. "Jealous, Stockton?"

Joe Stockton, one of the older guys who'd sit in the kitchen and shoot the bull all night, snorted from behind her. "Yeah, that'll be the day. Me, jealous of a n—"

"Hey!" She whirled, ready to get in his face. Furious—definitely furious.

He just laughed and moved away into the men's dorm area.

"Ignore them," said Irish, his voice low and close.

She turned and he was right there, close enough to touch. She could smell the menthol of his shaving cream, and for an instant it reminded her of her father, from when she was a little girl.

She swallowed some of her fury. "He was about to call you—" She faltered. "He was about to say—"

"You think I don't know?"

"You don't care?"

"Of course I care. But they're just looking to start trouble. I care about my job more."

They. She thought of the slamming lockers and male laughter she'd heard earlier. "Who else? You should report them."

He snorted and turned away, returning to the sink to let the water out. "You're funny. You going to report Stockton for what he just said to you?"

She thought about that for a second and wasn't sure what to say. Of course she wasn't going to report him. The best she could hope for was an eye roll and a promise from the chief that he'd talk to the guys.

And then the next time would be worse.

"It's not the first time, Blondie. Won't be the last."

All of a sudden, her firehouse nickname sounded belittling.

"Hannah," she said.

Irish smiled. "Hannah." Then he shook his head. "We can do better than that."

"What do you have in mind?"

Crap. It sounded like she was flirting.

Was she flirting?

She had no idea. Her brain was too tired, and the conversation had gone in too many directions in the last three minutes.

"I'll work on it," he said.

She turned away. "Close the door next time, okay? I don't need to see what else you guys have to offer."

Then she was through the door and into the parking lot before anyone could mistake the blush on her cheeks for anything more than a reaction to the early-morning chill.

CHAPTER 7

Michael sat on the edge of the concrete patio and put his bare feet in the grass. Sunlight beat along his neck and shoulders, fighting a losing battle against the lingering chill in the air. His breath made quick clouds that drifted away. He didn't have a sweatshirt, but Marshal Faulkner had allowed him to check his laundry room to see if any clothes had survived the smoke damage. Luckily, there'd been three pairs of jeans and a ton of T-shirts in the dryer.

Unluckily, those were all the spare clothes he had for five people.

Adam had some old sweatpants that made up the difference for now. Michael added clothes to the mental list in his head. He'd drive to Target right now if he weren't deathly afraid to separate from his brothers.

Every time he blinked, he saw the destruction of his neighborhood. Adam didn't have a television, but he did have a laptop. He'd pulled up the local news coverage of the damage, but Michael had walked out here to get away from the conversation. He didn't want to hear names and details. He didn't want to know who was battling for life—or who hadn't even gotten a chance to fight.

Now he'd been out here for an hour, and he could barely feel his fingers. At least his brothers had taken the opportunity to find a space to sleep for a while.

Michael unlocked his phone, tapped his text message icon, and then sat there, his thumb hovering over the keys.

He'd done this four times now. He had no idea what to say to Hannah. *Was* he okay?

No. He wasn't. She'd seen him near breaking, and if he let go, just a little, he'd completely fall apart with no hope of gathering up the pieces.

She'd known, though. She'd grabbed his hand at the right moment. *You're shaking.* She'd whispered it, leaving him a shred of dignity in front of her father.

He thought of those bookcases, charred almost beyond recognition. His whole house was unstable, but those damned bookcases were what his brain wanted to latch on to. His mother was long dead. Bookcases didn't matter. Nothing in that house mattered.

He locked the phone and set it on the concrete.

Dirt shifted under his heels, feeding him strength, but not much else. His element wasn't one for lightening a mood. He hunched over and rubbed his arms. *Damn*, it was cold.

He couldn't stop fidgeting.

He picked his phone back up. Put it down, then picked it up again and woke the screen to check the time. He couldn't call his insurance agent for another fifteen minutes. He could hold it together that long.

You can do anything for fifteen minutes.

His father's words, often repeated. Michael first remembered hearing them when he was nine and didn't want to do assigned reading for school. His father had set a timer on the stove and shoved the book in his hands.

His father had been right. He could read for fifteen minutes. He could do a lot of things for fifteen minutes.

Those words had haunted him after his parents' deaths. He'd broken time into chunks to get through every day. Fifteen minutes for breakfast. Fifteen minutes to get his brothers to school.

Fifteen minutes to travel between landscaping jobs. He could cook a frozen dinner in fifteen minutes.

Lights out in fifteen minutes.

His own words, when his brothers were younger, when he'd had no idea how to be a parent because he wasn't done being a kid. The minutes after they were asleep were both the best and the worst. The best because the house was finally quiet, and he was alone with his thoughts.

The worst for the exact same reason.

You can do anything for fifteen minutes.

He hadn't been able to save his parents. And the fire had killed them a lot quicker than that.

The door behind him slid open, and he inwardly sighed, wondering who else couldn't sleep, and how quickly their stress would double the weight of his own.

His money was on Chris, but the footsteps on the concrete were light and unfamiliar. Michael turned his head to find himself face-to-face with a travel mug, steam escaping through the hole in the lid.

"Hot drink?" said Adam, his voice quiet.

"Sure." Michael cleared his throat and forced his frozen fingers to wrap around the mug. He barely knew Adam, and he wasn't sure if he wanted this distraction. He turned his gaze back to the horizon. "Thanks."

"You're welcome."

He expected Adam to retreat into his apartment, but a blanket dropped over his shoulders, a weight of rich brown fabric that felt velvet soft to the touch.

Michael froze, unsure how to react.

Adam gave his shoulder a quick squeeze before moving away. "You were making me cold just looking at you." He sat cross-legged against the beam at the corner of the patio. His movements were unhurried and graceful, so different from Michael's brothers. He offered half a smile. "Nick ignores my chairs, too."

Michael glanced over his shoulder at the patio chairs. Saying he felt better with his feet in the grass felt like admitting vulnerability, so he kept his mouth shut.

Silence swirled between them, and though it wasn't strained, Michael wondered if he was being rude. "Thanks for letting us crash here for a little while."

"Stay as long as you need to."

Michael snorted. "You say that now."

"A houseful of Merricks isn't exactly a problem."

Michael studied him, trying to determine whether he was teasing, and what the right reaction should be.

Adam's expression went serious. "You'd do the same for me."

Michael looked back at the drainage pond. "You don't know that."

"I know Nick. So yes, I do know that."

Michael wasn't sure what to say to that, so he fidgeted with the lid of the mug.

After a long stretch of silence, Adam said, "Your brothers are asleep. You should get some rest, too."

"Yeah, right." Like he could sleep *now*, when he didn't know if they had a chance of surviving the next twelve hours. He took a sip from the mug, just to spare himself the need to say anything else.

To his surprise, warm chocolate and cinnamon swirled across his tongue, instead of the coffee he'd been expecting. It was good, and helped warm him from the inside. He took another sip.

Adam pulled his hands into the sleeves of his pullover and blew on his exposed fingertips. "Do you want another blanket?"

"No." Michael didn't mean to sound short, but the word ended with an edge. He added, "You don't have to sit out here. Go back inside if you're cold."

Adam didn't move. "I'm all right." He paused. "Do you want me to leave you alone?"

"Yes."

Again, the word was too short, too harsh. But Michael couldn't wrap his brain around social niceties, and he sure as hell couldn't face the stress of a conversation. Not because Adam's presence bothered him. Because Adam was a reminder that others could be caught in the crossfire if he made the wrong decisions. A reminder that Michael *couldn't* handle everything on his own, that once again they were dependent on the charity of others.

Tension crawled across his shoulders, digging in for a nice long ride. He wished they could run. He wanted to wake his brothers and pack them into the truck, then drive somewhere he wouldn't have to worry about anyone else.

He checked the time. Seven more minutes until he could call. He slammed the phone onto the concrete beside him.

Running would lead to problems with the authorities. It would paint him as guilty almost immediately. He and his brothers might be safe from the Guides—at least for a little while—but it would be hard to hide from the cops. He didn't have much cash on hand, and using credit cards would leave an indelible trail.

But staying made them a target.

Along with everyone around them.

Adam uncurled from where he was sitting. Michael hoped he was going into the apartment. But no, he edged over to sit next to Michael. Then he held out his hand.

"Here."

Michael looked down. A key chain sat on Adam's palm.

"Keys to the apartment," Adam said. "My mom's been whining that I'm never around much anymore, so I'm going to visit for a while. Maybe even spend the night."

Michael didn't touch the keys. Suddenly ashamed, he stared at his travel mug. "You don't have to *leave* leave. That's not what I meant."

"I know what you meant." Adam paused. "And I know what it's like to need time to regroup."

"I don't want to chase you out of your home. *We* can leave—"

"Sure, you can. Whenever you're ready. Or you can stay. But I have somewhere else to go—somewhere *free*—and it's not a hardship." He rolled his eyes. "Or it won't be for a while. You know how mothers are."

The words hung in the air for a moment. Adam seemed to realize what he'd said, because there was a little flinching around his eyes—but he couldn't unsay the words, and Michael appreciated that he didn't try.

Michael reached out and took the keys. He had to clear his throat. "I'll work on finding us somewhere else to stay once I talk to the insurance company."

"You should try to get some sleep."

"Yeah, yeah. You've said."

"Keep the keys with you if you leave. I'll get the spare from my mom."

Michael nodded. He knew he should say thank you, but emotion was clawing its way up his throat, and he was worried his voice would crack—or he'd say something angry, just to cover it up.

Keep it together. Your fifteen minutes is almost up.

It was enough to steady his breathing. "We'll be gone by tomorrow morning."

Adam didn't look away. "It's okay to let other people take care of you, you know."

Michael laughed without any real humor to it. "Yeah. Sure."

"Hmm. Well, at least now I know where Nick gets it."

That pissed Michael off. "You think I should let other people 'take care of us'? You think that would help? Let me tell you what happens when I try. When my parents died, they had people working for them. Good guys, I thought, who offered to help me figure out the business. *Good guys* who stole almost ten thousand dollars before I realized what was going on. Or how about when Nick and Gabriel were twelve and they snuck out of the house to be *stupid*, and they got caught. I asked a neighbor to come sit with Chris since it was the middle of the night. She was real helpful. She reported it to DFS. Told them my brothers were *running wild*. There are all kinds of people trying to help, but it always seems like they're really just waiting around for me to fuck up."

"I'm not waiting for you to fuck up." Adam paused. "Just because you can't trust everyone doesn't mean you can't trust *anyone*."

"I can take care of myself."

"I know." Adam stood and moved toward the door. "Those two things aren't mutually exclusive."

Michael turned to snap at him, because he couldn't take any more emotion or uncertainty, and "helpful" commentary from a veritable stranger wasn't all that welcome.

But Adam was already through the door, softly latching it behind him, leaving Michael sitting on the concrete, alone with his worries.

Hannah lay in bed, staring at the ceiling, willing sleep to slow her thoughts. She'd choked down a cup of coffee on the way home from the firehouse, knowing she'd have to be alert enough to get James to school, but now she was paying the price.

Some days her life was almost too surreal for examination. Six hours ago, she'd been performing CPR between burning houses during an earthquake. One hour ago, she'd been holding James close, inhaling his ever-present scent of sugar cookies and boy sweat, tickling him until he cried, "Mommy!" and collapsed in giggles on the front steps of his elementary school.

Then he'd gone through the double doors, and she'd walked back to her car, enduring the judgmental stares from the other mothers, most of whom were ten years older than she was.

When she'd been seventeen with an infant, she'd expected the stares. They validated a feeling she'd walked around with every day: shame.

Now, she wanted to scream at them all. *I'm a good mother, too.*

Some days she felt interminably lonely. Any friends she'd had in high school were finishing college now, looking at internships and getting ready to start their adult lives. Hannah had started her adult life five years ago, and she couldn't relate to young women whose biggest dilemmas were how to get their first credit card or how to deal with a roommate who had loud sex at all hours of the night. But she also didn't fit in with women whose days revolved around yoga class or desk jobs or picking up their husband's dry-cleaning. She felt squarely smashed in between life cycles, trapped by a mistake of her own making.

A mistake she wouldn't change for anything in the world.

She loved her son.

He just didn't cure the loneliness.

Hannah picked up her phone and checked for a text from Michael. Nothing. He still hadn't responded. Should she call? He was probably asleep by now.

She sent another text.

When you have a moment, please let me know you're okay.

She clicked off the screen and set the phone on her night-stand, not expecting a response.

The phone rang almost immediately, and she snatched it up. "Hello?"

"Hey." Michael. He sounded exhausted. His voice hadn't lost the roughness.

"Hey. Did I wake you?"

A low sound, almost a laugh. "No."

"Are you staying in a hotel?"

"No. Adam's place. At least for the day. The guys needed to sleep."

"Nick's boyfriend? Are they all crashed on the floor?"

"Nah, he left. They've taken over all the furniture."

"Where are you going to sleep?"

"You're funny."

Silence filled the line for a minute, as she tried to figure out how to respond to that. "I've been worried about you."

He didn't say anything for so long that she had to make sure the call hadn't dropped. He finally sighed. "We're fine." He paused. "Your dad let me get some clothes out of the house. The truck survived."

His voice sounded so *bleak*. She didn't have much experience with this side of firefighting, and all the intimacy of sitting in the back of the ambulance was gone now that their only connection was based on a cell signal. She wished she knew what to say. "Have you talked to the insurance company yet?"

"I just hung up. They're having a case manager call me back later."

She sat up in bed. "You sound . . . you don't sound good. Do you want me to come over?"

"No. No, Hannah. I want—look, forget it. I felt bad for not texting back." A long sigh, full of pain and so much emotion that she wanted to drive over there right now and wrap him up in her arms. Then his voice steadied. "We're okay. We'll be okay. You don't need to worry about me."

"Michael, I just watched your neighborhood burn down. I am worried about you."

That low not-quite laugh. "Don't remind me." A pause. An almost-shaky breath. "Please."

"Why don't I come over? I can bring coffee—"

"I said *no*, okay?"

His tone shut her up quick. Hannah blinked.

He made a shuffling sound with the phone, and his voice sounded distant for a moment. "I'm sorry. I'm—it's been a bad night. I don't even know what I'm saying."

"Did my dad give you a hard time? Are you in trouble—?"

"I need to go."

"Please don't go," she said. "Please don't hang up. Talk to me."

"God, Hannah. I wish I could. You have no idea how much I wish I could."

And then, before she could say a word, he ended the call.

CHAPTER 8

It had been a bad idea to call her. He'd almost lost it again.
The wind was picking up, stinging Michael's cheeks and eyes.
He welcomed the pain. It fed him irritation, which worked
pretty well to tamp down the anxiety.

His brothers and Hunter were sleeping soundly. He'd checked
a minute ago. Common sense dictated that he should be sleeping, too, but sitting inside the apartment left him feeling panicked and claustrophobic. He'd started to walk, hoping motion
would help tame his wild thoughts, but twenty feet from the
back door, he worried that he was leaving his brothers vulnerable again.

So now he was back on the porch, the blanket wrapped
around his shoulders.

Had Calla started those fires? They had a history, Calla and
his family. She wasn't the type to strike hard and not brag, but
anything was possible.

Michael had her cell number programmed into his phone,
and after gritting his teeth for a full thirty seconds, ready for her
taunting voice to mock him for not starting a war quickly enough,
he dialed. The line rang and rang and eventually ended on a me-
chanical tone telling him the number had been disconnected.

Michael stared at his phone, studying the digits as if he'd
somehow misdialed a programmed number.

He stupidly called again, sure there'd been some mistake. Same electronic message.

He sent her a text. Almost immediately, a return message appeared in his inbox.

The number you are attempting to contact has been deactivated. Please dial 411 for directory assistance. Standard voice and messaging rates may apply.

Nothing about this was reassuring. Did this mean Calla had done it, and she didn't want him to know?

Or did this mean Calla had disappeared again?

Or was she working with someone new?

Could one person have started five fires at once? Had they started simultaneously? The houses on his cul-de-sac weren't far apart, but it still would have taken time to set a fire in each one. He couldn't see how one person could have caused that kind of damage—but maybe a powerful Fire Elemental could. He and Hunter and Chris had been in the woods for maybe fifteen minutes, if that. Then he thought of the markings Hannah's father had pointed out. Elemental or not, laying out a pattern in accelerant would have taken time. Could someone have broken into five houses without detection, poured some kerosene or whatever, then lit five fires, all within in fifteen minutes?

He broke it down. Three minutes per house. That seemed *really* unlikely, even if each house didn't have an alarm system. He tried to remember which houses had the little stickers in their windows, but he was coming up with nothing. Alarm systems or not, two houses on the court had dogs. Dogs would have sounded their own type of alarm.

Unless the dogs had been taken care of ahead of time? He remembered his neighbors standing outside, screaming for their dog. Had the animal succumbed to the fire—or had someone else gotten to him first?

Ignoring alarm systems and dogs, this still seemed like a big job. This would have taken planning.

Maybe that's what you sensed in the woods every night.

It hadn't just been Chris. It couldn't have been—last night

had proven that. Michael had been ready for an attack on his family. He'd sat outside, ready to wake them if he sensed true danger, so they could fight or run.

He hadn't been ready for an attack on the whole neighborhood.

Guilt, quick and sudden, slammed into Michael. Maybe he should have been ready. Calla had set fires at a school carnival last month, just to get the attention of the Guides. She wanted a war. Her carnival fire hadn't started one, and Michael wasn't willing to do anything to draw more attention to his family. Had she given up on patience and turned to killing more people?

He needed more information. He wondered if the fire marshal would give him any. He fished the card out of his pocket and started to dial.

No. That was stupid. The fire marshal thought *he* was a suspect. He wasn't going to say, "Hey, sure, Mike, take a look at my files while you're at it. Want to walk through the crime scene?"

Michael ran a hand down his face. God, he needed some sleep.

His cell phone chimed.

Is this Michael Merrick?

He stared at it for a long moment. He didn't recognize the number, but the area code wasn't from Maryland or D.C. Sometimes landscaping customers would send him a text, but those had never been from an out-of-state cell.

Another bubble of text appeared.

We should meet to talk about last night. Free for dinner?

Wait. Was this the fire marshal? Was this Calla? Michael didn't move.

Another bubble.

It's in your best interest. I'm not sure I could limit a fire to five apartments.

Michael was on his feet in a heartbeat, letting the blanket fall.

He sent power into the ground, seeking information. He needed to wake his brothers. They needed to move. They needed to move *now*.

The phone vibrated again.

Good idea. Run. One truck is definitely a more convenient target.

Michael couldn't catch his breath. He searched the trees for movement, for anything out of the ordinary.

Nothing. The air was still and cold. The earth warned him of nothing.

Another message.

Relax. I'm not your enemy. But I could be.

Michael slid his fingers across the phone.

Who is this?

No message appeared, but instead, a photo.

Michael, sitting on the back porch of the Merrick house. Last night, before the fire.

Then another photo, taken from a distance.

Of him standing *right here*, looking at his phone.

Michael looked up, searching the trees on the other side of the pond. He begged the ground for information, but the earth returned nothing but contented vibes.

His phone vibrated with another message.

Dinner. Yes or no?

Michael wanted to punch his phone into the side of the building. He started forward, ready to search the woods himself. A new message appeared.

Don't go too far, Michael Merrick. Wouldn't want to leave your brothers alone, would you?

He froze. He had no idea if this was one person or several. If he walked away from this apartment building, would it go up in smoke like the house had last night?

New awareness shot off a flare in his head. Wasn't that exactly what had happened? He'd walked away, leaving them vulnerable?

He typed back with shaking fingers.

This isn't a game. What do you want?

I just told you what I want. Let's say 7 p.m.?

Who are you? Is this Calla?

No. Bring her if you like. I think she'll appreciate what I have to say.

Michael couldn't think. Lack of sleep and an abundance of adrenaline didn't help.

He looked out at the trees, then slowly slid his fingers across the face of his phone again.

You're obviously here. Why don't you come talk to me right now?

I think a crowded environment would be better for this meeting.

Interesting. Something about that statement dialed Michael's anxiety back a notch and fed him confidence. Photos taken from a distance weren't half as intimidating when you considered that it meant someone wasn't drawing close.

Was this mystery texter *afraid* of him?

Should I come alone?

Your choice.

What if I choose to bring the cops?

Go ahead.

Michael frowned.

Another message appeared.

As I said, I am not your enemy. Bring anyone who makes you feel comfortable.

And what if I don't come?

I'll be forced to make my point another way.

More pictures appeared, in frighteningly rapid succession. Homes on fire. Car crashes. Tornado damage. A bloated body, floating in murky water. Terrible images, but nothing personally terrifying.

Then more photos: Hannah in her fire gear, kneeling over him last night, her face exhausted but focused. Another of Nick, stopping the CPR efforts. Another photo of an ambulance in the cul-de-sac, Chris sitting on the bumper.

Michael clenched his jaw. His hands gripped the phone so tightly that he worried the case would snap.

Then another photo appeared. Hannah on the front steps of Southgate Elementary, James bouncing along beside her, his backpack hanging askew.

Michael felt his heart give a jerk. He made a sound before he could stop himself. His fingers wouldn't type, but his voice wasn't broken.

"You leave them alone!" he yelled, shouting at the trees, at the distance, at the very air. The earth rumbled and split, forming a crack that led from his feet to the fence around the drainage pond. "You hear me? You *leave them alone!*"

The phone vibrated.

You meet me, and I'll leave them alone.

Michael couldn't catch his breath. He stared out at the trees, then back at the series of photos.

Then back at the trees.

Nothing.

Sweat had collected on his neck. His heartbeat thundered in his ears. He wasn't cold now.

He forced his fingers to work.

Fine. Where?

Another text, this time a link to the web page of a little bar and grill on the outskirts of town.

7 p.m. I'll be in the bar.

Eventually, Michael couldn't take the quiet stillness. Seven o'clock was almost half a day away, and he had to *do* something.

So he walked. Not far, just a short walk along the fence blocking the drainage ditch. At first, he'd been ready for a chastising text. A warning, a threat, *something*.

Nothing.

As his brothers slept and no danger presented itself, Michael gained confidence. That picture of him on the patio had to have been taken from the woods, and even if no one remained, he should at least be able to seek information from the ground.

If nothing else, the movement would do him good.

But the woods didn't offer any answers, and they didn't offer enough space to walk and think, either. The dense trees barely covered half an acre before giving way to Ritchie Highway; they were more to give the illusion of nature than any real attempt to preserve the land. The air was still brisk, reminding him that he didn't have a sweatshirt, keeping his steps quick.

Every time his bare feet touched the earth, he asked for information.

Was someone here? Did someone cross this path?

Is someone here now?

Nothing.

Nothing.

Nothing.

He checked his phone a few times, examining the picture of himself, aiming his own phone at the now-empty patio. The photo was grainy—no surprise since it had been taken from a pretty good distance. He could estimate the angle, but now that he was out here using his own phone to try to recreate it, he realized that the picture hadn't been taken from the ground.

It had to have been taken from high up in a tree.

All of a sudden, Michael felt too exposed.

He cast his gaze up, searching the branches overhead. He put his hand against the trunk of the nearest tree, and as always, he could almost feel the tree leaning back into him.

Much like the earth, trees and plants didn't speak to him in words, but in general impressions. He sensed nothing malicious, nothing insidious. The tree liked him here.

Another tree. This one was younger, and a few autumn leaves eagerly fell around Michael when he touched the trunk. Again, nothing negative.

Another tree. This one didn't lean into him. The bark almost crumbled under his fingers when he touched it. Dead. No information to be found. He moved on to the next ones.

Nothing.

The young tree shed a few more leaves. One caught the wind and twirled to Michael. He caught it and spun it by the stem.

No one was out here. What had he expected to find? A journal detailing plans to destroy the Merrick neighborhood? He didn't even know what *he* was doing out here.

Yes, he did.

He remembered being young, being terrified of the strength of his affinity to the earth—but finding relief in it too. When he'd been fourteen, he'd snuck out of the house to sleep in the woods almost every night.

His father had found him, every time.

He'd been an Earth Elemental, too.

With a jolt, Michael realized that's what Chris had been doing: finding solace by the water. How had he missed that?

Being here, his feet in the dirt, his hand against a tree, brought Michael comfort. Some of the weight stacked on his heart eased, just a little.

Sorrow slid in to replace it. Sometimes he missed his father so much he almost couldn't stand it.

Like now. *Help me, Dad. What would you do?*

Another leaf, vibrant red, fell from the young tree and floated in his direction. Michael smiled and caught this one too. He stepped back to the tree and leaned against it, letting it lean back against him. He slid the two fallen leaves between his fingers and scanned his surroundings for the hundredth time. Whoever had been texting him knew how to move through the woods without leaving a mark. No broken branches or twigs. Nothing disturbed. No malice, no ill intent.

This didn't feel like Calla. Last night had, for sure. But *this*, this texting, it didn't feel like her at all. She didn't play games, and this definitely felt like a game. But there was something else, and he couldn't put his finger on it.

He glanced at the patio again. No movement, no sign of danger.

Maybe the clue was here, in the woods. Calla was a sixteen-year-old Fire Elemental. She would have set these woods on fire to send a message. Or she would have burned down Adam's apartment complex. She wouldn't taunt him with texts and then ask him to meet her in a bar.

A bar.

Calla wouldn't have asked to meet in a bar at all—she wouldn't be allowed.

So his tormentor was over twenty-one. That narrowed it down to about a bazillion people.

Well, not really. It couldn't be any of the middle- or high-schoolers who agreed with what Calla was doing. Who else did he know who was over twenty-one?

Bill Chandler, Becca's father. He was a Guide himself, but he was in hiding now, trying to keep Becca safe. He was also terrified of the Guides coming to town. He wouldn't have started a bunch of fires. Michael was honestly shocked he hadn't called yet to yell at Michael for letting his neighborhood get destroyed.

Bill was an asshole, but he wasn't behind this.

He scrolled through the text messages again, stopping on the one of Hannah at the fire. Fierce in her fire gear, then gentle and patient with her son.

Sudden fury welled up in Michael's chest.

He rolled forward onto his knees and punched the dead tree. Bark splintered and wood creaked. A few dead branches cascaded down around him. His knuckles were bleeding.

He wanted to do it again.

No, he wanted to do it to whoever had texted him.

Focus. Figure this out.

Another name came to him. Tyler?

Tyler.

Michael tried to make that work. Tyler had made it his life's goal to torment Michael—until he'd revealed himself to be a full Fire Elemental, just as cursed as the Merricks were. He'd saved Michael's life a few weeks ago, shooting a Guide in the head just before the man was going to kill Michael and Chris in their own living room.

Would Tyler do something like this? Why?

Michael couldn't connect the dots there, either, but he also couldn't eliminate Tyler entirely.

Who else? A complete stranger? A new Guide in town wouldn't taunt him. They wouldn't be like, "Hey, let's grab a beer."

They'd just shoot him.

Michael took a long breath and brushed bark off his knuckles. He picked up a dead branch and started snapping small pieces. He needed to think of a contingency plan, somewhere to send his brothers if he didn't survive this meeting tonight—because he wasn't naïve enough to think it was just a *talk*.

And he sure as hell wasn't telling them about it.

Snap. Snap. Snap. Each piece was easier to break than the last, the wood dry and lacking any energy.

His fingers went still. He studied the dead tree again. There was a gap of bark where he'd slammed his fist into the trunk.

But there were other gaps in the bark, and more broken branches higher up the trunk.

Someone had climbed this tree. Recently, too, considering the bare wood hadn't been exposed to the elements long.

Michael found himself climbing before he really thought about what he was doing. His feet caught the bark and gripped tight, his hands finding every available branch. In less than a minute, he was twenty-five feet above the ground, obscured by the autumn-darkened branches of the surrounding trees.

He had a perfect view of Adam's apartment.

And he had a comfortable seat, right in the crook of two strong branches.

He pulled out his phone and aimed the camera app at where

he'd been sitting. It was an almost identical match to the picture he'd received.

Gotcha.

Well, not really. The tree was empty now, the dead limbs offering no information. The air was silent up here, too, no breeze moving through the branches. Michael watched his breath fog for a while, thinking.

A Guide might be smart enough to climb a dead tree to avoid his notice. He'd have to ask Hunter if it would occur to him. An Earth Elemental *definitely* would.

Michael only knew one other Earth Elemental: Seth Ramsey. Tyler's best friend.

Seth and Tyler were totally the type to do something like this to fuck with him. They didn't necessarily have to be behind the fires in the Merrick neighborhood—they could have heard what had happened and known it was an opportunity to kick him when he was down.

But . . . how would they know to find him *here*?

Had they followed him? It was possible. Not likely—but not unlikely either.

Despite everything, Michael felt a twinge of disappointment. He'd thought he and Tyler had grown past that and found some middle ground. They'd never be friends, but he didn't hate the guy anymore.

Maybe he'd found a reason to renew that hate.

CHAPTER 9

M ichael heard a shout and bolted upright.

For an instant, he was completely disoriented. He didn't recognize these walls, this bedroom, this quilt.

Then he remembered all of it. The fires. Adam's apartment.

The threatening messages. The photo from the trees.

Another shout, more muffled. It sounded like someone was right outside the window.

Michael flung the blanket aside and staggered to his feet. Weak light filtered through the window blinds. He grabbed at the slats and pulled open a gap large enough to look through.

Just in time to see Gabriel tackle Chris hard enough to knock him to the ground.

Michael remembered chasing Chris through the woods. What the hell was—

Oh. Wait. They were laughing. An orange Nerf football lay in the grass a few feet away. Gabriel was letting Chris up. Nick retrieved the ball and pointed at something out of sight.

They were playing.

At once, Michael was simultaneously furious and terrified.

Playing. Outside, in full view of . . . whoever.

He grabbed his jeans from the floor and jerked them on, fighting with the button as he yanked the bedroom door open.

Hunter was sitting alone at the tiny kitchen table. He looked up in alarm as Michael burst out of the room. "You okay?"

"They shouldn't be outside. I can't believe they're—" He stopped short as the ball sailed past the glass door at the back of the apartment.

"They're what?" Hunter glared at the coffee mug in front of him. "I say leave them out there. I thought someone was going to get murdered in here."

Michael rubbed his hands down his face. The adrenaline was fading, leaving him standing in a puddle of mixed emotions. "What? Why?"

Hunter glanced around. "Why do you think?" His voice had an edge. "There are two rooms and you were asleep in one of them. No television. No one knows what's going on, or where we're going to go, or what might happen."

Michael looked out the door again, studying his brothers. At first glance, they'd looked carefree and happy. Under closer scrutiny, he could read the tension in their movements and see the worry in their eyes. Gabriel had tackled Chris a little too hard to be brotherly—and when Nick had thrown the ball, he'd propelled it like a missile. "How long have they been out there?"

"I don't know. Half an hour, maybe."

"You didn't want to play?"

Hunter shrugged, but didn't say anything.

Michael took a long breath and looked into the kitchen. The clock over the stove told him it wasn't much past five. He'd slept for three hours, which was two hours and fifty-nine minutes longer than he'd thought he would. The light on the coffee-maker was still lit, and half a pot sat there.

"Do you think we're in danger here?" said Hunter.

"Why would you ask that?"

"Because of how you came flying out the bedroom, all pissed that they're outside. Does anyone know we're here?"

Michael thought of those text messages. Would his brothers be any safer inside?

I'm not sure I could limit a fire to five apartments.

Maybe they were safer outside.

He had no idea.

"I don't know." Michael opened two cabinets before he found the mugs, then poured himself a cup of coffee. He sat down at the table across from Hunter, shifting his chair so he could see out the back window.

He had two hours to kill. An hour and a half, really, considering he wanted to get to the restaurant early, to walk the premises and see if the ground could offer further clues.

To see if Tyler or Seth was really behind this.

He could close his eyes and see the burned-out living room, the exposed beams in the ceiling, the destroyed furniture. He could still smell the acrid smoke and burnt insulation.

Before, he'd been tired and twitchy and panicked.

A few hours' sleep had brought focus. He wanted to kill whoever was behind this.

Michael took a sip of coffee—old, but not *too* old—and realized Hunter was still just sitting there, shoulders hunched, eyes fixed on the back door.

"You didn't say why you weren't out back," said Michael.

"I didn't feel like going outside."

"Did something happen?"

"No."

That *no* sounded like a whole lot of *yes*.

Michael waited, inhaling the steam from his cup, keeping his eyes on the backyard.

Finally, Hunter looked at him. His voice was almost belligerent. "Are you going to make me go home?"

Go home? But home was—

Oh.

Oh.

Michael looked right back at him. "I hadn't even considered it. Do you want to go home?"

Hunter didn't say anything, just kept staring back.

Michael traced a finger around his coffee mug, considering. "When I was a kid, I used to sneak out of the house and sleep in the woods. The first time my dad caught me, I thought he was going to drag me back."

"He didn't?"

Michael shook his head. "He brought sleeping bags and flashlights." He paused. "What do you want to do, Hunter?"

"Home would probably be better."

"Better for who?"

"You. Then you won't have to worry about me."

"I hate to break it to you, kid, but you're probably just as big a target with *your* family as you are with mine. And if you think I could drop you off with your mom and stop worrying, you're dead wrong." In fact, he'd probably worry *more*.

"I didn't mean worrying like that."

"Then what did you mean?"

"I made a bad call last night. We should have stayed at the house. Then we wouldn't have been gone—then those people—we wouldn't—" He caught himself before his voice broke, and shook his head.

Michael studied him. He'd been so wrapped up in his own guilt that he hadn't considered any of the others might be feeling it, too. "Hunter—"

"Chris was just being stupid, but I made you go after him, and now we don't have somewhere to live. I'm the one—it's my—"

"Hunter. Stop."

"If we'd stayed at the house, we could have stopped it. They were after us. It's our fault, and then—"

"All right, *stop*." Michael set the coffee down. "You didn't start those fires. And I have no idea what happened in the woods last night, but it *wasn't* just Chris, and you didn't start that either. No one is *making* you go back to live with your mom and your grandparents. If you want to go back, I won't stop you. If you want to stay here, that's fine, too. This was not your fault."

"What if I'd never come here? What if—"

"Then Becca's dad would have killed us. What if my parents

had never made a deal with the other Elementals in town? What if we'd never been born? Jesus, we can play *what-ifs* all day, Hunter. Things happen, and we deal with them."

Hunter still looked tense. Michael could read the warring emotions on his face.

"I don't want to go home," he finally said.

"Done."

Hunter sat there for a long minute, until the silence began to wrap around them. Michael listened to his brothers outside and told himself that Nick would sense danger before it could draw close—and Gabriel would sense anything to do with fire. They needed this time to burn off energy. Part of Michael was tempted to join them.

A bigger part of him was ashamed his family was in this situation.

He didn't move.

"I wish my dad was here."

Hunter's words came out of nowhere, and Michael was surprised when longing for his own father caught him around the neck and made it hard to breathe for a moment. His voice was rough and every bit as quiet. "Me too." He took his own shuddering breath. "God. Me too."

Hunter was looking at him again, and Michael realized Hunter was looking for reassurance, and here he was commiserating.

He smoothed a hand over the table and forced the emotion out of his voice. "When I was younger, I used to hate the music my dad played in the truck. The presets were all country and classic rock. But he said it was his truck and his rules, and when I had my own truck, I could pick my own stations."

Hunter studied him. "But that's what you listen to when you drive."

"It's still his truck."

They sat in silence for the longest time. Hunter finally said, "Is that your way of telling me we're supposed to do what we *think* they'd do?"

Michael shrugged. "I don't know. I spend more time wondering what he'd *expect* me to do. But maybe that's the same thing."

"Maybe."

It wasn't the same thing at all. Michael knew it. He had a pretty good sense that Hunter knew it, too. Michael's father had always been pretty clear about his expectations.

Hunter's father had never been clear about anything. At all. When Hunter had first moved here, he'd done it as an act of vengeance. His father and uncle had been killed when a rock slide crushed their car—while they were traveling to eliminate the Merricks. Hunter had been the only one to survive the wreck, and he'd assumed Michael and his brothers had been responsible.

They hadn't been. Calla had.

Michael wondered if some of Hunter's guilt was wrapped up in the fact that he'd once had an opportunity to kill Calla, and he hadn't been able to pull the trigger.

"I don't think you'd be a disappointment to your father," he said carefully.

Hunter didn't look at him. "When he was getting ready to come here, I wanted to come with him. He said I wasn't ready. He asked if I'd be able to do what needed to be done if you all turned out to be a danger to the community." He paused. "I had a chance to stop Calla once. I didn't do it."

"Hunter—"

Hunter looked at him, and anger was in his eyes. "You know, every time I see her, I'm reminded of that. I have to think about the fact that she admitted to killing them, and now we're letting her run around, harming innocent people—"

"We don't know that she's responsible for last night."

"She was responsible for a lot of other things."

"I know." Michael sighed and ran his hands down his face. "Honestly, Hunter, I don't know if I would have been able to pull that trigger myself. She's a kid. I'd rather turn her over to the authorities and let *them* deal with her. If we find her and shoot her, we're no different from the Guides. I'm not an executioner."

"Then turn her over to the authorities."

"I would. In a heartbeat." Especially after last night. Michael checked his phone again, as if there were some possibility Calla had magically texted him from a non-working number. "I don't have any idea where she is."

"The Guides say that everything they do to Elementals is for the greater good. Did you know that? They think it's better to kill someone who *might* be a threat than to take the risk of letting them cause any damage."

"They also think it's fine if innocent people get caught in the crossfire. According to your mom, your father didn't agree with any of that. He was coming here to help us."

Hunter's face twisted with emotion, just for a second. His voice was level. "I wish he'd made it."

"Me too."

The glass door slid open, and Gabriel stuck his head in. "Are you two going to start knitting, or do you want to come burn off some rage with the rest of us?"

Michael glanced at Hunter. Emotion still hung in the air, and he knew better than to poke at something fragile. "Nah, we're all right."

"Come *on*," said Gabriel. "Who knows if we'll ever get to play ball again?"

He dropped the serious words so casually.

Michael thought of his meeting tonight, of the secret he was keeping from his brothers.

He stood. "All right."

Hunter didn't move. "I'll stay here."

"Come on," called Gabriel. "You can tackle Chris if you want."

Chris said something from behind him. Michael couldn't make it out, but the intent was pretty clear.

Hunter must have picked up on it too. He shoved out of his chair.

When they lined up to play, Michael watched Chris, ready to make sure he and Hunter didn't push this aggression too far. But he was surprised to find that Chris's angry eyes didn't find a target in Hunter.

Instead, they found a target in Michael.

"Hey," Michael began.

But then the ball was in play, and Michael lost himself in a game with his brothers.

CHAPTER 10

Hannah woke to the smell of peppermint. She opened her eyes to find a half-eaten candy cane in front of her face.

"Grandma says you have to get up because Pop is bringing home someone from work for dinner."

Hannah groaned and rubbed at her eyes. "Dinner? What are you doing home already? What time is it?"

"Six-one-four. Grandma picked me up. We made cookies."

Hannah sat straight up in bed. The clock confirmed the numbers he'd read off. A quarter past six? She'd slept straight through the afternoon and into the evening. She'd missed picking James up from school.

Thank god for her mother.

Hannah looked at her clock radio. The alarm switch was off. Had she forgotten to set it? She never forgot her alarm.

"Mommy?"

His little face was full of sticky puzzlement. She grabbed him around the waist and tickled him until he shrieked with laughter, then pulled him close, inhaling peppermint backed by little-boy sweat and playground dirt.

"How was school?" she murmured.

He launched into a complicated story involving birthday donuts for a girl named Jovie, but Hannah lay there and held him, stroking the blond hair back from his forehead. Sometimes she wondered how her entire life could narrow down to one person, all her worries fading into the background when he was in her arms.

"Hannah!" her mother called. "Your father will be home in twenty minutes!"

Hannah made a face at James. He giggled.

She shoved herself out of bed and fished jeans and a T-shirt out of her dresser. Her parents had always made a big deal out of eating as a family, and that hadn't changed when James had come along. When she'd been a kid, Hannah had loved sitting together at the table every night, hearing her father's firehouse stories, grinning when he'd cut her food and arrange it into smiley faces and shapes.

Now, it seemed that her father used dinnertime as an excuse to list the ways she should be improving her life. Hannah used the time to ignore him when she could, choosing instead to focus on James and his table manners.

Her mother spent the time running interference.

At least her father was bringing someone home. She could eat in peace while he and some guy from the force traded BS stories.

She sent James down to help set the table, then pulled her hair into a clip. A glance in the mirror revealed dark circles under her eyes, so she spent an extra minute on lotion, some concealer, and a little bit of blush and mascara.

A far cry from the days in high school when she'd go all out. But seriously, who was she impressing? Some fifty-year-old firefighter with a beer gut and a smoker's cough? Some retired cop who wished for the good ol' days?

The door slammed downstairs. Male voices echoed in the kitchen. Hannah hustled.

Before dashing down the steps, she grabbed her phone. She'd been hoping for a message from Michael, but he hadn't sent her anything.

He'd hung up on her this morning, after sounding so . . . broken. Should she call?

Or should she leave him alone?

She sent him a text before she could think better of it.

Just checking on you.

She didn't think he was going to respond, but he did, almost immediately.

I'm okay.

She had no idea how to read that. Reassurance? Or a brush-off?

She told herself to stop being stupid. His life was in complete upheaval, and she was sitting here trying to read meaning into a message.

Her fingers slid across the screen.

Do you need dinner? I can bring you food.

I'm okay.

She hesitated at the top of the steps, wanting to call, but not wanting to push him. Another text appeared.

Thanks, though. I'm meeting someone at the Roadhouse at 7.

The Roadhouse was a little tavern that sat on the outskirts of town. At least once a month her engine company had to peel someone's car off a tree after they'd had too much to drink.

Meeting someone?

She realized immediately that he would read that as jealousy. It wasn't.

Well, not really.

Maybe. A little.

About a job.

Oh.

"Hannah! Are you coming down?"

Crap! She shoved the phone in her pocket.

Her mother was talking when Hannah got to the bottom of the stairs, in that engaged-yet-distracted tone she used when she was doing four things at once. "So you're interested in becoming a fire marshal?"

"Yes, ma'am. That's part of why I transferred to this area."

Hannah stopped short before turning the corner. She knew that voice.

She wondered if she should go upstairs and scrub off any trace of makeup.

Or maybe she should go up there and slap on a bit more.

"Hannah, is that you? Could you please fill water glasses for the table?"

Damn it.

She slipped into the kitchen, hoping her cheeks weren't pink. Her mother was chopping lettuce for a salad. Her father was reaching for something in the refrigerator.

And Irish was standing by the counter, looking almost as good as he had this morning.

When he'd been shirtless and shaving.

She smacked her brain into submission—but now she had no idea what to say.

He smiled when he saw her. "You look like you just woke up."

Oh. Nice. "You look like a man who wants me to spit in his water glass."

"Hannah!" Her mother sounded horrified. "That's disgusting!"

James came bursting into the kitchen. "Do it, Mommy! Do it!"

Irish lost the smile and glanced between her and James. His face went from pure amusement to pure shock.

Hannah knew that look. She was *used to* that look. She'd been getting it since she was seventeen, and it stung just as much now as it had then. She wondered if it would ever go away. Maybe when she was thirty. She ruffled James's hair. "Irish, this is James."

Her son leaned into her and looked up at Irish. "Are you a fireman?"

Irish still looked shell shocked. "Ah . . . yeah."

"Do you want to see my Lego house?"

"Um—"

"Maybe later," Hannah said. "Go wash up for dinner." She gave James a kiss on the forehead. "Especially this sticky face." He took off.

Her father held out a bottle of beer to Irish, keeping one for himself. "All I have is light."

It seemed to break through Irish's surprise. "No. Thank you, sir." He shrugged. "I'm still on call."

Hannah rolled her eyes at the *sir* and dutifully pulled glasses out of the cabinet, then started filling them with ice and water from the dispenser on the front of the refrigerator.

Irish appeared at her side and put out a hand. "I can help you."

"I've got it."

"You're going to carry four glasses at once?"

Something about him being here was pricking at her nerves. She couldn't decide if that was a good thing or a bad thing. Maybe it was the extra formality in front of her father. Maybe it was the look in his eyes when he'd seen James. "Sure," she said. "In one hand. While twirling. Watch." Then she picked up the four glasses—two in each hand—and carried them through the archway into the dining room.

Without twirling.

Irish followed. "I didn't mean to take you off guard."

That made her look up. "What do you mean?"

"By coming here. Marshal Faulkner invited me to join him for dinner, but I didn't know—"

"You didn't know he was my dad?" She placed the last two glasses. "Come on."

"No—I didn't know you still lived at home." He cleared his throat. "Or that you had a son."

She didn't know how to read his voice. It wasn't quite judgment, but it wasn't full of sunshine and flowers and acceptance, either. "Don't worry. You're not the father."

"Who is?"

The question hit her like a hammer to the temple. He hadn't meant it to be invasive—but it was, and she didn't have her usual deflection ready. She wiped her palms on her jeans and couldn't look at him. "I'm going to grab the salad bowl."

Her parents were speaking in low tones when she walked back into the kitchen, and they shut up quick when she came through the archway.

Her eyes narrowed. Everything about this evening left her feeling like she was missing something. "What?"

Her mother pushed the salad bowl across the island. "Your father and I are talking, Hannah. Please take the salad out and give us a minute of privacy."

Well.

It wasn't often her mother used her I-mean-business voice, and Hannah knew better than to argue with that. Unfortunately, it meant she had to go back in the dining room to entertain Irish. She grabbed the bowl, wishing she could fling it on the table and keep on walking out to the backyard.

And then keep on walking for miles.

No, she could never do that. Not with James at the center of her orbit, drawing her back from wherever life took her.

Irish looked abashed when she returned to the dining room. "I didn't mean to offend you. I didn't know—"

"It's fine." She dropped into her usual chair and ran her finger around a glass of water. "I didn't mean to be short. It's complicated."

"And it's none of my business, really."

She smiled. "That, too."

"Is it the guy from last night?"

Her eyebrows went up. "Didn't you just acknowledge that it's none of your business?"

"That doesn't mean I'm not still curious."

She gave a nod at the chair across from her, which was usually reserved for guests because it was beside her father. "Sit down if you want."

He hesitated, then sat. "I really didn't realize I'd be coming for a family meal. . . ."

"Don't worry. My mom is a better cook than whoever is running the kitchen at the firehouse tonight."

Irish smiled. "I'm not worried."

They fell into silence for a moment.

Hannah was very aware she'd never answered his question.

"Michael isn't James's father," she finally said quietly. "I've known him since high school, but we've only been dating a few months. Sometimes I wish . . ." She shut her mouth and cut herself off.

"You wish what?"

She glanced at the kitchen door. Her parents still seemed to be engrossed in conversation. She looked at her water glass. She never talked to anyone about these things, but she'd seen a different side of Irish this morning, and it had added a new level of closeness to their relationship. She always felt like an outsider at the firehouse, and now she knew he did too.

"This is going to sound ridiculous, but sometimes I wish he was."

"You guys are that serious?"

A blush found her cheeks. She hadn't meant it to come out that way at all. "No. Not really. Maybe. Ah—I don't know. I didn't mean—"

"What did you mean?"

Hannah hesitated and wondered how she'd dug herself in so deeply. She sighed. "I mean, Michael would have stepped up."

"You sound pretty sure about that."

"I am sure. He's a good guy, you know?" She paused, surprised by the sudden well of emotion in her chest. "He's been taking care of his brothers since his parents died. He's the type of guy who'd do the right thing, no matter what. He's sacrificed a lot, just for his family."

Irish frowned. "You know, your dad thinks he had something to do with those fires last night."

Hannah glared at the doorway to the kitchen and wanted to throw something at it. She didn't want to upset her mother, so she kept her voice down. "My dad is an asshole. He's looking for an easy target. Michael didn't set those fires any more than you did."

Irish put his hands up. "I'm just saying. Sometimes it pays to keep your eyes open."

James came flying into the dining room. "I washed my hands, Mom!"

His sleeves were soaking wet. Hannah couldn't help but smile. She looped an arm around his waist and pulled him in for a hug. "Good boy. Dinner isn't ready yet. Do you want to watch YouTube videos on my phone?"

"Yeah!" He took the phone and flopped on the couch in the living room.

Irish watched this exchange. "I don't think your friend Michael is the only one who knows something about sacrifice."

"What is that supposed to mean?"

"Are you the type of girl who'd do the right thing, no matter what?"

His voice was full of something she couldn't identify. She lost the smile. "I like to think so."

Irish shrugged a little. "I'm just saying. Sometimes right and wrong aren't easy to identify."

"You're a lot deeper than I expected, Irish."

He smiled. "Sometimes people see a big guy and they think *stupid*. I like to prove them wrong."

She smiled back.

Just as she wondered if his smile meant a little more, Irish stood, breaking the eye contact. He gestured at the back wall of the dining room, where more than fifty photos had been arranged in mismatched frames. Some were old: her parents' wedding picture, or a shot of Hannah as a baby. Some were new, like James's kindergarten photo.

He glanced down at her. "Your mom loves family photos, huh?"

"You should see the basement."

One broad finger touched the edge of an old photo in a faded frame. "Is this you?"

She noticed the one he was indicating and froze. These photos had been here for years, and she rarely noticed the old ones anymore. The one he'd touched featured her as a little girl, not much older than James, standing beside her father, who was kneeling. She was in a Sunday dress, all pink lace and frills and crinoline, her blond hair long and curled. Her father was kneeling in his fire gear, soot on his cheeks and hands, probably fresh from a fire. She was holding his helmet, a huge toothy smile on her face. Her father was smiling back at her as if she made the sun rise and set each day.

She couldn't remember the last time he'd looked at her like that.

"Blondie?" Then Irish caught himself and smiled. "Hannah?"

"Yeah." She coughed. "It's me. That's back when my dad was just a fireman." She paused. "He didn't start training to be a fire marshal until I was in middle school."

Irish studied her. He must have heard the bitterness in her voice. "You don't like what he does for a living?"

"Not as much as he does."

"I don't understand."

"He gets off on it." She smiled, and it felt a little sinister. "I'm glad you turned down the beer. I'd bet money he knows you're on call."

Irish's eyes lit with surprise—then settled into something like challenge. "Oh. So he's like *that*."

"Yeah. Keep up with the *sir* stuff. He'll eat it up."

Irish sobered. "Too much?"

"Nah." She paused. "Do you really want to be a fire marshal? Or were you just kissing ass?"

"Oh, that's real. My dad is a detective in Chicago. I think he always expected me to follow in his footsteps, but I wanted to make my own way." He shrugged and rubbed the back of his neck. "Sometimes I feel like there should be something more, you know? It's a career path to look at."

"You're a good firefighter," she said.

His eyes met hers again, and she blushed. "But don't let it go to your head," she added.

"I won't."

"You want to do something else?"

"I don't know." He looked back at the picture. "Maybe."

"My dad took a lot of crap when he made the decision to switch. It's a lot of work, and you've got your foot in both departments. Not quite a cop, and not quite a fireman either."

"He took a lot of crap?" His voice dropped.

She glanced at the kitchen doorway. Her parents were still having a heated conversation, but she couldn't make out anything but whispers. What on earth was *up* with them?

Irish was waiting for an answer, so Hannah looked back at him. "Yeah. He was in line to be chief, and he turned it down. He'd been a great fireman, but there was a massive fire and some people died during his shift. He couldn't get them all out in time. After that, he didn't want to walk into another active scene. The guys in his crew thought he got afraid. They thought he was running from his job."

Her father spoke from the doorway. "What do *you* think?"

Hannah straightened so quickly that she bumped the table and made the water slosh. "Dad. Sorry."

"What do you think?" he said again. His tone was even—not irritated, yet not warm either. Just level. Patient. His investigator voice.

Hannah hated that voice.

She looked back at him. "I guess it's going to have to remain a mystery."

"Your mother asked if you could get the rolls and put them in a basket."

She hated this voice, too. This was his dismissal voice.

Hannah was tempted to curtsey and mock him. Luckily, this wasn't high school. Besides, she had an audience.

She looked at Irish before she made her way back to the kitchen, and gave him one last warning. "Remember what I said. He's great at this job, too."

Then she brushed past her father without even looking at him.

CHAPTER 11

The Roadhouse Bar and Grill sat along Magothy Beach Road, a few blocks off the water and surrounded by an acre of trees. Beige paint peeled away from the siding in numerous places, and a few fake palm trees swayed in the November wind.

Michael had never been here, but it was obviously popular, given the packed parking lot. He found a spot for the truck at the back of the restaurant, between the back door and the Dumpster.

When he killed the engine, he just sat there.

He had half a mind to drive back to Adam's apartment, to tell his brothers that "the guy" never showed to talk about a landscaping job that didn't exist. Then he'd help himself to a few slices of pizza—if there was any left, given the way they'd attacked the boxes when the delivery guy showed up. They could break out a deck of cards and pretend their lives weren't skirting the edge of disaster.

And then the *real* guy who was threatening them would burn down the whole place.

Michael got out of the truck.

The gravel of the parking lot offered no information. No threat of danger, no hint of a problem.

He pulled his phone out of his pocket and sent a text.

How will I know you?

You'll know me when you see me.

Did that mean his mysterious texter wasn't here yet, but he'd arrive in a way that was unmistakable? Or that Michael would recognize him on sight?

He'd worried all afternoon that this was another way to lure him away from his brothers—but what choice did he have? He sure as hell wasn't going to bring them with him. And whoever set this meeting had implied that Michael could bring anyone he wanted—including the police.

Was that an extension of trust? Or a finely laid trap?

Maybe he should have involved the police. Hannah's father was still waiting to talk to him. Michael pulled the fire marshal's card out of his jeans pocket—now washed, though soot still stained the seams—and considered dialing.

Then he remembered the photo of Hannah and James on the school steps.

This was too close to home, for all of them. He wasn't putting anyone else in danger if he didn't have to.

Michael shoved his phone back in his pocket and circled around to the front of the building. Some older guys in layered flannel held the door for him on their way out. Jukebox music hit him hard when he crossed the threshold. He'd expected a simple bar with a few tables, but the place was bigger than it looked from the outside. A polished wood bar stretched across the rear of the restaurant, tended by an aging man with tufts of white hair. Swinging doors led to a kitchen beyond. A middle-aged waitress burst through them with a tray of steaming plates: gravy fries, nachos, Buffalo chicken wings. Bar food. At least eighteen tables crowded the open area, and all were occupied. The floor was littered with peanut shells, and Michael's boots crunched through them as he stepped out of the doorway.

His eyes swept the room once. Dim lighting didn't reveal much, and several people had their backs to him, but no one *looked* suspicious. Everyone seemed engaged, whether in food or a conversation. Mostly men over thirty, mostly blue collar, in for a quick drink or a dinner before heading home for the night. Flannel and denim everywhere. Laughter and loud voices carried over the music.

The waitress stopped in front of him on her way between tables, and he was so keyed up that for a second, he worried this forty-year-old frizzy-haired woman was his mystery person. Then she gave him a puzzled look and said, "It's seat yourself, sweetie."

He cast his gaze past her, at the bar, and then back to the door. "I don't—I'm meeting someone—"

"What's wrong, Merrick? Run out of lawns to mow?"

He recognized the voice, but with the noise and the low lighting, it took him a minute to spot its owner. About three tables over, with his back to the door, sat Tyler Morgan.

Tyler. *Tyler.*

You'll know when me when you see me.

Michael stormed between patrons. He hadn't thought Tyler was behind this. Not really. But now, with proof right in front of him . . .

He slammed his hand down on Tyler's table. It took everything he had not to drag the guy out of his chair and slug him in the face. "You think you're going to mess with my family?" He hit the table again, and he must have looked fierce, because Tyler shoved back a few inches. Michael got in his face. He was yelling and he didn't care. "You think I'm going to let you get away with it?"

Tyler didn't move. "Get out of my face, Merrick."

"Those people. All those people. You—"

"What people?" Tyler glared back at him. "Did you forget your medication or something?"

"You know what people." Michael shoved him, causing the chair to scrape back a few more inches.

Tyler gritted his teeth, but he didn't move. "I don't know what you're talking about."

"Do you think this is *funny*?" He was causing a scene, but

Michael didn't care. That Tyler would do this—that he would make jokes—that he could—his neighbors had died—

"What is your *problem*, Merrick?"

"You're my problem! Did you do this? Did you start those fires?"

Tyler's expression darkened. He didn't move from his chair. "Look," he said, his voice low and lethal. "I don't know what you're on, but if you don't sit down and act like a normal person, Tammy is going to call the cops."

Michael stared at him. The restaurant had gone silent except for the jukebox still cranking out tunes in the corner. Four men were standing nearby, ready to come to Tyler's aid. The waitress—Tammy?—had a phone in her hand, and she was looking at Tyler, as if waiting for him to tell her what to do.

Michael's breathing echoed in his ears.

Tyler raised an eyebrow. "Sit down and behave, or leave, Merrick. Your call."

Michael swallowed. He felt like he'd run a mile at top speed. "Did you text me to meet you here?"

"No."

"Don't you fuck with me, Tyler—"

"Jesus! I don't even know your number! Why the hell would I text you?"

"Tyler?" said Tammy. "Should I call?"

I don't even know your number. That was true. Michael had never given Tyler his number. Not that it wasn't listed with most of his business stuff, but still . . .

Michael couldn't catch his breath. He glanced around again. He was causing a scene—but no one else had come out of the woodwork.

Tyler gave Michael a clear up and down. "He's all right. He's going to sit down and have a beer. Right?"

Michael looked around again. The anticipatory tension in the restaurant was potent. God, what was wrong with him?

He collapsed into the chair across from Tyler. Normal activity slowly resumed around him. The four men returned to their tables. Tammy picked up her tray and slid the phone into a pocket of her apron.

Tyler scooted back up to the table. "You don't have dynamite strapped to you or anything, do you?"

Michael glared. "Don't be an idiot, Tyler."

"You come rolling in here like a psycho, and *I'm* the idiot. Okay."

"If you didn't text me, what are you doing here?"

"Having dinner."

Michael pulled a whole peanut out of a bucket on the table and crushed it between his fingers. He didn't want to eat it, but he needed something destructive to do with his hands. He glanced around again, ready for someone to jump out of the shadows and yell *Boo!* "Sure. Here. This is your scene."

"I don't know if it's my *scene*, but my family owns this place, so it's *free*." He paused. "What are *you* doing here?"

"Your family owns this place?"

"My grandparents did, actually. My folks inherited when they died. Want me to draw you a family tree?"

"No, I'm good."

But he wasn't good. This didn't make sense. Did . . . whoever-it-was know that this was Tyler's family's restaurant? Did it matter?

You'll know me when you see me.

Another glance around. The only person he recognized was Tyler.

But really, this whole thing—none of it *felt* like Tyler, just like none of it felt like Calla. Tyler had brutalized Michael's family for years, wanting the Merricks put to death because they were full Elementals. Then Tyler had accidentally revealed his carefully kept secret to Nick: Tyler was a full Elemental himself—a powerful Fire Elemental who had just as much reason to fear the Guides coming to town as the Merricks did.

They weren't friends now, not by a long shot. But Tyler hadn't bothered them in weeks. And no one *knew* Tyler was a Fire Elemental.

Michael took a long breath and let it out. "Our house was set on fire last night." He hesitated, keeping his voice low. "My whole street."

Tyler frowned, then went still. He leaned in against the table. "I heard about that on the news. I didn't know it was your neighborhood." He paused, and his voice sharpened. "And you thought I would do that?"

"No—I don't—" Michael shook his head. The adrenaline was fading, letting exhaustion settle in again. "I have no idea who did it."

"No wonder you look like shit."

"Thanks."

Tammy reappeared beside their table and unloaded two frosted bottles of Natty Boh, and then a platter of nachos. Tyler thanked her, and Michael smashed another peanut.

"Hungry?" said Tyler.

He hadn't eaten all day, but he couldn't think of putting food in his mouth right now. "No."

Tyler shrugged and took a chip. "You still haven't said what you're doing here."

"I got a text this morning that I should meet someone here about the fires."

"From who?"

"I don't *know* who. I thought it was you."

"Show me."

Michael hesitated—then unlocked his phone, clicked on the texts, and handed it over. It felt weird to trust Tyler with something he hadn't shared with his brothers, but this felt safer, too. His brothers had a big stake in this game. Tyler didn't.

Tyler scrolled. For a while.

Michael fidgeted. It was seven-fifteen now, and no one had come through the door.

"This guy said you could bring your brothers." Tyler handed back the phone, and Michael slid it into his pocket. "And the police."

"I know."

"And you didn't think maybe that was important?"

"I'm not leading my brothers into a trap."

"Do they know you're here?"

The question hit Michael hard. His brothers had no idea—but admitting it out loud seemed dangerous. "You're asking a lot of questions."

Tyler picked up another chip. "Jesus, Merrick. Maybe you could tone down the paranoia. Why didn't you bring the cops, then?"

"The cops think I'm involved in whatever happened to my neighborhood."

"So you're holding on to proof that you're *not*?"

"A bunch of pictures from a random phone number? That's not proof of anything. Hell, it's proof that I *am* involved. It's proof that more people are in danger."

Some of the aggression leaked out of Tyler's expression. "The blonde in those pictures. Your girlfriend?"

"Yeah." He paused. "Her father is the county fire marshal."

Tyler gave a low whistle. "So where is this guy you're supposed to meet?" He looked around. "You'll know him when you see him? What the hell is that supposed to mean?"

"I don't know." Michael sighed and rubbed the back of his neck. "I feel like I should be able to figure this out." He looked around again. The more time that went by, the more he felt certain this was an effort to separate him from his brothers. He twisted his hands together and fished his phone out of his pocket to send a text to Gabriel.

All OK?

His heart beat double time as he waited for a response, but he didn't have to wait long.

Yeah. What's up?

Nothing, just checking. Waiting for other guy to get here.

Michael blew air through his teeth and set down his phone again. "Why here? Why now? And why is he late?"

"Text him and ask."

Michael felt like an idiot for not thinking of it himself. He typed out a quick message.

Either I don't see you or I don't know you.

Then he hesitated before pressing *send*.

What was the worst that could happen? The guy could stand up and shoot him? And how was that any different from just sitting here waiting?

Fuck it. Michael pressed the button. The progress bar at the top of his phone showed the text going through.

And then the restaurant exploded.

Hannah pushed food around her plate and tried to ignore the way Irish kept kissing her father's ass. James had long ago abandoned the dinner table for his Legos, and Hannah was tempted to join him.

But no, when they had a guest, her father insisted that she remain at the table.

Like she was a teenager who needed a lesson in etiquette.

If her father were the only one at the table, Hannah would have walked out without question. But she wouldn't disrespect her mother that way.

Irish's alert pager went off with the chimes promising an urgent message. Out of habit, everyone went silent. No one in this house was a stranger to emergency alerts.

Commercial Box 13-3. Engines 131, 112, 104, 201 Truck 30, Truck 13, Medic Unit 11, Battalion Chief 2 respond for a commercial building fire, reported explosion, at 8503 Magothy Beach Road. Cross streets of Clover Hill Road and Riviera Drive. Respond hot on Echo—

There was more, but Hannah didn't hear the rest.

Commercial building fire. Reported explosion.

Magothy Beach Road.

She knew almost every road in this part of the county, right down to where each fire hydrant was located. She knew Magothy Beach Road like the back of her hand, and there weren't a lot of commercial buildings.

Except the Roadhouse.

Right where Michael was meeting someone about a job.

Her phone was pressed against her ear before she realized she had dialed.

Answer. Please. Answer.

It didn't even ring. Straight to voice mail.

She looked at his last text.

Meeting someone at the Roadhouse at 7.

It was now seven-twenty.

She tried to call him again.

"Pick up," she whispered. "Pick up."

"Hannah," said her mother, her voice concerned. "Hannah, you're white. What is it?"

Right to voice mail again. Irish was getting his coat from the front closet, calling his thanks for dinner. Her father was already on the phone, saying he'd be there in fifteen minutes, making notes on a small pad with details he'd never repeat out loud.

Hannah looked at her mother. "Can you watch James until I get back?" She didn't even wait for an answer, just pushed away from the table. "Irish! Wait!"

He stopped with the door halfway open. "Blondie?"

"But—Hannah—" Her mother was on her feet. "Where are you going?"

"I'm going to help."

CHAPTER 12

Even with lights and sirens, it seemed to take forever to get to Magothy Beach Road. Hannah was torn between keeping her eyes fixed on the controls inside the fire truck and looking out the window to see how bad it was.

Then Irish said, "Jesus," under his breath, and she didn't have a choice. She looked.

Half the building was gone. She didn't see much actively burning, but smoke plumed from the remaining structure. Several cars bore heavy damage, and almost none in the lot had escaped the flying debris. Fire trucks lined the road and the edge of the property, along with ambulances and half a dozen cop cars. She saw a lot of people in uniform or firefighting gear.

She didn't see anyone who looked like they'd survived an explosion.

She checked her phone again. She'd called six more times during the ride to the firehouse with Irish. No response from Michael.

"He'll be all right," Irish said quietly. "You don't know if he was still here."

"I don't even know if his brothers are with him."

"Can you call *them*?"

She shook her head. She didn't have any of their numbers.

The radio on her shoulder kept going off, but she hadn't been able to focus on any of it. Now she listened and realized why there were so many people milling around.

They'd been ordered to wait for the bomb squad and the collapse unit.

She turned to Irish. "We're waiting? We can't rescue—"

"Yeah, we're waiting." The truck rolled to a stop, and strobe lights from the other units reflected off his cheeks and clothing. "Have you ever worked a building collapse before?"

She shook her head, her eyes fixed on the smoldering structure. She didn't see any bodies.

Which meant they'd either been incinerated or they were buried under the rubble.

Michael. Her breath hitched.

Don't hang up. Talk to me.

God, Hannah, I wish I could.

Two major catastrophes in as many days.

"Maybe you should stay here," said Irish. "You weren't assigned to work tonight."

"I'm fine," she snapped.

"You're whiter than you were at your house. If you're looking for him, you won't be looking for anything else."

She unclipped her seat belt and stood. "There could be survivors in there! How can you just sit here and wait?"

"There could be another bomb in there, Hannah!" He got in her face and pointed out the window. "There are propane tanks sitting *right there*! You bet your ass I'm going to wait!"

She looked. There were two large propane tanks at the back of the restaurant, probably still intact because of nothing more than a huge stroke of luck.

But her eyes focused on what was parked right behind those propane tanks. A large red diesel pickup truck. Stray bits of lumber had landed across the cab, denting the roof and fracturing the windshield. The passenger door was clearly visible.

Along with the MERRICK LANDSCAPING logo.

"It's his truck," she said. Her voice almost broke as she swept her eyes across the rubble again. No movement aside from the wisps of smoke rising from the wreckage. "Irish, it's his truck."

Irish knocked on the glass separating them from the front part of the cab, where her battalion chief sat. When the glass slid open, Irish said, "Chief, she can't work this scene."

"I can!" she cried.

"Look at me." Irish put his hands on her cheeks. "Look at me, Blondie."

"His brothers—we have to find him. They're under eighteen—we need to find him—"

"Hannah. Look at me."

His voice was firm, and his chocolate-brown eyes were locked on hers. His hands were warm and strong against her face. She looked at him.

"We'll find him," he said. "I promise." He paused. "Don't make me rescue you too."

Something in his voice steadied her. She opened her mouth to respond.

Then the chief called for them to join the crew from the other trucks to form a plan of action. She pulled away from Irish, feeling warmth on her cheeks. He shifted past her to climb down from the truck.

When she moved to follow him, the chief said, "Not you, Blondie. Sit tight."

"But—"

"That's an order!"

His voice left no room for argument. She fell back into the seat.

Through the window, she could watch the flurry of activity. Groups of firefighters were getting orders. Some of it came across her radio. Police officers had blocked the roads, so no traffic could come through. A large truck from the county collapse unit rolled up—but still no one approached the structure. They were all waiting for the bomb squad.

She watched for any sign of survivors but saw none.

How long had it been? Twenty minutes?

Every minute counted. She knew. She'd been trained for this. *We don't trade lives for dead bodies, Hannah.*

Her father's voice, so clear, even years later. A hard and fast rule.

Had they found evidence of a bomb last night? Had that been the cause of the "earthquake"? Her father hadn't said—but he wouldn't tell her, anyway.

Her breathing echoed in the empty truck. Despite the chill in the air, her bunker coat felt stifling. She couldn't keep sitting here, wrapped in worry.

She climbed down from the cab, easing out of the truck on the side away from the rest of the crew. The chief couldn't imprison her in the truck, but he could yell at her for disobeying orders. She'd seen her dad's car, and all she needed was for him to hear her getting dressed down. He'd order her out of here in a heartbeat, and the only way she would leave was if she was handcuffed in a cop car.

She wouldn't put it past him.

Her radio squawked on her shoulder, and she quickly dialed down the volume. She moved to the back of the truck and pulled her helmet onto her head, hoping it would make her less recognizable. She opened the cabinet at the back, taking down some tools, then putting them back. Trying to look like she was standing here with a purpose.

She was really watching the site of destruction.

No movement.

Across the parking lot stood the crew from company ten. She knew some of them, but not many. They wouldn't know she'd been ordered to wait. She doubled back behind the fire trucks, walking with purpose, carrying a Halligan bar from the back of her engine as if she'd been sent to fetch something.

Yeah, right, like the guys from ten don't have a bar on their *truck.*

But what else was she going to carry? The fire hose? Might draw attention.

Her radio chirped again, only loud enough for her to hear. At first she ignored the radio chatter, but then her brain latched on to the message.

Thermal imaging showed no signs of life. All rescue units were ordered to wait for the area to be cleared.

No signs of life.

Michael. Her eyes flew to his damaged truck.

Keep moving. Find a task.

What task? What could she do?

She couldn't breathe. Had he survived last night only to die here and now?

Then she heard the *clink*.

At first her subconscious registered the sound and ignored it. *Clink*. Then she heard it again. And again. Clearly coming from beneath the wreckage. And then, a faint recognizable pattern. *Clinkclinkclink. Clink. Clink. Clink. Clinkclinkclink.*

Three short, three long, three short.

SOS.

Someone was alive.

She turned to run back to her crew. They had to know. She had to tell them—but then her radio crackled.

SOS observed. Pending clearance from bomb squad and collapse units. Hold all rescue.

They were right. She knew they were right. Attempting a rescue when a bomb could be sitting in there was *nuts*. Even without a bomb, nothing about the remaining structure looked secure. Those propane tanks could be leaking. There could be an active gas line leading to the stove. One spark could send the rest of the building sky high. One shifting board could send it all crashing down. She'd gone through the schooling and knew it as well as anyone.

But learning something in a classroom was different from handling it in practice.

Clinkclinkclink. Clink. Clink. Clink. Clinkclinkclink.

So faint, yet so clear.

"Hannah."

Her father. She'd lost track of herself, and she was now standing between units, staring at the wreckage, a bar clutched in one hand.

She looked at her father. His features blurred, just a little, then steadied. She blinked and tears rolled down her cheeks.

She was crying. She hadn't even noticed.

"Hannah?" he said again. His voice was quiet. Not harsh, but not gentle either.

Emotion clogged her throat and made it impossible for irritation to color her words. For an instant she wanted to be six years old again, for her father to be a hero again, for him to put on a helmet and rush into danger and walk out with a survivor in his arms.

But he wasn't. And now she was the firefighter. He was the fire marshal. The most heroic thing he did these days was harass people.

"Michael was here," she said.

"Was?"

She shook her head quickly. "Is. His truck . . ." She pointed. "Do you hear that?"

Clinkclinkclink. Clink. Clink. Clink. Clinkclinkclink.

The rhythm had changed. It was slower. Fainter.

Clinkclinkclink.

Clink.

Clink.

Clink.

And then it stopped.

"We all hear it," he said.

"It stopped," she whispered.

His own radio, tuned to the police channel, fired off a lot of codes she didn't know. He paused to listen, then said, "Bomb squad is en route."

His voice was so practical. Had he always been like this? She wanted to smack him. "Can't we send a crew in? Can't we—"

"That's up to your chief. Aren't you supposed to be somewhere?"

"Dad! Don't you want to help? Don't you think we should be rescuing them?"

"Hannah." His voice sliced through hers, cutting her off. His eyes were ice cold and furious. "I have a job to do here. There are more people involved than your boyfriend. There are *procedures* here, for your safety and everyone else's. Do you understand me?"

He might as well have hit her. She stared up at him.

She remembered that photo from her dining room wall, the way she'd looked up at him in admiration.

She'd been so stupid.

Hannah turned on her heel and started walking. She waited for him to call her back, but she wasn't five steps away when he was speaking into his radio.

And then her phone chimed.

A text from Michael.

Her heart cheered. It was almost enough to send her running into the wreckage, and procedure be damned. But no message appeared. Just a picture.

At first she didn't understand. It was dark, and the image was gruesome. A limb—and she couldn't even identify whether it was an upper arm or a lower leg—with a piece of rebar impaling it. Torn denim. Blood everywhere, speckled with dirt.

Then a line of text appeared.

Not me. Tell me what to do.

CHAPTER 13

When the text finally sent, Michael almost fainted from relief. He had about fifteen texts with a little red exclamation point beside them, showing that they hadn't gone through. Calls wouldn't connect at all, and he watched his battery percentage drop with each attempt. Water sprayed from exposed pipes overhead, creating puddles everywhere and misting his skin.

He was twenty feet below the surface, in a ravine of his own making.

Along with almost everyone else from inside the bar. Debris had fallen among them. And through them. Michael had turned on the flashlight feature of his phone and shined it around until he'd found familiar eyes staring back at him.

"Did it go through yet?" said Tyler. His voice was wispy. From what Michael could tell, they were the only two people conscious.

Michael was terrified that they were the only two people *alive*.

Tyler's leg was impaled on a steel bar—which was attached to a slab of concrete.

Hannah sent back a text.

DON'T MOVE BAR. Could bleed out. Conscious?

Yes.

Keep him talking. What else you got?

"She says we have to leave it," said Michael.

"Fuck that!" Sweat bloomed on Tyler's forehead despite the chill in the air. "Get it out!"

"She said you could bleed to death. Your call."

Tyler inhaled a long breath. It mixed with a sob. "Damn you, Merrick." He coughed and cried out. His fingers dug into the dirt surrounding him. "I need a fire. Sunlight. Anything."

"I know. I know." Michael slid his fingers along the face of the phone.

I smell gas. Open line maybe?

They're getting BG&E to kill the line. Anyone else hurt?

Everyone.

Michael held up his phone and took a picture. In the flash, he saw movement, but he couldn't identify the source. Had something fallen into the ravine? Or was that another survivor? He sent the picture, then turned on the flashlight again.

No motion. "Are you okay?" he called out to whatever he'd seen. "Move again. I'll try to get to you."

Nothing.

Dirt shifted and skittered from above, and Michael put a hand out, sliding his fingers along the wall. He sent power into the earth, begging for stability. This ravine might have saved his life, but it could just as easily end it for everyone else if it collapsed.

The sliding dirt stopped.

He took a long breath. His head pounded, and he wondered if he'd been hit by something in the fall.

Another text from Hannah.

Can you send me more injury pics?

I'll try.

We want to prep for rescue. Waiting on bomb squad. Need
clearance before we can enter.

"Don't move," he said to Tyler.

The response was slow, but it came. "You're funny, dickhead."

Michael crawled through the dirt to the next body he could
find. An older man, his legs bent at unnatural angles. Unconscious, but he was breathing, though it was shallow. He had a
pulse. No bleeding that Michael could see.

Michael took a picture and sent it.

Another man in a T-shirt and jeans, crumpled just beside the
first. The light reflected off his eyes, and Michael jumped.

Then he recognized the unnatural angle of his neck. Specks of
dirt clung to the eyeballs. No breathing at all.

He took another picture and added text.

No pulse, no breathing. I think his neck is broken.

Another man, bleeding from the head. Unconscious, but
breathing steadily. Good pulse. Michael took another picture,
sent another message.

Water was running across the face of the next man, and
Michael's flashlight app revealed a lot of blood. At first he couldn't
find a source of the bleeding, and he used slippery fingers to
send a pic with a message.

Blood everywhere. Breathing. Pulse. Help?

Head wound? Sit him up if you can.

He kept going, moving debris as he went. Some pieces were
large, and it took him a while to get past them. Three more dead
bodies, but then three who seemed alive. Two were moaning.
Michael sent pictures with as much description as he could.

Another man was ashen in the light from the app. Something
large had sliced across his thigh just above the knee.

Hannah's response was quick.

Rip a shirt. Tie a tourniquet HERE. Elevate if you can.

She sent a picture of someone else's leg, with a hand pointing.

He ripped a T-shirt off one of the dead bodies and tied as fast as he could.

"Tyler?" he called. "How you doing?"

No response. "Tyler!"

Nothing. Michael shined his flashlight in that direction. Tyler was still, his eyes closed. The metal bar still impaled his thigh.

But his chest rose and fell. He was still alive.

The light died, and Michael's phone chimed a warning at him. *Low battery. 5% remaining.*

Almost immediately, another text appeared from Hannah. When he opened it to try to reply, the phone died altogether.

Damn it! In the darkness, he patted the pockets of the next body he came to and found a phone. It was the older flip kind that probably wouldn't take a picture. He moved on to the next body. An iPhone! Yes!

Passcode protected.

"Christ," he muttered. Next body. An iPhone, though an older model. No passcode. A picture of a young girl and a boy as the background.

Kids.

Michael's breathing shook as he felt his way up the body to find a pulse.

He almost cried when he found one.

He opened the texts and started a new one. He typed in Hannah's number.

Phone died. Found a new one. Missed last message. – M

Asked if any burn victims?

This phone didn't have a flashlight app, but Michael had seen enough to know that he hadn't seen any burns.

No. Why?

Bomb squad investigating. Found fragments. Burn damage to building. Propane tanks intact. Still waiting on clearance to enter.

So a bomb *had* gone off. But no one was burned. And the propane tanks were intact? Had his ravine somehow insulated them from damage? Or had—

Then Michael realized.

Tyler. He was a Fire Elemental. Had his powers weakened the bomb, the way Michael's powers had offered a way out of the blast path?

More dirt rained down the walls. Splintered planks of wood fell from above. Michael shoved his back against the ravine wall and sent power into the earth again.

"Steady," he whispered. "Steady." He could feel vehicles moving now, where they'd been still for the longest time.

He texted quickly.

Don't move vehicles. Ground unstable.

It took a minute, but the motion stopped. Michael choked on his breath.

Hannah sent another text.

Are you in a basement? Can you send me pics of layout?

Michael aimed the phone up and started snapping pictures, trying to get the angles right. More debris fell from above and stung where it struck his face and forearms.

Then the flash lit up a face looking down at him from above.

"Hey!" Michael called into the darkness. He sent the photos to Hannah while he was peering up. "Hey! The edges aren't stable! Be careful!"

No response. Michael snapped another pic, hoping to get another image of the person. Was this a bomb squad technician? Or another survivor?

The flash went off. A gun fired.

Michael felt the bullet hit his shoulder. *Goddamn,* it hurt. It knocked him into the wall, and he lost the phone. More dirt poured down around him. The ground rumbled.

Another gunshot. He had no idea where it hit, but pain blossomed through his chest.

That wasn't good, right? He wished he still had the phone so he could ask Hannah. He couldn't see. He couldn't move.

Another gunshot.

Shouting erupted overhead. More gunfire.

Then nothing but darkness.

CHAPTER 14

Michael could move before he could see. Intermittent beeping filled his ears. His chest felt tight and painful, like someone had parked a car on his midsection. He shifted and felt soft cotton against his skin.

His eyes cracked open and found a blurred ceiling, edged by beige walls with a bland flowered border. Metal poles towered over him, complete with dripping bags. A small monitor showed jagged lines and beeped at regular intervals.

A hospital. He was in a hospital.

His brain didn't want to work. How—when—?

He lifted a hand to rub his eyes—but his arm hit resistance.

He tried again, and this time he heard the rattle of metal against plastic. He jerked hard and blinked his eyes before he figured out what was going on.

Handcuffs chained his right hand to the bed rail.

His heart rate tripled, making the beeping behind him accelerate. Every muscle in his upper body protested, but he forced himself upright. His chest felt as if it might cave in. More metal clinked and rattled.

His ankles were chained.

Now he was fully awake. He jerked at the handcuffs again, as if maybe he'd been wrong, and *this* time there'd be nothing there. His head pounded, keeping pace with his pulse. Breath rattled in his chest, every inhale like a stab through the heart.

If he was here, where were his brothers? Who had chained him to the bed? He didn't even know which hospital this was. The décor revealed nothing more than careful neutral blends of beige and pink.

The door stood partly ajar, and aside from a few people dressed in white passing by outside, he couldn't see anyone. A good thing or a bad thing? He didn't like this. He needed to be out of here.

"Hey," he called out. Speech forced a cough from his throat, and he almost doubled over from the sudden pain. He gasped and tried again. "Hey!"

The door swung open, and a policeman peered into the room.

Michael blinked in surprise. He'd expected a nurse or an orderly.

Then his brain caught up. Nurses didn't use handcuffs.

The man didn't seem much older than Michael himself—but he looked fierce and determined, like he enjoyed his job a little too much. His hand actually rested on the butt of his gun.

"You're awake," he said. "I'll let them know." Then he pulled the door almost all the way closed. Michael could hear him murmuring to someone—or maybe into a radio.

Handcuffs. A cop. He was being guarded.

What happened?

"Hey!" he called again. His voice sounded thin and reedy, and his entire rib cage really wanted him to lie back down.

The door swung open again. "Calm down. They'll be up in a while."

"Who?" Michael paused for breath. It took him a minute. "Why am I chained to this bed?"

The officer snorted and began to pull the door closed again. "Because we don't usually let bombing suspects wander free. Go figure."

"Hey. Hey!" Michael yanked at the chain restraining him to the bed rail. It felt as if his chest were being pulled apart from the inside. His muscles finally rebelled, and he collapsed back into the bed.

Bombing suspect.

Did that mean he'd been arrested? If he healed, would he be taken to jail? He couldn't catch his breath at all. His shirt felt too tight, like someone had grabbed hold and started twisting the fabric at the center of his back.

Then he realized he wasn't wearing a shirt. His chest was wrapped in bandages.

The door opened, and Michael gritted his teeth, ready to let loose on the policeman. But no, this was a nurse with a tiny cart. The officer followed her in and stood at the foot of the bed.

He looked like he was hoping he'd get a chance to draw his weapon.

The nurse—whose name tag read ELISSA—pulled a blood pressure cuff off the cart. She wore no makeup and her skin was barely lined, but there were traces of grey in her blond hair. Her movements were sure and confident. "Good morning," she said, as if she treated patients in handcuffs every day.

"We've been waiting for you to wake up." She pushed a few buttons on the monitor at the top of the cart, then reached for Michael's restrained arm. "May I get your blood pressure?"

"I didn't set any bombs," he said darkly, his eyes on the cop.

"I didn't say you did," the nurse said equably. She pulled the nylon cuff around his bicep and fastened the Velcro, then pushed a button on the machine to make it inflate.

Then she frowned and leaned closer. She pulled the sheet down, exposing the bandages around his chest. "We'll need to redo your dressing."

"He's fine," said the police officer.

"You can do your job and I can do mine," she said. "I need to check the stitches."

"Stitches?" said Michael.

She pulled a pair of latex gloves out of a little box on the cart. "Do you remember what happened?"

"I remember the restaurant. People were hurt." He glanced between her and the policeman. He remembered Tyler and the steel beam. He remembered exchanging texts with Hannah. He remembered finding people alive—and dead.

The blood pressure machine beeped and the cuff deflated. The nurse ripped the Velcro free. "You took four bullets."

Michael stared at her. His brain didn't want to process this information, and all he could say was, "I did what?"

"You were lucky. Only one needed to be removed." She gestured. "Your shoulder. The others glanced off your rib cage."

Only one needed to be removed. But he'd been shot four times?

She peeled at the edge of the bandaging. "I was going to yell at you for pulling your stitches loose, but these look great. You kids always heal fast."

His voice was tired. "I'm not a kid."

She chuckled. "One day, you'll wish someone was calling you a kid."

Michael hoped he'd live long enough for that to be true.

Then he realized what she'd said about healing. "How long have I been here?"

Her eyes flicked up to his. "Almost twenty-four hours."

A day! He glanced at the dim light peeking through the window blinds. It must be evening. The machine behind him kicked up its rhythm again. Michael swallowed. "My brothers. Do you know if my brothers are okay?"

"They're fine." A male voice spoke from the doorway, but Michael couldn't see past the nurse or the police officer. Then Hannah's father stepped into his line of sight. He carried a cup of coffee, and he looked about as worn and weary as Michael felt.

Then again, he was walking around unhindered, not chained to a bed with a bullet wound in his shoulder.

Marshal Faulkner clapped the police officer on the shoulder. "Thanks, Tony. You can take a break." He glanced at the nurse, then pulled a plastic chair away from the wall to sit down beside the bed.

Michael didn't want to look at him. He gritted his teeth as Elissa changed the gauze.

"Feel up to answering a few questions?" the fire marshal finally said.

"I want to see my brothers."

"Prisoners don't get visitors," he said.

Michael turned his head to glare. He tried to force as much fury into his voice as possible—because that was infinitely better than breaking down sobbing. "I shouldn't be a prisoner. I didn't *do* anything." His breath caught and he winced.

"Take it easy," said the nurse. She glanced at the fire marshal and gave him a stern look. "Not too much questioning. He just woke up."

Michael expected him to say something to put her in her place, but the marshal just nodded. "Yes, ma'am."

Then she was gone, wheeling the little cart beside her.

Michael stared at the ceiling. His throat felt tight. Maybe it was the fire marshal sitting here waiting to question him, or maybe it was the fact that Jack Faulkner was Hannah's father, but there was something extra-humiliating about being chained to a hospital bed, waiting for his fate.

He remembered the weeks after his parents were gone, how it had seemed he couldn't get through forty-eight hours without a social worker or a police officer or an attorney at his front door. He hadn't trusted any of them then, and he didn't trust Marshal Faulkner now. Then, he would have given anything for one of them to step in and tell him everything would be okay, that he could handle it if he'd just be patient with himself and let the right answers come to him.

Now, he knew it was up to him alone. He could get out of this if he kept the upper hand, if he didn't let emotion overrun his actions.

When he was sure his voice wouldn't crack and his eyes would stay dry, Michael said, "So I'm under arrest?"

The fire marshal sighed and rubbed at his eyes. "Maybe, Mike. I don't know."

That wasn't the answer he'd expected. Michael turned his head. "What does that mean?"

"It means I'll uncuff you, but I need you to be really honest with me."

"Fine."

The marshal unlocked the handcuffs first, and Michael felt his tension drop a few notches, just knowing he wasn't chained to this bed. The ankle chains were next. Everything rattled against the tile floor where the marshal dropped them.

Then the man straightened. "Did you start the fire at your house?"

"No."

"Did any of your brothers?"

"*No.*"

"Did you plant a bomb at the Roadhouse?"

"No."

"Do you know who shot you?"

"No." He remembered the flash of the phone's camera, seeing the edge of a face and some sandy-colored hair. It wasn't even his own phone, so he'd never be able to go back to it. A Guide? A cop? He had no idea. Still, it was something to offer.

"Someone was in the wreckage. He was looking down at me. As soon as I saw him, he was shooting."

The fire marshal looked interested at that. "Could you give me a description?"

"I only saw him for a second. Less than a second."

"But it was definitely a man?" Jack pulled out a notepad and a pen.

Michael thought. He'd assumed *man,* but really, his memories weren't even clear enough to confirm that much. "Maybe. I'm not one hundred percent sure."

"Race? Hair color? Height? Anything?"

Michael closed his eyes and tried to remember. All his thoughts would supply was a flash of movement, and then the sound of the gun firing. "Sandy hair. I don't know." He opened his eyes. "I don't know what happened to the second phone I used, but I might have caught him—or her—in one of the pictures."

Another quick note on the pad. "Why were you at the restaurant at all?"

Michael froze. His brain wasn't organized enough to lie, but he could go with the same story he'd given everyone else. "I was meeting someone about a job."

"Your brothers told an officer that, too. You know who *didn't* say that? Every single witness from the restaurant that I could question. They said you walked in and picked a fight with Tyler Morgan."

Michael fought to keep his voice even. "I didn't know Tyler would be there. The guy I was meeting never showed up. I thought—"

He stopped short. He'd almost said, *I thought Tyler had set me up.*

But that would lead to more questions.

"You thought what?"

Like that one. Michael shook his head. "Nothing. It's nothing. I didn't know he'd be there. I was supposed to meet someone else."

"Okay, give me a name."

Michael turned to stare at the ceiling again. "I don't remember."

The fire marshal pulled a plastic bag out of his pocket and held it up. "Maybe you should check your text messages."

Michael whipped his head around. His vision spun for a moment, and he had to blink.

His cell phone was hanging in a plastic baggie marked *Evidence*.

All he had to do was meet Marshal Falkner's eyes to know that his text messages had already been reviewed.

Michael had no idea what to say.

"You know what we found, don't you?" said the marshal.

The pictures. The texts. The threats. "Is that why I was chained to the bed? Because someone else was threatening *me*?"

"This is where the *really honest* part is going to be important, even though you haven't kept up your end of the bargain." The fire marshal paused. "I think this is bigger than just your neighborhood and that restaurant. Am I right?"

Michael had nothing to say. How could he explain? How could he even *begin* to wrap words around the scope of this?

Well. It began when I was a teenager, and my parents made this deal . . .

"This goes beyond the carnival, too, doesn't it?"

Michael didn't say anything.

"They're talking about bringing in the FBI," said the fire marshal. "You can talk to me or you can talk to them. I guarantee they're not going to give you the benefit of the doubt. You know something. It's obvious you know something. It's all over your phone."

Michael wished he'd run. This morning, when they'd made the decision to go to Adam's. He should have just gotten on the highway and started driving.

They had no proof, right? All they had were text messages he'd received.

"You mention Calla," said the fire marshal. "In one of your messages." He paused, waiting for a reaction. Michael didn't give him one, though the machine kept beeping out his heart rate, quicker than normal.

The man leaned against the bed rail. His voice was low, conspiratorial. "I'm sure it will come as no surprise to you that Calla was listed as missing after the fires at the carnival, and her body was never recovered. Want to tell me why you'd think she was sending you text messages claiming responsibility for the fires in your neighborhood?"

Oh, that's easy. Because Calla is a psychotic Fire Elemental who wants to start a war between the Elementals and the Guides. Oh, wait, you don't know about Elementals? Here, let me tell you . . .

Michael inhaled a long breath and set his jaw.

Marshal Faulkner held up the phone again. "You were texting Hannah around the same time. Did anyone else have access to your phone?"

No one had, but Michael was expecting a trap now, so he didn't answer.

You were texting Hannah at the same time.

And Michael thought it had been humiliating sitting here handcuffed to the bed. That had *nothing* on Hannah's dad reading their text exchanges. Michael racked his brain and tried to remember if he'd said anything incriminating—or embarrassing. For an instant he felt about fourteen, like he'd been caught in his bedroom with a dirty magazine.

Then Jack Faulkner said, "Are you putting my daughter in danger?"

Michael swung his head around. "No." His voice was rough and he had to clear his throat. "No. Never." He was trying to keep her *out* of danger.

"Someone is." For the first time, the fire marshal's voice held an edge. "And you know something about it. Do you understand what kind of position that puts me in?"

Michael met his eyes and realized he and Jack Faulkner were on opposite sides of the same coin. They both wanted to protect the people closest to them.

And they both felt powerless to do it.

"Yes," said Michael evenly. "I know exactly what kind of position that puts you in."

The fire marshal hit the bed rail and came halfway out of his chair. "Then tell me something!"

Michael recoiled. The movement was too sudden, and he felt every single one of those stitches pull this time. Stars danced through his vision.

A knock sounded at the door. "Everything all right in here?"

The marshal sat back down. He looked at the door, then cursed under his breath.

Michael glanced over. He recognized the sharply dressed man in the doorway, but he had to blink twice to be sure his eyes weren't playing tricks on him.

David Forrest was the father of Gabriel's girlfriend, Layne. He was also a high-powered criminal defense attorney with a price tag to match. He'd kept Gabriel out of jail when the town had been under attack from an arsonist, and even though he'd offered to waive his fees, Michael had looked up his consultation charges and sent him a check anyway.

The check had been cashed right away.

It had hurt the family bank account, but the damage to his self-respect would have taken longer to heal. Michael had never told Gabriel.

"I've spoken with the district attorney," David said. "I understand no charges are being filed at this time?"

"Not yet," said Marshal Faulkner. He didn't sound happy about it.

Michael glared at him. "You didn't tell me that."

David's eyebrows went up. "Did he tell you that you were under arrest?"

"He said *maybe*."

The fire marshal shrugged and sat back. "Depended on what you told me."

David looked back at Michael. "Did he read you your rights?"

"No."

Marshal Falkner picked up the handcuffs he'd removed and dangled them from a finger. "He wasn't in custody. It was just a conversation."

"I think you're done here," said David. "Unless we should pursue a complaint of harassment?"

For the first time, Hannah's father sounded pissed. "Go ahead."

"I want my phone back," said Michael. "And I want to see my brothers."

Marshal Faulkner and David Forrest exchanged glances. In that one look, Michael realized the fire marshal had hidden more than he'd let on.

"What?" said Michael. His voice did break, and he didn't care. He was going to crawl out of this bed and find them if he had to. He grabbed hold of the bed rail and pulled himself up. "Where are they? Are they okay?"

"They're fine," said David Forrest. His voice should have

been reassuring, but it wasn't. "They're in the cafeteria. I just saw them."

"And they're okay? What was with the look?" His chest felt like it might cave in again. "What's going on?"

Another knock, this one faint, sounded at the door. A young woman stood there, in thick glasses and a plain, shapeless suit, dressed more for function than for fashion. No makeup, hair in a simple ponytail. She carried a clipboard and a folder. "Mr. Merrick?"

"Yeah?"

"I'm from the Department of Family Services," she said. "I'm here to talk about your brothers."

Hannah shuffled the deck of cards and dealt around the table. She'd been playing poker in the hospital cafeteria for three hours, but she'd do it for three more if she had to.

Once everyone had two cards, Chris and Gabriel threw pretzels on the table to cover the blinds, and then the bet went to Nick.

Nick didn't glance at his cards, though he slid them between his fingers, leaving his eyes on Hannah. "You don't have to keep doing this."

She gave a meaningful glance at the pile of pretzels beside Nick. It easily dwarfed every other pile at the table, despite the fact that Adam kept eating from the stash. "Are you kidding?" she said, trying to keep the mood light. "My pride is at stake."

He ignored her attempted humor, but his voice wasn't unkind. "We'll be okay, Hannah. You don't have to stay."

His eyes, normally a bright blue, seemed dull and tired, leaving dark shadows above his cheekbones. His skin was pale, those few freckles on his face standing out as if they'd been drawn on. He looked exhausted. They all did.

She wondered what she looked like. She'd been here just as long as they had.

"I know I don't need to stay," she said quietly. "I want to."

"No one wants to spend twenty-four hours in a hospital."

"It hasn't been twenty-four hours yet. Are you going to bet or what?"

Now he did glance at his cards, then slid them toward her. "Fold."

She turned expectant eyes to Adam, who tossed two pretzels into the center of the table. Hunter followed suit.

Chris glanced at his cards, then looked at Hannah. His eyes were as tired as Nick's, cloaked with some combination of wary suspicion and fear. "Why?"

"Why what?"

"Why do you want to stay?"

"Because I care about your brother." She met his anger head-on, but she didn't take it personally. They were all ready to snap. The past day had been a careful mix of distraction and compassion and brutal honesty.

They'd been up all night long—and while she'd hoped Michael's brothers would fall asleep on the hospital couches at some point, they never had. *Adult Swim* on Cartoon Network had held their attention for a while, in a distracted kind of way, but that had worn off around dawn. They'd downloaded half a dozen new apps on their phones. They'd argued with hospital staff and begged for information on their brother—and later, they'd been surly and guarded with the policeman who'd come to ask them questions about what had happened at the Roadhouse.

Michael's brothers and Hunter knew less than she did.

Out of desperation, she'd tried to call her father, but he hadn't picked up, and he hadn't answered her texts.

Around dawn, she'd found board games stashed in a cabinet in the corner, but they'd glared at her when she'd asked if they'd like to play Uno.

"What?" Gabriel had said, his tone sharp since it was morning and no one had eaten. "No coloring books?"

"Actually, there are," she'd said. "Want to see who can make the most inappropriate picture out of Mickey Mouse Clubhouse?"

So they'd done that. She hadn't realized how . . . *creative* a bunch of teen boys could get. But at least it had cut through some of their tension.

Sometimes they'd sat in silence, just waiting, their worry permeating the very air. At one point she'd stood, planning to take a walk, wondering if maybe her presence was making them more uncomfortable, adding a layer of pressure to hold it together.

But they'd all looked up in surprise, full of questions about where she was going and whether she was coming back.

So she'd stayed.

Adam had shown up at some point this morning, bringing bags of pastries and a box of coffee that was ten times better than the crap in the hospital cafeteria. He'd spent the day here, too.

As the day had worn on into afternoon, Hannah's worry had begun to turn to dread. Michael's brothers should have heard something by now. Her father still wasn't answering her calls.

So she'd found a deck of cards. Poker was the first suggestion that had caught their interest. And held it.

Chris was still watching her with something like a glare on his face. "Can't you use some of your connections to find out what's going on?"

Hunter kicked him under the table. "Can't you stop being a dick for five minutes?"

Chris shoved out of his chair and went after him. Gabriel got a hold of him, but not before pretzels and playing cards scattered everywhere.

Hunter hadn't moved from his chair. His expression was full of derision. "Can't you grow up?"

Chris's breathing was too quick. "Fuck you, Hunter. What are you even doing here?"

Gabriel pushed him back in his chair. "Come on, Chris."

"Come on, *what*? He doesn't need to be here."

"Oh, because you give a crap?" said Hunter. "Sure looked like it when you were roaming the woods the other night."

Nick was picking up the fallen pretzels. "Stop," he said, his voice tired.

"Forget it." Chris jerked free of Gabriel's hold and walked away from the table. "I'm done."

They all picked up cards and pretzels in silence for a moment. "Should we go after him?" said Adam.

"Nah," said Gabriel. "Chris gets buried in his own thoughts sometimes. Leave him alone."

He's scared, thought Hannah. She knew guys like that, other firefighters who would lash out in anger when they were really scared shitless. But she didn't want to say it, not in front of his brothers.

"I'll go," she said. "Make sure he doesn't kill someone between here and wherever he's going."

No one stopped her, so she walked out of the cafeteria and into the main hallway. Since it was a Saturday afternoon, the hospital was crowded with visitors and staff, but she caught sight of Chris's angry form pushing through the double doors to the outside.

She hustled to catch him, expecting him to keep walking, but he dropped onto the painted bench just outside the doors and stared at the sky.

Hannah stopped beside him. November air bit her arms and tried to convince her to go back inside, especially when the clouds released a few droplets to sting her cheeks.

"Freezing rain," she said. "Want to come back inside?"

"No."

He wasn't looking at her, and she didn't know him well enough to know how far she could push. Crystalline droplets were collecting in his hair and on his jacket, melting where they found his face and hands.

If she had to put money on it, she'd say he was sitting here trying not to cry.

"Can I sit down?" she asked.

He looked away from the sky and met her eyes. "Is my brother dead? Is that why they won't tell us anything?"

His voice was so bleak that it caught her by surprise. She sat beside him. "No. He was alive when they pulled him out of the rubble."

"Then why can't we see him?"

"I don't know."

"Your dad is the fire marshal, right?" he snapped. "And you have no idea?"

"My dad doesn't exactly talk to me about active investigations," she said.

"I think he's a suspect," said a voice behind her.

She and Chris both turned. Hunter stood behind them, frozen droplets collecting in his hair and on his sleeves.

"Go away," said Chris.

Hunter ignored him and sat on the other side of Hannah. "I think he's a suspect in whatever happened at the restaurant."

A suspect? Hannah studied him. "Why?"

Hunter shrugged. His expression was just as bleak as Chris's. "He was at the scene of two major catastrophes. I'm pretty sure anyone in law enforcement can connect those dots."

"I told you to *go away*," said Chris.

His voice was so sharp that Hannah expected Hunter to snap back at him the way he had in the cafeteria. But out here in the cold, Hunter's expression looked almost wounded. He was silent for a long while. "Why?"

The freezing rain picked up, and each drop hurt where it struck her face. "Because you don't need to be here."

Hunter didn't say anything. He just kept letting the frozen precipitation beat down on him. Hannah wanted to ask if they should all move inside, but this conversation felt too precarious and she didn't want to upset the balance.

When Hunter finally spoke, his voice was low, and the words came slowly, as if he had to think through each one to get it out of his mouth. "You're right. I don't *need* to be here. He's not my brother. You're not my family."

Chris didn't say anything. He kept his eyes forward, unblinking against the rain.

"When I moved here," Hunter continued, "with my dad and my uncle gone, I didn't—" He stopped himself, seeming to search for words. "I didn't think anyone would ever *get* me, if that makes sense. When my grandfather threw me out of the house, I had like nine dollars in my wallet. I didn't eat for a day. Hell, your brother found me just before I was going to swipe cash from a Home Depot cash register."

Chris wasn't looking at him, but he was listening. She could feel it.

"When he offered to let me help with a job—" Hunter hesitated. "He could have just handed me a twenty and driven off. Most people wouldn't even have done that, you know what I mean? Hell, the school guidance counselor is *paid* to help me, but she just wanted to hassle me, and here your brother, who has every reason to hate me for everything I put you guys through—"

"He helped you," said Chris. His voice had lost the malice.

"Yeah."

Hannah knew this story. Michael hadn't just helped Hunter that one evening. He'd offered him a place to live. He'd stopped Hunter's grandfather from coming after the kid again. He'd opened his home and his family like it was nothing.

She understood Hunter's surprise. She'd been surprised when Michael had told her what had happened to Hunter—and what he'd done in return.

"No one has ever done something like that for me," Hunter said, then paused. "The other night, when I went after you—I really didn't know it was you. I shouldn't have . . ." He stopped himself. He pushed his hair back from his face and sighed. "I shouldn't have done what I did. I'm sorry. I just—it's been so tense, and I wanted to do something. I *needed* to do something. I wanted to help. I wanted—" He swore. "Forget it. This is stupid. Go sit with your brothers. I can sit out here."

Hannah didn't know this part, whatever had happened between Hunter and Chris to spark all this tension—and this apology.

Chris looked at him. "You don't have to sit out here."

Hunter's eyebrows went up.

Chris shrugged a little and looked up at the sky again. "We've been up all night. I shouldn't have been such a jerk."

Silence fell for a moment. Hannah glanced between them. "Friends again?"

"No," they both said simultaneously.

"I still don't trust you," said Chris. "I've seen you screw over my family too many times."

Hunter nodded. "I know." He paused. "I won't do it again."

"Prove it."

Hunter held his eyes. "I will."

CHAPTER 15

The day dragged on.

Hannah didn't dare tell Michael's brothers, but the sound of the gunshots still reverberated through her head. The gruesome pictures he'd sent her still waited on her phone. Even now, she couldn't close her eyes without seeing them.

Layne, Gabriel's girlfriend, and her little brother, Simon, had joined them at the table half an hour ago. Gabriel had looked so relieved to see them that Hannah had been surprised he didn't run out to hug them both.

Layne's father had been with them, but he hadn't lingered. David Forrest had left his kids at the table, saying he'd be back soon.

And then he'd hustled off.

He'd brought a new level of emotion to the table, though. Where before there'd only been thinly veiled panic, now there was a shred of something like hope.

Gabriel's hand was linked with Layne's, identical to the way Nick held on to Adam. He'd leaned into her and whispered, though not quietly, "I can't believe you got him to help."

Layne had leaned back into him. "Sometimes he surprises me."

Simon, who was deaf, had watched this, then made a disgusted noise. He signed something.

Gabriel had smiled thinly. "Whatever." He'd flicked a pretzel at him.

"What did he say?" Hannah had asked.

" 'Get a room.' "

And now they were waiting again.

It had been almost twenty-four hours.

When Hannah's father walked into the cafeteria, she almost did a double take. He was here? He'd been right here in this hospital and he *wouldn't answer her calls?*

He didn't look happy to see her either.

"Hannah. How long have you been here?"

She put the cards down. "Since last night."

"Who has James?"

"Mom. Who do you think?"

Michael's brothers watched this exchange like a game of tennis. Back. Forth. Waiting for something substantial to be said.

But her father was still fixated on James. "Have you talked to her? Is James okay?"

Something in his voice made her frown. "Yeah, he's fine. Why?"

His expression darkened. "You should be at home. You shouldn't be here."

"Have you seen Michael?" said Nick.

The question derailed her father's anger. His shoulders seemed to sag. "Yes. I've seen him. You can go up. He's in room forty-four-fifteen. He wants to see you."

They almost knocked the table over in their rush for the elevator.

Her father got in their way and put his hands up. "Family only."

Layne and Simon drew back to wait with Adam, but Gabriel got in her father's face. "Fuck that," he said. "They can all come. We've been waiting all day—"

"He's not alone," said her father. "For right now, family only."

That shut them up.

He's not alone. Her father's voice was full of foreboding. What did that mean? What had happened?

Hunter stepped back. His face was a little pale. "It's okay," he said. "Text me. It's okay. I can wait." When they hesitated, he gave Gabriel a shove. "Go!"

They went.

Hannah stood there for a minute, then moved to follow them.

Her father caught her arm. "You need to go home," he said. Then he looked past her, at the others. "You all need to go home."

"What's going on?" said Adam.

Hannah couldn't figure out the note in her father's voice, but it wasn't good. "What happened?" she whispered. "Is he dying?"

"No," he said. "Physically, he'll be fine."

Physically.

She jerked free of his hold. "What happened? What aren't you saying?" He wasn't responding, and it took everything she had not to hit him. "What did you do?" she demanded. "*What did you do?*"

"I didn't *do* anything, Hannah." He sounded tired. Exasperated. Weary. It wasn't a tone she was used to hearing from him. "There are laws here. Procedures I have to follow. This has nothing to do with me."

The elevator dinged, and David Forrest walked out. Apparently Layne thought she'd get more information from her father than Hannah had hope of getting from her own, because she rushed forward, full of questions. "Dad? Is he okay? What happened?"

Layne's father put his arm across her shoulders and squeezed. "He'll be fine. I'll tell you on the way home." He looked at Hunter. "Have you called your mother? I can drive you home."

Hunter had looked pale a minute ago, but now he looked positively sick. "No. Why do I need to call my mother?"

"Would someone please say what's going on?" said Adam.

Mr. Forrest glanced at him, then at Hunter. His expression

was grave. "Given the events of the past two days, and considering his brothers are under eighteen, the county has stepped in."

Now Hannah felt sick. The county couldn't do this. They *couldn't.*

"No," she said. "Can you stop them?"

"They have a court order. The Merrick house is unlivable and Michael is in the hospital. I can't stop them. It's temporary, but—"

"No," said Hunter. His voice was shaking now. "They can't."

"Wait," said Layne, her voice breathy. "Wait—you're saying—"

"I'm saying that Michael Merrick is losing custody of his brothers."

CHAPTER 16

Michael forced himself to sit on the edge of the bed. His chest still felt like it was being held together by nothing more than a few stitches. Every movement hurt. Every breath. Every thought.

Or maybe that was just the sensation of his world collapsing.

He'd been so worried about a Guide tearing his family apart. Not a nondescript girl with a clipboard in one hand and a court order in the other.

It felt as if hours had passed since everyone had vacated his room, but he was sure it hadn't been more than a few minutes. He couldn't even remember the social worker's name, but she'd agreed to wait in the hallway, to let him break the news to his brothers.

Some small, cowardly part of him didn't want to do it. He wanted to beg the nurse to come back, to pump him full of painkillers and let him drift off to a land of unawareness.

He didn't want to do this.

He didn't want to do this.

He didn't want to do this.

And then they were there, in the doorway, and he was going to have to do it.

A thousand words sat on the end of his tongue. He couldn't speak. If he didn't speak, it wouldn't happen.

They looked so young. He could remember them at eleven and twelve, staring at him just like this, silently begging him to make everything all right.

He'd failed. He hadn't made everything all right.

He couldn't breathe.

"Jesus, Mike," Nick said. He pushed past his brothers. "Are you in pain? Chris—get a nurse—"

"No," said Michael. He choked on the word. "Just—wait."

Wait. Stay here. If you stay here, I know you're here and I haven't failed.

They waited. He tried to breathe. The silence in the room pulsed with unspoken words.

They knew something bad was coming.

With each breath, the pain in his chest began to ease. Michael realized he didn't need to clutch at the bedrail to keep himself upright. The plastic railing felt slick under his palm.

As soon as Michael realized what was happening, he wanted his brother to undo it. He wanted to rip out his stitches and break his ribs. He wanted the pain.

He met Nick's eyes. "Stop, Nick." His voice almost broke. "Stop."

"I'm being careful. They won't know."

"Stop. Please. Just—stop."

"Okay," said Nick. His eyes had turned wary. And afraid. "Why?"

"I need—" He had to take another breath, and this one hurt for a reason that had nothing to do with his injuries. "I need—"

He couldn't even finish that sentence.

I need to tell you something.

I need you to forgive me.

I need you to know I never wanted this to happen.

Gabriel finally spoke, but he kept his voice down. "What the hell is going on here, Michael? Are they arresting you? Is that why there are cops in the hallway?"

Michael shook his head. Part of him wished that was why.

There were cops in the hallway in case his brothers resisted. Or in case he did.

Nick glanced at the doorway. "Close the door."

"No," said Michael. "They'll open it. Just—wait. Sit down. Wait."

There weren't enough chairs, but Nick and Gabriel sat, while Chris leaned against the small table beside the bed.

And they waited.

Michael wished for his parents to somehow be alive. He wished as hard as he had five years ago.

It didn't work any better now.

What would Dad do? What would he expect Michael to do?

He'd expect you to get your act together and pretend it's okay. Because if it's okay for you, it'll be okay for them.

It wasn't okay. This would never be okay.

He wasn't even sure he could fake it.

He looked at each of them and forced his voice to be steady. "This is temporary. I need you all to understand that." His voice wavered, and he caught it. "This is temporary."

"What's temporary?" said Nick. A lick of fear had crawled into his voice. "Michael. What's—"

"You're all under eighteen, and we don't have a house to live in."

"No," said Gabriel. "We're fine. We can stay at Adam's."

"Please," said Michael. "Please, listen to me."

"You can't do this," said Chris. His voice was quick and frightened. "Becca's mom said we can go there. We can—"

"I've tried," said Michael. "I'm sorry. I tried. It's already arranged."

Gabriel was out of his chair so fast, it almost fell over. He glanced at the door. "What's already arranged? What the fuck are you talking about?"

Gabriel's anger helped steady Michael. *This* he could deal with. He strengthened his voice. "DFS has ordered emergency custody. You're going to spend a few nights in a youth home, until I can get before a judge—"

"You can't do this," Chris said again. He was breathing like he'd run a race.

"We'll run," said Gabriel. His eyes were furious, and the

lights in the room flickered. "They can't keep us there. God-damn it, Michael, I can't believe you agreed to this—"

"I didn't! I didn't agree to any of it! Don't you know I'd do anything—"

"Not enough!" Gabriel's voice was full of fury, but his eyes were full. "You could have stopped this."

"I tried. David tried. It's already in motion."

Gabriel looked at the door, then back at his brothers. "Then we can't stay here. Nick. Chris. There's a stairwell at the end of the hallway—"

"Stop it." Michael had hold of Gabriel's arms before he even realized he was on his feet. Nick's powers had worked quickly—his body didn't protest the motion. "Damn you, Gabriel, don't you understand that I need you?"

Gabriel stared back at him, and under all that anger and bravado, Michael could see the little boy who was scared shit-less.

"If you run, they'll run with you. If you go along with this, they'll go with you. Don't you know that? I need you, Gabriel. *They* need you."

His brother's eyes were so full of fury and defiance that Michael was ready for Gabriel to jerk free and tell him to fuck off.

Instead, Gabriel's face crumpled, and he threw his arms around Michael. "Please don't do this. Please."

"We'll get through it," Michael said. His brother's grip made his chest ache, but this was a good kind of pain. "I promise. We can get through this. It's just a few nights until I can get before a judge."

"I can't do this, Michael. I'm not like you."

Michael's heart broke a little at those words. "You can. I know you can."

"What if the Guides find us?"

Michael's greatest fear, spoken out loud. "Then you run," he said, keeping his voice as low as he could. "You run, and you hide, and you keep your brothers safe. But that's the only rea-son. Do you understand me?"

Gabriel drew back and nodded. "What if they come after you?"

"Then you stay hidden. No powers."

"No," said Nick. "What if they come after *you*?"

"Then you take care of each other." Michael looked at Nick. His eyes were also red, his shoulders tight. "I need you, too. Someone has to keep Gabriel from veering off the rails."

Nick nodded. "I know."

Michael looked at Chris, who was still standing with his back against the side table. His fingers gripped the edge of the table so tightly that Michael could see white across his knuckles. "Chris—"

"We can't stay with you anymore." His breathing was shaky, and he wouldn't look over. "Got it."

"Chris—"

A gentle knock sounded at the door. The social worker was back. "How is everything going in here?"

His brothers shifted away from her, as if she were more imposing than a hundred-pound woman in a cheap wool suit.

"They're fine," said Michael. "They know."

They didn't look fine, but he kept his voice casual, and the grip of tension on the room loosened a notch.

She looked at her watch. "They'll be finishing up dinner in the home, and from what I understand, it's game night, so now would be a good time to head over, if everyone is ready."

Gabriel turned steely eyes his way. Michael could read every word in his expression. *Game night? Are you fucking kidding me?*

Michael looked back at him. "That sounds like a lot of fun. Don't you think?"

For an eternal instant, Michael waited for Gabriel to snap and turn this whole thing on its head. He'd done it before, and Michael could almost see him charging past the social worker and the police officers, getting thrown to the ground and Tasered, making everything three thousand times worse than it needed to be.

But then Gabriel let his shoulders drop, and he glanced at Nick and Chris. His voice was bland. "It sounds great. Come on, guys."

And just like that, they filed out of the room.

Silence fell around Michael like a cloak. He dropped onto the side of the bed and waited for something to happen.

Nothing did.

His brothers were gone. He was alone.

CHAPTER 17

Near midnight, Hannah found herself outside Michael's hospital room. The door was partially ajar, and the lights were off. He was curled on his side, the blanket draped over his form. The monitors cast an eerie glow on the edge of the bed, but she could tell his eyes were closed.

She slipped into the room, moving as silently as she was able. His breathing was soft and even, so she eased into the chair with barely a whisper of sound.

His eyes shot open anyway, and he shoved himself up on one arm.

"Easy," she whispered. "I'm sorry. I didn't want to wake you."

"You didn't." His voice was rough, and he ran a hand down the front of his face and pulled himself all the way to sitting. He must have been on a boatload of painkillers to move so easily this soon. His shoulders drooped as he looked at the door. "What time is it?"

"Almost midnight."

He nodded, but didn't look at her. "Do you know?" When she didn't answer right away, he turned his head. "Do you know what they did?"

The pain in his expression took her breath away. She nodded. "Yeah. I know."

He folded his arms across his stomach and seemed to curl in on himself. His breathing shook.

Then Hannah realized he was crying.

It took her by surprise. He was so strong—so *stoic*. Seeing Michael crying silently in the dark in a hospital bed surprised her as much as it would to find her father the same way.

She pulled the lever to drop the railing on her side of the bed and sat beside him.

"I'm sorry," she whispered. "I'm so sorry." She put a hand on his arm gently, unsure he'd welcome her touch.

He unwound his arms and pulled her closer. It put his face against her shoulder, his arms tight around her back. She could feel him shaking. The only other person who ever clung to her like this was James, after the really terrifying nightmares.

Only this wasn't a nightmare.

"I don't know where they are," Michael said, his voice thick with emotion. "They wouldn't tell me where they were taking them."

Hannah drew back enough to speak. "They wouldn't *tell* you? Don't they have to?"

"No. Said it was safer if I didn't know." He pulled back and seemed to gather himself a bit. "I've spent five years drilling it into their heads that I have to know where they are, and now it's the middle of the night and I have no idea." He glanced at the side table, then at the door. "I don't have a phone. I can't even call—"

"Shh. It's okay. They're okay." She stroked a hand down his face.

"I promised them, Hannah." His voice was rough and harsh and the pain in his words almost hurt her ears. "I promised I wouldn't let anyone take them away. And now—"

"You didn't fail them, Michael."

"I did." He put his face in his hands again. "I did."

"No. You didn't."

His voice took on a panicked edge. "What if I can't get them back? What if the judge says no?"

"That won't happen."

"Don't you know what happens in those kinds of places?" He dropped his hands and looked at her. His eyes were shining in the darkness. "If someone picks a fight with Gabriel—if someone finds out Nick is gay—" Another shaky breath. "And Chris. Chris hates me for this."

"He doesn't hate you."

"He's so young sometimes—" Michael shook his head. "He wouldn't even look at me."

"He's afraid."

Michael gave a laugh that was more of a sob. "That makes me feel better. Thanks."

She found his hand and held it. "They're together. They'll take care of each other."

"I hope so."

"I know so. They barely left each other to go to the bathroom."

Michael turned his head to look at her. "When?"

"Last night."

"Where were they last night?"

"Here. Well, downstairs."

He looked bewildered. "Wait. They weren't at Adam's?"

"No. They came here as soon as they heard. Hunter, too. And Layne and Simon and Adam."

"All night? They were sitting down there alone all night—"

"I stayed with them. They were okay."

Michael stared at her. His voice was soft with something like shame. "You didn't have to do that, Hannah."

"Your brothers were ready to climb the walls." She brushed another finger across his cheek, pulling a stray tear away. "Consider it a public service."

"What about James?"

"He stayed with my mom. He's all right. I went home for dinner and his bedtime story." She didn't mention that she'd had to wait for her father to fall asleep before she could sneak out again. She'd sent her mom a text message so she wouldn't worry, and hoped the woman would run interference if her dad decided to pitch a fit.

"I'm sorry you had to waste your time here."

"They're your brothers, Michael. It wasn't a *waste of time*." She paused. "I was worried about you, too. No one would tell us anything."

"I'm all right."

Said the man crying in the dark. She stroked a hand across his cheek again, feeling the beard growth there. He bowed his head and leaned into her touch. He always took her by surprise in these moments when he was quiet and passive, like an untamed lion that would only settle in her presence.

"I should leave so you can get some sleep," she said.

He shook his head. "I don't think I can sleep." He rubbed his hands down his face, catching her hand in his own, holding it against his face. "Every time I close my eyes, I see too many things."

She didn't mention that he'd seemed asleep when she'd walked in here—but then again, he'd startled so easily. "Do you think you could lie down? Rest?"

"No, I—no." His breath shook again, just a little. He kept a grip on her hand as if he worried she'd leave him here.

"Try," she said. "If you don't sleep, you won't heal." She kicked off her shoes and leaned back against the pillows, giving his hand a tug. "Lie down. I'll rest with you."

After a moment, Michael shifted to lie beside her. He pulled his hand free to stroke her hair back from her face. His fingers were warm against her cheek. After a moment, he shifted closer, until his forehead rested against hers.

She thought he might kiss her, but he didn't. Somehow this was more intimate, lying in the dark, dried tears on his cheeks and trust in his eyes. She was seeing a side of him that he didn't often show. To anyone.

For the longest time, he didn't move beyond touching her, his hand stroking the length of her cheek or the slope of her arm.

After a while, his movements slowed, and his eyelids fluttered. He fought it.

She put a hand against his face. "I'll stay," she whispered. "If that's okay."

He nodded and took a long breath. His eyes drifted closed. "Always."

Michael woke to a cart rattling past his room and sunshine peeking through the window blinds. He was alone in the bed, and the sheets were cold.

Hannah. Had he dreamed her?

His hand shifted, crumpling a piece of paper. He held it up.

Had to be home to get James breakfast, then on first shift.
I'll be back as soon as I can.

She'd signed it with an H.

And a heart.

It made his own heart sing.

He had so little *good* to hang on to that he wanted to clutch this silly little note to his chest and never let go of it. He folded it in half and tucked it beneath the card from the social worker.

A nurse knocked on his door and announced it was time for vital signs. She was different from the nurse the previous evening. Her name tag read MARY PAT. He obediently let her take his blood pressure and temperature.

She made a note in her computer, then said, "I hear you get to go home today."

"I do?" But then he realized that *home* didn't really mean home. They just weren't keeping him here.

She nodded and pulled the blood pressure cuff from his arm. "The doctor will be around with your discharge instructions later this morning."

She was gone, wheeling her cart into the next room, before he realized he had a dozen questions. Where would he go? How would he get there? What had happened to his wallet and the clothes he'd been wearing at the bar?

His brain couldn't process all these questions. Not yet. He curled against the pillow and read the note from Hannah again. He could still smell her on his sheets.

Other memories started to crowd those thoughts, darkening his mood. His house, burning. The bomb. The bodies in that ravine. The gunfire.

His brothers, walking through the doorway as DFS took them away.

His throat felt tight again. He'd never felt so alone.

A hand rapped on the door, and a hushed voice said, "Wait. He might he asleep."

"He's not asleep. He's wallowing. Mike, get up."

Hunter's voice. Michael lifted his head. Hunter and Adam stood in the doorway.

He frowned. "What are you doing here?"

"We aren't allowed to see the guys, so we figured you were better than nothing." Hunter came into the room and dumped a duffel bag unceremoniously onto one of the plastic chairs. "Here. I hope they fit. If they don't, blame Adam."

"Wait. What—?"

Hunter snatched the piece of paper from the side of the bed. "What's this?"

"Hey! Give that—"

Hunter's eyes flicked up to him, and his lips twisted into a shadow of a smirk. "H? And a *heart*? She'll be back? Dude. This is a *hospital*."

"Shut up, Hunter." Michael snatched the note out of his hands. "How did you guys get in here?"

"Walked," said Hunter. "Well, from the parking garage. Up until then we were *driving*—"

"They said you could have visitors," said Adam.

"And we knew you didn't have clothes," said Hunter. "Though now that I'm this close to you, I kind of wish we'd brought you a toothbrush."

The banter reminded him of his brothers, and while it hurt, it felt good, too. He scrubbed his hands down his face and thought a toothbrush sounded delightful. Maybe he could get one from the nurse. "No—seriously. What are you doing here?"

Hunter raised an eyebrow. "We. Brought. You. Clothes. And—"

"Come on."

"We're being serious." Adam came over to lean against the wall. His voice held some of the emotion Michael felt. "We saw them when they left. They're *not* allowed visitors. Not at first."

Them. Michael hadn't thought of what his brothers' being taken away would mean to anyone outside his family. Becca. Quinn. Adam. Layne. Would his brothers be in school tomorrow? How would that work?

Michael had to clear his throat. "Were they okay?"

"Shaken up," said Adam. "They said their phones would be confiscated for the first three days." He smiled, and it was a little sad. "So Nick slipped me his. He said to give it to you." He pulled it out of his pocket and held it out.

A phone! Michael felt like he'd been handed a missing limb.

But then he realized what Adam had said.

Three days.

"It won't be three days," he said. Now he understood why Hunter and Adam had come here: this separation was too new, too raw. The county had torn his family apart without warning, and here their friends were trying to glue the remaining scraps back together.

"How long do you think it'll be?" said Hunter.

"At least another day. I can't get in front of a judge on Sunday." He used to love Sundays because it was the one day a week he didn't schedule landscaping jobs—but he'd give up Sundays for the rest of his life if he could accelerate time right now. "David said he'll try to get me a hearing tomorrow."

"They'll be okay," said Adam.

"Did they tell you where they were going?"

"No," said Hunter. "The social worker lady said it's to prevent a 'conflict of interest,' whatever that's supposed to mean."

She'd said the same thing to Michael. "It means they've had

issues with people breaking out—with outside help. Or people breaking in to cause harm."

"Breaking out?" said Adam. "It's not prison."

Michael looked at him. "It's not home either." He frowned and admitted a truth he didn't want to share. "I'm glad they're locked down. It'll keep them safer than being with me."

Hunter and Adam exchanged glances. "What does that mean?" said Adam.

Michael glanced at the hallway, which wasn't busy, but still had a fair amount of traffic. "Close the door."

Adam did.

Michael kept his voice low anyway. "It means Friday night was a setup. Whoever started the fires in our neighborhood set that bomb as a trap."

"For you?" said Hunter. "So you think whoever wanted to meet about that landscaping job was—"

"There was no job, Hunter." Michael hesitated. "When you guys were sleeping at Adam's, whoever started the fires in our neighborhood asked me to meet him." Now he realized the insidious threat behind those text messages. *Bring your brothers. Bring the police. Bring anyone that makes you feel comfortable.*

It was supposed to be reassuring.

Now, in retrospect, it was terrifying.

What if he'd listened? What if he'd called the police and they'd stormed that bar? How many more people would have been killed?

Hunter folded his arms across his chest. "So you lied."

"I didn't lie! I did it to protect you. All of you."

"Do your brothers know?"

"No."

Hunter's expression had turned into a glare. "Everything we've been through, and you lied. We could have come with you. We could have *helped*. Do you have any idea what they're saying on the news? Do you have *any idea*?"

"Damn it, Hunter, of course I have an idea! I was there! And you all could have been killed!"

"Easy," said Adam. He glanced at the door.

Michael sighed and dropped his voice. "It was *too dangerous.*"

"Fuck dangerous," said Hunter. "We've been through worse. *With you.* You know that. We could have *helped.*"

Michael glared back at him. "I'm not apologizing for this. I'm not putting all of you in danger."

"Too late! You don't even know where your brothers *are*, and they have no idea someone could be after them! You didn't even *warn them*!"

"I know that! You don't think I know that?"

"Hey." Adam got between them, his hands up. "Fighting isn't going to solve anything."

Michael didn't realize he'd swung his legs onto the floor, or that Hunter was on his feet, ready to get into it.

He knew better than this. Michael sat back. "You're a kid, Hunter. Like it or not, *you are.* All of you are. I'm not putting you in harm's way if I can help it."

"I'm not helpless," said Hunter, his voice full of acid. "Your brothers aren't either."

"I know you're not—"

"And you're obviously not doing the greatest job keeping everyone safe, are you?"

Michael flinched.

"Stop," said Adam. "Both of you. Stop."

But Hunter's words lingered in Michael's head, an arrow of guilt when he least expected it.

Hunter was right. He hadn't kept them safe. That's why he'd lost them.

"This isn't just about you," Hunter snapped.

"I know that!"

"Fix it," said Hunter. "Right now. Fix it. Tell us what really happened."

Michael froze, not wanting to give in. But keeping everything a secret hadn't kept anyone safe—and in fact, he'd ended up putting more people in danger. With a sigh, he explained everything he knew, from the text messages he'd received while he was sitting on Adam's porch to the fact that whoever was attacking them had hidden in a tree. He tried to recount the text messages as well as he could, but his phone was still *evidence*, and he doubted he'd be getting it back anytime soon.

When he was done talking, Hunter still looked pissed—and Adam looked thoughtful.

"How'd he get your number?" said Hunter.

"I have no idea. It's not like it's private. I have business cards, a website. . . . He could have gotten it from anywhere."

"How do you know it's a *he* at all?" said Adam.

They booth looked at him, and he shrugged. "Nick said a sixteen-year-old girl was responsible for the last round of arson, right? Could she be responsible now?"

"Yes," said Michael. "But Calla has fallen off the map again. I tried reaching out to her, but her phone has been disconnected."

"Was it really a bomb?" said Hunter. "Not a gas line or something?"

"The fire marshal said they'd found fragments," said Michael. "I don't have details, but they seem convinced."

Hunter shrugged. "A bomb would mean some kind of sophistication. I'm not saying a teenager couldn't have done it, but for the level of damage they showed on the news, especially if it were on some kind of timer or remote control . . "

"I agree," said Michael. "And I think I saw the person who shot me."

Adam's eyebrows went up. "Did you tell the police? Maybe they could hook you up with a sketch artist or something."

"No. It was too fast. I might have seen the side of his face." Michael closed his eyes and tried to remember, but nothing was clear. It was as bad as when he'd been questioned by the fire marshal. No details. "I haven't seen him before."

"But he had a bomb," said Hunter. He leaned back in his chair and looked at the ceiling. "And he had a gun, too. A Guide? Any pentagrams?"

"None," said Michael. "At least none that I've seen yet." He paused. "Your father was a Guide. Would he have set a bomb to trap an Elemental?"

Hunter thought it over. "According to my mother, he wasn't

in the business of trapping Elementals at all. He was more *hands-on*, anyway. A bomb wouldn't have been his style. He used to tell me that guns made killing too impersonal, but they were a necessary evil. He said that even from a distance, a death should *mean* something. I can't imagine him setting a bomb and walking away." He shrugged, rolling his shoulders, thinking about it. "That said, he would have known where to find someone who could do it. He and my uncle were in the Marines together. Special forces. They had contacts—and that's not uncommon among Fifths. Just because my dad wouldn't have done it doesn't mean there's not someone out there who would. If I pull a trigger, I know where the bullet is going to end up—but not everyone is the same way. Some people don't care about collateral damage. My dad used to talk about Elementals who could use their power to enhance a weapon, making them more dangerous. An Air Elemental could guide a missile, or spread an airborne agent, right? A Guide could use his power the same way. There's a reason the Guides say the ends justify the means."

Adam was staring at him, his eyes a little wide.

"What?" said Hunter.

"Nothing."

Hunter gave him half a smile. "Gonna sleep with one eye open tonight?"

"Maybe both."

Michael glanced between the two of them. "You didn't go home?" he asked Hunter.

"No." He sobered. "If this guy hasn't connected me to my mother, I don't want to put her in danger. My grandparents, either. Their farmhouse is too remote—I'd never be able to control the perimeter, or escape quickly, if I needed to. Adam is right in town. I could disappear in a heartbeat if necessary."

"Thanks," said Adam.

Hunter grinned. "We. *We* could disappear in a heartbeat."

"I'd rather we not disappear at all," said Adam.

"Actually, that brings up an interesting point," said Hunter.

"Disappearing?" said Michael.

"Yeah," said Hunter. "Whoever did this destroyed the neigh-

borhood on Thursday and blew up the bar on Friday. Today is
Sunday. Where'd he go?"

"I don't know," said Michael.

"I have a better question," said Adam.

They both looked at him.

"Where's he going to strike next?"

CHAPTER 18

Sunday mornings were usually the only time Hannah had to herself: Sunday school for James, volunteer time at the church for her mother, and paperwork in the office for her father.

The whole family had gone to church every Sunday when she was growing up. Hannah and her mother had participated in every potluck or holiday bazaar. Hannah had helped in the nursery school and sung Christmas carols with the children's choir. When her father wasn't on duty, he'd joined them.

Then Hannah had gotten pregnant. It shouldn't have been a massive scandal—but it had been, Suddenly, she hadn't been welcome in the nursery school. When she'd tried to serve food at the pancake breakfast, she couldn't miss the whispers. The judgmental looks. The comments behind her back.

And to her face.

Her mother had been supportive, but Hannah couldn't take it. She'd stopped going. As soon as she'd stopped, her father had, too.

So much for the perfect family.

When James had grown old enough for Sunday school, Hannah's mother had insisted, and since he had friends in the class, Hannah didn't object. Luckily, he wasn't a target of open mockery and shame. She usually used the time to catch up on classwork for the college courses she was taking—especially since she was already behind this week.

But by the time she dropped James off at church, Hannah was ready to drop. She couldn't remember if she'd missed one night or two nights of sleep, but whatever, she was going to take a shower and crash into bed for a few hours before heading to the firehouse.

Her father's car was waiting in the driveway when she got home.

Hannah sighed. She didn't want to get out of the car.

His presence shouldn't have left her with a sense of foreboding. They lived in the same house, for goodness sake—though they rarely did more than pass like ships in the night. Her father had spoken more to her at recent crime scenes than he'd said in weeks.

Maybe she could just walk inside and go up to her room.

She didn't understand why every time she had to face him, it was as if the last five years vanished and she was seventeen again, walking around with shame riding on her shoulders.

Well, if she sat out here in the car long enough, he'd definitely come to investigate.

Hannah closed the car door as quietly as she could and eased into the house like she wanted to rob the place.

This is pathetic. You're pathetic.

She didn't see her father on the main level, so she quickly loped up the steps, springing silently on the balls of her feet. She could grab some sweats from her dresser and be in the bathroom before he even knew she was home.

Except for the fact that her father was sitting on her bed.

He looked like he'd been up all night, too. The few lines on his face seemed more pronounced, and she could see dark circles under his eyes.

Hannah frowned at him. He hadn't been in her room in *years*. "What are you doing?"

"Where were you?" he said.

"I took James to church," she said.

Something in his expression tightened. "He's with your mother?"

"Yeah. He'll ride back with Mom after lunch like they always do. What's with the look?"

"Where were you earlier?"

She shrugged and began digging through her dresser.

"Hannah."

She looked at him. "What? I need to take a shower, Dad."

"I'm not stupid. Did you go back to the hospital?"

"I'm an adult. It's none of your business. "

His voice remained level. "I'm not trying to police your behavior. I'm trying to keep you safe."

"Yeah, okay. Is this more of your procedures nonsense?" She pulled a jersey T-shirt and cutoff sweats from the bottom of the drawer and went to move past him. *I'm not trying to police your behavior.* That was rich.

"What are you talking about?"

Hannah glared at him. "How could you report Michael to social services? How could you *do* that?"

He looked incredulous. "How could I *not*, Hannah? His brothers are minors. You want me to leave them out on the street? You think that's better?"

"No, I expect you to show a little compassion. He's not some stranger. He's not some deadbeat dad who left a toddler home alone. He just lost his *home*, and you took his family away."

Her father's face didn't change. "Every time you talk like this, I wonder when you're going to grow up."

"If that's what growing up means, I hope I *never* do. Does Mom have any idea of what you did?"

"Your mom has nothing to do with this."

"Sure. Because she would have done the *right* thing. She would have made them meals, or heck, she would have invited them to stay here. She would have treated them with kindness, instead of acting like Michael is some felon."

"This is an active investigation, Hannah. People are dead.

The FBI is involved. Do you understand that? Do you have any idea what a conflict of interest that would be?"

"Yeah, I do. And somehow I still manage to treat people with common decency. You think you're so smart that you figured out I was at the hospital all night? Clearly you weren't concerned enough to head over there and find out for sure. You took his family away and you didn't even wait to see if he was okay. He was *alone,* Dad."

Finally, her father's expression shifted, but only for a second. "I'm not at fault here, Hannah. I haven't done anything wrong."

"No, you never do. Trust me, I get the memo every day."

"I'm not going to argue this with you. I have a job to do. I did it. End of story."

"Yes, sir." She saluted.

He set his jaw, but he didn't lose his composure. "Until this investigation is over, I don't want you seeing Michael Merrick anymore. Do you understand?"

"Are you for real?"

"Yes, Hannah, I'm *for real*. This is a matter of life and death, and as much as I want to share details with you, I can't. So I'm asking you—begging you—to listen to me. For once."

"For once. God, you really are an asshole. Move." This time she didn't even wait for a response. She just ducked under his arm and headed for the bathroom.

She fully expected him to grab her arm, but he didn't. "What does that mean?" he said.

She turned in the bathroom doorway. "It means I listened to you for seventeen years. Every word. You know how many times I didn't listen to you? *Once.* And I've been paying for it ever since. Guess what, Dad? I'm a grown-up. No matter what you think, I'm a good mother. I'm a good firefighter. And I'm going to be a good paramedic. Michael is not a criminal. He's doing the best he can, despite people like you making it impossible. If I want to see him, I'm going to see him. And if you don't like it, that's just too bad for you."

With that, she slammed the door and turned on the faucet,

glad that the sound of the shower would drown out anything else he had to say.

The nurse had a toothbrush. Toothpaste, too. And a razor and shaving cream. She removed Michael's IV and examined his stitches, then told him he could take a shower. Adam and Hunter said they'd wait.

Michael turned the water as hot as he could tolerate and stood under the stream for a while.

He still had no idea where to go. Back to Adam's for the night? And then what?

Guilt tweaked his thoughts. He should have warned Hannah. But what would he have said? *A crazy bomber/arsonist took a picture of you and James to threaten me. Watch your back. Oh, and he might have Elemental powers.*

Sure. Maybe he'd like another night in the hospital—in the psych ward.

No matter what Michael thought of the fire marshal, he was glad Hannah lived with a man who could provide some protection for her and James.

Unlike you.

He told his conscience to stick it.

The water felt good across his shoulders, but eventually his skin began to prune. He'd need to face reality sooner or later. It might as well be sooner.

The clothes still had tags on them, and Michael added another line to his ongoing mental list. He'd have to pay Adam back when he found his wallet. Everything felt starchy and new, and the shirt was nothing he would have bought for himself, but it all fit. Even the shoes.

When he walked out of the bathroom, he found another visitor waiting in the chairs next to his bed.

"Wow," said Tyler. "That is one teal shirt."

"What are you doing here?" Michael threw the bag on the bed. Hunter and Adam didn't seem fazed by Tyler's presence, but they didn't have the history with him that Michael and his brothers did.

If he didn't know better, he'd say Tyler looked hurt. "Gee, Merrick. Glad to see you made it through okay." He stood, and Michael realized he had crutches with him. "Guess I'll leave you alone, then."

"He came to check on you," said Adam.

"Said you were trapped under the restaurant together," added Hunter.

Michael sighed and sat on the edge of the bed. He'd been so caught up in the drama with his brothers that he hadn't even *thought* to ask if Tyler had survived.

Pretty shitty, especially considering that Tyler had probably kept them all from burning to a crisp.

"Stop," he said to Tyler. "Wait. I'm sorry."

Tyler turned, and one crutch squeaked against the floor. "Did you just say you're *sorry*?"

"Don't make me take it back." He paused and gave Tyler a clear once-over. "I'm glad you didn't lose your leg or anything."

"They said I might need surgery. Screw that. I told them to give me the good pain pills and let me get the hell out of here."

Michael raised his eyebrows. "And they listened?"

"Nah, but Quinn brought me a lighter. My second ultrasound looked amazing. They must have read the first one wrong. The crutches are really just for show. " Tyler half smiled. "Maybe I should have brought you a bag of sand or something."

"I'm all right. Nick helped." Michael swallowed.

Tyler glanced at Hunter and Adam. "Yeah, they told me what happened." He paused. "What are you going to do?"

"I don't know." He gave a laugh though nothing was very funny. "I don't even know where my wallet is, much less—"

"Here," said Hunter. He pulled a plastic bag from beneath his chair. "The nurse brought this by. She said it was everything you had on you."

Michael began pulling things free. His jeans: filthy and torn. His shirt: filthy, torn, *and* bloody. His shoes followed the trend.

But at the bottom of the bag was his wallet—with everything

intact, from what he could tell—and his watch. He pocketed the first and slipped the second over his wrist. In the pocket of his jeans he found his keys.

He pocketed those, too. "At least I have access to a vehicle," he said. Maybe his day was looking up.

Adam and Hunter exchanged glances.

"What?" said Michael. "Jesus. I can't handle one more thing. *What?*"

Hunter winced. "The truck isn't drivable."

"Define 'isn't drivable.' "

"Like . . . you can't drive it."

"Hunter!"

"You were parked behind the bar," said Adam. "Hannah said most vehicles took some damage, but the truck had a beam through the cab. They towed it. You can probably—"

"Stop. God. Stop." Michael ran his hands down his face. His truck. His *truck*.

No. Not his.

His father's.

He waited for this news to tighten his chest and bring tears to his eyes, but surprisingly, he felt nothing. Maybe all his emotion had been used up.

"Have you been back to the house?" he said, his voice bleak. "What about the SUV? Is that drivable?"

"They're not letting anyone on the court," said Hunter. "Well, not us anyway. We tried, but they've got it cordoned off, with an officer standing guard."

"Great."

"I have a truck," said Tyler.

"Good for you," Michael snapped. "I'm sure you have a place to live, too."

"Maybe if you'd quit with the shitty attitude I could say, yeah, I do, and yeah, you can stay with me."

Now they were all staring at him. For the first time, Tyler looked uncomfortable. He shrugged and looked back at the door. "If you need a place. I have a spare bedroom. I'm just saying."

"Why would you do that?" said Michael.

"Because it's the right thing to do."

Michael didn't buy it. "You? Altruistic? Try again."

"Because it's what my sister would want me to do."

That, Michael bought. It had been years since Tyler's sister had died, but Michael still had clear memories of Emily Morgan. She'd been the first Elemental in town who treated him like a human being instead of someone who needed to be put to death.

"Won't it piss off your parents?" he asked Tyler.

"You going to call and tell them?"

"No, but I don't want to wake up chained to the bed and set on fire, either."

"Look, man, whatever you want to do with your sex life is your business—"

"I'm serious," said Michael. Tyler and his friends had once trapped Michael in a parking lot. They'd pinned him to the ground with a truck chain and Tyler himself had put a butane lighter against Michael's face.

It had been years ago, but Michael hadn't forgotten. Tyler's sister had rescued him—but that moment had led down the path that had ended with Emily's death.

Tyler hadn't forgotten either. He looked at Michael. "I can't play both sides anymore. I'm either one of you or one of them." His expression didn't waver. "I don't know who blew up the restaurant, but I don't think it's a coincidence that he sent you to a place my parents own. A place where I'd be. Do you?"

Michael hadn't considered it. He'd been focused on the people he'd been told to bring: his brothers and the police. He hadn't thought about the people who'd already been there.

"No," he said. "I don't think it's a coincidence at all." He paused. "What if he targets your place?"

Tyler's expression darkened. "He already tried to get rid of me once."

"You afraid?"

"Fuck that," said Tyler. "I dare him to try. What do *you* say, Merrick?"

Michael looked at him, and realized he could see something in Tyler that couldn't be said for anyone else in his life. Tyler was an adult. He was a powerful Fire Elemental—possibly more powerful than Gabriel. He owed Michael nothing—and vice versa. Tyler wasn't an obligation or someone who needed protection.

Tyler was an equal.

Michael smiled, and for the first time in forever, he felt a shadow of genuine emotion behind it. "I say bring it."

CHAPTER 19

Michael sat at Tyler's kitchen table and studied the list he'd made. He couldn't decide if it made him feel better or worse about the state of things.

1) ~~Check on brothers~~
2) ~~Reassign cell phone number~~
3) ~~Buy more clothes~~
4) Find out status of truck
5) Find place to live
6) Cancel jobs? Rent truck?
7) Talk to David about custody stuff
8) Talk to David about legal stuff
9) Call insurance. House secure?
10) Repay Adam

He'd taken care of the easiest things first. He wasn't allowed to talk to his brothers, but as soon as he'd had access to a working phone, he'd called the social worker to find out if they were okay. She'd assured him that they were fine and she would pass on that he'd asked about them.

Her manner had been cool and distant, but Michael couldn't hate her for it. He'd tried to sound as confident as he could while telling her he'd straighten out their living situation over the next day or so, and he'd be arranging a court date with his attorney as soon as possible.

She'd wished him luck and hung up.

Tyler had let him borrow his truck to run errands, and Michael had taken Nick's phone to the wireless store to see if he could move everything from his phone to this one. He was half lucky: he could have access to his old number, but his contacts, photos, and messages would all have to wait until he had his old phone back.

But still. Something was better than nothing. He'd been able to text Hannah to tell her what was going on.

She'd promised to call him after her shift.

Clothes had been next, and it had been so long since he'd bought new clothes for himself that he'd had to check the tag of the jeans Adam had bought, just to find his size.

Now he was back at Tyler's, sitting at the table, staring at his list.

He left a message for his insurance agent.

He left a message for David Forrest.

He thought about leaving a message for the fire marshal, but he didn't think he should speak to anyone in law enforcement until he spoke with an attorney first. David had made that abundantly clear yesterday.

He didn't have the pictures he'd taken. He had no way to contact whoever had been sending those text messages—not that he wanted to. Anyone else he could think to call was either a liability—Becca, or maybe Hunter's mother and grandparents—or a complete jerkoff who wouldn't help anyway—Bill Chandler, Becca's father, who was also a Fifth like Hunter, and a former Guide.

He tapped his pen against the paper and thought.

"What did you come up with?"

Michael looked up. Tyler was across the table, surrounded by textbooks and notebooks and loose paper.

"Not much," Michael said. He sighed and rubbed at the back

of his head. This felt weird, sitting here with a guy he'd spent much of his life hating. "Where's your girlfriend? I thought Quinn would have practically moved in by now."

"She lives with Becca, which means Bill has them both under lock and key until this is over." He paused. "I wouldn't want her here right now anyway."

Michael understood that. They lapsed into silence again.

He couldn't take it. He fought for something to talk about. "How's schoolwork?"

Tyler opened a bottle of Mountain Dew and gave him a look. "You don't give a crap."

"You're right." But sitting here made him wonder if this was what his life would have been like if his parents hadn't died. Tyler was a year or two younger than Michael, but he'd followed a traditional path: graduating high school, going to college, moving out and getting a place of his own. Tyler had beer in his refrigerator and cabinets full of food. Michael would buy a six-pack every now and again, but he'd always kept it hidden in the back of the garage—more so he wouldn't have to explain it during a surprise social worker inspection than because of any worry his brothers would snatch one. Their own cabinets were always a little barren because four people went through food *fast*.

But the biggest surprise for Michael had been the *quiet*. Tyler's apartment didn't have four teenage boys banging doors or stomping up stairs or blasting music or roughhousing in the living room. Tyler's apartment was *his*.

"Sorry my place isn't a thrill-a-minute." Tyler gestured at the television. "Watch TV or something if you're bored."

Bored. Was that what this was? Michael couldn't remember the last time he'd been bored. If he wasn't actively *doing* something, he was usually sleeping.

"What do you Merricks usually do?" said Tyler.

"They go to school," said Michael. "I work. You know that."

Tyler was silent for a moment. He sat back in his chair and

balanced a pencil between his fingers. "What are you going to do about the landscaping stuff?"

"I don't know." Michael looked back at his list. "I need my laptop so I can call people. I don't even know what jobs I had lined up this week. I know my regulars, of course, but it doesn't matter. I can't pull a trailer on my shoulders." He tried to guess how many people would drop his service if he canceled this week. He didn't want to think about it too hard—especially since they were coming into winter.

"If you can drive me to class, you can take my truck during the day," said Tyler.

Michael almost snapped, but he reminded himself that Tyler wasn't setting him up to watch him fall. Even so, he didn't like feeling obligated to someone who once would have used it against him. "Thanks." He paused. "It's going to depend on whether I can get access to my stuff."

"You want to go see?"

"Hunter said he and Adam were stopped at the end of the road."

"Yeah, but it's *your* house. You don't think you can flash some ID and get access?"

"I don't know," said Michael.

"So I'll ask you again." Tyler leaned in against the table. "You want to go see?"

No cop car sat at the end of the cul-de-sac, but yellow sawhorses blocked the pavement and declared that the road was closed.

They still had a pretty clear view of the damage that had been done.

Tyler blew out a breath. "Holy shit."

In the bright light of day, everything looked worse than Michael remembered. Family homes turned to nothing more than piles of charred lumber and rubble—with the exception of his own, which stood alone, dark and smoke damaged. The pavement had buckled in places, sometimes severely, and the sidewalk had the appearance of a shattered pane of glass, with broken lines scoring the surface. Beyond the homes, he could see downed trees along the edge of the woods. It looked like the set of a post-apocalyptic movie, not the barren shell of the neighborhood he'd grown up in.

He didn't want to be here. He didn't want to see this.

Tyler took his foot off the brake, and for an instant, Michael wondered if he'd spoken the words aloud, if Tyler was going to turn the truck around.

But no, Tyler pulled up on to the fractured sidewalk and drove around the barriers. They rocked and swayed with the motion of the truck moving across the broken pavement, and Tyler stopped at the top of the loop, just at the end of the Merrick driveway.

"Do you want me to drive all the way up to the house?" he said.

"No." Michael swallowed.

"Do you want me to leave you here to have a good cry?"

"Shut up, Tyler." But the words hit their mark. Michael unbuckled his seat belt and pushed the door open.

Nausea hit him as soon as his feet touched the ground. He had to hold on to the door for a moment.

Tyler stopped by the front of the truck. "You all right?"

"Yeah."

But he wasn't. A lot of people had died here. He didn't just know it. He could *feel* it. The emotion, the energy, the memories and terror and destruction, all trapped in the ground.

He remembered a school field trip to Antietam back in eighth grade, during a class unit on the Civil War. He'd stepped off the bus and almost puked on Annabel Scranton. The entire day was a hazy memory, but it was the longest six hours of his life. He'd never been more relieved than when he was allowed to climb back on the bus for the ride home.

He'd thought he was getting the flu or something until they were driving down the highway and all the queasiness disappeared. He mentioned it to his parents that night over dinner, and his father had put down his fork and told Michael to grab his coat.

They'd gone to an old cemetery at the edge of town.

Michael had been glad he hadn't eaten much dinner.

It had been one of the first signs that he was going to be far more powerful than his father ever had been.

He let go of the truck. "Come on."

The still silence pressed down on Michael as they walked. His street was *never* silent in the middle of the day. Too many kids, too many cars, too many lives. Now there was nothing.

"Can you feel it?" said Tyler, his voice almost hushed.

"Yeah." Michael glanced over. "How did you know?"

"I feel something too. From the fires." He made a face as if he smelled something distasteful. "I don't like it."

Michael expected the front porch steps to flex and shift under his weight, but the wood was strong, though he could see a few panels farther down had cracked and split—whether from the earthquake or the fire, he had no idea.

The door wasn't even latched, the frame splintered and broken where the firefighters had broken in.

Michael didn't want to go inside. He could see blackened walls and melted carpeting from here, and he didn't have any desire to get a closer look.

He felt like such a wuss. *Suck it up.*

Tyler touched the door frame and picked at a few splinters. "We should go back up the street to Eighty-Four Lumber and get some plywood. Board this up while we're here." He gestured at the shattered windows. "Those, too."

The fire marshal had said the same thing, but Michael shrugged. "I doubt there's much worth stealing now."

"Still. You don't want animals in here."

Valid point. They went back to Tyler's truck. They were a mile down the road before Michael realized that maybe Tyler had needed a breather, too.

Unfortunately, it didn't take long to get plywood and supplies, because they were driving around the barriers again less than fifteen minutes later. Michael was better prepared this time, and the nausea didn't hit him as hard.

They stacked the plywood and materials on the front porch, and then Michael stood there, facing the front door for a second time.

This was stupid. He'd gone through this door a million times. He'd already seen the damage; it wasn't like it would suddenly be worse.

But somehow now was different. Staring at this damaged door hammered home just how little he had left.

Nothing. You have nothing.

This was so much worse than looking at the charred bookcases. Michael put a hand on the door and pushed it open.

The foyer still reeked of smoke and melted synthetics. Light poured through the front windows, displaying all of the damage in full color. Footprints were everywhere, but Michael had no way of knowing if they were all from that first night, or if someone had been in here since.

Tyler stepped up beside him. "Wow."

Michael pushed through. He needed to keep moving or he'd collapse into a pile of despair. His shoes crunched on grit as he made his way through the dining room—where everything was a mere shell of what had been there. Table? Chairs? Burned and blackened. One of his brothers had left schoolbooks out, and they were just as unrecognizable as the rest of the room.

When he'd been fourteen, Michael's mother had wanted the room painted in alternating stripes of high-gloss and flat maroon paint. Michael remembered measuring and taping lines on the wall with his father before breaking out the rollers.

Now, he couldn't have told where the stripes began or ended. Everything was just *black*.

Tyler pointed at the destroyed books on the table. "I hope that's not your landscaping stuff."

The words spurred Michael into action. "No. That's all in the kitchen."

Luckily, the kitchen was somewhat better. Smoke damage extended in here as well, but instead of black walls, they faced a gray haze over everything.

Almost everything: the counter where he usually kept his laptop sported a familiar-sized rectangle of clean granite, untouched by soot.

His laptop was gone. So were the two binders where he kept invoice copies and paper records.

"Fuck!" Michael slapped the countertop. A crack split and tore across the stone surface before he could stop it.

Tyler raised his eyebrows. "I'm going to assume you didn't just misplace stuff?"

"No," he ground out. Michael wanted to hit something. Someone. He had no idea whether his things had been stolen or if the cops had taken them for evidence against him, but he'd never be able to contact all his customers without his records.

And he'd thought he had nothing five minutes ago.

A common thief wouldn't have taken his notes. This had to be the cops, right? He wondered if David Forrest would be able to pull strings and get his laptop back.

Because Michael could *totally* afford to keep paying the guy seven hundred and fifty dollars an hour to do things like chase down his laptop.

He ran a hand across the back of his head and drew a long breath. "Let me see if I can find the keys to the SUV. Then we can get out of here."

But he couldn't find the keys. They might have been burned, or lost, or seized like his work stuff. No way to know.

At this point, Michael didn't even waste energy being surprised or disappointed. He walked back to the front porch and picked up a piece of plywood and a hammer.

Tyler didn't say a word. He simply did the same.

The physical labor helped ease some of his rage. His thoughts funneled down to each whack of the hammer. He slammed every nail into the plywood with enough force to crack the window frame behind it. Tyler matched him, nail for nail—though without the rage.

It was funny, but Michael had always thought of Tyler as a do-nothing slacker, but the guy kept pace and worked hard beside him.

Once the windows were covered, Michael picked up another piece of plywood and held it against the door frame. He brushed sweat from his forehead and placed another nail.

"Wait." Tyler grabbed his arm before he could swing the hammer.

"What?"

"Just wait."

Michael glanced over, but Tyler was already yanking the plywood out of Michael's hands and dropping it to the porch.

"What are you—"

"Your house." Tyler shoved past him, through the door. "It's on fire."

CHAPTER 20

The front of the house was dark and untouched, but Michael could smell the smoke as soon as they were through the door. He followed Tyler, who strode through the dining room with clear purpose, stopping short as soon as he entered the kitchen.

The room had quickly filled with smoke, making Michael recoil immediately, but not before he saw the flames licking over the floor.

Tyler, however, was moving forward. "Come on. Your back door is open."

Flames had already caught the walls and table and were climbing upward, reaching for the ceiling with alarming speed. Either Tyler couldn't stop it or he didn't see the point, because he sprinted through the flames and out the back door.

After a moment's hesitation, Michael followed.

He didn't realize how intense the heat and smoke were until he stumbled onto the porch, into the cool November air. He coughed, trying to catch his breath.

"Look," said Tyler, unaffected by the smoke or the heat. He circled the porch. "Do you see anyone? Anything?"

"I don't need to see anyone." Michael stepped off the porch and sent his own power into the ground, the way he'd done the first night he'd sensed someone out here.

It wasn't Chris this time; he knew that much.

The ground offered nothing: no panicked movement, no nearby vehicles, no whisper of danger at all.

But Michael knew that whoever had watched him at Adam's didn't have to rely on the ground.

He looked up, at the trees. Many had already shed their leaves, but enough red and gold and evergreen clung to branches to hide one person, even two.

"Come on." He stepped beyond the tree line, opening his senses fully, reaching out to the trees, asking for any hint of movement.

Nothing.

"He couldn't have gone too far," said Tyler.

"He didn't," said Michael. "He's waiting us out."

"I can be patient."

Michael glanced at him. "Me too."

The quiet bothered him, though. He didn't like that this Guide could evade his senses so effectively. He needed to talk to Hunter, to find out just how strong a Fifth's powers would be.

His cell phone vibrated against his thigh, and Michael fished it out of his pocket. Another number he didn't recognize—but this time he had no doubt who was screwing with him. He tapped on the message.

Maybe you want to put that fire out.

"Fuck you," Michael muttered. He slid his fingers over the screen to reply:

Like it matters at this point.

"Who is that?" said Tyler, standing close enough to read over his shoulder.

"Whoever we're tracking right now." Michael looked up, scanning the trees again. His senses remained quiet.

Another message appeared.

Feeling confident, Michael?

He wasn't. Not at all. But he knew how to fake it.

I've got nowhere to be. You'll have to come down sometime.

That's funny. I have a question for you.

Michael waited, but nothing else appeared. He *hated* playing
these games—but he had no idea how else to move forward. He
sighed tightly and typed back.

What's your question?

Cold wind blew through the trees, rustling branches and
stinging Michael's cheeks. Leaves fluttered into the air, spinning
wildly, obscuring his vision further. He waited, phone in hand,
keeping his eyes on his surroundings.

The phone vibrated again.

Right now, who is hunter, and who is prey?

Michael frowned.

"What does that mean?" said Tyler.

Michael looked up—and saw a red laser dot flicker across a
tree trunk to land on Tyler's forehead.

He shoved Tyler to the ground before he'd even thought
about what it meant. A bullet cracked into the tree behind them.

"Move!" shouted Michael.

But Tyler was *already* moving, digging his feet into the underbrush to run. Michael was right behind him.

A loud crack split the air. Then another. Michael thought of
gunshots or lightning—but then he felt the power through the
ground.

Two trees fell in their path, bringing down smaller saplings as
they fell. Michael and Tyler skidded to a stop.

The gun fired again. Another bullet took out half the trunk of
a sapling just to Michael's right. Another bullet, even closer—
Michael felt a burn and flare along the outside of his arm. He
swore and jerked back.

"Jesus," said Tyler. "Where is he?"

"I don't know yet." Michael's power flared, almost against

his will. Undergrowth thickened between his feet, growing along the tree branches, building a wall to hide them.

"Handy," said Tyler.

Wind, ice cold, blasted between the branches, stinging his eyes and tasting of winter. For an instant, Michael couldn't see anything.

Then he heard the crack and split of another tree trunk.

Michael barely had time to drag Tyler out of the way before it crashed through their hideout. His heart slammed against his ribcage. He hadn't even *felt* that tree pull loose from the ground.

This guy had a lot of power.

Fury flared. Michael sent more power into the earth, feeling his way through the soil. He picked three at random. The earth loosened and the trees began to fall.

The gun fired a third time.

This time Tyler shoved him sideways. They both crashed to the ground. Undergrowth swelled to offer cover. More trees fell, making the earth shake as they landed. The ground pulsed with power, with potential, and for the first time, Michael felt someone else's Earth talent fighting against his.

It made him want to level this entire forest.

He pushed his fingers into the soil, stretching his abilities far and wide. He could bring every tree down. Trap anyone moving in undergrowth. Bury them alive if he wanted. Decompose the body before they'd even stopped breathing.

At one time, these thoughts would have terrified him.

Now, they reassured him.

The ground gave a small tremor, waiting for his order.

And then, for the first time, Michael felt malice through the earth. Footsteps. Someone moving toward them.

He told the trees to wait. "He's on the ground," he said to Tyler, his voice very soft.

Tyler's voice was steady, focused. "Where?"

"There." Michael nodded east. Another icy blast of wind tore through the trees, slicing through the undergrowth to find them. This time it stung his cheeks so violently that Michael could swear the air drew blood. He choked and tried to breathe, but the air hurt his lungs.

"Just one?" said Tyler.

"I don't know." The air felt thinner, and Michael gasped for a breath. His leafy barrier thickened, responding to his panic, creating an impenetrable wall.

"Could one Guide be this powerful?" choked Tyler. He wheezed a long breath. The edge of his lips had turned blue.

"I *don't know*." The last Guide to come to town hadn't been alone. Michael spun in a circle, trying to determine the best direction to go. Power had his chest in a vise grip now, and lack of oxygen was making it tough to think.

Then his natural barrier began to wilt. Leaves and branches dried up and died, crumbling away from the stems. At first, Michael wanted to blame the cold air, but it happened so quickly that he knew they'd been found.

In a heartbeat, all of the undergrowth had wilted down to nothing, giving him a clear view of his surroundings. Michael couldn't have felt more exposed if his clothes had melted away.

But he didn't see *anyone*.

Then he saw the laserbeam again, and the tiny red light hit Tyler's forehead.

Michael shoved him again. *Hard.*

Tyler cried out anyway. Blood found the earth.

"Shit," said Michael. He gasped the word. Lack of oxygen wouldn't let his thoughts organize. He grabbed Tyler's arm and pulled. "Run," he said. He had no idea where Tyler had been hit, but he found his feet. "Run! If you fall, you're dead."

Tyler took a few stumbling steps. He was wheezing, too, his face ghost white. Michael half dragged him toward the house, clambering over the trees that had fallen.

And then, suddenly, the leaves underfoot were on fire. Smoke surged from below, surrounding them with heat and darkness.

Michael swore again, looking for new escape.

"It's me," Tyler gasped. "My fire. I'll hide myself." He stumbled against Michael. His leg must have given out. "Let me go."

"That's not how I work, Tyler." Michael tried to shift Tyler's weight so he could support more of it, but Tyler went down on one knee. He put a hand against a tree.

The smoke had thickened into a black cloud behind them, but it didn't offer Michael any confidence—especially when that icy wind sent the smoke scattering.

He felt more of Tyler's blood hit the earth. Too much, too fast. That didn't inspire confidence either.

"Where are you hit?" said Michael—but then he saw the wound, a long slice along the outside of Tyler's thigh.

"I need five minutes," Tyler said. "The fire will help—"

"If you think we have five minutes, you are out of your head."

Tyler winced. The fire spread. "Just run, Merrick. I'll be okay."

"Would you shut up and *try*?" Michael got Tyler's arm across his shoulder, and fought to drag him to his feet. "We need to run. Now."

Cold steel touched the back of his neck. "No, you need to freeze. Right there."

Shit. Michael froze. The voice sounded familiar, but—

"Hands on your head. Turn and face me."

Michael let go of Tyler, who collapsed against a tree, though he managed to get his hands up.

Michael turned, his heart in his throat, certain he was living his last moments right here and now.

But he turned around and found himself face to face with Jack Faulkner. Hannah's father.

"Are you not speaking to me now?" asked Irish.

Hannah glanced across the short space between them. Outside the fire truck, trees raced by and the sirens screamed the path to their next destination, but in here, it had been dead quiet until he'd spoken.

She hadn't realized Irish had been reading the silence as tension.

She raised an eyebrow at him. "Not speaking to you?"

He looked at her like he wasn't sure if she was yanking his chain. "Yeah. Because I stopped you from working the building collapse."

So much had happened since the restaurant bombing that until now, she hadn't even thought about how he'd told the chief to make her stay in the truck.

She probably owed him a thank-you, considering that she never would have seen Michael's texts if she'd been actively working the scene.

"I'm just tired," she said.

"Just tired? I'm pretty sure that's the girl equivalent of 'still pissed.' "

She smiled. "I am tired." The smile fell off her face. "It's been a long weekend."

He studied her. "Thinking heavy thoughts?"

"Something like that."

But it was *exactly* like that. She'd been thinking about her dad's words all afternoon. She'd been full of vitriol and judgment when he'd started playing the overprotective parent, but now she wasn't so sure. Maybe he had been obligated to report Michael and his brothers. He wasn't wrong—the Merricks *were* in trouble. A lot of trouble. She had no idea how deeply Michael was buried in debt or work or anything. If she lost her job or her car or ran into financial difficulty, she knew her parents would provide a safety net. Michael didn't have that luxury.

"Want to share?" said Irish.

"I'm thinking about Michael. And my dad." She frowned and looked out the window. "I still can't believe what he did."

"He said you'd be pissed about the arrest. I think he was *more* pissed that the attorney pulled strings with the county prosecutor."

The words hit Hannah like an assault, completely unexpected, and just as unwelcome. "Wait a minute. What are you talking about?"

Irish raised an eyebrow. His level voice didn't change. "I'm talking about your dad arresting your boyfriend."

"He *arrested* him?"

"It didn't stick for long. Like I said—"

"Wait." Hannah thought her head might explode. "My dad told you all that? He talked to you about the case?"

"Not a lot." Irish looked surprised that *she* was surprised. "He knew I was interested—"

"Do you have *any idea* how long I sat around that hospital trying to get information out of him, and he wouldn't even *answer my calls*?" She wanted to punch the window. "He tried to *arrest* him? It wasn't bad enough that the county took his brothers away?"

"Hannah." He winced. "I didn't know. I didn't mean to come between you and your father—"

"You didn't. He did." She scowled and felt like a petulant teenager. "I've never wanted to move out as badly as I do right now."

But she couldn't. Because of James.

She'd never spent a second resenting her son, but sometimes she resented this situation, the way she was trapped by an obligation of her own making.

She thought of Michael's brothers, holding it together in the hospital by barely more than a thread. She thought of Chris, the way he'd nearly broken down in the rain, or Gabriel, a hairbreadth away from picking a fight with hospital security to find out information about his brother. Even Nick and Hunter had seemed frayed at the seams, trying to maintain the peace while wanting answers just as badly.

And she thought of Michael, her own age, sacrificing his own life for an obligation *not* of his own making.

An obligation he took so seriously that he'd cried in the dark over losing it.

In that instant, she felt outrageously spoiled.

"If you need a place to crash," said Irish, "I've got room."

She gave him a look, wondering if he was mocking her—or worse, putting the moves on. "That's sweet, but I can't leave James."

"I didn't say you had to." Irish shrugged, like it wasn't a big deal. "I'm almost never there."

"Big-time party animal?"

"Biggest time," he said flatly. He paused; then his voice dropped. "It's a standing offer, Hannah. Just know it's out there if you need it."

She stared at him, watching storefronts fly by along Ritchie Highway behind him. "Thanks, Irish."

He inhaled as if he wanted to say something else—then hesitated.

She narrowed her eyes. "Say it. What?"

Another hesitation. "I don't want to dig myself deeper, but . . . have you ever just *asked* your dad to tell you what's going on?"

"I've heard the confidentiality lecture about a dozen times, thank you very much."

"I don't mean asking him to break the law, Hannah." He paused. "The other night, you implied that he doesn't care about you. I think you're way off base."

Hannah wanted to snap and disagree, but she kept hearing her father's voice in her bedroom this morning. *I just want to keep you safe.*

"He knows Michael," she said, her voice losing some of the anger. "It's not like I've been spending time with a foreign arms dealer or a drug smuggler."

"No, you're attached to a guy who's been at the scene of two major crimes in the course of twenty-four hours."

Fury flared, hot and quick, and Hannah almost came off the bench to get in his face.

Irish put up a hand. "I don't even know the guy. I'm just saying. You can support someone and keep your eyes open at the same time."

Her brain wouldn't even wrap around this possibility. "He's never given me any indication that he could be involved in *anything* like this."

"Didn't you mention to me that he'd been distant the last few weeks?" He paused. "And wasn't his brother involved in something recently?"

"Yeah, but—" She stopped herself. Laid out like that, she wondered if she *was* being an idiot.

I don't want you seeing Michael Merrick anymore.

She'd spent years resenting her father for the way he treated her. Was that blinding her to truths that might be right in front of her face?

The fire truck slowed to make a turn off Ritchie Highway, and she glanced out the window, catching a glimpse of the road sign.

"Chautauga?" she said. "There's another fire in this neighborhood?"

Irish slid open the window separating them from the main cab. "What are we running, Chief? Another fire down this way?"

The fire chief glanced over his shoulder. "Looks like another dwelling fire on that last house on the cul-de-sac. At least we know it's vacant. Report came in from law enforcement."

"What?" said Hannah. "Wait. The last house—"

"That's your boyfriend's house, right?" said Irish.

She stared at him, thinking of the destruction on the first night, of the bombing on Friday. "Someone came back to finish the job?"

"Sounds like it," said Irish. His tone was grim. "Or maybe someone is destroying evidence."

CHAPTER 21

Hannah stared at Michael's house as the fire truck rumbled across the broken pavement. A truck she didn't recognize sat on the road in front of his driveway—and beside that was her father's work truck. Someone had boarded over the front windows of the house, but the door hung open. Smoke billowed from the back of the house.

Despite what the chief had said, she hadn't believed it until she'd laid eyes on the house.

"You okay for this one?" said Irish.

She met his eyes, wondering if he was teasing about the bombing. But his eyes were serious.

"I'm fine," she said. Then she straightened, remembering something that had been a concern on the night of the first fire. "The garage. It's full of landscaping equipment. Lots of fertilizer and chemicals—"

Irish jerked open the window to the main cab again. "Chief. You need to hear this."

Within two minutes, they had a plan.

Within five minutes, she had an oxygen mask and helmet in place, and she was following Irish into the house, dragging a hose with them.

It was different this time, knowing Michael and his brothers were safe and far from here, that she could keep her mind focused on firefighting. She tried not to think of what Irish had implied, that this could be an attempt to hide evidence. The house was dark and clouded with smoke, but some of the other guys from her unit were prying the plywood away from the windows to allow oxygen back into the home.

They found the fire in the kitchen, already eating away at the walls. She and Irish attacked the wall closest to the garage first, working methodically to ensure the fire didn't spread back to areas they'd already cleared. They worked backward, chasing flames away from the walls, leaving only the floor on fire.

Someone had to have spread accelerant for the floor to be burning this hot, this long.

Not Michael, she thought. He wouldn't have done this.

Right?

She could see the vinyl flooring melting into a clear pattern of lines below the flames. She turned the nozzle, ready to attack the floor next.

Irish grabbed her hand and kept the water directed at the wall. His voice came across her radio. "Hannah. Wait. What do you see?"

She stared. She saw fire. A lot of fire.

But then a pattern started to emerge. "A message?" she guessed. Then she looked more closely. "A star? What does that mean?"

"That's not a star," said Irish. "But it's definitely a message."

"It's not a star?"

He let go of the hose, and water streaked across the flames on the floor.

"No," he said. "That's a pentagram."

Michael had never been so glad to see the inside of a police car.

He was handcuffed beside Tyler, and they were alone in the vehicle, but Hannah's father was just outside, speaking to the officer who was going to be driving them to the police station. The cul-de-sac was again lined with fire trucks and ambulances, but the terrified urgency from Thursday night was conspicuously absent. The radio in the front seat kept crackling with orders and updates, but Michael didn't understand most of the codes, and he didn't learn anything more than he already knew: his house was empty, yet on fire. A brush fire was burning in the woods.

He'd searched the faces of the firefighters he'd seen milling about, but he hadn't seen Hannah. At least he didn't have to be worried about her getting involved here.

Tyler shifted beside him. "I've never been arrested before," he said. "I don't know whether to be relieved or not."

Michael stared out the window at the woods behind his house. "I prefer it to being dead."

When Marshal Faulkner had put the gun against his head, Michael had worried that the Guide would burst out of the woods and kill them all—Hannah's father included. But it was as if Jack Faulkner's appearance had broken some sort of spell. Once he'd appeared to take them into custody, Michael hadn't sensed their pursuer at all.

He had no idea what that meant—but he wondered if he should be giving Hannah's father a bit more regard. Hadn't the man been at every crime scene?

Yeah, because he's the fire marshal, you idiot.

"Did you see anyone?" said Tyler.

"No." Michael kept his eyes on the woods. "I didn't."

And that bothered him, too. Everything had happened so fast that Michael was still trying to piece it together. Had a Guide affected the air, making it thin and difficult to breathe—or had Michael been panicked, leaving adrenaline to do the same thing? Tyler had started the fire on the forest floor, right? Had the Guide made trees fall? Or had Michael done that?

His cell phone vibrated in his pocket. It hit him like a live wire. Michael jumped and swore.

"What?" said Tyler.

"I got another text."

Tyler's voice dropped, though they were alone in the car. "From the guy in the woods?"

"My hands are cuffed behind my back, Tyler. It could be from anyone."

But it wasn't. He *knew*. This was bait. A trap. A taunt.

He looked out the window at Jack Faulkner and wondered if he should tell him. The earlier text messages weren't a secret—was there any reason to keep these hidden? He'd probably lose this phone too, but hell, he'd lose it anyway when he got to the police station and they booked him.

Arrested. Michael swallowed. He kept thinking of his brothers, waiting for him to go in front of a judge so he could get them out of that group home. An arrest record would definitely throw a wrench in those plans.

Especially if his new lodging was a jail cell.

His phone vibrated again. Michael stared at the woods. Sweat collected between his shoulder blades despite the arctic chill in the air.

"It's gotta be him," Michael said. "He's fucking with me."

"Can you break the cuffs?" Tyler said. "Steel comes from the earth, right?"

"I can try." Michael flexed his wrists against the restraints. The edge bit into his skin, but he used a little power, feeling it out. He could barely get a read on the cuffs. "The more processed something is, the harder it is to manipulate." He paused and looked at Tyler. "If I break out of here, there's no coming back from that."

He'd be a criminal—and he'd have no chance of getting his brothers back.

Tyler looked back at him. "Do you think we're safe here?"

"I have no idea."

Tyler glanced at the woods. "What about everyone else?"

The radio in the front seat crackled to life again. A man's voice, talking about the brush fire, giving orders to survey the scene.

Then a woman's voice responding, agreeing to check the woods.

Michael froze. "That's Hannah."

"Your girlfriend?"

Michael didn't even respond to him. He threw power into the cuffs, and though they flexed from the tension, they didn't break. He kicked the door, trying to get the fire marshal's attention.

Marshal Faulkner looked over, but didn't stop his conversation with the police officer.

Michael kicked the door again, then slammed his shoulder into the window. "Stop her!" he called. "You have to stop her from going into the woods!"

The man looked aggrieved. He opened the door. "What was that?"

"Hannah," said Michael. "She's going in the woods. You need to stop her."

Jack's expression tightened, but he didn't move. "Why?"

Michael gave another pull on the handcuffs. The steel gave a little, bending under the pressure. "Whoever started these fires is hiding in the woods. *Stop her.*"

If anything, the fire marshal looked exasperated. "There are cops in those woods, Mike. They haven't found—"

"Damn it, *listen to me.*" Michael swung his legs out of the car. "You need to—"

His feet hit the ground, and he stopped short. He could feel the potential for danger again, even from here. They were all in danger. Not just him and Tyler—everyone here, on the scene.

Bring anyone who makes you feel comfortable.

This guy didn't have a problem killing cops and firefighters.

"I need to what?" said Marshal Faulkner.

"Stop her. Them. All of them. Whoever is in the woods. Right now."

"Mike. I'm telling you the police are already searching the woods, and there's no one there." His eyes narrowed. "What happened? You've been in the car for fifteen minutes. What else do you know?"

"You know they're not just after me," Michael said, his voice low. He pulled at the cuffs again. The steel flexed a bit more, but not enough for him to slide his hands free. "You know they've threatened Hannah, too. You need to get her out of the woods."

Jack held his eyes for a moment longer, and then he reached into the front of the vehicle to grab his radio.

Michael kept his feet on the ground. The earth practically trembled with possibility. If his brothers were here, he had no doubt they'd be able to sense more through the other elements.

His phone vibrated in his pocket again.

A gun fired somewhere behind the house. The fire marshal swore and dropped beside his open door. The radio went crazy with reports and requests for assistance.

Shots fired.

"Fire," said Tyler. "He's trapping them with fire, too."

"Hannah!" Michael flexed his wrists, throwing more strength into it. Almost—*almost* . .

"This'll hurt," said Tyler. "Brace yourself, Merrick."

"What? What are—" Then Michael cried out. The handcuffs were burning, searing into his skin.

Another gunshot fired behind the house.

The cuffs snapped. Michael ignored the shouts behind him. He ran.

CHAPTER 22

As soon as he crossed the tree line, the woods turned into a war zone. The underbrush blazed with fire, creating a dense covering of smoke, hiding everyone from view. Random gunshots fired, and Michael pressed his back against a tree, getting low, trying to orient himself.

Too many people crowded the woods now, and he couldn't get a grasp on who was an ally and who remained an enemy.

He knew Hannah was out here, though, and right this second, that's all that mattered.

His cell phone vibrated in his pocket again, and Michael jerked it free. Half a dozen messages were lit up on the preview screen.

His eyes read them each in quick succession.

Do you really think a jail cell will keep you safe? That's funny, Michael.

As if you'd even get to a jail cell.

As if I'd let you leave this neighborhood.

Your girlfriend is adorable how she plays fireman. Maybe I should introduce myself.

Footsteps approached rapidly, sending panicked fury into the ground. Michael swore and looked up. Smoke had swirled closer to him. The fire was spreading.

His power flared without warning, drawing defenses from the earth. Before he had time to mentally process his actions, Michael had fractured a rock in one hand, and he was spinning to meet this new threat.

When a body appeared through the smoke, Michael didn't hesitate. He threw a punch with his hand wrapped around stone. He connected and his quarry cried out. Michael hit him again, feeling the jagged edges of his stone tear into skin. The man fell. Earth and vegetation grabbed hold of the man to trap him there.

Michael dropped to pin the man's arm with a knee, kneeling above him to hold the sharp edge of the rock to his neck.

Then Michael got a good look: Hannah's father.

On his face was a hell of a mark. The rock had broken the skin.

Michael still felt power in the ground. Leaves and underbrush smoldered all around them. Smoke curled between them, and Michael wondered how long they had before a police officer or a Guide stumbled across them.

The fire marshal looked pissed, but his voice was low and even. "Let me up, Mike."

Michael didn't move. "We need to get people out of the woods."

"Sure. I'll get on my radio and we can clear all this up—"

"Don't patronize me." Desperation filled his voice, but Michael couldn't stop it. "You don't understand. I didn't start these fires. I'm trying to *protect* people—"

"Is that what you're doing right now?"

His voice hadn't changed, but his words hit their mark. Michael drew a tight sigh—and realized how deeply he'd dug himself in here. He'd assaulted an officer of the law. He'd broken free of the handcuffs and run. He was twenty-three years old and already a suspect in the bombing—to say nothing of the house fires on the cul-de-sac.

There was no way in hell he was going to walk away from this.

For an instant, he wished the Guide would find him and shoot him and put him out of his misery.

"Please," said Michael. "I didn't do any of this."

"We can talk about it. Let me up."

"If I let you up, you're going to arrest me and haul me out of here. There's someone with a gun who's going after Hannah, and I need to find him—"

"You found him, Michael Merrick." A gun hammer drew back and clicked behind Michael's head. "And I have all the proof I need."

Michael went still. His world centered on that moment, the space of time between the click of the gun and the explosion of the bullet.

And in that moment, he realized he truly had *nothing left to lose.*

The jagged rock was still clutched in his fist, and Michael didn't hesitate. He ducked and spun off his knee, driving the edge of the stone into the man's abdomen. The rock glanced off bone. Michael felt a rib fracture. Skin tore and blood rushed over his hand.

It should have horrified him.

Instead, he kept on pushing. He thought of all the people who'd died over the last three days, and he kept on pushing.

Another rib broke.

The Guide stumbled back, yelling. Michael didn't recognize him at all. He could have been the same guy from the restaurant bombing—or not.

He was also aiming his gun again, but Michael's free hand had already found another rock.

That rock smashed into the man's knee. The Guide fell. The gun fell.

The fire marshal was yelling, but Michael couldn't comprehend his words. His element had taken over, and his brain was focused on nothing more than survival.

The Guide was on the ground, surrounded by smoldering underbrush. Michael trapped him there, holding him with power from the earth below. The Guide wasn't powerless, however. The air had turned thin and ice cold again, and Michael couldn't catch his breath.

He didn't care. He pulled the jagged rock free and put it to the man's throat. Blood was everywhere, running down his fingers, dripping along the man's neck to find the earth. Michael felt every drop.

"I'll kill you before I pass out," he said, and meant it.

The Guide smiled. "You can try." The smoldering underbrush burst into full-on flame.

Fire caught Michael's clothes—and then his skin. He recoiled, smacking at his clothes, trying to ignore the burn. The fire seemed to burn hotter. The pain was *intense*. Michael sucked in a breath of cold air—but he got a lungful of hot smoke instead. His vision went hazy.

The Guide raised himself up on one arm. Blood smeared across his face. He found his gun and pointed.

A gun fired—but not his. Michael heard the shot just beside his head.

The Guide fell. The fire died so quickly the flames seemed to be sucked back into the earth.

The sudden silence was so absolute that Michael could swear his ears were ringing. He couldn't move.

Then Marshal Faulkner stepped past Michael, his gun still in his hand. He dropped to a knee beside the Guide and reached out to check for a pulse.

He must not have found anything, because he holstered his gun, then looked up, at Michael. "You okay, kid?"

Michael couldn't even generate his usual fury at being called a kid. His breath shook, but he nodded.

"You need an ambulance?"

He shook his head, then had to clear his throat. "No."

"Any more surprises for me?"

"I hope not." Michael couldn't quite believe how quickly that had all happened.

The Guide was dead. He was safe. His brothers were safe.

"Thank you," he said.

"Don't thank me yet." The fire marshal picked up his radio and spoke into it, requesting assistance, and probably explaining what had happened. More codes Michael didn't understand. Then he looked at Michael. "Are you going to take off again?"

"No."

"You want to tell me how you broke the cuffs?"

Michael blinked. He'd forgotten about that part. The handcuffs were still attached to his wrists, a short stretch of chain dangling from each. "Adrenaline," he said flatly.

Hell, it was sort of true.

Jack Faulkner's mouth settled into a straight line. "You know I'm going to have more questions, don't you?"

"I figured. Am I still under arrest?"

The fire marshal sighed. He looked back at the body, then at Michael. His eyes were tired—no, exhausted. "Wait and see, Mike. Wait and see."

CHAPTER 23

Hannah found her father at the police station.

She didn't find that out from him, of course. He'd been gone from the scene before she and Irish had been ordered to bag the body of the man he'd killed. He wouldn't answer her texts or her calls, and he wasn't at his office by the courthouse—she'd already checked there. Her mother only knew that he'd said he'd be *late*—without anything more specific than that.

So Hannah had been left to find him like a child who'd lost her mommy at a grocery store: by asking any adult who might have a clue. In this case, it meant someone with a badge.

Even when she walked into the precinct and found him sitting at an empty desk, surrounded by forms and file folders, he barely looked up at her.

"I'm busy, Hannah."

She didn't move. Police officers moved about the room, creating dense background noise, but his words and the tone behind them came through loud and clear. It should have felt like a slap to the face, but for some reason, right now, his words hit her as nothing more than that: just words. He didn't sound angry; he sounded worn out. In the bright fluorescent lighting, she realized she'd never noticed just how much grey had spread through his hair, or how many lines had etched the skin around his mouth and eyes. Her mind always thought of him as the hero fireman, maybe mid-thirties, with blond hair and a bright smile.

Not as this stern taskmaster who lived and breathed by procedure and code, who looked as if life had chewed him up and spit him back out.

Her father looked up more fully when she kept staring at him. His eyes were hard, a cold blue. "I'm not kidding, Hannah. I've got a mountain of paperwork—"

"I see that."

"Then what do you want?"

I wanted to see if you were okay. But she could never say that. They didn't have that kind of relationship.

Then again, she knew he'd never killed anyone before. Maybe she was just remembering the man he'd been, the firefighter who took every life as seriously as if the victim were a member of his own family. Ten years ago, this would have bothered him. A lot. After his last job as a firefighter, when he'd failed to save everyone, he hadn't slept for a week. She remembered.

She didn't want to think too much about the flip side: that he wouldn't have used deadly force unless his own life was in danger.

At first glance, he didn't seem bothered. But his knuckles were white, as if he gripped his pen too tightly. The set of his shoulders looked almost painful.

"Hannah?"

"I wanted to see if you were okay."

Maybe she could say it after all.

His eyes widened a little. Just enough that she knew she'd surprised him. His voice softened. "I'm fine."

"You didn't tell Mom what happened." Her mother had seemed startled that Hannah was even questioning her father's whereabouts.

"I don't talk about active investigations. You know that." His voice was automatic. Hannah thought about what Irish had said in the fire truck. He looked up at her. "Did you tell her?"

Hannah shook her head. "No."

"Good."

Hannah wet her lips and dropped her voice. "You don't want her to know?"

"No reason for her to know."

"Dad. You shot someone." A pause. "You *killed* someone."

"I was there, Hannah."

A small steel chair sat beside the desk, and she glanced at it. "Can I sit down?"

She honestly expected him to refuse, but after a moment, he slid the paperwork into a file folder and nodded at the chair.

She eased into it, wishing for privacy. This room was too open. Too many people swarmed around. If she said the wrong thing, her father would shut his mouth and order her out of here.

"I'm surprised you're not in your office," she said. "I looked there first."

"I had people to question."

Hannah hesitated. "You mean Michael?"

She didn't expect an answer, but he nodded. "And his friend."

She'd tried to reach Michael, but his phone had gone straight to voice mail, and he hadn't responded to her text messages. "Did you arrest them?"

"No. They just had to give a statement." Her father put his pen down, then rubbed his eyes. "We found evidence on the gunman linking him to the fire in the home."

"And the bombing?"

"I can't say."

Which meant yes. Probably.

"What about the other fires?"

"Hannah—"

"No. It's okay. I'm sorry. I shouldn't have asked." She hesitated again.

He studied her. "Why did you come looking for me?"

She gave him a look. "Because you wouldn't answer your phone."

He pulled his cell phone out of his pocket, took a glance at the screen, and grimaced. "I can't believe it's after seven. I missed one from your mother, too." He centered on Hannah, and his voice turned brusque again. "That doesn't answer my question. What do you need?"

She blinked. "I don't *need* anything."

"Were you just trying to find out the fate of your boyfriend? I've already told you that I'm not going to let personal feelings get in the way of—"

"Dad." This was so typical. She almost slapped her hand on the desk to get his attention. "I'm not here because of Michael. Is that what you think? That I came here to beg you not to arrest him?"

"I sure hope you're not here to make your case about being an *adult* again—"

"I'm not here to argue at all!" She stood up. It was a struggle to keep her voice low. "God, you make it impossible to talk to you."

"I'm not the only one."

That made her stop, a quick retort dying on her tongue. For the first time in a long while, he was looking at her—really *looking* at her—and his expression revealed that maybe he was as frustrated by their relationship as she was.

When she'd been a child, all she'd needed to do was shed a tear, and he'd swoop her up in his arms and make her feel better. She wished he would do that right now.

Because that wouldn't be awkward right here in the middle of the police station.

She took a long breath to ensure her voice would be level. "I really was worried about you. That's the only reason I came looking for you."

And because she couldn't take any more rejection from him, especially now, she turned on her heel and headed for the door.

By the time she made it to the parking lot, she realized she'd expected him to follow her. He didn't.

Shocking.

She climbed into her car and put the key in the ignition. She felt like such an *idiot*. It didn't help that his last comment kept pinging around her brain, making her question her own actions.

I'm not the only one.

He wasn't right. He couldn't be right. She'd made one mistake in high school, and he'd turned into a different person. He'd gone from someone who always did the right thing to someone who'd barely give her the time of day. Nothing she did was ever good enough.

Fuck him. She didn't need this. She shoved the gearshift into reverse and pressed down on the accelerator.

A hand knocked on her window. Hannah jumped and slammed down on the brakes. Her car was half out of the parking place, and her father stood just outside the driver's-side door, about six inches away from being squished between two cars.

She rolled down the window. "Are you *crazy*? I could have killed you!"

His eyes were dark and shadowed in the darkness. "Maybe you shouldn't back out of a parking place at forty miles an hour, then." Before she could get all up in arms, he leaned closer. "You're a paramedic. I would have been all right."

She looked at the windshield. Her eyes were burning, and she was ashamed to realize she was a breath away from crying. "I'm not a paramedic yet."

"That's all right. I already know you'll be a good one."

Hannah turned to look at him. She expected a patronizing smile, maybe even a mocking one. But shadows still darkened his face, and he looked serious as ever.

It was possibly the kindest thing he'd said to her in *years*.

That didn't mean she had to take the bait. "What do *you* want?" she said.

He glanced at the open lane of traffic behind her. "Could you park your car for a moment?"

She was tempted to refuse, to press down on the accelerator, and then zoom off, leaving him standing here.

But she didn't want that any more than he did.

She pulled back into the parking place, rolled up her window, and got out of the vehicle, slamming the door behind her. Her breath fogged instantly, and she rubbed her hands together, leaning back against the driver's-side door.

"Parked," she said. "Now what?"

He leaned against the adjacent car. "I try not to tell your mother too much because I don't want to worry her."

"You were a fireman for years. You don't think she's used to it?"

He laughed, but without any real humor to it. "Not anymore. She thinks this job is code violations and safety inspections. Most of the time, she's right, so I don't spend much time correcting her. But your mother hated it when I was a fireman."

"No, she didn't. She loved it."

His expression didn't change. "No, Hannah. *You* loved it."

Hannah stared at him, too shocked to come up with an immediate response. He was right about her, of course. She'd been so proud of her father when she was little. Her mother still had a massive box of crayon drawings from when she was a child, and just about every picture featured a fire truck on its way to a blazing building, or a tall, blond fireman rescuing a kitten.

Her father spoke into her silence. "Don't get me wrong. Your mother loved it when we were first dating. But after we were married, she seemed to realize that firefighting carried a little more risk than a desk job. Every time I had a tour, I had to watch her choke back a handful of anxiety pills."

Hannah thought about her mother, the perfect homemaker, the perfect mother, the perfect *grandmother*. Always calm, always even-keeled. "Mom never said a word about that."

"You think your mother would have wanted to pass that along? To tell her ten-year-old that every time her father walked out the door, they might never see him again?"

Hannah watched her breath continue to cloud. She tried to wrap her head around this new information, but there were too many memories, too many years to scroll through quickly. "But she's been so supportive of my becoming a firefighter. She watches James at the drop of a hat."

Her father gave her a look. "He's her first grandchild. Your mother would watch James if you were jumping out of planes all day long." He paused. "I probably shouldn't tell you this, but . . " He trailed off.

"Yes. You should definitely tell me."

"I don't want to drive a wedge between you."

"You don't have to worry about my relationship with *her*."

He winced, then hesitated so long that Hannah worried she wouldn't get an answer at all. "She hates it just as much that you're a firefighter. She's counting down the days until you get your paramedic license."

"She's never said a word!"

Her father narrowed his eyes. "Are you sure? She hasn't encouraged you to find a less stressful job?"

"Well, yes, but . . " Hannah stopped. Her mother *did* encourage that, all the time. Hannah had never realized it had anything to do with her choice of occupation. She'd always thought it had more to do with being a working mother while trying to go to school.

"When you enrolled in fire school," her father continued, "she wanted to forbid it."

Hannah set her jaw. "She couldn't have stopped me."

Her father smiled—the first real smile she'd seen from him in forever. "That's what I told her."

Hannah jammed her hands in her pockets. "Don't try to turn this around, like you've been the perfect parent all along, and this has all been some misunderstanding."

He lost the smile. "That's not what I'm doing."

"You expect me to believe that you gave up a job you *loved* because you didn't want Mom popping a few Xanax?"

"No, Hannah." His voice went low and dark. "I chose to be a fire marshal because I didn't want your mother to *leave*."

If her car hadn't been right there, holding her in place, Hannah might have fallen back a step. She studied his face, looking for any clue that he was exaggerating.

He looked just as steady as ever.

She couldn't handle this. She wrapped her fingers through her key ring and turned to open her car door. "I don't believe you."

"You don't have to." He paused. "I was just explaining why I didn't tell her about the shooting."

"It doesn't explain anything. I wish you'd never told me."

He didn't have anything to say to that.

Hannah slid back into the car and turned the key, ready to throw it into reverse despite the fact that her father was still standing against the opposite vehicle. He reached out and tapped on her window again.

Against her better judgment, she rolled it down.

This time, she didn't give him a chance to speak. "You can pin all this on Mom if you want to," she said, "but I think you're being a real coward. You're the one who hates that I'm a firefighter. I see it every time I run into you on a job."

"Hannah—"

"And I know you hate that I got pregnant when I was seventeen. You know what? I made a mistake. I can't undo it. You're just going to have to get over it."

He frowned. "Wait—"

She didn't want to wait. She'd been waiting for years, and now she was done with it. She slid the car backward, then pulled out of the parking lot without a backward glance.

CHAPTER 24

Michael couldn't believe he was sitting at a dining room table, eating Chinese food with Hunter and Tyler like it was an ordinary Sunday evening.

He couldn't believe it was over. He couldn't believe he was still alive.

And the Guide was dead.

Every time he blinked, he saw the gun. The blood on his hands as he'd driven that stone into the man's body. The fire that had threatened to destroy him.

The rage had never fully dissipated, leaving Michael feeling somewhat charged, ready for another threat. The past three days had been so full of terror and panic and worry that he couldn't talk himself down. He'd found it hard to keep still while talking to the fire marshal. He barely had any recollection of what he'd said about the events in the woods, but it must have sounded good, because they'd let him go. The cops had even bought his "adrenaline" excuse about the handcuffs—because what else could they think?

He'd thought for sure that they'd take his cell phone, but they didn't. They didn't need it. Any text message evidence was on the phone the police had taken from the shooter. They'd found evidence tying him to the fires. The fire marshal had killed him, so Michael was off the hook.

The man was dead, so there'd be no need for a trial.

Dead. Another dead Guide. Michael wondered how long he'd have before they sent someone new.

It didn't matter if it was five months or five days or five hours. This time, he wasn't screwing around. He'd get his brothers out of that group home and then they were *leaving*. There was nothing to tie them to this area anymore. Nothing.

Hannah, his brain whispered. *And your brothers have ties here, too.*

He told his brain to go to hell. Those ties weren't worth anything if they were all dead.

"You're quiet," said Hunter.

Michael didn't look away from his food. "What do you want me to say, Hunter?"

"I think we should talk about what happened."

"He's dead. It's over."

Tyler stabbed a piece of broccoli with his fork. "You really think that means it's over?"

Michael shook his head. He pushed chicken around on his plate. "They'll send another one."

"Should we have a plan?" said Hunter.

Michael didn't answer that. Any plan he came up with now would be violent and vicious. He was done with hiding. He'd spent his entire life trying to hide his nature, and look where it had gotten him. He'd lost everything.

His hand almost missed the feeling of the sharpened rock he'd clutched in the woods. He shouldn't have stopped. He should have pushed the edge all the way through that man's body. A couple of times.

These thoughts should have scared him. They were risky— and the whole reason the Guides were a threat in the first place.

It wasn't as if he'd never used his abilities fully before. He'd used his powers on more than one occasion to help the earth absorb a dead body into the soil, leaving no trace of a person's death.

He'd never used his own strength and power to directly affect another man, seeking death so effectively.

He thought of what he'd said to Hunter, about how he tried to live according to what his father would have expected of him. Would his father have expected this? His parents had fought to keep him and his brothers safe from the Guides—but would they have wanted him to employ this kind of violence? Or was this exactly what they *didn't* want him to do?

He had no idea. And it wasn't like he could ask them.

Hunter hit his fork against his plate. "Earth to Michael. Should we have a plan?"

"I have a plan. I'm going to get my brothers and we're leaving."

The room went silent. Michael could feel them looking at him.

He finally looked up. "I can't do this anymore. We don't have a house to live in. I don't have a truck. We have too much history in this town. We're too big a target." He paused and looked at Tyler. "Maybe I should have paid attention to the signs five years ago. I don't know."

"This isn't just about your family anymore," said Tyler.

"Then you should leave, too." Michael dropped his fork against the plate. "You should all leave."

"Fine," said Hunter. "I'll go with you."

"You can't." Michael refused to let guilt affect him—but it was hard to meet Hunter's eyes. "It's one thing to stay at the house with your mother's permission, when she lives a few miles down the road. But I don't have a legal claim to you, Hunter. Like it or not, you're a minor—"

"So you're just—you're going to leave me here, knowing more Guides are coming—"

"I'll talk to your mother. Explain the situation."

Hunter shoved his chair back from the table. "Wow, that's helpful. She moved *here* because she couldn't afford to live on her own. What do you think we're going to do—"

"What do you think *I'm* going to do, Hunter?" Michael was too charged with adrenaline. He couldn't keep his voice level. "I'm not made of money, either. It's not my responsibility to protect every single person I come in contact with."

Hunter was glaring at him. "What about Hannah and her son? They were threatened, too—"

Michael glared back. "You think I don't know that? Jesus, Hunter, I can't even spend fifteen minutes with Hannah without some kind of crisis falling at my feet. In the past week, I've spent more time worrying about her than I've actually spent *with her*, and you think I'm not aware of what my presence here does to her family? To my family? To *your* family?"

"My father and my uncle were coming here to help you, and now you're going to run, and you're going to leave me behind."

"Your father and your uncle *never made it*, Hunter."

Hunter flinched.

Michael immediately regretted his words. He took a long breath. "Look—"

"Forget it." Hunter didn't look at him. He dug his keys out of his pocket and headed for the door.

For two seconds, Michael didn't move. He watched Hunter go. He told himself it was better this way. He'd need to separate himself from everyone, and soon.

Then he found himself at the door, a hand above the dead bolt, holding it closed. "Stop. Hunter, stop."

"Let me go."

"No. Listen. We'll figure something out. I won't—"

"You won't what? You won't leave me to deal with this alone? Guess what. You wouldn't be the first."

Michael stared at him. Hunter barely had any more ties to this area than Michael himself did. The poor kid was staying with Adam—almost a stranger—because he didn't want to endanger his family. And here Michael was about to turn his back on him too.

Michael winced. "I don't want to be the second, either. Finish your dinner. We'll figure it out, okay?"

After a moment, Hunter returned to the table. So did Michael.

Tyler hadn't even stopped eating. He looked vaguely amused—but also pissed off. "What happened to 'it's not my responsibility to protect everyone'?"

"Shut up, Tyler." Michael hated this. He hated that he couldn't turn off his thoughts and obligations and let someone else take the reins for a while.

Hell, fate had already dealt him those cards by taking his brothers away, by offering him a chance to live *free* of obligation, and he could barely consider it.

Tyler picked up a carton of rice and dumped half onto his plate. "Where are you going to go?"

"I don't know yet."

"You want my opinion?"

"No."

Tyler shoveled a bunch of cashew chicken on top of the rice. "You're getting it anyway. If you want to run, run. But remember that text message from the woods, about who's the hunter and who's the prey?"

"Yeah?"

"I don't think you're cut out to be the latter."

Was that a compliment? Michael wasn't sure how to respond.

Tyler kept talking. "I've never seen you run from anything. Even when I hated you, I knew you wouldn't back down."

"Are you an idiot? We ran from the guy in the woods until Jack stopped us."

"Yeah, and as soon as you thought Hannah was in danger, *you ran back in.*"

Michael didn't have anything to say to that.

"What really happened in the woods?" said Tyler. "Give me details, because you weren't this keyed up before."

"I told you." Michael set his jaw. "The Guide pulled a gun and the fire marshal shot him."

"Then why were you covered in blood?"

Hunter's fork went still against the plate. He was watching this conversation like a tennis match.

"It's not important," Michael said.

"Fuck that. It *is* important. What happened?"

Michael didn't say anything.

Tyler leaned in against the table. "What did you do?"

"He was going to kill me. So I tried to kill him first."

Hunter finally spoke up. "Hand to hand?"

"Yeah." He paused. He almost didn't want to say what had happened, as if admitting it would make it more real. It was plenty real. He'd scrubbed the blood off his hands forever. He still felt like he hadn't gotten it all. "I stabbed him. A couple of times. Broke some ribs, too."

"Holy crap," said Tyler. "What did you stab him with?"

Michael met his eyes. "A rock."

"And they think he was the same guy who bombed the restaurant?" said Hunter.

Michael shrugged. "I don't know. But I think so."

"Interesting." He paused, and his expression said he was working through something in his head. "If he was the kind of guy to work from a distance with a bomb, I'm surprised he confronted you in the woods like that."

"There was a lot of smoke and fire in the underbrush," said Michael. "Poor visibility. He was shooting at us to begin with."

"Huh." Hunter picked at his food again.

"What?" said Tyler.

"I don't know. I just think people tend to fall into two camps: those who prefer to be violent from a safe distance, and those who prefer to be an active participant. My dad and uncle were opposite sides of that coin. My dad had lots of experience in hand-to-hand combat. He wouldn't work from a distance unless he had to. He thought violence should mean something. My uncle was a cop, and he'd been trained to take care of a situation from a distance, if he could. It was a safety thing: why engage with a bad guy if you don't have to?"

"So what's that all mean?" said Michael.

"I don't know. Maybe nothing." He paused. "But there wasn't just one Guide last time, right?"

The question made Michael's heart stop for a moment. "No. But why wouldn't the other one step in to save the first?"

Hunter rolled that around for a long moment. "I don't know. I can't see any advantage to letting you leave if the first was going to kill you. Especially since the police have a body and a name and someone to investigate."

"What was his name?" said Tyler.

"Warren Morris," said Michael.

Tyler snorted. "He sounds like he should be preparing taxes, not walking around hunting people with a gun."

"Maybe he does prepare taxes," said Hunter. "He doesn't *have* to be military. Guides come from all walks of life. Look at Becca's dad. He works for the Department of Natural Resources. Not exactly the front lines of the militia."

"So there could be another Guide in town," said Tyler.

"Right," said Hunter. "And it could be anyone."

Not for the first time, Michael was glad that he didn't know where his brothers had been taken. They were safe. Hidden.

Michael pushed his food away. He'd barely touched it, and he didn't want it now. "There's always a chance of a Guide being in town," he said. "Nothing different about today."

"You have a bigger target on your back," said Tyler.

Michael scowled. "Nothing different about that either."

His cell phone chimed. Michael tensed and fished it out of his pocket. Another message from Hannah.

I'm worried about you.

He didn't respond. He hadn't answered any of her texts since leaving his neighborhood with the fire marshal.

It was *killing* him.

But hearing those gunshots and knowing she was in the woods—he couldn't take it. He couldn't go through that again. He needed to end this. She'd never be safe while involved with him.

His thumbs hovered over the phone anyway. He wanted to reply. He wanted to invite her over. He wanted to spend one night away from fear and anger and worry, to just be a guy and a girl.

But that wasn't possible for him.

For her either.

He shoved his phone back in his pocket.

A knock sounded on Tyler's front door, and they were all instantly on high alert.

Tyler stood up, but Hunter put up a hand. "They could shoot you through the door."

No one moved.

Finally, Michael stood up. "Wait. I'll answer it."

"It's my house," said Tyler.

"Yeah, but I'm the one they've been trying to kill."

Tyler considered that, then stood back.

Michael stopped in front of the door. He looked through the peephole, but the person was wearing a ball cap and looking at a phone. Through the distortion of the fish-eye lens, he couldn't even tell if it was a man or a woman.

He held his breath and turned the dead bolt, ready for a bullet to hit him in the chest.

Nothing happened.

Then a female voice from the other side said, "Are you going to open the door or what?"

Michael opened the door. "Hannah."

She stood there in a cap and raincoat and jeans, everything speckled with raindrops. Her eyes were red rimmed yet furious. "I don't know whether to hit you or hug you."

"Do both," he said.

She did one better. She kissed him.

CHAPTER 25

Hannah hadn't realized how much she'd missed Michael until she was pressed against him. She'd taken him by surprise with the kiss—but it wasn't long before he caught her waist in his hands and kissed her back. She loved the way he kissed: slow and strong and sure, nothing hurried, as if he needed to memorize each moment.

Someone cleared his throat from farther back in the apartment, and Michael broke the kiss, but he only drew back a few inches. His brown eyes were close and intent on hers.

"You left that out of the options," he said.

"My bad." Her anger had dissipated, leaving only relief that he was safe and well and *here*, right in front of her.

He caught her face in his hands. His palms were warm against her cheeks, and she thought he might kiss her again.

Instead, he sighed and closed his eyes. "You need to go home," he said, letting go of her face and taking a step back. "You shouldn't be here."

Talk about a one-eighty. She frowned. "Why?"

"I don't want—" He hesitated and made a frustrated noise. He sat against the back of the couch and gripped the edge hard enough to turn his knuckles white. "I want to keep you safe, Hannah. It's not safe for you to be around me right now."

Her day had been too long and too intense, and she didn't even want to attempt to make sense of that. "Why?"

"I can't tell you."

Her anger had burned off during their kiss—but it flared right back up again. "You can't tell me."

"No." He met her eyes. "I can't tell you."

"Bullshit. You can't say something like that and expect me to turn around and drive home."

"That's exactly what I expect," he said. "You can't throw a fit and expect me to explain things that are a hell of a lot bigger than just me, okay?"

"A fit? You think I'm throwing a *fit*?"

He inhaled like he wanted to placate her.

"Don't," she said. "Don't bother." She wanted to hit him. Hard. Right in the face. She knew how to throw a punch, and it would probably feel *fantastic* to drive her rage into something.

But she didn't. She was bigger than that.

"Don't talk down to me," she said. Her hands were still in fists at her sides.

"I'm not talking down to you." His jaw was tight, and he looked like he wouldn't mind getting into it either. "I'm trying to *protect* you—"

"Screw you, Michael. You think I'm some damsel in distress? You think I *want* your protection? You don't know what I can handle. You have no idea."

"I'm not getting into a pissing match with you, Hannah." He stepped forward, into her space. "You don't know what you're dealing with."

She didn't back away. "I know that if you can handle it, so can I. I'm so sick of men trying to protect me for my own good. My father tells me to stay away from you, but he won't tell me why. Irish tells the chief that I'm not fit to work a scene. Now you tell me that I have to stay away from you, because it's just not safe. Well, that's bullshit. I'm an adult. I'm raising a child. I'm a goddamned *firefighter*, Michael. You don't know what

I've seen. You don't know what I've dealt with. And if you think that I'm the type of girl to sit in a corner and paint my nails while the big, strong men do their thing, then you're a jackass, and I don't know why we're wasting our time."

She was breathing hard. So was he.

"Talk," she said. "Tell me what's going on."

"Hannah." His eyes had gone hard. "You don't want any part of this—"

"Try me."

He glared at her for the longest moment, until she was sure she'd pushed him too far and he was going to yell at her to get the hell out of here. Regret began elbowing its way into her thoughts. She wasn't angry at Michael. Not really.

This rage was all about her father.

She realized she expected Michael to shove her out the door with dismissive words, the way her father would. To treat her like a little girl who couldn't deal with the big, bad issues of the world.

But Michael straightened and pulled his cell phone out of his pocket. "Here," he said. "I'll show you."

He unlocked the screen, went to the text messages, and handed it to her.

She read the first few on the screen, and they didn't make sense.

Right now, who is hunter, and who is prey?

Do you really think a jail cell will keep you safe? That's funny, Michael.

As if you'd even get to a jail cell.

As if I'd let you leave this neighborhood.

The tone was chilling, even from the relative safety of a cell phone screen. Someone was stalking him? Were these messages from the man her father had killed? Why didn't Michael want to tell her about this?

Then she stopped on the next line.

Your girlfriend is adorable how she plays fireman. Maybe I should introduce myself.

Her eyes flicked to the top of the screen to see that these texts had been sent from a random number, not from anyone in his contact list. She directed her gaze up to Michael. "Who sent these?"

"Warren Morris. The man your father shot in the woods."

She glanced at the phone again, then back up at him. "Does my dad know about these text messages?"

"Yes."

He put out a hand, but Hannah took a step back and held the phone out of reach, scrolling up, reading through a brief exchange. "Do you know this guy?"

"No." He paused. "Sort of."

"So someone has been threatening you? For how long?"

Michael didn't say anything. She glanced past him, to where Tyler and Hunter were sitting at the dining room table. "Do they know?"

"Yes."

"Oh, so they get to be in on all the secrecy."

"Hannah—"

She glanced at the text messages again. "Did this just start today?"

"No." Michael took a long breath. "It's complicated."

"Is this related to the fires in your neighborhood?"

He hesitated. "Yes. And the restaurant bombing."

He didn't say anything else, but she kept looking at him expectantly. "There's more," she said. "I can feel it."

He glanced away, but he talked. "Your father doesn't even know all of it. Like I said, it's bigger than just me. The recent arson attacks. The fires at the school carnival—"

"*That long?*" She wanted to hit him again. "And you didn't think maybe I should *know*?"

"I'm trying to keep you *out of it*, Hannah!" He shoved away from the couch and stood over her. "You don't think it kills me to get text messages like that? To know that the more we're together, the more of a target you are? Do you have *any idea* what it was like to get those messages when you were in the woods, just trying to do your job?"

She punched him in the chest with his phone. "Do *you* have any idea what it's like to know that you kept this from me?"

He drew back. His expression looked bleak. "I didn't want to tell you like this."

Hannah looked from him to Hunter and Tyler and back. So much secrecy. She wanted to storm out of there right now.

She didn't. She needed to piece it together, but she didn't have enough clues yet. There'd been so much violence and destruction that she probably should be afraid of whatever Michael was involved in, but she'd known him too long and she wasn't the type to back away from a threat. What could he and his brothers be into? Were they arms dealers? Drug smugglers? That didn't seem to fit. Michael always seemed so concerned with doing what was *right*. He was a solid role model for his brothers.

She almost couldn't believe they were having this conversation. "What are you involved in?"

"Nothing like you're thinking. My parents struck a deal five years ago, and it didn't work. Now I'm just trying to keep my family safe." He paused, and his expression turned desperate. "Not just my family. *Everyone.* You and James. Hunter and his mom. Becca and Quinn. Adam. Layne and Simon and—"

"They're all involved?" Hannah stared at him. "All those people?"

He nodded. "Like I said, it's bigger than just me."

"But they know. They know the risks?"

Michael hesitated, then nodded.

It had been months since the carnival fire and the arson attacks in town. He'd been keeping this secret—whatever *it* was—for *months*. Years, if she believed what he'd said about his parents. She gritted her teeth. "And now I'm a part of it."

His voice was very soft. Almost ashamed. "I'm sorry, Hannah. I didn't want—"

She didn't care what he *didn't want*. "But it's over, right? The man is dead?"

"The guy who sent those texts is dead." Michael paused. "But I don't think he was working alone."

"What else do you know?"

"Nothing!" he cried. "I don't know anything else! Don't you understand? I'm not in control here." He swallowed hard, and she could swear the tension in the apartment was going to rip him apart. "Jesus, there's a part of me that's *relieved* my brothers aren't here. If no one I know has any idea where they are, they're *safe*."

He looked so distraught that part of her wanted to hug him, to tell him they'd figure it out, if only he'd tell her everything.

Another part of her thought it was way too late for all that.

"All right," she said. "You think I'm safer if we stay apart?"

He winced. "Hannah. Please—I don't—"

"Good call," she said. She opened the door and walked out, easing it closed behind her.

He didn't follow. Of course.

In the parking lot, she thought of her father, coming after her at the last minute. She waited, wondering if Michael would make an appearance.

He didn't.

She told herself not to cry. She'd never needed a man before, and she sure as hell didn't need one now. Especially not one with a box of secrets that would rival Pandora's.

She didn't want to go home. It was after nine, and her father would be there for sure. She didn't want to see him. She didn't want to see her mother, either, because Hannah was worried she'd demand truths she just wasn't ready to hear. James would already be in bed, dreaming of SpongeBob and Legos by the time she walked through the door.

She had no girlfriends she could call. Anyone she knew was more of an acquaintance than someone she could dump all of this on. The guys from the firehouse weren't much better.

Except one.

She pulled out her cell and typed out a text.

What are you up to?

Irish responded immediately.

Going to bed. On at 0500. :-/

She frowned.

Sorry. Talk to you tomorrow.

She locked her phone and shoved it in her bag, not wanting to see if he responded. She shifted into reverse and began to ease out of the parking place.

Her cell phone rang. Hannah sighed and put the car back in park.

The display was lit up with *Irish* across the screen in black letters. She slid her finger across the bottom to accept the call.

"Hey," she said.

"What's wrong?"

She swallowed. Her throat felt tight. "Nothing's wrong."

Silence hung on the line for a beat or two. "You've never texted me before."

"Well, we can text more tomorrow. I didn't realize you had an early tour."

"It's all right."

A long pause, during which neither of them said anything. Hannah knew she should talk or hang up, but she didn't like either of those options. The words were all jumbled in her throat and couldn't make it out. But hanging up meant she was really alone for the evening.

So the silence dragged on.

Her throat tightened further. God, she'd never hear the end of it if she started crying.

"You know," said Irish, "I really can't sleep. I was going to make a pot of coffee. Want to join me?"

She started to decline. She actually opened her mouth to say no. Instead, she found herself saying, "Sure. Text me your address."

CHAPTER 26

Irish lived in a tiny two-story duplex right on the water, down at the end of a quiet street. His front yard was barely bigger than a postage stamp, and parking was along the road, but the lawn and a few bushes were kept neatly trimmed. She pulled her cap down to keep the rain out of her eyes and stepped out of her car.

He opened the door before she knocked. "Come on in," he said. "I hope you're not expecting much."

"Four walls and a roof, mostly," she said. But when she walked inside, she realized there really wasn't much more than that.

No, that wasn't true. He had a sofa and a television and a small two-seater kitchen table, but that was pretty much it. The television was tuned to the local news, though it was muted, with closed captioning scrolling across the bottom of the screen. A heavily made-up anchorwoman spoke animatedly into the camera about a crime in a neighboring community. A fluorescent bulb hung over the kitchen sink, casting the rest of the space into a maze of shadows. No pictures hung on the walls, no books anywhere, no knickknacks.

Irish noticed her looking around. "I told you there wasn't much. I haven't lived here long, so . . "

She smiled. "It smells nice, though. Like apples and cinnamon. Baking?"

"Yeah, right." He pulled mugs out of a cabinet and gave her a wry glance. "I literally plugged in an air freshener the minute I hung up the phone. How do you take your coffee? And keep in mind that I only have milk and maybe a few Splenda packets if you're lucky."

"Just milk is fine." She eased into one of the chairs at the table. Almost immediately, something alive wound around her ankles, and she gasped.

A small, orange tabby cat looked up at her and meowed.

Irish looked over. "Snap your fingers at him if he's bothering you. The cat's on a hair trigger."

"He's not a bother." She trailed her fingers along the back of the animal's head and got a *prrrrow* in response. "What's his name?"

He shrugged. "I don't know. Cat."

"Original."

"I picked him up as a stray when I lived in Chicago." Irish picked up the mugs and joined her at the table. "Never got around to naming him. He's never seemed to mind."

"You don't strike me as a cat person."

"I'm not. But sometimes life sends things our way for a reason."

She mock gasped. "Did you get that off a fortune cookie?"

He smiled. "Funny." He paused and wrapped his hands around his own mug. His expression went serious. "What's up, Blondie?"

A hundred things. A thousand. But now that she was sitting here with a—with a what? A friend? It felt like such a foreign concept. But now that she was sitting here with an audience, she couldn't find the words. "Nothing."

"I don't think you'd be here for nothing." He paused and turned his mug in circles. Waiting.

Hannah stared into her coffee, inhaling the familiar scent.

She had no idea what she was doing here.

After a moment, she pushed the mug away. "I'm sorry, Irish. I didn't mean to bother you."

He put a hand over hers before she could stand up. "Hannah. Stop. You're not a bother."

She stared at his hand where it rested over hers. He had

strong hands, warm yet rough from work. It didn't feel like he was hitting on her. It felt . . . supportive.

Her eyes lifted to meet his. "It's been a long day."

"Tell me about it."

So she did. All of it. Everything her father had said, even the bits about her mother leaving. Everything Michael had said, including the parts that didn't make sense. Irish was a good listener, and he kept quiet while she talked. He stared at his coffee as if he was taking it all in.

By the time she finished, the cat was in his lap, and her coffee had gone cold.

"Wow," he said. "It has been a long day."

"I still can't believe I woke up in the hospital with Michael this morning. That feels like it happened *weeks* ago."

Irish didn't say anything, but he was studying her.

"What?" she said. "If you have any thoughts, feel free to share them, because I'm not sure what to think anymore."

He winced. "I don't want to throw my hat in the ring with the rest of the men trying to control you, but it sounds like both your father and this Michael guy agree on one thing, and maybe you shouldn't ignore it."

"You mean staying away from him?"

Irish raised his eyebrows and nodded.

"Don't worry," she said, scowling. "I'm pretty sure we're going to be avoiding each other regardless."

Irish tapped his fingers on the table and didn't say anything.

"I can feel you thinking," she said. "Come on, out with it."

He lifted one shoulder in a shrug. "It sounds like you're determined to show them you don't need them. I don't know about Michael, but I'm sure your dad knows what you're capable of."

She frowned. "I have a pretty good idea what he thinks I'm capable of."

"I don't know what that means."

This felt painfully personal, but it was easier to share secrets in the shadowed darkness of Irish's quiet apartment. Her voice dropped. "He's never forgiven me for having James."

"Do you really think that's true?"

"I know it's true. He practically didn't speak to me for the entire time I was pregnant." But now that she was saying that, she thought back to the exchange with her father at the police station.

You're impossible to talk to.

I'm not the only one.

She remembered getting the positive pregnancy test, how she'd cried to her mother for an hour straight. By the time her father had come home, she'd been so ashamed and humiliated that she'd screamed at him and hidden in her bedroom.

She hadn't been able to make eye contact with him for weeks.

Had she started it? Had she been blaming him for something she'd initiated years ago?

Maybe. But he hadn't helped.

Hannah looked up at Irish, and she felt a familiar shame creeping up her cheeks. "I don't know who James's father is." She hesitated. She'd never shared this whole story. Not even with Michael. "When I started high school, my father got super strict. I didn't mind, really—I'd always done everything my parents expected of me. But it almost wasn't good enough. He'd grill me on where I was every minute of every day. I'd go to the library after school, and if I wasn't home exactly when I said I'd be, he'd flip out. Once he sent police officers to a friend's house to make sure I was really there for a sleepover. Just because I didn't answer my cell phone. Can you imagine how humiliating that was?"

Irish smiled. "I don't need to. My dad was a cop, too. He used to treat my friends as if they were smuggling pot and whiskey into my house. I wouldn't accept a ride home from anyone because my dad would be standing in the driveway, wanting to smell their breath."

Hannah faltered. "Really?"

"Yeah, really." He shrugged. "I think some of it is just being a parent, and some of it is knowing the consequences of poor choices. Well—you know all about that, right? With James?"

She blinked. James wasn't old enough for her to humiliate

him, but she *was* more cautious than other parents. She'd seen too many injured children to be otherwise. She never let anyone other than her parents drive him around. Michael and his brothers were the first non-family members she'd *ever* let babysit. When James was invited for a play date, one of the first questions she asked the other parent was whether they had a gun in their home and how it was secured.

Irish was right. She knew too much.

Was that her father's issue too? Did he know too much?

"I didn't mean to interrupt your story," said Irish.

All of a sudden, she didn't want to finish. She'd always felt a little self-righteous about this part, but now, in this new light, she felt more foolish.

She traced a line in the wood of the table. "During my junior year, a friend's brother was going to a frat party. He invited her. She invited me." She shrugged a little. "It was your typical college party. Lots of guys, lots of music, lots of alcohol. I snuck out of my room and we went. I was so ready to break free of all those expectations that I just completely let loose. I met some guy, one thing led to another, and . . . well, you know."

"I can connect the dots."

"The party got out of control, and someone must have called the cops. I don't even know what happened to the guy, but he must have gotten away."

"And you didn't."

She gave him a look. "No. I didn't. And you can guess who was waiting for me when his underage, drunk daughter was dragged into the police station."

Irish gave a low whistle. "I bet that was a good time."

She scowled. "It *sucked*. It was humiliating. I would rather have been thrown in jail. I sure as hell didn't give my dad all the details of what had happened. And what sucked more was that I didn't give the guy another thought until I peed on a stick six weeks later and came up with two pink lines. By that point, I didn't even remember his name. My friend's brother didn't know who he was. It was this one-time random hookup."

"So you think your dad has been blaming you for all this time."

"Yeah!"

He spun his coffee mug on the table again. "You don't think maybe you've been blaming yourself?"

"Okay, Dr. Freud—"

"I'm serious, Blondie." He smiled. "Hannah." He glanced up at her. "I didn't even know you had a kid until I showed up at your house. It's not like you tell everyone about him."

She had good reason for that. She was sick of being judged by everyone. "You have no idea what it's like, Irish."

"You're right. I don't. I'm sure it was hard as hell being a mother at seventeen." He hesitated. "But you're not seventeen anymore."

She narrowed her eyes. "Are you telling me to grow up?"

"No. I'm telling you that you already *have* grown up." He paused. "It's okay to act like it. You don't need anyone's approval."

Wow.

She blushed. "Thanks, Irish."

He nodded. "You're welcome."

"I'm glad you joined the station."

He made a frustrated noise. "You're one of the only ones."

She remembered the comments she'd overheard. "Are you still getting crap from the other guys?"

"We're south of the Mason-Dixon line. I'm sure I'll still be getting crap in twenty years." He paused. "It's not bad. I've heard worse. It just makes it hard to cover some guy's ass when you know what he thinks of you."

"Are you going to say something?"

"I'm going to keep doing my job as well as I can."

"But that's not *right*, Irish."

"I spend a lot of time thinking about right and wrong," he said. His eyes were very serious. "Sometimes it's worth losing a few battles to win the war."

"Maybe," she said.

"Not maybe. I—" He stopped short and frowned, looking past her. "Look. Is that local?"

She looked at the television, which was still muted. The reporter was in a box at the upper left, but the majority of the screen showed an aerial shot of a large home on an even larger plot of land.

Or what used to be a large home. Because the building on the screen had been destroyed. Fires blazed in four areas that she could see. Smoke streamed from the structure, which was surrounded by fire trucks and ambulances.

Her eyes locked on the closed captioning flashing across the bottom of the screen.

. . . in Annapolis. First responders have yet to identify any survivors. Local sources estimate that twelve to fourteen teens may be in residence at the group home at any given time—

Her heart stopped. What had Michael said?

There's a part of me that's relieved that my brothers aren't here. If no one I know has any idea where they are, they're safe.

This couldn't be a coincidence. Couldn't be.

The guy who sent those texts is dead. But I don't think he's working alone.

Shit. She fished her phone out of her pocket and dialed with trembling fingers.

"What's wrong?" said Irish. "Do you know where that is?"

"Yeah," she said.

She didn't expect Michael to answer, so she almost dropped the phone when he did.

His voice came across the line, rough and gravelly. "Hannah. I'm sorry—"

"No. Michael. Listen to me. I'm not calling about that." Her voice almost broke as she looked at the screen again. "You need to turn on the news."

CHAPTER 27

They were stopped at the end of the road. The police had set up a barricade. The hell with that. Michael almost shoved Tyler out of the driver's seat to floor the accelerator.

He must have actually started trying to do that, because Tyler grabbed his arm. "Hey. Take it easy. I'll park down the road a bit, okay?"

Hunter was in the back seat, but he'd come to the edge to peer around them. His breathing was almost as quick as Michael's. "Do you think they're here?"

"I don't know," said Michael. After Hannah's call, he'd stared at the news for a solid minute. His brain hadn't wanted to process the images or the words—until it all burrowed into his brain with the force of a speeding bullet.

Another bombing. At a group home for teenagers.

Guilt and panic had wound through his thoughts, leaving no room for anything else, and they showed no sign of leaving. To think, a few hours ago, he'd been relieved that his brothers had been taken. *Relieved.* He'd thought this meant safety for his brothers.

Gabriel had wanted to run from the hospital. Michael had stopped him.

He hadn't been able to get out of Tyler's apartment fast enough. Thank god Tyler had followed him to the parking lot, because it wasn't until he was out in the cold November air that Michael remembered he had no truck, no way to go anywhere.

While Tyler drove, Michael had called the social worker. No answer. No surprise, either, considering it was after eleven on a Sunday night.

Next, he'd called David Forrest, who didn't have any information, but at least he was awake and concerned and said he'd find out what he could immediately.

After the bombing at the restaurant, Tyler had been able to deflect some of the fire damage. Did Gabriel have the strength to do the same? Were his brothers hiding here somewhere? Would they have tried to rescue the other residents, or would there not have been time?

He texted Hannah. She'd have access to a radio, and she'd know what was going on.

Have they found any survivors?

Not yet.

He gritted his teeth and typed another message. His finger shook as he pressed *send*.

Have they found any bodies?

No text came through, but his cell phone rang. Hannah.

"We're five minutes away," she said. It sounded like she was crying. "I'm trying to reach my dad to get more information, okay?"

"Do you know anything now?" His voice was hollow.

"They've found—" Her voice broke. "They don't know— Michael, I'm sorry."

"What, Hannah?" He had to choke the words out. Her emotion said more than her words did. "What have they found?"

"No bodies," she said.

"No bodies," he echoed. It should have been a relief, but it wasn't. He felt as if someone else were having this conversation. "Then what?"

Tyler parked the truck beneath some trees a little way down

the road. He killed the engine and didn't move. Michael held his breath, waiting for Hannah's answer. Hunter shifted closer, trying to listen.

Her breathing kept shaking. She was still crying. "Let me find out more, okay? Wait for me to call you back."

"No! Hannah! What did they find?"

She choked on a sob. "Parts, Michael."

"Parts?" He couldn't make sense of the word.

"From the explosion." Another hitched breath. "But they don't know, okay? They haven't identified anyone. Just wait. Wait 'til we get there."

Michael couldn't speak.

Parts. From the explosion.

"Thanks," he said, and again, it was as if someone else were speaking for him, because his thoughts were tied up in panic and rage.

No wonder the building was still burning. No wonder they hadn't found any survivors.

His brothers hadn't been able to stop it.

Michael grabbed the door handle, but Tyler hit the locks.

"Stop," he said. "Think about what you're doing. We should have a plan."

Michael could barely process that. Smoke was in the air and he needed to *get out of this truck*. He clawed at the lock as if he'd never seen one before. He needed—

Tyler grabbed him. "If some Guide blew up this place," said Tyler, "he might still be here."

"Good," said Michael. The rage he'd felt earlier was nothing compared to this. His power was already reaching for the earth below the truck, ready to lay waste to the entire county if that was what it took. "I'm going to find him and kill him."

"Not if I get to him first," said Hunter. Metal clicked in his hands. Light glinted off his gun.

"Jesus," said Tyler. He reached over and unlocked his glove box.

When he pulled out a gun of his own, Michael turned wide eyes his way. "You had a gun when we faced that guy in the woods?"

"I didn't have it *on me*. I didn't think I'd need to be armed to board up your front windows."

Michael's cell phone chimed, and he pulled it out of his pocket, expecting a text from Hannah. His heart leapt, hoping for good news.

But this text wasn't from Hannah. It was from a new unknown number.

Did you honestly think I was working alone?

Michael didn't hesitate. He typed back.

I'm going to find you and kill you.

The response appeared almost immediately.

Go ahead and try. Save me some time.

Michael started to reply, but another message appeared below that one.

I already took care of your brothers.

Michael stared at that sentence until it burned itself into his eyeballs.

I already took care of your brothers.

The letters blazed and blurred until he couldn't make sense of them anymore. To think, earlier he'd thought he'd lost everything.

He hadn't felt this kind of despair since his parents had been trapped in that fire.

"I need to get out of the truck," he said. His voice was a wisp of what it had been.

Tyler hit the button to unlock the doors. The air was cold and still when Michael stepped out of the vehicle. He stood and inhaled, realizing that he was waiting for . . . something. A blast of wind, either too cold or too warm for the weather. Some sign of Nick's presence or power.

Nothing.

It had been raining before, but the clouds had dissipated overhead, revealing a heavy white moon staring down at him.

Had the earlier rain been a sign of Chris trying to draw power? Or just nature playing out? Michael wished he'd checked a forecast. He had no idea.

But there was no rain now.

And the fire continued to blaze from the home. Gabriel would have tried to stifle it, to contain it somehow and help with the rescue efforts.

He kept seeing them in that hospital room, remembering how they hadn't wanted to be taken away—but they'd gone. For *him*, because he'd asked. They'd gone with the social worker, and willingly, too.

Hunter stood beside him, immobile. Michael couldn't look at him. If he looked at Hunter, all he'd see was the brothers he'd lost.

His phone chimed, and Michael almost chucked it at the ground. But he had to look. Just in case.

Just in case what? Just in case your brothers aren't in pieces and they magically found a cell phone?

It was Hannah.

Where are you?

He didn't answer.

"Kill the lights on the truck," he said to Tyler. "I want to walk the property line."

They all walked, clinging to the shadowed darkness beneath trees and along the fence line. Tyler might have been cautious, looking for hazards, but Michael paid no attention. He simply walked, and they followed. If the Guide confronted him, Michael was ready to fight.

If the Guide simply shot him . . . well, right now that might be okay too.

Another chime from his phone. Hannah again.

My dad wants to talk to you.

He didn't respond. After a moment, she texted again.

Please, Michael. Tell me where you are. Please call me.

He kept walking. Tyler and Hunter were silent behind him. Michael found that if he kept putting one foot in front of the other, feeling the power of his element, he could go on living.

If he stopped, he worried that he'd fall down and let the earth swallow him up.

When they reached the edge of the property, he could see rescue workers swarming around the house. The heat from the fire warmed his cheeks, even from here. He finally turned to look at Hunter and Tyler. "Do you feel anything? Any power at all?"

"No," said Tyler.

Hunter's face was white in the moonlight, leaving his eyes hopeless and desperate. He looked at the house and then back at Michael. And then away. His voice was a cracked whisper. "Nothing." He had to wet his lips. "I thought we'd find them. I thought maybe they'd be hiding, and they'd sense us walking. I tried to use power, to see—to see if—"

And then his voice broke and he was crying.

· Michael grabbed him. Held him. He didn't cry. Every motion still felt like someone else doing it.

"I shouldn't have come here." Hunter pulled away and swiped his eyes on his jacket. "I shouldn't have started this—"

"You didn't start this," Michael said. He couldn't take his eyes off the burning home. He kept seeking information from the ground, but he felt *nothing*. "You're a kid, Hunter. Your dad and your uncle started this. Or maybe Calla and her followers did, when they started that rockslide. Or maybe my parents did, by forming the deal."

"None of them started this," said Tyler. "This is the way it's always been."

Michael looked at him. "It shouldn't be this way."

"No," said Tyler. "It shouldn't."

But it was. And Michael couldn't fix it. He felt like he'd been fighting forever.

And now he'd failed. The past five years seemed so pointless. Just borrowed time.

"Someone is coming this way," said Tyler.

Michael straightened, suddenly alert, ready to fight. He was surprised to find himself *eager* for it, to have a target for all this rage. For the first time, he didn't care about setting an example for someone else. He didn't care about what his father would have expected him to do.

If the Guide showed his face, Michael was going to find a way to kill him.

The man who walked through the haze and smoke with a flashlight wasn't the Guide, though. It was Hannah's father, the fire marshal.

Jack flicked the flashlight over each of their faces. Michael couldn't see his face clearly, but his voice was tired. "Hannah told me you were here. Come sit in the car. I don't have any information yet, but—"

"Were they here?" said Michael. "Is this the place?"

The fire marshal didn't even ask for clarification. He just nodded. "Yes."

Michael felt his face start to crumple. He hadn't realized there'd been a shred of hope left curling in his thoughts.

Gone now.

Marshal Faulkner put a hand on his shoulder. "Come on." He didn't offer false hope. He didn't say anything else. He just left his hand there and waited until Michael started walking.

Every step brought them closer to the house. The bomb had done its job, and thoroughly. Most of the structure was gone, and what was left was burning. Michael kept hoping for some kind of miracle, that maybe after *this* step, his brothers would appear from the darkness. Or after *this* step, the rescue teams would declare that they hadn't really found body parts from the explosion, that it was all a joke. Or his brothers had escaped, and they were looking for a pay phone—

His cell phone rang.

Michael choked on his breath and grabbed for it. He didn't recognize the number.

Please. Please please please—

A girl's voice spoke across a poor connection. "Michael?"

He didn't recognize the voice, but she sounded young. His thoughts were too jumbled to make sense of this. "Yeah?"

"It's Calla Dean."

He stopped walking. He pressed the phone more tightly against his ear. "Calla?"

"Yeah." She coughed. "I need you to get here."

Her plea was surreal enough that it chiseled through his panic and despair. "You what?"

"I need you to get here. They had me trapped, but I got free." She coughed again. A burst of static came across the line. "I don't know how long—"

"Wait—you what? Who had you trapped? What are you—"

"I'm by the water. At the abandoned park at the end of Fort Smallwood. There's an old storage shed—" More coughing, then silence.

"Calla? Calla?"

Hunter and Tyler and the fire marshal were staring at him, but he didn't care. Michael pressed a hand over his other ear. "Calla? Are you there? You're at the abandoned park? What are you talking about?"

"I'm here. I need you to come. I knocked one of them unconscious, but it won't be long—"

"You knocked who unconscious? Calla, I don't understand."

"One of the Guides, Michael. They're in town. There's one here, but he's unconscious. I need you to come here."

"Okay," he said, breathless. "Okay, I'll get there."

"Hurry," she said. "Before the other one gets back."

CHAPTER 28

Michael had been sure the fire marshal would stop him from leaving. Too many recent interactions had ended with him in handcuffs.

But he'd turned on his heel and walked away, and no one had stopped him. Tyler and Hunter had hurried after.

Michael knew the old park well. A few acres of land made a narrow peninsula, with a beach on one side and a rundown pier on the other. He'd played there as a child, when the playground had been in good repair and the swing chains had still had all their seats. Now, there were nicer parks in more accessible parts of the county, and this one seemed to have been forgotten. None of the streetlights in the parking lot worked, leaving the entire place bathed in moonlight.

When he got out of Tyler's truck and put his feet on the pavement, power swelled up to greet him.

A lot of power. Enough to make him hesitate. The Guide had hidden before, and pretty effectively. This was a deliberate display.

"Do you feel that?" he said to Hunter.

"Yes." Hunter's gun was already in his hands. He looked focused now that they had a task, as if he'd compartmentalized all the horror of the past few hours.

"Do you think it's a trap?" said Tyler.

Michael hadn't considered that. "Maybe you two should stay here."

Tyler snorted. "Fuck that. *I* don't work that way, Merrick."

"We're safer together," said Hunter. "Not . . " He hesitated, as if unsure he wanted to finish that sentence. He swallowed. "Not apart."

They'd be safest with all five elements represented. That's what Hunter wasn't saying.

They didn't have all the elements anymore.

He couldn't start thinking about any of it or he'd never be able to move again. He needed to do something, to *act*.

"Come on," Michael said. "The storage shed is by the old playing fields."

As they crept across the park, Michael kept his focus on the earth, feeling for signs of anyone nearby, whether friend or enemy. Trees here were few and far between, and the moon cast a silver glow on the baseball diamond and the two soccer fields. A storage shed sat between them. At one point, it had been a bright, sunny yellow, but now it looked gray in the moonlight, and some of the wood from the sides had broken and fallen off.

Silence hung over everything, broken only by the water hitting the rocky breakers on the east side of the peninsula.

They stopped as a unit.

Hunter kept his voice low. "Are you sure this is where she said she was hiding?"

"Yeah." Michael hesitated. Maybe his sense of self-preservation had kicked in since the numbness at the bombed house had worn off, but he didn't want to walk into a bullet if he could help it.

"I'll stay back here," said Tyler. He cocked his gun and aimed at the shed. "Cover you both."

Michael nodded and moved forward, asking the ground for silence. He and Hunter circled the shed, looking for any sign of movement. Tyler followed, going wide to keep them in his line of sight.

On the far side of the shed, Michael stopped short. "Jesus," he whispered.

Calla was on the ground. Her clothes were torn and filthy and streaked with blood. Her skin was mottled with bruises. Blood stained her lips and trailed out of her mouth, dripping onto the ground.

Behind her was a man—what was left of one, anyway. He'd been burned beyond recognition. Clearly dead. Michael could smell the charred flesh.

Hunter knelt beside Calla. He reached out and touched two fingers to her throat. "She's alive. Barely."

Michael took a knee beside him. Her blood had touched the earth, and he tried to send power into her. "Calla." He touched her face and her head moved limply. "Calla."

"We should get her back to the car," said Hunter. "She needs a hospital."

Michael nodded and bent to lift her.

Calla's eyes opened halfway. "Michael Merrick." She coughed, and more blood wet her lips. "You came."

"I did."

Her eyes rolled, and she blinked as if trying to focus. "And Hunter Garrity. How funny." She started laughing. More blood came up.

"Why is that funny?" said Hunter.

"She's out of her mind," said Michael. "Let's get her to the truck."

"I'm perfectly lucid," she said. "Is he dead?"

Michael glanced at the charred corpse. "Yeah. I thought you said he was unconscious."

"He was." Her head lolled as he shifted her into his arms. "You weren't fast enough. He woke up."

"And you did that to him?"

"You would have done the same," she said. Her voice gained strength. "I wasn't going to give him the chance to trap me again. He's not the one who really deserves it, though."

"How many more are there?" said Hunter.

"There were three. I thought they were just going to kill me, but it turns out they were pretty mad at me for causing the accident."

"What accident?" said Michael. They were never going to get any information from her like this. And she was responsible for so much, he was tempted to leave her dying beside the shed.

"He kept crushing me with rocks," said Calla. "Over and over again. Then healing me in fire. Said it was poetic justice. Do you understand what that *felt like?*"

Tyler joined them as they stepped onto the path back to the parking lot. "There were three?" He nodded toward the charred body. "That's one. The fire marshal killed the other. So there's one left?"

"Just one. Hunter knows. He remembers."

Hunter made a disgusted noise. "What the hell are you talking about? I remember that you're a psychopath who doesn't mind killing people. I remember how you conned us all into starting a war we wanted no part of. I remember how you said you started a rockslide to kill my dad and my uncle—"

"Yeah, that." She coughed and it took her a while to catch her breath again. "And let me tell you," she said—but then she broke off to catch her breath.

"Let me tell you what?" said Michael.

She drew a long breath., "Jay took that rockslide *really* personally."

Hunter stopped in the middle of the path. "What did she just say?"

Calla giggled, but it launched a new round of violent coughing. "This—this is why it's—why it's funny—"

Hunter jerked her out of Michael's arms. She stumbled against him and could barely hold herself up. He shook her. "Talk, Calla. What did you just say?"

"I said—"

A gun fired. Calla's head snapped sideways and blood was spattered all over Hunter's face and shirt.

Hunter yelled and dropped her.

She was dead. Just like that, she was dead.

"Put down your weapons," said a male voice. "Now."

Michael turned, lifting his hands as he did so. A man stood at the junction where the trail split off to the parking lot. In the moonlight, Michael could see him clearly, but it didn't matter. He could have been any man off the street, maybe late thirties, with lighter hair and dark clothing.

And a gun. Something large, like a rifle—with a red laser sight.

He'd snuck up on them. Even with the man this close, Michael couldn't feel any threat through the ground. He couldn't feel anything at all.

Hunter's breathing was shaky, and his eyes were wide. "It's okay," he called. He put his gun on the ground and put his hands up. He didn't sound frightened or angry now. He sounded . . . awed and a little determined. "It's okay."

"It is *not* okay," hissed Tyler. "We're fucked." His gun didn't leave his hand.

That red laser sight centered on his chest. "Put the gun down. Now. Three. Two—"

"All right!" Tyler dropped the gun and put his hands up.

"It's okay!" Hunter yelled again, a little more desperately. "It's me! You don't have to shoot them."

"I know who you are, Hunter." The man didn't lower the weapon.

Michael was replaying the last words between Hunter and Calla.

I know you started a rockslide to kill my dad and my uncle.

Yeah. And Jay took that really personally.

Michael remembered the man he'd caught sight of during the restaurant bombing, the victims' photos where he'd caught the edge of a man's face, with a flash of sandy blond hair.

Just like Hunter's.

They'd spent so much time talking about his father's experiences that Michael almost felt like they should have considered this a possibility.

How would you consider this a possibility? Dead people don't come back.

"It's your father," said Michael. "Isn't it?"

"No," said Hunter. "It's my uncle."

He looked like a kid greeting a parent after a long business trip. His voice was full of eager longing, so at odds with the specks of blood on his face.

And the fact that his uncle was still pointing a gun in their direction.

"I hate to break it to you," said Tyler, "but this dude doesn't seem to care who you are."

"Quiet," said the man. He walked toward them, his gun still pointed in their direction.

Hunter stared at him, his eyes widening with each step the man took. "How are you . . . ?" His breath caught. "My dad— is he—?"

"Still dead." No emotion in that voice.

"But—but I went to your funeral. I saw you—in the casket— they *buried* you—"

"Yes, they did. It took me a while to get out, and longer to piece together our records. You and your mother were long gone. All our old files were gone." He stopped about ten feet away. "I honestly didn't expect this much trouble once I got here." He glanced between Michael and Tyler. "Or this many Elementals in town. You've created quite a little community, haven't you?"

"Fuck you," said Tyler.

The Guide shot him in the shoulder. Tyler went down yelling.

"Stop!" Hunter surged forward. "Stop! I said you don't need—"

Michael grabbed his arm and jerked him back, physically blocking Hunter when the Guide swung the gun around.

Michael put his hands back up, but he kept Hunter behind him. He took a step back, very aware of how close that gun barrel was. "Easy," he said. "He's a kid. He's your family. Just tell him to get out of here. He doesn't need to be a part of this."

"I might have believed that once," said the Guide. "Before I found him living with the enemy." He gestured with the weapon. "Move, Hunter. Out where I can see you."

"You don't need to do this," said Hunter. He shifted to the side. "Please. Uncle Jay. Mom said Dad wasn't coming here to kill them. I know them now. They're not dangerous."

"Your dad and I didn't always agree." Jay made a sound of disapproval. "John was still trying to talk sense into them when they pulled us out of the wreckage. He honestly thought it was an accident. He didn't see it for what it was: an execution."

"Kind of like this one?" said Tyler. His voice was strained. The scent of blood hung in the air.

"Exactly," said the Guide. He gave Michael a wry glance. "I thought you were going to 'find me and kill me.' How's that working out for you?"

"I'm halfway there," said Michael.

"They haven't done anything wrong," said Hunter, his voice full of resolve. "Uncle Jay, you have to listen to me—"

"Don't," said Michael. "He's not the uncle you remember, Hunter." Calla's body was proof enough of that. Even without the bombs and fires.

"Funny how death changes us," said Jay.

Michael knew that better than anyone. "Let Hunter go," he said again, his voice low. "Let him go, and you and I can finish this."

"You and I?" Another wry smile. "I'll finish it. Don't you worry."

"No elements," said Michael. "Tyler and I won't fight you. Just let him go."

"Speak for yourself," said Tyler.

"I'm not leaving you," said Hunter.

"Nice offer," said the Guide. "But I want you to call elements. The bigger, the better. Here, I'll help you." Jay pulled the trigger.

The pain was so sharp and immediate, Michael didn't even know where he'd been shot—just that he was falling. Hunter was shouting, but Michael couldn't make out a single word. The earth responded to his pain and the quick flare of panic. Deep cracks shot out from where he landed. The ground rumbled and shook and settled. Michael thought he might throw up.

"Stop!" yelled Hunter.

"Oh, we can do better than that," said Jay.

Michael tried to catch his breath, but his lungs burned with each inhale. "Why?" he gasped. "Why are you doing this?"

"Because I need you." He pulled the trigger again.

Pain exploded in Michael's left leg. Upper thigh this time. The earth shook harder. Michael wished for clarity, for something useful. He wished for the singular focus he'd found while fighting the Guide in the woods behind his house.

He couldn't think through the pain.

"Why?" he said again. "Why do you need me?"

"Easy," said Hunter's uncle. He pulled the trigger again. "You're bait."

CHAPTER 29

Hannah fought Irish, but he was built like a linebacker, and she wasn't. His arms were wrapped around her rib cage and his hand pressed over her mouth.

She wished his hand were over her eyes. Or her ears. Especially when the man shot Michael a second time.

The earth shook and rumbled beneath them, but Irish had a tight grip. He stumbled, but he didn't let her go.

"Stop fighting me," he said, his voice low and close to her ear. "I need you to stop so I can call for help. Okay?"

A sob worked its way up her throat, but she choked it off.

"Come on, Blondie," Irish whispered. "We aren't armed. If that guy finds us . . " He left the rest of the thought unspoken.

She nodded.

She hadn't known what to expect when she'd gone after Michael.

But she hadn't expected this.

Irish's hand eased off her mouth.

"I want my dad," she whispered.

"I want the National Guard," he said back, his fingers dialing.

Another gunshot. She flinched and slapped a hand over her mouth to keep from crying out. Another earthquake, this time hard enough to send cracks across the pavement and between the small cluster of trees where she hid with Irish. One of the trees gave a loud creak, and she gasped and started shifting backward, ready for it to fall.

Irish put a hand against the trunk. "It's okay," he said. "It's steady."

But nothing was steady. The earth kept shaking, until tiny cracks began to form between Hannah's fingers. The gun fired again, and the packed dirt and pavement buckled and gave way. She felt herself falling. She scrabbled for purchase.

Irish grabbed her arm and yanked her sideways. She found herself looking into a ravine—six feet deep and three feet across. It stretched from Michael all the way through the parking lot and out of sight. It wasn't the only one.

And the ground hadn't stopped shaking.

"Make it stop," she said.

"I can't," said Irish. "He's too strong."

"He—what?" Wind whipped through her hair, chilling her cheeks, carrying the scent of the water. Another gust picked up grit and debris from the ground, sending it skittering into the ravine. Thunder boomed overhead, an almost deafening roar from the sky. A bolt of lightning hit a tree and branches exploded everywhere.

"What's happening?" she cried. The wind picked up, beating her hair against her face.

"He's setting a trap," said Irish.

Thunder cracked again. This bolt of lightning skipped the trees and raced straight for earth.

The man with the gun laughed. He turned in a circle. At some point he'd hurt Hunter—now he was the only one standing.

"Come out, come out, wherever you are," he called.

"A trap," said Hannah. "Who is he trapping?"

"Us," said a voice.

She looked up. There, coming out of the darkness, wearing torn, bloodied clothes and covered in bruises and lacerations, were Michael's brothers.

Michael had to be dying. That would explain the sudden wind on his cheeks and the mist in the air.

At this point, he'd welcome it. He'd lost track of how many times he'd been shot. At some point he'd realized that his brothers couldn't be dead, if the Guide was using him to lure them here now. He tried stopping his power from reaching into the earth, but his body had taken so many injuries that he had no control left.

And of course the Guide was strong enough to keep any damage away from himself.

Tyler had long since gone silent, and Michael suspected one of those bullets had gone into him.

Hunter was crying.

"I'm sorry," he said. "Michael, I'm sorry."

Michael didn't even have the strength to answer him. He slid his hand sideways, toward Hunter, knowing it wouldn't be enough.

But Hunter must have seen, because he took Michael's hand and held it.

"Sweet," said the Guide. "Hunter, you're such a disappointment."

Michael squeezed his hand. *You're not*, he wished he could say. *You're not*.

Hunter squeezed back. "No," he said to his uncle. "You are. You killed so many people. Why? Just to get to the Merricks?"

"Oh, this is bigger than your friends, Hunter. Don't you see that?"

"No," said Hunter, desperation in his tone. "I don't see it. Why?"

"You're proof. Your father was proof. The Guides have lost focus. Priorities are no longer clear. Did you know your father wanted to *help* these Elementals? Can you imagine?"

"Yes," said Hunter. "I can."

The Guide pointed to the ground, at the cracked earth. "Look at this damage he's done already."

"That's happening because you're *shooting him*!" yelled Hunter.

Another gust of wind pulled at Michael's cheeks. The air seeped into his injuries, and he felt a surge of power.

"Nick," whispered Hunter.

No, thought Michael, feeling relief and despair battle for dominance in his thoughts. *Run. Hide.*

But they wouldn't. He knew they wouldn't.

"Good!" called the Guide. "Call more power. Try to destroy me."

"We will," said Hunter. His hand was tight on Michael's.

The wind was a solid force now, flinging loose bits of earth through the air. Lightning arced to the ground, and the water surrounding the peninsula surged high against the rocky breakers.

They'd done this once before—called elements with a full circle and sent the power directly into another Guide. With Silver, they'd held back. They hadn't killed him.

Now, they weren't holding back. Through his link with Hunter, Michael could feel each element as clearly as his own. His wounds carried no pain now. There was simply earth, air, fire, and water, combined and strengthened through Hunter's connection to the spirit.

The winds' force reached hurricane strength. Michael lost track of how much lightning coursed to the ground. Rain spit at his cheeks. He'd never felt this much power. It was choking him, threatening to rip him apart if he and his brothers didn't give it direction.

"Do it," said Jay, and his voice was terrible. "You know what we say, Hunter. For the greater good."

The power stood ready to destroy him. All it needed was Hunter's direction.

Michael had one clarifying thought: *This is too easy.*

He remembered Hunter's lecture about violent combat, how his father preferred hand-to-hand fighting, to be an active participant in someone else's demise. But his uncle—he preferred to fight from a distance. Jay knew about explosives—he'd already proven that. Hadn't Hunter said that a Guide could use power to give his weapons an extra *kick*?

For the greater good. Wasn't that what all the Guides said?

That anyone's death was worth it, if it led to the destruction of pure Elementals?

Michael squeezed Hunter's hand, hard. He couldn't feel his injuries now. He couldn't hear over the roar of the wind and the rumble of the earth and the thunder. All this power needed to go somewhere.

"A bomb!" he said to Hunter. "He has a bomb!"

Hunter's eyes shot wide. His hand was tight on Michael's.

This much power combined with the outward force of an explosive—it would level the county. Maybe even the state. Hundreds of thousands of people would be killed.

All for a few Elementals.

Hunter was trying to dial it back, but there was too much. His skin practically glowed. "You'll die with us," he said through clenched teeth.

"Of course," said Jay. "I understand sacrifice. I'm doing what's *right*."

"No," said Hunter. "I am."

He jerked his hand out of Michael's. The cord of power snapped.

A burst of white light exploded from Hunter's body, taking all the wind and rain and lightning. Power surged outward, over everything. Michael felt it strike his body, healing the damage the Guide had caused. It went farther, finding the earth, the air, the water, an explosion of light and warmth spreading across the peninsula.

For an instant, Michael couldn't see. He couldn't feel.

And then he could.

Hunter was gone. Gone. Not lying dead at their feet.

Simply *gone*. The power had torn him apart.

Michael couldn't breathe. What had Hunter done? What had he *done*?

The Guide was on the ground across from Michael, struggling to get to his feet. The guns lay on the ground between them. Michael scrambled for one, hoping he'd be faster.

But the Guide's eyes lit with fury, and he started pulling

at something in his waistband. "I can still take some of you with me—"

Michael shot him in the head. The Guide fell.

Then Michael sat there in the sudden silence and waited for his brothers to find him.

CHAPTER 30

Early morning light was breaking across the park. The parking lot was packed with official vehicles: fire trucks, ambulances, police cars, a bomb squad technician—even a van from the FBI.

Hannah hadn't been able to see Michael or his brothers yet.

She wasn't sure she wanted to. She had too many questions, and she wasn't sure she was ready for answers.

She'd seen Michael and Tyler get shot. She'd *seen* it.

She'd also seen them get off the ground as if it had all been staged. She'd seen Hunter vanish into a burst of white light and heat. A bomb? But no one else had been injured.

And then there was the earthquake damage.

Or the lack thereof.

She sat on the back of an ambulance and studied the ground, which was slowly going from gray to green as sunlight found blades of grass.

Every mark from the earthquake was gone. No ravines. No cracks. Nothing. The grass itself looked lush and full.

"How are you holding up?"

She looked up to find Irish standing in front of her. "I have no idea how to answer that question."

"Your boyfriend and his brothers are fine."

"He's not my boyfriend. I don't know *what* he is."

"I do."

She remembered what he'd said when he was holding her, when she was begging for the earthquake to stop. *He's too strong.*

"How much do you know?" she said warily.

"Not all of it." His voice was careful. "I can put together the pieces."

"How, then? How do you know?"

He hesitated, then glanced around. "That's not really a conversation for here and now."

"Were you involved?" she said. "All this time? Were you part of this whole thing?"

"No." Irish shook his head. He looked aggrieved. "Though I might have known a little more than I was letting on when I encouraged you to listen to your father."

"Then what are you doing here?" she asked.

"I've always told you the truth about that," he said. He glanced across the grounds, to where Michael was sitting in one ambulance and his brothers were sitting in another. Michael was alone, but his brothers were being checked over.

Michael was watching their interaction, Hannah realized.

She couldn't look at him.

She looked at Irish instead. "You've always told me the truth about bizarre weather events? I don't think so."

"About why I'm here. I came looking for a new opportunity."

"What kind of opportunity?"

He sucked his breath through his teeth. "Again, not a conversation for here and—"

"Yeah, yeah." She suddenly realized she was so tired of secrets. "Over coffee, then?"

His eyes widened. "You want me to tell you—"

"Everything," she said. "I want you to tell me everything."

Michael sat in the back of an ambulance and watched Hannah's partner approach.

He'd rather be watching Hannah approach, but he'd seen her

conversation with Irish, and had seen her very deliberately turn away from his gaze. Now, he'd lost her entirely among the crowd of rescue personnel.

Irish didn't mince words. He simply climbed into the ambulance and dropped onto the bench in front of Michael. "My secret's out," he said.

Michael kept staring at him. He had Tyler's gun shoved into the back of his jeans, and he'd bet good money that Irish knew it was there. "My brothers tell me you're a Guide," Michael said.

"A Fifth," Irish said. "Not a Guide."

Too much had happened for Michael to play this any way but aggressively. "Tell me why I shouldn't shoot you, too."

Irish took that question at face value. "I'm not like him. I wasn't here for you."

"Then who are you here for?"

"Myself." He paused. "I moved here to get away from all that."

Michael's eyes narrowed. "Why?"

"Because my father was a Guide. I saw what he had to do. I wanted no part of that." He paused. "I think your Hunter was the same?"

Your Hunter. Michael had to put a hand over his chest, the ache was so strong and sudden.

Irish reached out, and Michael jumped. He had the gun pointed before he'd finished a breath.

Irish put his hands up. "Take it easy. I'm sorry. You're hurting—"

"That's none of your business."

"Fine," Irish said equably. "But I'm not your enemy."

"We'll see." After a second, Michael put the gun away.

"There are more of us than you'd think," Irish said. "The Guides don't like us much either, for what it's worth."

"Why?" said Michael.

Irish shrugged. "Younger generation. New way of thinking." He paused. "A lot of us think it's time for a change."

"Me, too," said Michael.

"Maybe we can make that happen together," said Irish. He held out his hand.

After a moment, Michael shook it.

When Irish tried to pull away, Michael held fast. "What's going on between you and Hannah?"

"She asked me to tell her everything."

Michael felt that like a bullet. He winced. He should be telling her.

He *should have* told her.

But maybe it was better this way. He'd never be safe. Not really.

"Good," he said. But he still didn't let go of Irish's hand. "You didn't really answer my question."

Irish raised his eyebrows.

Michael repeated himself. "What's going on between you and Hannah?"

Irish smiled. "Ask her."

CHAPTER 31

Michael's brothers sat in the back of an ambulance, wrapped in blankets. They'd been examined and questioned and told to wait.

So Michael sat on the tailgate and waited. He didn't want to move. He felt like if he stayed right here, he could keep his brothers safe.

They hadn't said much since the paramedics had left them alone. Michael couldn't blame them. He didn't feel like talking, either.

He kept turning around to look at them, though. He couldn't quite believe they were safe and unharmed, as if one of these times he'd swivel on the tailgate, and the ambulance would be empty and this whole night would be a cruel joke.

He kept hoping he'd turn around, and Hunter would be sitting there with them.

When he'd done it one too many times, Gabriel said, "We're still here, Mike."

"I know." He studied them, their drawn and filthy faces, the way they sat huddled together. "I thought . . ."

He couldn't finish that sentence.

Nick nodded as though he knew what Michael was trying to say. He glanced at his brothers. "We thought we were dead, too."

Michael swallowed, remembering images of the bombing

he'd seen first on television, and then firsthand. He'd never be able to forget the sound of Hannah's voice in his ear, saying that they'd found body parts.

But here were his brothers, safe and sound in front of him.

Someone else's kids hadn't been so lucky. Hunter hadn't been so lucky. Neither had Calla Dean—regardless of whether she'd deserved it.

Tyler had been lucky. Hunter's power burst had healed him as well as it had Michael.

"We tried to warn them," said Chris.

"Warn who?" said Michael.

"The people in the house," said Gabriel. His face was paler than usual, and he kept glancing at the trail where the Guide had fallen—and where Hunter had vanished into a plume of power and elemental energy. "Nick felt it first—that someone had broken in—"

"I didn't know it was a bomb," said Nick. His face was white, too. "I just thought the Guide was after *us*. We wouldn't have run if we'd known. We would have helped—"

"It's not your fault," said Michael. "I'm glad you ran. I told you to run."

"We tried to warn the others that someone had broken in, that we were all in danger—"

"Yeah, we tried," said Gabriel. "But they wouldn't fucking listen."

Chris picked up his rage and ran with it. He scowled. "They thought we were trying to run away."

Michael understood the anger—it was so much easier to deal with than grief, which would sucker punch you when you least expected it.

Hunter had given up everything to save them. And not just them—possibly the whole county. Maybe more. Michael thought of their conversation at Adam's kitchen table, when he'd told Hunter that he tried to do what his father would have expected of him.

Had Hunter taken that to heart? Had his decision been a direct result of that conversation?

Was this really what Hunter's father would have wanted? Or was that just what Hunter had believed?

Michael had no idea. And he wasn't sure it really mattered.

He wasn't sure he was worthy of the sacrifice.

"How did the Guide know where to find you?" said Michael.

"We don't know," said Nick.

"We thought—" Gabriel started, but he stopped himself.

"We thought he'd killed you," said Chris. "We thought he'd gotten the information out of you somehow."

Michael realized that while he'd been feeling lost and alone, his brothers had been feeling the same. He shook his head. "They wouldn't tell me where you'd been taken. Even David didn't know."

Shoes crunched on the broken pavement behind him. "Didn't know what?"

Michael turned to find Marshal Faulkner standing there. He considered lying—but there'd been so many lies and secrets and half truths, and he just couldn't find the strength anymore.

"How did this guy find them? How did he know which home to target?"

Marshal Faulkner glanced into the ambulance and then back at Michael. His voice was heavy. "Because he was a cop." He paused. "He knew who to call, what to say, what to ask."

Of course. Michael didn't know how to respond to that.

He shifted and looked into the ambulance again. "When can I take my brothers and get out of here?"

"You can't."

"What?" Michael stood, and he was so tired and furious and desperate that his powers flared too. He fought to keep the earth still. "Why not? Am I under arrest again? Am I—"

"Calm down. You're not under arrest. Your friend, Tyler, either. Hannah and Irish have already made a statement. That guy had enough explosives strapped to him that I don't think we're going to have too hard a time proving self-defense. That doesn't mean I don't have some questions for you, however."

"I can answer your questions later. I want to get out of here. I want to take my brothers home."

"Oh yeah?" The fire marshal raised an eyebrow. "Where's that, Mike?"

Michael took a step forward. "Don't fuck with me—"

"I'm not." Marshal Faulkner held his ground. "I'm telling you that there's a court order in play, and if you want to have any hope of getting custody back permanently—"

"You can't seriously think I'm going to let them out of my sight again. You failed to keep them safe."

"So did you. If you'd been up front with me about the danger—"

"I'm taking them out of here."

"Then you'll be charged with kidnapping. I'm trying to *help* you here—"

"Whoa!" Gabriel was suddenly on the ground, pushing Michael back. "Back off, Mike. It's fine."

"It's *not* fine. You know what we're dealing with, and—"

"Yeah! I do!" Gabriel shoved him in the chest, some real fury behind it. "We all do! And we dealt with it."

Michael stared at him, more surprised by the anger than anything else.

"We're not twelve anymore," Gabriel said.

"You're not adults, either—"

"Yeah, well, we're almost the same age *you* were when Mom and Dad died."

Michael didn't want to fight—but he kind of did. Fighting with Gabriel felt easy, natural, and crowded thoughts of darker things out of his head. "I know how old you are. Maybe you could act like it."

Chris burst out of the ambulance with a vengeance. "Maybe *you* could! You don't have to protect us all the time, Michael. You're not our father. You're our *brother*."

"Don't fight," said Nick. He stepped out of the ambulance, too. "There's been enough fighting." Then his eyes met Michael's. "But I agree with them. We're not helpless. You don't have to keep acting like we are."

He knew they weren't helpless. He'd known that for a long time.

But if he didn't have to watch out for his brothers, what else did he have?

Marshal Faulkner put a hand on his shoulder. "They'll be okay. Aren't you appearing in front of a judge in a few days anyway?"

Michael looked at his brothers. They looked so defiant—but strong and capable, too. He didn't know what to say.

"It's not safe," he started.

"It's never safe," said Nick. "Never. And what are you going to do? Load us into the truck and take off?"

"The truck is totaled," Michael said. But yes, he'd been planning something exactly like that.

His brothers looked stunned. "The truck—is totaled?" said Gabriel.

"Yeah. From the restaurant bombing." Michael leaned against the edge of the ambulance. He rubbed at his eyes. The fire marshal was right. Nothing had changed. He had nowhere to take his brothers. No vehicle to take them *in.*

The night had been terrifying, and he'd been so relieved to have his brothers back that he hadn't considered practicalities.

This sucked.

"What do we need to do?" said Chris.

Michael looked up and sighed—but Chris wasn't talking to him. He was talking to the fire marshal.

Marshal Faulkner glanced between Michael and his brothers. "Same as before." He hesitated. "You'll stay with someone approved for emergency custody for a few days."

"Fine," said Nick.

"Fine," agreed Gabriel. "Let's go."

"*Not* fine," said Michael. He couldn't let this happen again. He couldn't go another night without knowing where his brothers were. Not now, not this soon. "I told you—"

"Wait." Marshal Faulkner held up a hand. "Would you feel better if you knew where they were?" He looked at each of them again. "If you all agree to behave until your brother has a court date, I can pull some strings."

Michael hesitated.

"We agree," said Chris.

"We agree," said Nick. He punched Gabriel in the arm and got the same response.

"Besides," said Gabriel. "You can't be a pain in the ass from jail, so you'd better do this the legal way."

"I didn't agree yet," said Michael. "I want to know where you plan to take them, *first*."

"That's easy," said Marshal Faulkner. "I plan to take them to my house."

CHAPTER 32

Hannah arrived home to find her mother carrying a stack of pillows and blankets into the basement.

She stopped short in the foyer. "What are you doing?" she asked.

"Shh." Her mother tilted her head at the kitchen. "Talk to your father."

Like that's what she wanted to do after the night she'd had. Hannah considered springing up the steps and locking herself in her bedroom, but she kept hearing Irish's words. *You are an adult. It's okay to act like it.*

Her father appeared in the kitchen doorway before she could decide what to do. The early morning sunlight filtering through the window was still weak, so she couldn't make out his expression, but it sure didn't feature a big ol' jolly smile.

"Where've you been?" he said.

She wanted to snap at him, because it wasn't any of his business, but maybe she could start working on that whole communication thing.

"Went for coffee with Irish." She hesitated, thinking of all she'd learned, about Elementals and Guides and all the reasons Michael had hidden the truth from her. "I needed to unwind."

"I've been thinking a lot about what you said," he began.

"Oh yeah?"

He nodded. "Yeah." He paused. "Do you want to come sit in the kitchen so we can talk?"

She opened her mouth to say *not really*, but now her father's words were an echo in her head.

You're impossible to talk to.

I'm not the only one.

She shut her mouth and headed for the kitchen. Instead of sitting, she leaned against the cooking island. "Don't tell me. Mom found out about the shooting and you have to sleep in the basement."

"No." His eyebrows went up. "You haven't talked to Michael?"

"No." She shrugged but wouldn't meet his eyes. "Tonight . . . he kept a lot of secrets, Dad. I don't . . . I don't even understand all of it."

But she understood some of it. Thanks to Irish.

She had no idea what to do. At least she'd been able to make a coherent statement to the cops.

She had no idea where things stood with Michael—or where she wanted them to stand. He had a second life. A secret life, full of magic and danger and mystery. In a movie or a book it would have made him sexy and desirable.

To a real live woman with a young child to raise, it made him terrifying.

Her father gave a heavy sigh. "I don't understand much either." He paused. "That's not really what I wanted to talk to you about."

"Fine." She turned to the refrigerator and pulled out a bottle of Gatorade. "What, then?"

"I don't hate that you're a firefighter. And I don't hate that you got pregnant." A moment passed. "And I didn't mean for you to think I was trying to pin anything on your mother."

She stood there with the refrigerator door open, unsure how to respond. He was so *direct*. She kept her eyes on the bright white shelves and didn't say anything.

"I was disappointed," he continued. "I won't sugarcoat it. I think any father would be. I think any *parent* would be."

"Trust me," she said, slamming the refrigerator door. "I got the memo."

"I don't think you did," he said. "I don't think you understand me at all."

She waited, listening.

"When you went to that party, when you got arrested—" He shook his head. "You acted like I was the one who showed up and shoved you into a cop car. You wouldn't speak to me for *weeks*."

Her cheeks warmed. She remembered that.

"I was worried," her father said. "I didn't want you to miss out on anything you wanted to do, because of one mistake."

"James isn't a mistake." The words came out of her mouth like an attack.

"I didn't say he was." He paused. "Going to that party to prove a point to your overbearing father was a mistake."

She flinched. He was right. "I didn't miss out on anything," she said. Her voice was small.

"I know. You've worked very hard. I'm proud of you."

Anything she could have said was trapped in her throat by sudden emotion. He said it so simply, like anything else. Like he didn't realize how long she'd been waiting to hear him say those exact words.

Before she could change her mind, she crossed the kitchen and threw her arms around his neck.

If he was surprised, she didn't feel it. He hugged her back as if he held her every day. His arms were warm and secure and familiar, despite the fact that she hadn't hugged him in *years*.

"I missed this," she said.

"Me too." He didn't let go.

Then she remembered the pillows and blankets. "If Mom's not making you sleep in the basement, then what's going on?"

James came bursting into the kitchen, full of the energy only kindergartners could find at five o'clock in the morning. He tackled her and her father at the same time, as if they did group hugs on a daily basis. "Mommy! Mommy! The big kids are here for a sleepover, and they said we could play the Lego game on Xbox later!"

"The Lego game?" She drew back to look at him. "The big kids? What—"

"I took your advice," said her father. "You were right. I should have been more compassionate."

She was too tired. Her brain couldn't process this. "What?"

"Michael still doesn't have custody. So his brothers are staying with us."

CHAPTER 33

The day had been overcast for the funeral, but now the sun was peeking through the clouds. Michael took that as a sign. He turned his suit coat inside out, laid it on the grass, and sat.

Casper curled up at his feet.

He'd tried to give the dog back to Hunter's mother, but Casper kept escaping from her house—and showing up on Tyler's doorstep, scratching and whining to be let in.

After the third time, Mrs. Garrity had asked Michael if he'd like to keep him.

It hadn't seemed as if it was up to him—and how could he refuse?

Anyway, it was nice to have company.

He felt someone coming across the field at about the same time as Casper raised his head, his ears alert. The service had been over for hours and his brothers had all gone home with the fire marshal. He wasn't sure who else would be walking out this way.

He glanced over his shoulder, expecting Hunter's mother.

No. Hannah.

Surprised, he got to his feet and brushed dried grass from his pants. He'd seen her at the funeral, of course, but she'd stood with her parents and James while he'd stood with his brothers.

They'd barely spoken all week—and when they *had* talked, it had seemed accidental, as if he'd caught her by surprise when he was stopping in to see his brothers.

Here he'd thought it was awkward *before*.

"Hey," he said, when she drew close. He couldn't keep the confusion out of his voice.

"Hey yourself," she said in return. She gave him a clear once-over. "You look good in a suit."

Michael found himself blushing and told himself to knock it off. "I had to buy it for court." He wanted to tell her she looked good in her wool skirt and boots, but he wasn't sure how that would come across.

But she did. She somehow looked soft and gentle, yet strong and fearless at the same time.

His brothers had offered to talk to Hannah on his behalf, and he'd told them to stay out of it and keep their mouths shut. Right now, facing her, he regretted that. He'd do anything for a little insight.

Hannah looked around. "At first I thought this was an odd place for a funeral, but now I think I kind of get it."

They stood at the edge of a large, open field by the water, part of Lake Waterford Park. Hunter's mother had chosen the location—she'd wanted to have a service somewhere her son would have enjoyed spending time.

A gravestone would be going next to his father's, back at some cemetery in Pennsylvania.

Michael preferred the atmosphere here. He was glad there'd been no body to bury. Watching a box get lowered into the ground, feeling every shovelful of dirt—he wouldn't have been able to take it. His parents' funeral had been bad for exactly that reason, but Hunter was different. Hunter was a kid. He'd trusted Michael. Relied on him.

Michael wouldn't get over this easily.

He cleared his throat. "I get it, too."

Hannah looked up at him, wincing a bit at the sunlight. "Want to go for a walk?"

He blinked, surprised, then grabbed his coat. "Sure."

So they walked, Casper ambling along between them. Maybe she wanted closure. Maybe his brothers were making her crazy. Michael had no idea. He expected her to talk, but she walked in silence.

He didn't mind.

Eventually, she glanced up at him. "I'm sorry the judge denied custody."

That had happened yesterday. After everything he'd lost, Michael had hoped fate would cut him some slack.

Fate had punched him in the gut. He still felt the blow.

But it wasn't permanent. The judge had given him thirty days to figure out a suitable living situation.

A month without his brothers. He thought back to his dad's mantra: *You can do anything for fifteen minutes.*

Thirty days was a hell of a lot longer than fifteen minutes.

But he understood it. When he'd been eighteen, he would have fought like hell to challenge even that. Now? His brothers' lecture the night they'd lost Hunter still echoed in his mind. They were old enough to take care of themselves—a little.

He needed the time anyway. To get his life back together.

He glanced at Hannah. "I understand why the judge did what she did. Your dad—he's been amazing. It's a relief knowing they'll stay together, and that I know where they are. . . " He stopped walking and looked at her. "Wait. This isn't why you came out here, is it? Have your parents changed their minds about letting them stay? I know a month is a long time, and—"

"No! No, Michael, they didn't change their minds. Are you kidding? My mother has practically adopted them already. It might break her heart when they *leave.*"

Michael smiled. His brothers could be charming when they wanted to be. "The guys said she bakes them cookies every day."

"Just about."

"That's good. They could use some mothering."

She didn't answer, and he lost the smile. They fell into silence again.

He peeked over at her. The sunlight was bright on her hair, and the chill in the air had thrown pink on her cheeks. She rubbed at her arms, and he realized he'd been an idiot.

"Here," he said, shrugging out of his coat. "It's cold with the wind."

She straightened in surprise when he dropped it around her shoulders, and he thought she might refuse. But then she grabbed the lapels and pulled it closer.

Her eyes flicked up at him. "Too bad we don't have Nick to make it stop, right?"

That felt a little too pointed. Michael frowned.

She looked up at him. "What's with the look?"

"I wish I'd told you," he said. "If I could go back and do it over, I would."

She didn't say anything to that.

She kept walking, though, so he kept pace with her.

"That night you came to Tyler's," he said, "when you implied that I didn't think you could take care of yourself . . . that's not what I think, Hannah." He paused. "That's not what I think at all."

Now she did stop, and she got in front of him. "Then what do you think?"

He studied her. "Why did you come out here?"

She shook her head. "Don't do that. Answer the question."

He rubbed a hand across the back of his head and looked past her, at the field. "I think I spent five years wondering if I'd ever meet someone who could handle my life. Not just my brothers or the Elemental stuff. All of it. Then I met you, and I thought . . . maybe." He paused. "I've been carrying this all by myself for a while, Hannah. I couldn't figure out how to share some of the load without dropping all of it." He glanced at her, then away. "I don't just mean you, either. My brothers, too. I forget that they're not little kids anymore." He shook his head. "The morning after the fire, Adam told me that it was okay to let other people take care of me. The problem is that I've forgotten *how*."

She was still looking up at him. "I can understand that."

"I know you can." He gave a short laugh. He wanted to touch her so badly that it hurt. He jammed his hands in his pockets. "Probably better than anyone else."

"Irish told me that it was okay for me to start acting like a grown-up, instead of like a kid with something to prove. I don't think I'm the only one."

"You're not." He paused and looked down at her. "So . . . you and Irish . . . ?"

He let that thought trail off.

She turned and started walking, but she didn't torture him too long. "We're friends."

Michael fell into step beside her. "That's all?"

"That's all. I'm still too hung up on someone else."

His heart tripped and stumbled and raced to catch up. "Oh yeah?"

"Yeah."

He caught her arm and turned her to face him. "Hannah— you've seen what we're up against. It won't stop."

"Irish says that things are changing. That the Guides are losing the power they once had."

It was so surreal to hear her talk about it like she'd known all his secrets all along. Bemused, Michael shook his head. "Maybe. But change is never immediate."

"Maybe we could deal with it together?"

He didn't say anything.

She grabbed his arms and shook him. "Damn it, Michael, this is one of those times when you can let someone else carry the load."

He grinned. "Like I said, change is never immediate."

She smiled back and started walking again.

He reached out and caught her hand. "So we're okay?"

"Nope."

Her voice was light, so his eyebrows went up, and he matched her tone. "Nope? What do you want from me?"

"A grown-up relationship."

"You mean we should argue about home equity loans and where to find the cheapest gasoline?"

She smacked him on the arm. "No. I mean no more hiding our relationship from your brothers." She paused. "Or my father."

"I was never hiding you, Hannah."

"I don't mean hiding, exactly." She paused. "I mean no more acting like we don't have a right to be together."

"Oh." He nodded and stopped her again, but this time he slid his hands under the jacket to catch her waist in his hands. "I think I can do that."

"No more big secrets, either."

"I can do that, too."

He leaned down to kiss her, but she put a finger against his lips. "If you kiss me like a grown-up," she said, "are you going to start earthquakes and stuff? Just how dangerous are you?"

Her voice was still teasing, but he heard the honest question there, too. He caught her face in his hands. "Let's find out together," he said.

He pressed his lips to hers.

And despite the fact that it was mid-November, every single wildflower in the field burst into bloom.

FEARLESS

CHAPTER 1

Hunter Garrity ducked behind a copse of trees and waited. The last week of school, and those jerks were still pulling this crap.

He held his breath and listened. Nothing.

But someone was still back there. He could *feel* it. He'd been feeling it the entire walk home, but sometime during the last fifteen minutes, they'd drawn close.

They'd never be able to wait him out. He knew that from experience. He had patience in spades and could sit here all night, letting the air and the earth feed him information. His talents weren't strong enough to demand answers from the elements—yet—so he had to wait, to pay attention to what they were willing to offer.

But if he missed dinner again, his dad would be *pissed*.

A branch snapped underfoot about twenty feet behind where he was hiding.

Hunter eased out a breath and waited. Another branch, a rustle of leaves.

It seemed like one person, which was surprising. None of them ever had the guts to face him alone—not anymore, anyway. Freshman year, sure, before he'd come home with one bruise too many and his father had taught him to put up a fight.

This year had started differently. Jeremy Rasmussen had been the first one to find out the hard way. On the second day of school, he'd walked into the boy's bathroom and slammed Hunter face-first into the tile wall.

Hunter had slammed him face-first into a mirror.

Jeremy had earned a broken nose, stitches across one cheek, and a chipped tooth. Hunter had earned two days' suspension and some greater regard from his classmates.

But they didn't leave him alone, though they wouldn't mess with him at school. No, now his walk home was a challenge. A gauntlet. They kept coming up with more creative ways to screw with him.

He kept coming up with more creative paths to travel.

Like this afternoon. He'd turned his walk from one mile to three, cutting through the dairy farm at the end of his road, easing between fence boards until he reached the acre of corn that led to the woods backing his parents' property.

Just because he *could* fight didn't mean he wanted to.

The crunching underbrush stopped, but Hunter couldn't look without giving away his hiding place. He held his breath again, wondering what their weapon would be this time. Bricks? A two-by-four? Once they'd actually thrown cow manure at him. Idiots. Maybe one day they'd shock him with something effective.

He let a breath out, drew one in, and held it.

Another step, another snap of underbrush. A breeze kicked up and whistled through the leaves overhead, whispering across his cheeks. He focused, waiting for information about his pursuer, but the wind cared for nothing more than the sunlight and the trees. He touched his fingers to the ground, and the earth confirmed it was one person.

One person, drawing close.

Hunter braced himself. Time slowed down, an eternity passing before the next crunch of leaves.

His eyes registered movement beyond the edge of the trees, and then he was all motion. When he fought, his brain tracked the activity like stop-action photography. The toe of a boot, a denim-covered knee, a powder-blue shirt, a flash of brown hair.

His arm, flying out to block any weapon. His leg, hooking an ankle to bring his attacker to the ground. A gasp and a shriek and an *oof*.

And a bright pink backpack, sailing through the air to land somewhere nearby. Papers fluttered into the wind and scattered.

Pink.

He stared down at the person he'd pinned. "Clare?"

"Ow." She grimaced and put a hand to her head. Strands of her hair were tangled in the dead leaves littering the ground. "That kinda hurt."

Clare Kasten was in his fourth-period government class. Cute, in a gentle way, with wide brown eyes and soft features. Shy, too. He couldn't remember a single word they'd ever exchanged.

Hunter swore and braced a hand against the ground so he could get some distance. "I'm sorry. I didn't mean . . . Are you okay?"

"I just wanted to talk to you." She made another face. "I didn't realize I'd be risking my life."

It would figure that the first time a girl *wanted* to talk to him, he'd knock her flat.

"I'm really sorry," he said again. He rolled up to one knee and held out a hand. "Are you all right?"

She took his hand. Hers was slight and soft, and it practically disappeared inside his. He pushed to his feet and pulled her along with him.

She wavered and he caught her elbows. It put them very close, probably closer than he'd ever been to a girl. "You sure you're okay to stand?"

She pulled an arm free to rub at the back of her head again. "I probably should have just passed you a note in class."

A note? No one had ever passed him a note. What kind of note? He had no idea how to play this. He had no idea what she wanted. Had she followed him?

"Could you let me go?" she said. "I need to get my papers."

"Crap. Yeah. Sorry." He'd been *staring* at her. He let her go and started grabbing for wayward papers, straightening them into a pile. "Do you want my phone? You could call your parents—"

"I'm not sure I really want to explain this to my parents."

"Look . . " Hunter couldn't meet her eyes. He focused on getting the last of the papers together. "I didn't think it was you."

"I sure hope not." She rubbed at the back of her head again and winced. "Holy crow, just who were you expecting?"

"It's not important." Despite the fact that he could kick Jeremy's ass blindfolded—not to mention most of his friends—being a target always left Hunter feeling less than dignified. He shrugged a little and looked at her sideways. "Seriously. You all right?"

"I think so."

He picked up her bag and slid the papers inside, then yanked the zipper closed. "How far do you have to walk?"

"I don't know. How far do you live?" She held out a hand for her bag.

"You want to come home with me?" God, he should tackle girls more often. He hoisted his backpack onto one shoulder and slung her bag over the other. "I can carry it."

"I live just on the other side of the dairy farm. But I wanted to ask you about the presentation you made in class yesterday."

"Oh. Sure." Talk about slamming the brake pedal. He should have figured she wouldn't be interested in him. But he couldn't really figure why she'd be interested in his presentation, either. Their government final had consisted of preparing a speech on Constitutional amendments. Two kids in class had actually fallen asleep while he was talking.

He sighed inwardly and pointed west. "I live on the other side of these woods. What did you want to know?"

She kept pace beside him, carefully picking her way through the underbrush. "Do you really believe what you said?"

He glanced over. There was a leaf stuck in her hair, but he didn't have the courage to pick it free. "Which part?"

"The part about guns being harmless?"

"I'm not sure I said that."

"You said people shouldn't be afraid of guns."

"They shouldn't. They should be afraid of people who don't know how to *use* guns."

"Do you?"

He grabbed her arm and hauled her to a stop. "Careful. You're about to step in poison oak. Do I what?"

She stepped around the leaves. "Do you know how to use a gun?"

"Yeah."

She gasped a little and stopped short. "Really?"

He shrugged. "My dad was in the military. He still works defense jobs. I've known how to handle a gun practically since I could walk." He paused. This might be the longest conversation he'd ever had with a girl, and he couldn't tell what that gasp meant. "It used to freak my mom out, but Dad always told her that I'd be a lot safer if I knew what I was doing with a firearm."

She was staring at him, wide-eyed. "You don't, like, have a gun on you now, do you?"

God, he wished he could carry weapons to and from school. Flashing a handgun would certainly save time with those idiots. "No. Are you crazy? That's a good way to get expelled." Not to mention his dad would go ballistic if Hunter took one out of the house without permission.

"But still." Clare started walking again. "Wow."

He had no idea how to take that, either. And she didn't say anything else. Their feet crunched through the leaves.

Hunter wondered if there was any possible way he could have made this interaction more awkward.

Here. Let me give you a concussion and then scare you.

"Sorry," he said. "It's never been a big deal in my house."

"My parents are total pacifists," she said, and there was something bitter in her voice. "They're completely against guns, and war, and . . . well, you know."

He didn't know. But he said, "Yeah. I get it."

"My older brother graduated last week, and he'd secretly enlisted in the army. He left on Saturday." She hesitated. "Mom and Dad are having a really hard time with it."

Clare was, too. He could tell from her voice, could feel the uncertainty in the air around her.

"My mom would have a really hard time with it, too," he said. He had no idea whether that was true, but it felt like the right thing to offer.

"Your dad would probably be proud, huh?"

"He'd probably throw a party." Then again, maybe not. His dad wasn't exactly the celebratory type. But he never lost a moment to impart a lesson that would fit right in with the military. Even when he was younger, Hunter had known that each gun lesson, every moment spent in self-defense was twofold: part knowledge, part training.

Sometimes he liked that. Even now, barely sixteen years old, there was some self-assurance in knowing he could take care of himself, that his father's rigid adherence to discipline served some purpose. With his connection to the elements, control could be a fleeting thing, and he'd take what he could get.

But sometimes he wanted to say screw it, to grow his hair out and get piercings all over, to let his abilities run rampant, just to break free of the mold for a minute.

"Does it scare you?" said Clare. "Living in a house with guns?"

Hunter smiled. "It's not like I wake up in the middle of the night to find them staring down at me."

"Shut up." She gave him a light shove. "No, I mean, are you ever worried you'll accidentally get shot?"

"You mean, when I catch the assault rifle raiding the refrigerator? Like maybe it'll turn on me?"

Her breath caught again. "You have an assault rifle *in your house*?"

"Sure. It's partial to lime Jell-O."

"Hunter. Seriously."

He liked the way she said his name, the way her tongue lingered on the *T*, just the tiniest bit.

He lost the smile. "Seriously."

They'd stopped again, and she was staring up at him. Her

eyes were a little wide, her breathing a little quick. There was a slight flush of pink across her cheeks.

"Scared?" he said, amused.

"Yes," she said. That flush deepened. "A little."

"I've never caught a gun wandering the woods yet."

She shoved him again. "Don't tease."

He started walking before he had to analyze all this touching too closely. "Sorry. I'll be nice."

She fell silent again, and he bit at the inside of his lip, sure this silence meant she was done with the conversation, that she was ready to find some other way to spend her afternoon.

"So," she said quietly.

Yep. This would be it. Hunter didn't even know how to prolong the interaction. He didn't look at her. "So."

"Your dad has a lot of weapons."

He shrugged. "I don't know about a *lot* .. "

Clare looked up at him. "Would you let me see them?"

His dad would definitely have a problem with this.

Thank god his dad wasn't home yet.

Hunter had worried his mom might be home, though she was the polar opposite of her husband: She never interfered in Hunter's activities. It didn't matter, anyway. A note hung from a magnet on the refrigerator, something about a trip to her store in town and a snack on the top shelf.

He looked at Clare. He felt jittery now that she was in his house. Somehow the kitchen felt both larger and smaller with her presence. "Are you hungry?"

"Not yet. Your mom has a store? What does she sell?"

Hunter shrugged. "Odds and ends. You know." His mother really worked for a New Age store in the antique district, but that usually launched a whole line of questions he didn't feel like answering.

Clare stepped forward and leaned close. His pulse jumped, but she was only reaching out a finger to touch a photo stuck to the refrigerator. "Is this you and your dad?"

"And my uncle. Yeah." The picture was from a camping trip last fall. They'd gone into the Appalachian Mountains, and it had rained almost the entire time. In the picture they were drenched and smiling.

"You look just like your dad."

"Everyone says that."

She touched another picture. "You have a dog?"

"My uncle does. Casper is a police dog. Uncle Jay is a cop."

Clare looked up at him. "You're close."

He shrugged. "You know. Family."

"Must be nice."

The tone in her voice reminded him of the uncertainty when she'd talked about her brother. He wondered just how upset her parents must be—and where Clare fit in.

Hunter reached on top of the refrigerator to grab the keys to the gun locker before he could think better of it. "Everything is in the basement. Come on."

The gun locker wasn't really a locker at all; it was more of an extra bedroom with a steel door, a dead bolt, and a six-key combination lock.

He wanted to cover his hand while he punched the numbers, but that would look stupid, and what was the difference if she knew how to get in here? She was scared of the very mention of guns; it's not like she was going to be back later to steal something.

Clare watched him push the buttons until the door clicked and the lock released. "What's twelve-fourteen-twenty?"

He stopped with his hand on the knob. "Our birthdays. My dad's is the twelfth, mine is the fourteenth, and my uncle's is the twentieth."

"Not your mom's?"

Hunter had never thought about it. He shrugged. "I guess he ran out of numbers." He hesitated before pushing the door open. Now that they were down here, he was having second thoughts.

Clare put a hand on his arm. "Are you going to get in trouble for showing me?"

Her fingers were warm, and when he turned his head to look at her, her lips were close.

Stop thinking about her mouth.

He had to clear his throat. "No. I mean, I don't think so."

Because no one was going to know about this.

Before he could think better of it, he threw the door wide.

"Holy crap," she whispered.

Hunter tried to see the room with fresh eyes, but it was tough. He'd grown up with this stuff. The hunting rifles in racks along the far wall, the Peg-Board on the right with hooks for the handguns, the military-style guns hanging on the left. Low cabinets lined the sidewalls, the counter space clear. A table sat in the middle of the room, empty, of course. His dad had way too much military training to leave anything out of place.

Clare had sucked back a bit, and Hunter gave her a smile. "They won't jump out and bite you."

"Am I being ridiculous?"

"I don't know. I've never showed this room to anyone."

Ugh. Why did he say that?

"Can I go inside?"

"Sure." He stood back, then followed her through.

She walked to the wall of military-style weapons first. He couldn't really blame her; those were definitely the most impressive.

"Do you know how to use all of these?" she asked, her voice hushed.

"I haven't fired all of them, but most guns work on the same principle." He took down the AR-15, which looked pretty badass but was really rather simple.

She flinched.

"Relax," he said, more at ease now that they were in here. With weapons, he knew what he was doing, and it fed his confidence. He did what his dad always did, unclipping the magazine and checking to make sure it wasn't loaded. Each click was loud, heavy steel sliding into place. When he was sure the gun was safe, he held it out to Clare.

She shook her head quickly.

"No bullets," he said. "You can hold it."

She gingerly started to take it from him, just her fingers wrapping around the barrel. Hunter shook his head. "Don't do it halfway. It's heavy. Just take it."

He didn't let go until her hands were wrapped solidly around the weapon. She held it at a distance from her body, like a poisonous snake.

He had to smile. "Here. Like this." He positioned her left hand on the front of the gun, supporting the barrel. "Now put your right hand on the pistol grip—"

"I don't want to shoot anything."

"Bullets don't magically appear. Work with me." He reached around for her right hand.

And then, somehow, her back was against his chest, and he was holding his hands over hers, positioning the rifle against her shoulder.

Her hair smelled like mangoes. Her cheek was right by his face.

Hunter dropped his voice. "What do you think?"

"I think my parents would die if they knew."

He laughed softly. "What do *you* think?"

She didn't say anything for a moment, and when she finally spoke, her voice was soft. "The day after my brother graduated, he went out and bought a gun. My parents don't know."

"Does he keep it locked up?"

"I don't know. He took it with him." She paused, and her voice almost wavered. "I kept worrying that I'd accidentally find it, or he'd accidentally shoot it, or . . . I don't know."

"If you want to learn how to handle them, I could show you."

She turned her head slightly. "Yeah?"

"Sure. When—"

The basement steps creaked; then heavy footfalls were coming down the stairs. "Hunter?"

Hunter jumped and almost dropped the gun. Thank god it

was unloaded, because Clare started to spin with the weapon in her hands.

Hunter got a grip on it before she turned all the way, but it left his arms wrapped around Clare, the gun in their hands, just as his uncle came through the door.

CHAPTER 2

Hunter tried to think of a way out of this.

He was coming up short.

"That better be unloaded," said his uncle. He was still in uniform, and it always made him look taller, more official.

"It is," said Hunter. He let go of Clare, keeping the barrel pointed downward, trying not to meet his uncle's eyes.

There was no way his dad wouldn't find out about this.

"I figured we'd catch you with a girl one day, but this isn't quite the scenario I imagined."

Hunter sighed. Humiliation was going to kill him.

"It's my fault," said Clare quickly.

"Really?" said Uncle Jay. "You stole the keys and guessed the combination? Was Hunter trying to get the weapon away from you, then?"

He couldn't be in *too* much trouble if his uncle was going to stand here and joke about it. "It's not her fault."

"Should I give your girlfriend a ride home?"

"Let me guess," said Hunter. "You mean in your police cruiser?"

"Oh, I can walk," said Clare. She was already edging toward the door.

Hunter wished he could go with her.

She didn't look back at him as she dashed for the stairs.

Well, that had been short-lived.

But at the top of the steps, she ducked back to look at him. "I'll see you tomorrow at school."

Then she was gone, and the gun room was completely silent.

Hunter held out the gun, stock first. "You want to just shoot me and save Dad the time?"

Jay smiled and took the weapon, checking the magazine before putting it back on the wall. "He's not going to shoot you."

"That would be too quick?"

Now Jay laughed, but then he quickly sobered and gave Hunter a *look*. "We've talked to you about girls before."

"It wasn't like that."

"I'm pretty sure I know exactly what it was like."

Hunter scowled. "I did a presentation on the second amendment at school. She had some questions about firearms."

"Is that the new lingo for saying you're her *anatomy tutor*?"

Jay's voice was easy, but Hunter knew that the questions behind it were serious. "Look, I said it wasn't like that. I haven't even talked to her before today."

"Hunter, our abilities are a blessing and a curse . . . it's very easy to get taken advantage of."

"She wasn't taking advantage of me! We were just talking!"

"No. *This*"—Jay gestured at the space between them—"is talking."

Hunter flushed and looked away.

His uncle straightened and put his hands on Hunter's shoulders. "You're a Fifth. While that means you're connected to all the elements, it also means you're connected to the people around you."

Hunter rolled his eyes. He knew this rhetoric better than a nursery rhyme. "And when people are drawn to me, I'll be drawn to them, and it's hard to remember my own purpose—"

"Don't mock it, Hunter."

Hunter shook Jay's hands off. "We were just *talking*. You're acting like she was trying to—"

"I don't care what she was trying to do. I'm trying to tell you that it can be hard to distinguish what *you* want from what others want. You're going to want to help everyone, and that's not always a good thing."

"How is that not a good thing?"

His uncle leaned back against the table. "What if I wanted to help every criminal I had to arrest? What if your dad went on assignment and empathized with the bad guys?"

"Did you really just say 'bad guys'?"

Now Jay didn't smile at all. "You need to take this seriously. Your abilities are going to get stronger. That means it's going to be *more* difficult instead of less."

"So I can't ever have a girlfriend."

"You'd probably be better off if you had *lots* of girlfriends. You know what your dad used to tell me when I was your age?"

"What?"

Hunter's dad spoke from the doorway. Even in khakis and a polo shirt, he looked like he'd stepped right out of a recruitment poster. "He's too young for that, Jay."

"If you'd walked in here five minutes ago, you wouldn't think so."

Hunter wanted to roll his eyes, but his dad was a lot less tolerant of attitude than his uncle was. He kept his voice mild. "Uncle Jay is overreacting."

"Is this about the girl I just saw walking down the driveway?"

"Clare." Hunter couldn't read his dad's expression, but the man wasn't an idiot. He'd probably figured out half of it already. "She's in my government class. I did a presentation on firearms and she had some questions."

"Did you answer them?"

Hunter wasn't ready for a question. He was ready for lecturing. "Most of them."

"Good." He looked at Jay. "Thanks for coming over. You have time to stay for dinner?"

That was it?

"You're not mad?" said Hunter.

His dad glanced at him. "Not yet."

Hunter frowned. "Yet?"

"You're about to teach yourself a lesson a lot more effectively than I ever could. I'll be mad if you don't learn it the first time around."

"I don't understand."

"You will." His father looked back at Jay. "The file for this weekend is upstairs if you want to take a look."

His uncle straightened. "Sure. I have time."

"File?" Hunter's ears perked up. If Uncle Jay was involved, that meant it was Elemental business. His father worked private security jobs on his own. "You have a job this weekend?"

"Nothing you need to worry about," said his father.

"Let him listen," said Jay. "You said it's just surveillance for now, right? He'll be doing it himself soon enough."

Hunter's dad smiled and smacked his brother on the back of the head good-naturedly—but his eyes were serious. "I said, it's nothing he needs to worry about."

"You know I can keep a secret," said Hunter.

Hunter's dad lost the smile. "It's not about keeping secrets. I don't want you in on this stuff any sooner than you need to be."

"But *why?* You tell me about your private-duty stuff all the time. But *this* is the stuff I should be learning—"

"No," said his dad, and his eyes were fierce. "It's not a game, Hunter. You're *not ready.*"

Hunter gritted his teeth. He took every lesson seriously. He followed every rule his father laid out. His skills with a rifle could rival real sharpshooters. Any challenge his father set, he could do it. He *had* done it.

"I know it's not a game," he said.

"Good. Then forget we mentioned it."

"Is this because I brought a girl home?" Hunter wanted to punch the wall, but he was well practiced in maintaining control, especially when his father was around. He kept his voice even. "You said you weren't mad."

"I'm not. And this isn't a punishment."

"What good is all this training if you're never going to let me *use* it?"

"Hunter."

"Maybe if you would let me have the *chance*—"

"*Hunter*. I said no."

That tone was final, like throwing up a wall. A point of no return. For a bare instant, Hunter wanted to knock it down, to rebel and throw a fit.

But that would just make his father throw up a new wall, a stronger one.

His father wasn't waiting around for him to make a choice, anyway. He turned and started through the door, saying, "Lock up when you're done in here."

Like Hunter would sit down here and sulk.

Actually, he would have if his dad hadn't said something.

Now he stood back and waited for his uncle to go through the doorway, then flipped the light switch and locked the door.

But he stopped Jay at the bottom of the stairs.

"Hey," he said, his voice low, "what *did* Dad tell you about girls?"

His uncle laughed and clapped him on the shoulder, and Hunter thought he was going to brush off the question.

But Jay leaned in and lost the smile. "Use them before they use you."

Hunter thought about his father's and uncle's warnings all night.

He couldn't line it all up in his head.

If Clare was using him, it was just for information, and that seemed kind of weak. She could learn practically anything about guns from Wikipedia. It didn't seem worthwhile to follow him home from school for something she could find in zero-point-six seconds on Google.

And regardless of whether she was using him, he sure didn't want to use *her*.

Clare's apprehension about guns was real—his abilities were strong enough to sense that. Her concern for her brother felt real, too. Maybe she just craved some kind of *experience,* some way to understand what her brother would be handling.

And she'd hung close to him in the gun locker. She hadn't

minded when his arms went around her, when he'd placed his hands over hers and showed her how to grip the weapon.

But still, his father's lessons were never something to be treated lightly. Hunter could feel the seeds of future disappointment taking root already.

I'll be mad if you don't learn it the first time around.

What did that mean? Did his father expect him to cut Clare off now, before anything else happened?

He could do that. It would be easy enough. They hardly knew each other, and this was the last week of school.

But it felt . . . *wrong*. He was sixteen years old, not six. He didn't have to brush off some girl just because his daddy didn't think they should play together.

Maybe he didn't have to worry about it at all. The way they'd been caught had been plenty embarrassing. Today was his alternate schedule, too, so he didn't have Government. Maybe he'd walk into school and find her giggling about him with her girlfriends. Even better, maybe he'd make it through the whole day without seeing her at all.

No. He found her waiting at his locker after last period.

Sleeveless sundress, brown hair shining, a splash of freckles across her shoulders.

He tried not to think of what it would be like to show her how to hold a weapon while she was wearing *that*.

She smiled at him. "I've been worried about you all day. Did you get in trouble because of me?"

He shrugged a little and worked the combination lock. She smelled like mangoes again, and it took effort to keep his eyes on the spinning numbers. "Nah. My dad was actually cool with it."

"Really? So I can come back?"

"Sure—"

Then a hand smacked him on the back of the head, hard enough to slam his face into the locker.

Stars blossomed in his vision, but Hunter was already spinning automatically, an arm coming up to block, the other swinging a fist.

The other guy barely got out of his way. Garrett Watts, a heavyset junior who usually trailed after Jeremy Rasmussen. His brown eyes were small and beady above doughy cheeks, and the only thing about him that gave Hunter pause was the fact that this guy had to have seventy pounds on him.

But at least he couldn't run fast. It was probably a lucky miracle he'd missed Hunter's first swing.

Hunter was about to remedy that when a teacher appeared in the hallway. Miss Janney, the first-year Spanish teacher. She had guts getting between them. "Boys. Take a walk. In opposite directions."

Hunter didn't move. Clare had shrunk back against the lockers. Garrett looked like he was ready to come around the teacher— or through her. If Hunter turned around and started walking, Garrett wouldn't follow his lead. He'd strike again.

Hunter could feel the promise of violence in the air. He wondered what he'd done to draw Garrett's attention today.

Once he had the attention of Jeremy's crowd, it was insanely hard to lose it.

He started planning how he could minimize the damage.

"*Walk,*" Miss Janney said. "There are two more days of school. I'm sure you don't want to spend them on suspension."

Garrett didn't move. "He started it."

Hunter opened his mouth, but Miss Janney held up a hand. "I don't care who started it. Walk or I'm calling security."

"Whatever." Garrett shrugged his backpack higher on his arm as he turned to walk. "I know where to find him later."

New way home. Check.

Once Garrett was walking, Miss Janney disappeared back into her classroom, muttering something about forty-eight more hours until peace.

Clare left the safety of the lockers and touched Hunter's arm. Her eyes were full of concern. "Are you okay?"

He would let Garrett punch him again if this was the result.

"Yeah," he said, and his voice sounded slightly thick. His cheek had taken the brunt of the hit, but his nose felt sore, too.

"I think you're bleeding," she said. "Do you want to go to the nurse?"

Bleeding? He touched a hand to his nose and felt wetness. Crimson drops clung to his fingers.

Clare was fishing through her backpack. "Here."

Tissues. He held one to his face. This was just *great*. Maybe he could pee his pants next.

"You were going to fight him," said Clare, her voice soft.

"I wasn't going to let him kill me."

"Aren't you afraid of him?"

"I used to be," he said honestly.

"Did your dad teach you to fight, too?"

"Yeah." He checked the tissues. Ugh. "God, I look like a total wuss."

"No way," said Clare with a smile. "I think you look totally fearless."

CHAPTER 3

The early summer air was soft on Hunter's face as he trudged through the woods to the edge of the cornfield. He'd shoved some apples and two cans of soda in his backpack, along with a box of ammunition and two unloaded handguns.

Clare was walking by his side.

He was going to teach her to shoot.

His father's lack of anger left him feeling more worried instead of less. The warning still rang in his ears, and he told his brain to knock it off. What could she be using him for? Shooting lessons?

Stupid.

She'd been mostly quiet on the walk to his house, and he'd been walking a cord of tension himself, ready for Jeremy or Garrett or one of those morons to come flying out of the trees.

But nothing had happened.

"You could take them, couldn't you?" she said out of the blue.

He didn't have to ask who she was talking about. After that display in the hallway, he wasn't surprised those thugs were on her mind, too. He smiled. "*Take them,*" he mimicked. "I don't really want to fight them."

"Why not? Don't you think they'd leave you alone?"

Hunter stopped at the edge of the tree line. There was a long stretch of grass here before the cornfield started, and his dad had set steel targets of varying heights into the ground. He set his backpack gently on the ground.

"That's not how it works," he said, dropping to sit in the grass. He unzipped the nylon. "If it were that easy, I'd have done it at the beginning of the year."

She hesitated, then dropped to sit beside him, pulling her skirt over her knees. The grass was warm here, the sun beating down. "I don't understand."

"People don't really leave me alone," he said. "Kind of an occupational hazard."

She frowned. "I still don't understand."

Hunter smiled and shook his head. "Sorry. I just mean, when I fight them, it seems to inspire them to fight more. You know how sometimes when you put up resistance, it just makes people push harder?"

She was staring at him, and he couldn't figure out the tension in her expression.

"What?" he said.

She shook her head quickly. "Nothing. So they keep coming after you?"

"Yeah." He shrugged and started snapping bullets into an empty magazine. "It's like they keep coming up with more creative ways to try to kick my ass. And if I fight them at school, it just gets me in trouble. Getting in trouble pisses off my dad. I mostly try to avoid them. Want an apple?"

"Sure."

He snapped the last bullet, then slid the clip into a 9mm Beretta. He'd chosen this one because it was smaller and might not make her so uneasy.

Even so, she swallowed when the metal clicked.

"We don't have to do this," he said.

"No. It's fine. It's good."

Hunter made sure the safety was on, then stood. He showed her all the parts to the gun, going over the safety features, glad for his father's and uncle's thorough instruction, because he could talk about this stuff in his sleep. He paid close attention when she started to take the gun from him, and it was a good thing, because she almost pointed it directly at him.

"Downrange only," he said, holding her wrist. "Always pay attention where you're pointing it."

Her breath was shaking, just a tiny bit. "What are we shooting?"

"Just cardboard. The targets are backed with half-inch steel. The bullets won't go through."

"What if I miss?"

"Shooting this way, we're almost a mile from the nearest house," he said. "Besides, we're only twenty feet from the target. You'll hit it. Just hold on to the gun. There's a kick to it."

"I'm scared I'm going to shoot myself."

"Come on. I mean, if anyone should be scared here, it's me."

She gave him a look, and he smiled. "Here. I'll shoot first." He took the pistol and aimed. "Put your hand on my wrist. You'll feel it."

As soon as her fingers closed around his wrist, Hunter almost couldn't focus. He was acutely aware of her closeness, of the scent of mangoes and cut grass and summer corn. He took a deep breath. It didn't help.

"What's with the bracelets?" she said, her thumb brushing one of the strands of twine wrapped around his wrist. Her touch was making him crazy.

"Just rocks," he said.

"Very New Age."

"My mom's into that stuff," he said. It was a half-truth. His mother *was* into rocks and charms and talismans, but the difference between the crap she sold in town and the rocks on his wrist were that his rocks actually did help him focus power.

Really, it was a miracle he could even remember to keep it a secret.

Focus. "Ready?"

She nodded. He pulled the trigger.

The sound was near deafening. She flinched hard but didn't let go of his wrist. Her fingers were trembling against his skin.

"You all right?" he said. His ears felt thick. He probably should have thought to bring earmuffs.

"Yeah," she said. Her breathing sounded too quick, but she glanced up at him. "I want to try."

He showed her how to hold the weapon again, how to look down the sight to find the target. "Don't do it halfway," he said. "My dad always says *commit to the target*."

Her grip tightened, but she didn't pull the trigger.

"Whenever you're ready," he said.

Her eyes were narrow, staring down the line on the barrel. "Do you ever wish you could just shoot them?"

"Sometimes," he said. "When I'm in the moment." He hesitated. "I don't think I could do it, though. We can talk about bullets and safeties and target practice all day, but the bottom line is that guns are made to kill people. It's stupid to forget that."

"And you don't want to kill them."

"Not for a bloody nose, no." He paused again. "I don't know what it would take."

"I do." She pulled the trigger.

He wasn't ready for it, and it made him jump a mile.

"I did it!" She had a huge smile on her face, and he grabbed her wrist before she turned toward him again.

"Downrange," he said, breathless. "Not at me."

Her eyes were shining up at him. "Take the gun."

He took it and flipped on the safety. "That's it?" he teased. "One shot?"

"I need my hands free."

And before he could even ask why, she put her hands on both sides of his face and kissed him.

Hunter sat at dinner and pushed his food around the plate. His brain had turned to mush. Criminals could storm the house right now, and he'd probably just sit here and watch them do it.

He kept thinking about Clare. Her hands in his hair. Her lips against his. Her mouth. Her fingers. The thin fabric of her dress, the warmth of her skin, the way he'd traced the freckles on her shoulders with his fingertips first, and then his tongue.

He'd almost missed dinner.

He wouldn't have minded.

Clare had been the one to bring him back to reality, telling him she'd have to sprint for the house just to make it back before her mom got home from work. He'd barely made it home in time himself. The guns were still in the bottom of his backpack, waiting to be put back when his dad wouldn't notice him going downstairs.

"Hunter?"

He dropped his fork. It clanked against the plate. His dad was staring at him intently. Hunter had to clear his throat. "Yeah?"

"I asked what happened to your face."

Hunter stabbed a piece of grilled chicken for an excuse to look away. He'd checked the mirror when he got home, and there was a pretty decent bruise along his left cheek.

"Accident at school."

"Those boys still hassling you?"

Hunter never knew how to answer that question. Did his dad want him to admit it? Or did he want to know Hunter could take care of himself? "Just guys being stupid. School's almost out anyway, so . . " He shrugged.

His mother tsked and reached out to put a hand over his.

Hunter pulled his hand away. No matter what his father meant, Hunter hated taking her sympathy in front of him.

"And the girl?" said his dad. "How are things there?"

Hunter almost choked on the piece of grilled chicken. "She's great. Good. She's good."

"Girl?" said his mother. "There's a girl?"

"It's nothing," said Hunter. He shoved another piece of chicken into his mouth.

"Learn anything yet?" said his father.

Yes. He'd learned that the world could narrow to a single breathless moment when he was kissing Clare.

He met his father's gaze head-on. "Not yet."

"Make sure you're paying attention." His father stood to take his plate to the sink and dropped a kiss on his wife's head. "Thank you for dinner, darling."

Hunter watched this and wondered about Uncle Jay's warning last night. It seemed like a direct contradiction to the whole *use them before they use you.*

Then again, he kept thinking about Clare's question in front of the gun locker, about the fact that his mom's birth date wasn't part of the combination. It was such a minor, inconsequential thing—but it felt like such a *big* thing when combined with that harsh warning.

His father doted on his mother. Hunter watched it every day. They really were the most unlikely pair—his mom even commented on it to strangers with a laugh. How the die-hard military man had fallen for the New Age neo-Wiccan.

But for the first time, Hunter started to wonder if what looked like doting was really . . . tolerance. Indulgence.

As soon as he had the thought, Hunter shoved it out of his head. They'd been together for seventeen years. They never fought. He'd never questioned their love for each other, because their love for him was an unwavering constant.

But now that he'd considered it, he couldn't *stop* thinking it.

A hand rapped at the back door, and Uncle Jay stuck his head in. "Am I late for dinner?"

"There's plenty left," said Hunter's mom.

Jay opened the door fully, and Casper burst into the room, jogging immediately to Hunter, who rubbed the scruff of his neck and slid him chicken from his plate.

"That dog loves you," said Jay.

Hunter gave Casper another piece. "I love him back."

Casper sat by his side and put his head in Hunter's lap.

Jay pulled out a chair and dropped into it. He glanced at his brother. "Did you get more info?"

Hunter's dad cast a glance at him. "Yeah. We'll talk upstairs. Later."

Hunter pretended he didn't notice. But after dinner was done, he lingered in the kitchen, washing dishes, playing with Casper, giving his dad and uncle time to finish shooting the shit and get down to real business.

Then he crept up the stairs, easing around the step that creaked, holding his breath as he edged as close as he could to his father's office door.

Their voices were low, and he could only make out a few words, none of which made too much sense.

He eased out a breath, then took another one in. He slid a bit closer.

"Hunter."

Damn it.

His father's voice. Hunter didn't move. Maybe this was a bluff.

Then the door opened. Uncle Jay stood there. "Really, kid?"

Hunter sighed and looked up at him from where he crouched on the floor. "I don't get what the big deal is. You said it was just surveillance."

"Come in here," his father called. He didn't sound happy.

Hunter shoved to his feet and went to the doorway.

His father was sitting at his desk, two files on the surface in front of him. Both were closed.

"First," he said, "I'm not happy about the spying."

"But you never tell me anything! I'm sixteen years old, and—"

"And you're acting like a teenager. *Not yet,* Hunter."

"I can handle it."

"Like you handled those boys at school?"

Hunter flinched. "I don't know what that means. What do you want me to do, break their necks? Get expelled? They're just playing stupid pranks. I can't exactly kill them for that."

"What if I told you they would grow up to be criminals? What about then?"

"What *about* then?" Hunter glanced at Uncle Jay, but there were no answers there. His uncle was leaning against the doorjamb, his arms folded.

His father leaned forward in the desk chair, bracing his arms on his knees. "If I told you they would grow up to be criminals, that they could potentially hurt people, could you kill them then?"

Hunter licked his lips. This felt like a trick question, and the wrong answer wouldn't be something he could take back.

His father didn't wait long. He shook his head. "You're not ready."

"I'm not ready because I didn't say I could *kill my class-mates*? You're not making any sense. What does this have to do with one stupid surveillance job?"

"Sometimes watching leads to action."

Hunter felt like the right answers kept springing up in front of him; he just couldn't grasp them quickly enough. "Fine. If it comes to that, I'll stand back and let you guys do the action part."

"That's not how this works. If you're there, you're there. Nothing halfway, right?"

Hunter nodded. "Right."

"This is a different surveillance case." His father flipped open the file folder. "These aren't full-blown Elementals causing major problems."

"Then . . . what are they?" Hunter reached for the file, but his dad snapped it closed.

"They're teenagers. Your age. They haven't come into their full powers yet."

"So it's safer—"

"No." His dad laughed, but there wasn't any humor about it. "There's nothing safe about this one. Not from what I'm read-ing. These could be four of the most powerful Elementals to sur-face in *years*."

"What have they done?"

"I don't know yet. There are conflicting reports about deaths and threats and . . . hell, I can barely wrap my head around what's going on in that town. But really, Hunter, it's not about what they've *done*."

"What's it about?"

His dad leaned back in his chair. "It's about what they can *do*."

Hunter stared at him.

"Say I agreed, and I took you along as a decoy. You're a teenager; you could fit right in." He glanced in the file again. "Your mom's folks even live right in the area. We wouldn't have to think of an excuse for you to be there."

"Yes," said Hunter. "*Yes*. I'll do it."

"And what if you determined they were as powerful as these reports say? Could you kill them?"

Could he kill complete strangers? "If they were using their powers to hurt people, I would do what I had to."

"What if they're not using their powers to harm anyone?" said his father. "What if they're good kids? Boy Scouts? What if they help people?"

Hunter swallowed. "Then . . . why would you kill them?"

His father smiled, a little sadly. "You're not ready."

"But—"

"Enough, Hunter. We have work to do." He lost the smile. "And if I catch you spying again, you're not going to like the results. Do you understand me?"

Hunter walked out and slammed the door behind him—before realizing he was probably driving his father's points about immaturity home.

He went back to the kitchen and grabbed his backpack. He should probably put the weapons back before he got in trouble for that, too. He slammed the door to the basement, too, wanting to punch a hole in the drywall. He jammed the key into the gun locker door and punched the buttons, practically breaking a finger in his fury.

Only when he reached into his bag was he careful. He pulled the zipper free on the table and looked inside.

Then he kept on looking.

One gun and a fully loaded magazine were missing.

CHAPTER 4

Hunter wondered if this was what a heart attack felt like. The bag had been sitting in the corner of the kitchen all evening. Unless someone had broken in and stolen the gun in the last hour—while there was a police dog lying on the mat in front of the sink—then he'd either left the gun in the clearing or Clare had taken it.

He had no idea why Clare, someone who was obviously afraid of firearms, would take the weapon.

But he knew he hadn't left a fully loaded handgun lying in the grass, either.

If his father found out, he was so dead.

He grabbed the cell phone out of his pocket—just as he realized he'd never gotten her number.

Like she'd answer. What would he say? "Did you maybe accidentally take a gun from my bag?"

Hunter ran a hand through his short hair and tried not to panic.

How. Could he. Have let. This happen.

His father's stupid comment kept running through his head.

You're about to teach yourself a lesson a lot more effectively than I ever could.

Or his uncle's: *Use them before they use you.*

It didn't make any sense. Clare didn't seem like the type.

God, what did he know about *types*?

He needed to figure out a solution. Otherwise he might as well just load the remaining handgun and shoot himself.

No. He could handle this. First, he needed to get out of the gun locker before his dad realized he was down here and decided to come see what was going on.

Hunter locked the room. He almost put the remaining gun away, but if Clare had totally played him and was some kind of marksman, he didn't want to go facing her unarmed.

Marksman. Who was he kidding? He'd felt her hand tremble on his wrist when he'd fired that first shot.

Why would she take a gun?

Hunter went back to his bedroom and logged on to Facebook. Clare wasn't his friend, but maybe he could find her cell phone number.

No cell number. No address. Her status message was set to public, and it was last updated two days ago. *The cafeteria macaroni and cheese doesn't actually include cheese. I read the ingredients!!!*

Seriously. Like there was any chance it would say *I stole a handgun from Hunter Garrity this afternoon! He can totally find me at 123 Main Street!*

Uncle Jay was a cop. He could find out where she lived.

Yeah, and his dad said he'd be pissed if he caught Hunter *spying* again.

Why the hell hadn't he offered to walk her home this afternoon?

Wait a minute. What had she said yesterday?

I live on the other side of the dairy farm.

Hunter grabbed a flashlight.

The sun was fully down now, but humidity still clung to the air. Hunter had the other handgun, a .45 ACP officer's model, in one hand, a flashlight in the other. Casper had followed him out of the house, which worked well—so well that Hunter had gone back in to yell to his uncle that he was taking the dog for a quick run.

And he could have been running, as fast as his heart was racing. It felt like it took forever to cross the pastures to the far side of the dairy farm, but he could see a small house between the trees, the porch light like a beacon.

He had no idea what he was going to do when he got there. He couldn't exactly knock on the door with a gun in hand. And if Clare had stolen his weapon, it wasn't like she'd hand it over.

Hunter stopped in her backyard and waited, deliberating. He wasn't even sure this was the right house. The back patio offered no answers. Only the upstairs lights were on, although it seemed early.

Casper waited by his side, bracing against Hunter's legs.

"Damn it," Hunter whispered. He bit at his lip.

Could he break in?

Yeah, if he did that, his dad *and* his uncle would kill him. How long had he been gone? They might be starting to wonder already.

What he needed was for Clare to come running out here with the gun.

He took a deep breath and blew it out.

And then he heard the yelling.

Hunter held his breath. He couldn't make out words, but it was definitely a man, very loud and almost incoherent.

And then a girl's voice, high pitched and almost shrieking.

Casper growled.

Hunter put a hand on the scruff of his neck. The air was whispering all kinds of hints about this altercation, and none of them were good.

Then a gunshot cracked the night.

Hunter dropped and dashed to the side of the house, staying low. The shot had come from inside.

The screaming had escalated.

Another gunshot. This round went through a window, because glass shattered and rained down on the patio about ten feet over from where Hunter crouched.

He could barely hear over his breathing.

More screaming. A woman, but Hunter couldn't tell if it was

Clare. No one was dead yet, because they sure were making a racket. Casper barked.

Another shot. A bullet hit the storage shed across the yard. Hunter flinched.

If that was the 9 mm, there would be at least six bullets left, unless shots had been fired before he got here. He and Clare had fired one in the field, and now someone had fired three.

Hunter should have grabbed a bulletproof vest out of the locker.

He fished his phone out of his pocket. He started to dial, but the screaming upstairs cut off abruptly.

Casper growled softly.

Hunter held his breath again. If he made a call, they might hear him.

He didn't exactly want to be noticed by someone shooting wildly.

He switched to text message and found Uncle Jay's number—his dad's texting was sporadic at best.

Shots fired at house on opp side dairy farm. Send help.

A text came back almost immediately.

U OK?

Hunter moved to text back, but another gunshot exploded somewhere above him. He shoved the phone back into his pocket and slid toward the front of the house.

The front door was half open, the lower level a well of darkness. Was this a robbery in progress? He might have believed that—if Clare hadn't already stolen his gun. Hunter ducked inside. He waited for his eyes to acclimate, then eased around furniture toward the staircase.

Someone was crying upstairs.

Clare?

But then he heard Clare's voice, cold and hard and definitely not full of tears.

"You leave her alone. I swear to god I will shoot you."

Then a man's voice. "Shoot me. They'll lock you up, and then what'll you do?"

"I'll shoot. I will." Clare's voice sounded strong, but Hunter heard the slightest waver beneath the words. He kept the .45 in his hands and eased up the steps.

And then he turned the corner and they were right there, in the hallway. Clare had the gun in her hands, held at chest level in both hands, just like he'd shown her.

The gun was pointed at a man in his forties wearing nothing but a pair of jeans. Hunter could smell alcohol from here.

And on the floor behind Clare lay a crumpled woman, crying, her hands over her face. Hunter could see blood between her fingers.

Hunter trained the gun on the man. "Clare," he breathed carefully, not wanting to spook her with the gun in her hands. "It's okay. I called the cops."

Almost on cue, he could hear the thready sounds of a siren.

"Hunter," she said. Her voice broke. "Hunter, you have to go."

"It's okay," he said again. "I'll hold him. Just . . . just put the gun down. Slide the safety, remember?"

The man sneered at him. "You won't hold *shit*, kid."

Hunter snorted. His own gun didn't waver. "Some pacifist."

"I just said . . . I just said that because—" Clare's voice broke again. She still had the gun pointed at the man, but her grip was wavering badly. "My brother used to stop . . . used to stop him—"

"It's okay," said Hunter carefully. "It's okay. Just put the gun down. The cops are coming. You don't need to shoot him."

The sirens were very close now. Tires crunched on the driveway, and a car door slammed.

"See?" said Hunter. "They're here. You need to put the gun down so they don't shoot *you*."

"They're here?" said Clare.

"They're here. They won't let him hurt you. Or your mother."

"Okay." Clare turned toward him with the gun in her hands.

"No!" Hunter dodged to get out of her line of fire—especially since her father had lunged forward to grab for the weapon.

The gun went off. Clare cried out. She fell to the ground, just as her father raised his arm, pointing the gun at Hunter.

Hunter didn't think.

He pulled the trigger.

CHAPTER 5

"So what did you learn?"

Hunter slumped in the free chair in his dad's office. He'd been up all night—and his dad had already made it clear that he expected Hunter to go to school.

Clare and her mother were in the hospital.

So was her father, under police guard. He had a bullet hole through his left shoulder.

"A lot of things," said Hunter.

"Specifically?"

"I should have told you she took the gun."

His father smiled, but there was an edge to it. "No, that one I understand. What did you learn about *her*?"

Hunter set his jaw and looked out the window, where sunlight was just beginning to crawl into the sky. "She was using me."

"And what did Jay tell you about girls?"

Hunter rolled his eyes. "To use them first. That doesn't even make sense. You want me to go through life using everyone I meet?"

"If it will keep you safe, yes, I do."

Hunter didn't say anything.

"Even last night," said his father. "Even knowing she'd stolen from you. You wanted to help her. Didn't you?"

"Who *wouldn't* want to help her? Can't you imagine what she must have been going through? Do you *blame* her?"

"She could have told you, Hunter. If she cared about you, if she trusted you, she would have. Jay was here in uniform last night. She could have told *him*."

Hunter scowled.

"If nothing else," said his father, "say you used her for the lesson."

"What about you?" Hunter snapped.

"Me?"

"Do you use Mom?"

"You keep saying the word *use* like it's a bad thing. As if there's nothing given in return. Your mother wanted security. A family. A husband who would take care of her. She got those things."

Hunter snorted. "You make my whole existence sound like a barter transaction."

"Good. Start thinking of every relationship in your life that way."

"What fun."

"You can think about it while we're gone. I think you'll figure it out."

"Gone?" Hunter straightened in the chair. "You're leaving?"

"We got another message about this family in Annapolis. It sounds suspicious. We've decided to go a few days early, get the lay of the land before they know we're there. Jay's packing the car now so we can beat traffic."

Hunter looked out the window. "This is bullshit."

"Excuse me?"

Hunter flew out of his chair. "I said *this is bullshit*. I can do this. You know I can do this. I should get to go. You even said yourself—I could be a decoy. I could help. I could—"

"You're not ready."

"I am ready! Look at last night! Look at—"

His dad raised an eyebrow. "I am looking at last night, Hunter."

Hunter flushed. "I don't mean the . . . the *using*. I mean—"

"I know exactly what you mean. I also know that man had every thought to kill you, and you shot him in the shoulder." His father paused and put his hands on Hunter's shoulders. "You're *not ready*. And that's *fine*."

Hunter shoved his hands off and moved to brush past his father. "Fuck you."

Hunter didn't realize his dad had grabbed him until he'd been spun around and pinned to the doorjamb.

His father didn't even raise his voice. "Want to try that again?"

The door frame was pressing into his cheek exactly where he'd gotten the bruise yesterday—and Hunter could swear his dad knew that. "Let me go."

"Acting like a cocky teenager isn't the way to convince me you're ready." But his dad let him go.

Hunter shoved him, hard.

And then his dad came after him.

"Hey. *Hey*." Uncle Jay was there, dragging them apart. "Leave him be, John. The kid's had a long night."

"Forget it," said Hunter. "I've got to get ready for school." He didn't look at his dad, just turned for the steps. "Have a great time on your *trip*."

When Hunter came out of the shower, his father and uncle were gone.

It figured.

Hunter slammed through the underbrush surrounding the property. He was exhausted, but fury rode him hard. He kept replaying those last minutes with his dad.

And a small nagging voice at the back of his head kept insisting that his dad had left for a potentially dangerous assignment, and for the first time, he hadn't said good-bye.

Hunter hesitated and pulled the phone out of his pocket. He tapped out a text to Uncle Jay.

Tell Dad I'm sorry.

Before he could press SEND, someone tackled him from behind. The phone went flying, disappearing beneath the leaves.

"Payback's a bitch, huh?"

Jeremy Rasmussen.

A foot kicked Hunter in the side. "*Someone*'s a bitch."

Garrett Watts.

Normally Hunter would fight them enough to stay alive, to keep his dignity. Anything more always seemed to up the ante.

Today wasn't the day for that.

It took him less than three minutes to have them both on the ground. Jeremy's head had collided with a tree trunk, and he lay unconscious in the leaves. Garrett's arm was pinned behind his back, and he was whimpering. Hunter was all but kneeling on his throat.

And for the first time, Hunter considered driving his knee down, crushing Garrett's windpipe.

He thought of his father's question, of whether he could do it. *Thinking* and *doing* were two very different things.

The world would be a better place without a jerk like Garrett Watts.

Just like the world probably would have been a better place without a man like Clare's father. Hunter's dad was right—he should have shot to kill.

But Garrett was a *kid*. He still had time to figure out what kind of man he was going to be.

So did Hunter.

He stood. "Get your friend out of here," he said. "If you guys ambush me again, I won't stop there."

Then Hunter picked up his backpack and started walking. But he headed for home, instead of school. If his dad was gone, there was no one to crack the whip. He had a lot more use for a day spent sleeping.

When he got there, the car was back in the driveway.

His dad and Uncle Jay were in the kitchen.

They didn't say anything when Hunter walked in, and he

wondered if he could feed them a line about forgetting a text-book.

Then his dad said, "I changed my mind."

Changed his mind? After everything? Hunter could count on one hand the number of times his father had *changed his mind*. Now it made Hunter wonder whether he'd made the wrong decision in the woods just now—or the right one.

He dropped his backpack. "You . . . what?"

His dad glanced at Jay. "Your uncle convinced me. Go pack a bag. You can come with us."

Find out where it all started! Read on for a sample of *Storm*, the first in The Elemental Series by Brigid Kemmerer.

CHAPTER 1

The self-defense class had been a waste of sixty bucks.

Becca hadn't felt like a victim going in, but she sure did now. When she'd seen the flyers around school advertising a three-hour session with a "women's defense specialist," she'd been eager to sign up. But the instructor—really just some college kid named Paul—had been texting half the time, happy enough to pocket their cash in exchange for halfhearted instructions about body blocks and eye gouges. She'd lose another Saturday scrubbing kennels to make this money back.

She'd left her cell phone in her locker, so after class she went to get it. Her best friend had left fourteen texts about some drama with her mom, so Becca stood in the shadowed corridor to write back. Quinn wasn't exactly patient.

The night air bit at her flushed skin when she slid out the side door, making her wish she'd brought a heavier jacket—but at least the promised rain had held off. Darkness cloaked the now empty parking lot, and her car sat alone near the security lamp in the middle of the cracked concrete.

This was exactly the kind of situation Paul had warned them about: secluded and solitary, offering little visibility. But Becca welcomed the darkness, the silence. She almost wished she smoked, so she could lie on the car's hood, flick a lighter, and make up names for the constellations while nicotine burned her lungs.

You should be so cool.

Her key found the lock, but the door handle to her aged Honda refused to release. She muttered the obligatory prayer, but nothing happened. Sometimes it took a curse.

Then she heard a muffled shout, a distant scuffle on pavement.

She froze, more curious than afraid. A fight? Here? She saw the combatants, just at the edge of the security light over by the east wing. Three guys fighting, two on one, it looked like. One caught another in a headlock, and the third swung a fist at the captive's midsection while he struggled.

They weren't saying anything, making the violence cartoonish and unreal, like watching an action movie on mute.

The kid in the headlock twisted free, his liberty quickly rewarded with a fist to the head, sending him into a stagger. Another punch brought him to the ground.

Then he didn't move. One of the other guys kicked him in the stomach.

She heard *that*. And the sound made her remember that she was just standing in the middle of a parking lot, watching.

Becca dropped beside her car. Breath whistled into her lungs. She didn't want to open the door and have the sound or the light draw their attention. She'd call the police. An ambulance. The whole frigging cavalry.

She thrust her hand into her bag for her cell phone.

Dead.

Damn Quinn and her fifty bazillion texts. Becca swore and punched the phone against the pavement. The cover snapped off, skittering away under her car.

Helpful, Bex.

She peeked around the front bumper. The fallen boy lay in a crumpled pile.

They kicked him again.

"Get up," she whispered.

He didn't.

She tried to make out who the kids were. Some senior boys

got off on violence. She knew a few of them firsthand—some only by reputation. The Merrick twins, maybe?

They were circling now, like vultures. One nudged the fallen boy with his foot.

Then he kicked him. "Get up."

"Yeah," said the other one. "How'd you get rid of them?"

The voices were sharp, cruel. She held her breath, wishing she could help somehow. But what could she do? Run at them with her water bottle and the splintered plastic of her cell phone? Maybe she could practice that "confident woman's walk" Paul had demonstrated.

If only she had a weapon, something to level the playing field.

You idiot. You do have a weapon.

Her car.

Adrenaline made for a good ally. She'd barely thought it before she was crawling through the back door and climbing into the driver's seat, driving straight at them.

She had the satisfaction of watching her headlights illuminate their panic; then they were scrambling, diving to get out of the way. Not the Merrick twins, not anyone she could make out at all. Her foot punched the brakes at the last second, jerking the car to an abrupt stop.

"I called the cops!" she shouted out the window, feeling her heart kick against her ribs. "They're on their way!"

But the boys were already bolting into the darkness.

Her fingers refused to release the steering wheel for the longest moment. She finally pried them free, and, leaving the engine running, eased out of the car.

She wished she'd turned the car differently, because the boy was mostly in shadow, away from the headlights. He lay face-down, the thick dark hair on his head matted with blood at one temple. They'd done a number on his face: More blood glistened on his swollen brow. Abrasions scored his cheek in various directions, as though he'd met the pavement intimately, and more than once. His black hoodie had taken a beating, and his jeans weren't much better, sporting a tear down the side of one leg. He was breathing, a rattle of air pulling into his lungs, ending on a slight wheeze each time.

She'd never seen someone beaten so badly.

"Hey." She gave his shoulder a little shake. He didn't move.

Those boys had run off on foot. She had no idea if they'd stay gone.

Now what, genius?

She left her car engine running, its headlights cutting a path in the darkness. She reached inside the door and pulled out her half-empty water bottle. She crouched beside him, feeling the cold grit of the pavement through her jeans. Then, using her hand to slow the flow, she trickled water down the side of his face.

At first, nothing happened. She watched in macabre fascination as the water pulled blood across his jaw, trailing over his split lip.

Then he came to with a vengeance.

Becca wasn't ready for that, for him to explode off the ground in a fury, his fists swinging before his eyes were open.

She was lucky he was injured. She barely got out of his way.

His momentum didn't last long, however. He staggered to a knee, planting a hand against the pavement. He coughed and it shook his body; then he spit what looked like blood.

Now that he wasn't lying on the ground, she recognized him. Christopher Merrick. Chris. He was a junior, like she was, but she couldn't think of two words they'd ever exchanged. He was the Merrick twins' younger brother, the type of guy who'd slouch in the back of the classroom and stare at the teachers with disdain, daring them to call on him. People left him alone, but that's how he seemed to like it. An outsider by choice.

Unlike her.

"You gave me water," he rasped, his head down.

His voice startled her, made her realize she was just standing there, clutching her water bottle so hard it made the plastic crackle.

"Yeah," she said. "Those guys—they could come back—"

"Are you stupid?"

The derision in his voice was like a punch to the chest. "Funny. I was just asking myself that."

"No. I just—I could have hurt—" Chris coughed again, then pressed his forehead to the ground, making a low sound in his throat. He spit blood again. She felt like she was standing in the middle of one of those cable crime dramas—the kind where the violence is too much for network television.

"Do you have a cell phone?" She cast a quick look out into the darkness, but the night remained still. "You need an ambulance."

"I need a damn rainstorm." He seemed to laugh, but it choked him. "A drizzle. Fog even."

He was delirious. "Can you get into the car? I can drive you to the hospital."

"No. Home."

"*Whatever*. Climb in the car. Those guys could come back, and I'm not—"

A hand closed on her arm, hot and meaty and painful. A voice spoke from the darkness. "Did you think we wouldn't wait and see?"

"Big surprise." The other voice now. "No sirens."

That hand swung her around. This guy didn't go to her school. He looked older. College, maybe. Short blond hair framed a severe face, all angles and lines.

Something scraped on the pavement. "This is going to suck," said Chris.

The other one was dragging him to his feet.

Becca knew how to swallow pain and keep emotion off her face. "Let me go. I didn't call the cops, but he did."

Those sharp features cracked into a smile. "We took his phone."

"Good try," said Chris. He coughed again. The other guy punched him in the side, and he dropped to the pavement.

The one on her arm shoved her up against her car. It hurt. She squealed before she could help it.

"You should have driven away, sweetheart."

"Nah," said the other, his dark hair making him look sinister. "That right there is dessert."

Then she recognized his voice. Seth Ramsey. A senior. And part of the reason she'd been in that self-defense class.

His friend reached out to cup her chin. "Yeah. Dessert."

Maybe it was Seth's presence; maybe it was the implication in their words. Whatever, her mind didn't think, her body just moved. The water bottle went flying and her arm swung.

Eye gouge.

Something squished under her fingers. He dropped her arm like a hot potato, shoving her away, flying back to put a hand to his face. "Bitch! You bitch!"

Holy crap! It works! She was choking on her breath, but she was free.

"Shut *up*, Tyler," Seth hissed. "She might not have called the cops, but you're gonna—"

"Freeze. Right there."

At first she thought the cops *had* shown up. But it was Chris, her water bottle in his hand. He'd found his feet somehow, and though he looked a little unsteady, their assailants went still.

Chris drew a shaky breath. "Back off. Or I'll mean that literally."

Mean what literally?

"Yeah, right," said Seth. "It's one bottle."

Chris shook it. The water sloshed. "Try me."

GREAT BOOKS, GREAT SAVINGS!

When You Visit Our Website:
www.kensingtonbooks.com
You Can Save Money Off The Retail Price
Of Any Book You Purchase!

- **All Your Favorite Kensington Authors**
- **New Releases & Timeless Classics**
- **Overnight Shipping Available**
- **eBooks Available For Many Titles**
- **All Major Credit Cards Accepted**

Visit Us Today To Start Saving!
www.kensingtonbooks.com

All Orders Are Subject To Availability.
Shipping and Handling Charges Apply.
Offers and Prices Subject To Change Without Notice.